SIGNAL 13

Chronicles of a Calvert Trooper

A Novel

by

S. Eric Briggs

Booklocker.com, Inc.
2008

Dedication

This book is dedicated to my immortal "lost brothers" who will never, ever, be forgotten. My sincere thanks and gratitude to Jon, my always encouraging brother and kindred spirit, to Linda, my special, indefatigable "go to girl," and to my ole pal Bruce "Bientot" Williams, for trying to help me tame this beast. And to the Maryland State Police family of yesteryears and today...*I salute you!*

To that Garber guy, my ole high school hunting, fishing and spitting buddy......

Thanks for arranging my stay on the SPHS football team, ole pal ... and for all those other memories that make me pee my pants whenever I conjure them up!

"Ahhh .... when we were troopers once, and young."

Cheers and beers forever,

Eric

PS: wher the hell we goin fishin again?

" *Fatti Maschii Parole Femine* "

Chapter 1

THE TOAST

He doggedly clung to his days like a diffident priest clutching a cross on his first exorcism, but the pervasive demons, the "restive tiger" in his head, savaged his nights.

Standing hunched over in the half moon's silky luster, he peered ahead at the vaguely familiar tobacco barn. He shook his dependably fickle state trooper flashlight in a vain attempt to give it life, cursed it, then edged closer to the looming behemoth. Deja-vu sensations washing over him, he warily gazed back at the hanging crescent for reassurance. Nothing. For a fleeting moment, a shooting star stole his attention as it streaked to its fiery death high above. When he turned around, she was standing there, stoop shouldered and wide-eyed, frozen beside the open barn door. In the pale moonlight he could see she was barefoot, dressed in a simple peasant skirt, and she had a distorted, all-knowing smile on her opaque face. On his approach, the little girl dreamily waved him on before she drifted into the barn and faded into the darkness. He gnawed on his lip and paused, wondering if she was just one more apparition on another long, tiresome night shift. Years of honed intuition begged otherwise. *Damn* !! The first signature strands of Jimi Hendrix's *Purple Haze*, shrill and grating like never before, echoed crazily in his head when he started her way. This one was gonna be a real doozy!

The strong, pungent smell of the tobacco leaves drying overhead greeted him as he entered the dark cavernous structure. He flinched as the barn door creaked shut behind him, but forced himself to stand still, hoping to see her Lilliputian figure somewhere up ahead. In front of him, merely a few steps away, the child's soft plaintive voice suddenly broke the silence. "Jesus loves me, yes he I know, for the Bible tells me so." Blindly, he pitched forward after the verse was sung again, only to stumble across something on the packed dirt ground. He froze for a moment before squatting down to find out what it was—hoping it wasn't. It was just one piece of many scattered at his feet, but the touch of the mangled arm, cold and clammy, sticky with coagulated blood, announced his return to that hideous Parker Creek scene again; the hacked up remnants of the hapless Bowen girl, an unsolved grisly murder from many years past. *PURPLE HAZE !!* The hair on the back of his neck rose, and his throat went dry as blood iced in his veins. And from the dark it came again, the child's voice more sluggish and deeper, falling off at the end. "Jesus loves me yyes I knowww...for the *BI*...for the *BIBLE*...!"

For several gut-wrenching seconds there was deafening silence, a sweet prelude until her buoyant giggles filled the air, then silence again. He shuffled closer and was rudely greeted by a shrill hiss and the acrid stench of death. His eyes jerked wide open as the hooded animal-like specter with the beaded ember eyes floated from the shadows. Vaguely discernable in the shards of moonlight filtering through gaps in the barn siding, there was a double bladed, long-handle axe at the end of the towering specter's appendage. Horrified, he broke out of his near paralysis and eased himself up, his service weapon already drawn and aimed at whatever it was.

A warm stream of urine ran down the front of his trousers, but he didn't notice. The deranged hissing grew louder, the embers blazing brighter, as the entity came on. Firing pointblank and dead-on, he emptied the revolver at the massive bulk. Unfazed, it kept coming as he frantically pulled the trigger, the hammer finally falling on empty chambers. *Click!! Click !!* He stumbled backward, wildly off balance, and the gun flew from his hand when he fell against a pile of tobacco sticks. Throwing his arms in front of him, he tried to scream. But nothing came out, as the axe cleaved through the electric air.

He woke up with a start, gasping, with sweat rolling off his face. Welcome daylight was finally piercing the musty, cramped bedroom of the stucco cottage. He never could sleep late, but during the last few months it'd gotten worse, with more incessant nightmares and damning, maddening, headaches. Fitful sleep amounted to maybe an hour of real shuteye a night. Insomnia, after his career's very *last* late shift, was an uninvited beastly guest at another maniac party he was forced to attend.

Catching his breath, he rolled over and pushed himself up from the cold tile floor. Poised on the edge of the platform bed, he stretched his arms over his throbbing head and yawned. Recoiling from the reek of his stale, funky breath, he stared blankly at the cobweb cracks on the blood-streaked mirror above the dresser. His eyes strained against the midmorning sunlight beckoning under the faded vinyl blinds of the tiny bedroom window. What glared back at him was, questionably, one of "Maryland's Finest," a stubble-chinned, bleary-eyed fifty-one year-old Sergeant Dalton Bragg of the Maryland State Police, who, in just two days, was metamorphosing himself back to civilian status after a twenty-six year hiatus.

"Sweet Jesus, have all those ball-buster twenty-six frickin' years *really* added up to tomorrow?" he muttered lamely at his callous reflection. His smile rolled up into a tight grimace when he held up his right hand and studied his flayed, blood-crusted knuckles. He sucked on each violated knuckle until it stung enough to stop. Nice, another bout with the tiger.

Skittish fingers combed through the thinned out tangles of blonde hair before his scruffy face escaped the mirror to stare at the heap of boxes cluttering the floor. Dalton studied several duct taped boxes of career trivia and uniforms, along with the rules and regulations books he'd gathered for the conclusive equipment turn-in at the Supply Division tomorrow. Yeah, like someone would give a royal rat's ass if anything was missing, right?

His jaded blue eyes darted back to the MSP regulations books, the yellow manual marked "Patrol," and the black one marked "Administrative." He sighed and shook his head. "Ahhh, the "rules of life" in the MSP...the dual nemeses and bane of too many potentially great troopers," he mused out loud. The first MSP rules and regulations book was a mere thirty-five rules to abide by, totaling only thirty-one pages. Even twenty-six years ago, there was only the puny, two-inch thick, MSP bible "guide." Now, there were two grossly-obese manuals serving as a testament to the changing times and too many vain job justifications as dictated by the Wizards of OZ on the third floor planning and research unit in the Executive building.

Being on sick leave for his last two days wasn't a total cop-out either. No doubt the cheeky first sergeant had changed his sick leave report to indicate an ailment other than the incurable case of "draggin ass due to lobotomy complications" Dalton had scribbled out on the much-abused form. They weren't about to mess with him at this stage of the game, knowing he'd yank his papers out if they did, an irksome aspect they definitely had to avoid. So, it'd be a truce, more or less. He'd paid his dues several times over, but he also knew it was time to leave, as others eventually realized when the sun set on their fading careers.

Dalton had spurned the grandiose idea of a few cohorts who were willing to throw him a customary retirement party. He'd deferred, avoiding the stereotyped, genuinely meaningless accolades and tributes from hollow department figureheads and plastic politicians who'd never met him, those who hadn't walked in his shoes.

Divorced, as most of his fellow troopers had been at one time or another, houseless, and with kids flown from the coop, Dalton eventually found a quaint cottage to rent in Calvert Beach, a beach community on the bay in mid Calvert ("Culvert") County. There, in this pivotal life's moment, he lived—very much alone. When the cottage walls closed in on him, as they too often did, he had only to walk a short distance to the open sandy beach to bask in the welcome solace that nature invariably granted him. He particularly relished spending time at the special place he called Purgatory Ridge, the lofty outlook on top of the regal Calvert cliffs, a scant mile north of the beach entrance. High above the bay, his more frequent sojourns to the haven aptly served as a dependable antidote for his problems. Today's "antidote" session would be lengthy, one badly needed to assuage his dark, increasingly convoluted life perspective.

His bleak outlook was never manifested in his physical self, as he took great pride in his regimented approach to staying in shape, daily pushing himself hard with weights and grueling miles of running along the beachfront. At six feet even and a strapping one hundred and ninety-five pounds, the blond-haired sergeant with the boyish good looks knew he was in better shape than most troopers half his age. No, his steely mindset pushed him harshly, usually to total exhaustion, giving him that welcome euphoria, however fleeting it was. But within hours, the sleeping tiger in his head would rouse itself to prowl again. As usual, he'd try to restrain it any way he could, evidenced by the slew of beer cans cluttering the kitchen sink each morning.

Dalton tugged on a faded pair of jeans, pulled on a sleeveless camo T-shirt, then jammed his bare feet into the ragged running shoes he'd kept far too long. To loosen up some, he forced himself through a series of sit-ups, grueling crunches and blood pumping pushups. Warm-ups finished, he plucked a frayed canvas knapsack off a closet shelf, brushed off the cobwebs, then tossed it on the bed. Next, he eased the shiny Sam Browne belt from the shelf and removed his service weapon, the state-owned, highly venerated, 40-caliber, locked and loaded Berretta semi-automatic. The handgun and two full magazine clips were tucked into a knapsack side pocket. Today, his most reliable "friend" was coming along for the jubilee.

Unlike some former MSP cohorts who'd digressed from friends to persona non grata types, his sinister looking metallic pal had never failed him. Funny thing how the job warped people so badly! Dalton stuffed the knapsack with a sundry collection of beer, throwing in a half empty pint of Jose Cuervo tequila and a few munchables for good measure, before scribbling out a short message on the chalkboard hanging on the side of the wheezing refrigerator. Had to give a heads-up to Diane, his long-term squeeze, just in case she showed up unannounced again, perplexed by yet another one of his odd absences.

Everything in order, Dalton shouldered the knapsack, adjusted the straps, and strode out the front door. When he passed his Ford Crown "Vic" cruiser in the driveway, he solemnly patted the hood. After a few steps, he stopped abruptly and slowly turned around. Dalton's eyes roamed over the olive-green and black patrol car which bore the distinct State of Maryland emblem on the driver's door. His gaze drifted to the *State Trooper* decal on the front fender, then up to the red and blue roof lights, and finally down to the yellow tag bearing the designation U-17. He always thought they were sharp, quasi-military looking cruisers, really something to be proud of, very much unlike the pale, baby-puke, "Chiquita Banana" rollers that were foisted on the troops years ago. Minutes later, he was standing on the warm sandy beach with the welcome sun on his face.

Staring over the calm, blue water bay to the Eastern Shore, the sergeant spotted the familiar outlines of several sparsely wooded islands on the surprisingly clear morning. A school of silvery iridescent alewives, just off the beach in the shallows, suddenly shattered the still water, chased by a cow-nosed ray whose dual wingtips cut the surface right behind the big-eyed bait fish. High above, he saw three ospreys circling lazily overhead, chortling to each other as they rode the thermals. Only the muffled grumbling of the work boat manned by the sun-baked, leather-skinned watermen checking their crab pots just offshore, hinted of any other human presence on this otherwise pristine day. He always relished the rarity of such treasured times.

Smiling broadly, Dalton began hiking over sand, shells, shark teeth and other fossils marking the way to Purgatory Ridge, some twenty minutes away. He effortlessly jumped over a shallow stream next to a crumbling concrete barrel seawall, then hurried on to where the beach narrowed and the cliffs loomed high. Heavy recent rains had caused more erosion in the cliffs, he noticed. Along with a few mammoth poplars that had lost their earthen grips to tumble down the cliffs, there were also several new dirt slides. No doubt the fossil hunters searching for prehistoric evidence of past life had scrambled about in ecstasy after the recent storms.

Dalton was fascinated, knowing that the very fossils and shark teeth he was treading came from the Miocene Epoch, millions of years ago. The entire area, even up to the cliff tops, had been under salt water once upon an unfathomably long time ago. Although adept at finding shark teeth along the beach, he had never found one from the Great White shark or XXXXX, as the efficient marine eating machine was fondly known to the avid fossil hunters. Flashing back to an earlier time in his career, Dalton recalled a fossil hunting incident that occurred along the cliffs, barely a mile to the south. A young schoolteacher trudging along the shoreline during a spring thaw had been crushed, killed instantly, when a large clay boulder suddenly broke off from the cliff top. He also vividly remembered being ordered by his gonzo ID sergeant to stay with the gruesome, crushed corpse until it was removed by the rescue squad. Of course, there was no advice given as to how he was supposed to hold back the cliff sections that were steadily collapsing around him. Damn new guys always had too much to prove.

Dalton hurdled over another fallen poplar tree and was startled when he nearly landed on an exploding blur of gray and blue feathers. With a loud, panicky squawk, the ungainly bird took to the air, its strong wings flapping hard to escape. With a racing heart and a smile, he watched the large blue heron soar away to settle down on a large, mossy rock, several hundred yards beyond. Continuing on, Dalton approached to within yards of the pterodactyl-like bird before it gave a raucous cry and flew off for needed privacy.

Beads of sweat dotted his forehead when Dalton stopped to gaze up at the large clump of branches and sticks marking the bald eagle's nest high atop the oak near the edge of the cliff. Motionless, he waited, hoping to catch another glimpse of his much revered, magnificent raptors. Eyes beaming, he finally spotted one in the distance as it gracefully soared back and forth over the warm air currents rising above the cliff.

Several weeks ago, just before the dusk of a glass-clear day, he and his nature loving girlfriend, Diane, were meandering along the beach at this very spot. When they heard the shrill cries of the two eagles cavorting high overhead, they immediately plunked themselves down on the sandy beach. Open-mouthed, they watched the acrobatic birds make dazzling loops and dives, once even swooping close enough to briefly grasp each other's talons.

Yes, if there were any validity in the reincarnation theory, Dalton knew without a doubt that he'd return as an eagle, a vision he'd mentioned to Diane months before. From his interest in Native American lore, he knew that the natives saw the eagles as sacred messengers from the creator of them all. They were the ever-vigilant watchers who looked over them, the regal sentinels who flew the highest and saw the farthest of any other living creature in their mystic worlds.

Graced by the eagles' appearance, Dalton trudged further down the beach, eventually arriving at the rotted pilings and scattered scraps of weathered plywood, all that remained of the on-shore duck blind marking the spot that led to his Purgatory Ridge, high above. He took off the knapsack and rubbed his shoulders, then sat on the shell-strewn beach for a short rest. Minutes later, he grunted and slung the knapsack over his back for the big climb. He gazed up at the majestic cliff, his Chesapeake Himalaya, in silent admiration, marveling at the evidence of a million years before. His eyes roamed over several levels of packed sediment, from the bluish-gray clay base, on up past the higher saffron and ruddy-colored sand and clay layers, before they rested on the towering trees of his favorite refuge.

"Here we go again, big boy," he muttered out loud before starting up the unmarked stairway leading to his coveted overlook.

At first, he scrambled straight up the face, moving slowly in a crouch, grabbing any convenient roots to pull himself upward. Soon he was crawling on hands and knees, struggling to keep himself at the lowest gravity point. Sweat trickled from his forehead and ran down his back, while the pack straps bit into his shoulders. Finally, with the help of an outcropped tree root, he pulled himself up and over the top of the one hundred and ten-foot cliff. Once again, king of the mountain!

Prone on his stomach, he wiped the sweat from his face and rested until his gasps tapered off. He rolled over onto his knees, unlimbered the pack from his aching shoulders and set it against the base of a massive oak. Behind him, as far as he could see, there was nothing but oak, poplar and sweet-gum trees, surrounded by several mountain laurels and heavy undergrowth. No residences for a good half mile or so. Dalton stood up and turned around to savor the panorama. The warm easterly breeze felt good as it stroked his sweaty face and mussed up hair. Time after time, ever since his first climb to this treasured ridge, it always had the same humbling effect on him. Just standing on fossils which had actually been part of a seabed millions of years ago, was mind-boggling in itself. He could only imagine the alarm of those early native hunters, four braves of the proud Piscataways, on that June day in 1608, when they gawked at the "Great Canoe," the pretentious Captain John Smith's shallop, the Discovery Barge, as it sailed north to explore uncharted waters.

Dalton could make out the faint outlines of houses and piers on the Eastern Shore, miles across the brilliant blue bay. There were several listless sailboats, "blow boats," plying the waters in search of good wind, and just to the south, he spotted a small armada of charter-fishing boats shifting for position, trolling deep along the shipping channel for rockfish, he imagined. Scanning to the north, he saw a massive container ship heading south and making good headway. And several miles beyond, the Bay Bridge, with its majestic twin spans, came vaguely into view.

Combined with the sweet and salty tang hanging in the air, Dalton was once again transfixed into his world of solace. He stood there for several minutes, arms slack by his side, sucking it all in. Satiated, he knelt down and rummaged his knapsack until he found his treasured, weather-beaten "dream-catcher" of native Indian lore. Almost twenty years ago, while hunting for elusive whitetails in the deep woods of Battle Creek Swamp, Dalton found the webbed, feather-laden dream-catcher. Strangely, it was hanging from the lower limb of a scraggy pine next to an abandoned, tumbledown farmhouse. Although it was badly weathered, Dalton was captivated enough to bring it home and hang it beside his bedroom window, wishing beyond a prayer that it'd work its magic.

Today, he mused to himself as he tied it to a sapling branch, he would set it free again. He gently ran a finger down the rim of the small hole in the middle of the web where the "good dreams" were thought to be snared. A reflective moment later, he brushed the hanging feathered tail with the back of his hand and gazed at the outer webbing where the bad dreams were snagged in the dead of night, taking care not to touch it.

Satisfied, he liberated the first can of beer from the knapsack and hunkered down against the deeply furrowed tree trunk. Dalton glanced down at his watch and scowled when the Casio confirmed that 11:00 AM hadn't quite yet arrived. For a fool's moment, he thought about setting it ahead to five o'clock—*Here*, not just somewhere. Instead, he took it off his wrist and pitched it over the cliff edge. Chuckling to himself, he popped the beer tab, wedged the can between his legs, then lit the cigar to relish the sweet smell of the tobacco smoke he'd never allow himself to inhale. "Let the party begin," he carped to the beer can now held aloft in a mock salute.

"Sooo...Sergeant Bragg," he muttered lamely, "How the Hell ya *really* been during the last twenty-six years of your dubious existence, huh?" He grinned and drained the beer can, tossed it out a few yards and studied it closely as it rolled to a stop, a silver round end taunting him. This might be a tough one, he mused, as the Beretta came up. He quickly focused on sight alignment and squeezed the trigger. *Blam!* Instantly, his efforts were rewarded as the can spun several feet beyond, a perfect round hole in the center of its perfect round end. It was also a perfect violation of one of those puritanical departmental rules pertaining to service weapons too. Probably found in the grossly obese, yellow patrol book, somewhere under pukey Commandment Chapter 25, Sec. 8, subsection b "Thou shall not use departmental weapons for the desecration of dead beer cans, or some shit like that," he thought, as a chorus of giggles engulfed him.

Fresh beer in hand, the sergeant settled back against the tree, took another drag on the cigar, and blew out a few dislocated smoke rings. With the "tiger" fast asleep, he closed his eyes and drifted back twenty-eight years ago, searching for the lightning bolt that had zapped him hard enough to become obsessed with the prospect of being one of "Maryland's Finest." Unable to find the electrifying moment in his faulty memory bank, he only remembered the dumbfounded look and stony silence coming from his girlfriend Cindy when he told her he was quitting the band to become a Maryland State Trooper.

She was quizzically gazing back at a longhaired twenty-five year old, one hundred and sixty pound, gangly-built, hard rock drummer who she'd presumed was trying to emerge as a rock-n-roll star—some day. Years earlier, he'd initiated a pen pal relationship with her after he'd been smitten with the tall, thin-boned, blonde Scandinavian beauty while he was home on leave from the Army, the Army he'd enlisted in after signing a medical waiver, and in the midst of the Viet Nam war at that! He'd volunteered as an obligation to the country, and for the chance to be a "warrior," to test his mettle amongst so many others who were destined to be a part of the only big game being played at the time. His brother, however, had usurped that reckless, youthful desire.

Dalton's orders for the *Nam* were abruptly changed when Uncle Sam learned that his older brother was already there, humping the hills in the central highlands. Dalton had several friends who'd served on the front lines, and a few of them came back in flag draped caskets. Those who made it back said they had seen the wretched tragedy of war firsthand as it rambled and wrecked lives, spirits and countries. Dalton would be guilt ridden forever for not being there, guilty for being alive today, a status that probably wouldn't have been, if he'd visited the *Nam.*

It began with a not-so-innocent, curious letter, and soon enough, their written exchanges turned intimate. Every letter he wrote to Cindy screamed of his aspirations to come home and form a band to pursue the Beatles with a vengeance on a quest for fame, riches, and too many other naive etceteras of youthful, carefree days. And then, merely two and a half years later, he was altering his life's course 180 degrees, to become—a cop? Dalton knew that proclamation would go over like a lead balloon, yet he decidedly couldn't continue without suffering serious repercussions to his body, soul and spirit. Being a hard-rocker in the volatile late sixties, was the ticket alrighty, but he never fathomed being part of the sordid drug world he'd brushed against along the way. Time to return to his true self—if he could still find it.

Dalton was athletic, and he thrived on challenges. Morally, his integrity was rooted, although he did have a scampish Dennis the Menace streak infected with a warped sense of humor, an impetus which foddered countless provocative pranks: frogs in toilets, snake shows in the den room, BB-gun battles with neighborhood pals, under-age joyrides in the family car late at night, cutting school to go fishing or skinny-dipping, chucking eggs or cherry bombs at the Good Humor truck on listless summer evenings, and other shenanigans. Rampant boredom was judiciously staved off with juvenile buffoonery. On the flipside, Dalton embraced a few attributes that tempered such flaws, including a heartfelt tendency to help others when he could.

Yes, it was prime-time to challenge himself and hope to become a member of what he felt was the most elite and prestigious agency in law enforcement—a trooper in the quasi-military, highly-disciplined Maryland State Police!

Weeks later, Dalton drummed out the last gig with his befuddled band members. The next day, after shearing his hair, the trooper-wannabe paraded into the Annapolis Barrack and proudly requested an application to the MSP, hoping to pass the challenging entry hurdles in time for the next academy class. The gauntlet included a written test, which he passed easily. Dalton was later interviewed at by a poker-faced, anemic-looking investigator who'd lost his personality somewhere, obviously not interested in finding it, on Dalton's lucky day. Weeks later, he reported to the Pikesville MSP headquarters gym for the "cattle call" physical and an easy agility test, and a month later he took a nerve-wracking polygraph test at the Annapolis Barrack, a nigh exorcism performed by all-knowing Corporal Floyd White, which satisfactorily released all the shrieking skeletons in his closet.

The final step in the trooper application process was the applicant interview board. All those awaiting interviews lined up anxiously along the long hall of the MSP training academy at Pikesville. Sharing restless gibberish, they waited their turns to be dissected via interviews conducted in stuffy, vacant academy bedrooms. The prim captain and the other two uniformed board members were polite and courteous, yet direct and assertive, and while Dalton felt he'd handled himself well, the interview ended way too soon. His rock drummer background yielded several headshakes and a few consternated scowls. When the captain delved more into his "hippie" rock drummer lifestyle, Dalton jokingly quipped that *hippie* really stood for Highly Intelligent Person Pursuing Interesting Endeavors. The pregnant pause afterwards, told him that with this granite-faced group—all three in dire need of a courtesy colon flush—the comment had gone over like the fart in church. Still, Dalton thought he'd be a slam-dunk for the next class.

Obsessed with lofty aspirations, Dalton, working full-time, evening hours at a local concrete plant, enrolled in a law-enforcement curriculum at his community college. He also toned up physically, pushing himself hard, in hopes of gaining acceptance to the conservative department. It took him *two and a half* more years, four more polygraphs, physical agility tests and interview boards, and an enduring dissection of his dubious "hippie" background several times over, before the MSP closed its eyes, held its breath and invited him into the club.

After his first rebuff, Dalton requested an appointment with the commander of the personnel division to review his tenuous applicant status. He'd never forget the stern-faced, Irish molded Captain Moran when he shut his door, locked eyes with him, and stated emphatically that he'd never get on the job if *he* had anything to do with it. Dalton felt the eye-daggers pierce his back as he left the captain's office—but they didn't stick, however, and more important, they were no match for the fuel that had just been poured on his burning obsession to become a Maryland State Trooper.

Dalton was cooling down after finishing a grueling three mile run along the winding dirt road to the summer cottage he and his new wife Cindy were renting on the Magothy River near Arnold. Short of wind, with his pulse racing madly, he checked the mailbox and yanked out a thick manila envelope. His eyes sparkled when he saw the Maryland State Police return address. *Yes!* Such positive news, right before Christmas, signaled an approaching new dawn in his life, and Dalton was deliriously giddy—and totally oblivious to Cindy's muted reaction upon learning of his acceptance to the MSP academy.

* * *

"Ahhh...the frickin academy," the sergeant sighed with drifting reflection. Smiling broadly, he pitched out another dead beer can. True to form, it was sent spinning with a second, neatly placed Berretta round direct to mid-center. Uncanny at the least, he never seemed to have a problem with putting holes in things where he wanted them.

Chapter 2

THE MSP ACADEMY

Riding motorcycles in their 1935 debut, the first tough and determined bunch of Maryland State Troopers, quickly established a glowing reputation for staunch law enforcement. Growing in numbers and responsibilities, the MSP established its own headquarters complex in 1949 when the Old Confederates Home in Pikesville was renovated and turned over to the elite force. In 1954, the State Police academy was added at the complex. From that day on, all trooper candidates received their six months of basic training there.

Open House—MSP Says Hello!
(December 1973)

It was a cold, blustery Sunday afternoon, and the Baltimore beltway traffic was light when trooper candidate Dalton Bragg and his wife drove to the State Police Headquarters at Pikesville to attend the open house activities for the new academy class. Driving past the front entrance of the MSP complex, Dalton gazed at the red brick patriarchal facade adorned with the colorful state emblem and the bold Maryland State Police lettering overhead. He parked their rundown Ford Pinto next to the torture chamber he'd heard too much about already, the MSP gym.

Other candidates were milling anxiously in the parking lot with parents, wives or girlfriends, and Dalton and Cindy joined them as they migrated toward the Spartan three story academy building. Meandering down the hallway, Dalton was impressed with the sundry State Police plaques and mementos displayed in the glassed cabinets.

They were greeted at the classroom door by two lean, clean-shaven, slick-sleeve troopers who stood tall in their signature Class A dress uniforms. Dalton took it all in, from the snug brown blouses and glittery badges and medals, to the glossy Sam Browne gun belt with the cross shoulder strap, the tapered olive-drab slacks with the black stripe, and finally the shiny, ink-black shoes. They exuded an aura of proud confidence, and Dalton was impressed with their cordial, professional demeanor. Smiling knowingly, Dalton couldn't decide what was more impressive, however, his impression of them, or their impression of his radiantly beautiful wife who was getting uncomfortably edgy as too many wandering eyes devoured her.

A balding, astute looking captain strode to the wood podium bearing a large MSP shield and greeted them. After a half-hour welcoming presentation, which included a brief history of the MSP along with an overview of the academy training, they were shown a grainy video film depicting the academy activities. The academy instructors, all beaming like wayward choirboys, were then introduced, and soon the candidates were free to tour the training facility.

Entering the gym, Cindy crinkled her nose at the odors of musky sweat, vinyl, and fresh varnish. Dalton stared at the chin-up bars attached to the walls and the thick climbing ropes dangling from the ceiling rafters. On one side of the gym were rolled-up padded mats and various types of pain inducing exercise devices. The back wall displayed a large painted State of Maryland emblem with a motivating State Police motto underneath, while the other end was decorated with wall plaques attesting to fitness achievement records set by previous trainees.

Dalton snatched Cindy's elbow and escaped from the gym to tour the upstairs boxing ring and weight room. Afterwards, they hurried down the hallway to the official State Police "training tank," or swimming pool he could call it, for now. Beyond the double door entrance the air was thick and heavy, over-seasoned with nauseous chlorine. Moments later, they were standing on the sidewalk outside the dungeon complex, sucking in gulps of fresh air. Suddenly, their attention was drawn to the loud buzzing of the MSP Bell Jet Ranger helicopter taking off from the four-story Executive building roof. Dalton had already been apprised of the location of the Superintendent's third floor office, along with a warning to avoid the exec building if at all possible while a candidate. If *they*, the Lords of the Third Floor, grew too familiar with a trooper candidate's name, more than likely it'd be a bad omen for the trainee.

When she saw the candidates' dorm rooms, Cindy frowned and remarked how impersonally bleak they were. Dalton laughed, telling her that the setup outshone what he'd endured in army basic training at Fort Polk Louisiana years ago. At the dingy army base deep in the Louisiana Cajun country, dozens of recruits were stuffed like sardines in one modest-size barrack room attached to a latrine with non-partitioned, shoulder-to-shoulder toilets. At least during this basic training, he wouldn't be fretting about angry water moccasins, creepy scorpions, wily alligators, upper bunk masturbators or a drunken drill sergeant with the loose fists. Yup, if he could take "Fort Puke's" sweet ambiance, he'd thrive here.

Leaving the academy, they took the front granite steps down to the grass courtyard. It was a tranquil enough setting with a few towering red oaks, a splotchy sycamore tree, and two flagpoles adorned with the stars-and-stripes and the colorful state flag. The courtyard was bordered on three sides by redbrick buildings with slate roofs which housed the various State Police supportive units such as the medical, finance, crime lab, and central records divisions. Even had a garage and cafeteria, too, Dalton noted, wondering if the meals here would bear any semblance to what passed for sustenance in Uncle Sam's army.

All told, the Maryland State Police was a self-supporting, quasi-military force not far removed from the Army life he begrudgingly grew to appreciate—but only after his stint was up. Easily surpassing Uncle Sam's offerings, the MSP gig came with a starting trooper salary of $8,980, a few coins more then four dollars an hour!

Minutes later they were southbound on the beltway, Dalton chattering up a storm while Cindy was hoping she'd be in a much better mood after a glass or three of Chianti. She duly smiled and squeezed his hand when she thought he expected it, making sure Dalton never saw her doubting side glances during the long ride home.

Hell hath no fury…

"*Stand by!* Dalton and two other candidate trainees slammed their backs against the hallway wall, dropped their arms stiffly to their sides, and stood at rigid attention. Three pairs of bulging eyes locked onto the opposite wall, as the academy instructor zipped past. '*At ease!*" the stern instructor shouted, and the trainees deflated themselves and scurried back to the classroom sanctuary like spastic mice. The first two weeks of academy acclimation were pure hell. When they first set foot on the academy grounds, the candidates were greeted by several pissed-off looking instructors who bombarded them with frenzied orders. "*Move, People...MOVE!* This ain't no Goddamn Boy Scout jamboree!" barked a badass corporal. "And neither your momma or your smarmy state senator's gonna help your sorry asses now! Left, left, right, left! Your other left, you damn idiot! Drop down and give me another ten pushups, you dick-head!"

From the start, the candidates quickly grasped they couldn't do *anything* fast enough to please *any* of the eagle-eyed cadre hovering around them like raging wasps. While still in their civvies, they were corralled into ranks outside the gym to endure hasty lessons on military commands. Much sooner then expected, they were doing knee bends and jumping jacks because a jittery fellow candidate gave a wrong hand salute. Running to and from *anywhere* on academy grounds was mandatory, as was the saluting of all sworn officers wherever confronted. Dialogue with anyone other then the instructors or fellow trainees was strictly *verboten!*

Due to acclimation shock, the class of forty-eight candidates incurred its first dropout after only one day. Suitcase in hand, he scurried out the door under the cover of darkness with a hearty: "*Screw this shit!*" Over the next three weeks, several others would follow.

Being the first state police academy class with females, it was a diverse one, to say the least, or the most, depending on one's take of political correctness. With looming Federal mandates and possible discrimination suits, the gate to the all-male bastion was begrudgingly opened to the fairer sex. Initially, the eager female candidates were told they'd be special trooper agents, an undefined role labeled by the MSP hierarchy which remained stupefied about the coerced feminine inclusion. Dalton could only imagine the anxiety they were experiencing in the testosterone-packed environment.

Much to the chagrin of the old school, hardcore troopers, there were other changes. Under the glare of the judicial spotlight, the mandatory minimum height requirement of five feet ten inches was scrapped, along with the long-standing twelve-hour workdays. Several members of the class had previously been police officers or cadets, either in Maryland or out of state. Like Dalton, a few were military veterans, and most had graduated from or had several years of college. They all sought to answer the challenging call of police work, not only to serve and make a difference, but to also avoid the drudgery of the normal nine-to-five rut. It was good to have a sizable class to commiserate with each other during the daunting adaptation to the MSP realm, which, luck prevailing, would be theirs for the next six months.

For the first few weeks, the candidate's training itinerary was routine. The class was broken down into squads, with squad leaders rotated weekly, and every joyful, blessed day started with each bug-eyed candidate standing half awake in formation on the back parking lot at 0600 hrs. First came the warm-up calisthenics, followed immediately by the fast-paced mile-and-a-half run in the nippy, wind-blown January. Afterward, it was back for a quick shower and cleanup, followed by work detail assignments and a hasty breakfast. Later, the sleeping quarters were scrutinized by the instructors who chaffed at their bits, hoping to find any minute discrepancy that warranted a demerit. From a mere speck of dust on a door ledge, a rack not made military-style tight, or heaven forbid, the stitching of a shoe sole not treated with black polish ala a worn-out toothbrush, demerits easily flowed.

Academy rules were enforced through the feared, highly subjective demerit system.

Simply put, the instructors were empowered to cite any wayward trainee with, depending on the offense, one, or up to five demerits. If five demerits were accumulated during assuring a two-day repentance as a member of a special work detail. *Joy!* Of course, the instructors took great care to compare notes with each other, and if an errant trainee's name became too familiar, he'd be put under the spotlight to assure proper attitude-adjustments were rendered.

After the daily inspection, half the class would double-time it to the gym for PT, while the other half settled down in the main classroom to endure endless blocks of lessons. After lunch, the half-class activities were switched to continue until minutes before the dinner meal, when the entire class crammed together in ranks in front of the academy to salute the flags during taps.

Mandatory study hours followed the dinner meal, with an hour of free time mixed in until the strict "lights out" at 2200 hrs. Unless granted permission by *God* or his academy instructor disciples, no lowly recruit was allowed off academy grounds.

The six female candidates had their separate enclave on the other end of the academy third floor—far, but not far enough from their randy male counterparts. Academy roommates were assigned two to a room, and halfway through the training program, new roommates would be assigned. The modest "sleeping quarter" rooms were furnished in the expected Spartan style, each room equipped with two military-surplus maroon metal dressers, two steel-framed beds with rigid mattresses and two rudimentary study desks. On the second floor was a large military-style men's latrine, complete with open showers and urinals, and partitioned toilets.

Aching, drained and mentally numbed, the class was granted a sorely needed weekend pass after the first week. After the first weekend, and up to the second month, several candidates predictably failed to return, their vacancies quickly filled by other masochistic applicants from a standby list.

Maynard Bowman, a demur, twenty-two year-old, physically unimposing candidate from Western Maryland, was Dalton's first roommate, and Dalton quickly perceived that while Maynard was a nice guy, he was a tad naive about what lay ahead. Barely enduring the third week of academy chaos, Dalton's mild-mannered roommate was teetering badly, perilously close to caving in. Tonight was his reckoning. Dalton woke up with a start and gaped at the red glow of a cigarette several feet away. "Don't think I can cut it here anymore, Dalton," Maynard muttered after realizing his roommate was awake.

Never having left home before, Dalton's doleful roommate with the hound dog droopy eyes sorely lacked real-life experiences. After graduating high school, Maynard bounced idly from aimless jobs, finally accepting his father's overtures to help him out on the farm. Now, emotionally torn like never before, his heart was tugging him back to his pregnant, seventeen year-old girlfriend and his family's diary farm in Thurmont, the God's Country he'd left to become a trooper. Dalton hadn't a clue as to what Maynard's expectations were when he first applied to MSP, and to his own chagrin, Maynard didn't either. Nevertheless, the relentless pressure was wearing him down, making him grope for the "throw-in" towel to call it quits.

Dalton had already made up his mind that no roommate of his, or any more classmates, were going to throw in the towel if he could help it. Having fallen asleep in class that morning, Maynard received his fifth demerit, the clincher that sentenced him to his second academy weekend. When his heavy head slammed down hard on his desk, it startled not only the instructor, but several other starry-eyed trainees. Panicky heads snapped up upon hearing the resounding "*thunk*" which left a nifty red knot on Maynard's forehead.

Staying awake in class after lunch was becoming one of the greatest academy challenges, Dalton realized. Usually, thank God, the candidate next to you, or behind, was able to kick your leg or jam an elbow in your side if he saw your head slipping south. They did seem to choose the drollest classes after lunch though, courses like the narcoleptic Motor Vehicle Law taught by a quirky, burned-out sergeant gifted with a catnap-inducing, monotone. "Ahhh...umm, now listen up y'all, that's right, umm...Ok, a stop sign is an "*O-Fee-Shoal*" traffic control device, heh, heh, not just a...umm...red and white sign that's an acronym for Stupid Trooper On Patrol. Ahhhh...OK?"

Dalton's biggest challenge in class was conquering his daydreaming penchant, or maybe it was his libidinous musings about Margot babe, one of the female candidates who sat in front of him. And once, when an instructor called on him, he was just about ready to put the hook to a lunker bass at his favorite farm pond in Arnold, but somehow managed to respond with a fairly credible monkey-talk ad lib.

"Damn, Maynard, just hang on for two more weeks! It'll get better, I promise you that," Dalton whispered in the direction of the red glow. "Just gotta shrug things off like a bad dream...gotta keep on plugging with your head focused on graduation day, Ok?" Maynard took a long drag from his cigarette, slowly blew the smoke out through his nose and silently nodded.

During the next hour, in the darkness of their stuffy room, they diagnosed and solved most of the problems related to academy survival. As their tongues loosened, discussions turned to other enlightening matters, inevitably ending with an intimate critique of the lithe chassis owned by a particularly alluring, blonde candidate.

"Yeah, Dalton, like ya said, Margot Trott's a real babe, that's for sure, a solid nine on my personal erection scale," Maynard blurted out. He coughed and pounded his chest with a fist while tracing a thin circle of flaring red with his cigarette. "Maybe my ass'll get lucky enough to spend the next academy weekend with her, huh buddy?" "*Now* you're thinking, Maynard, my man," Dalton replied, trying hard to stifle a yawn. "*Hey!*" Maynard suddenly spouted out. "Wanna rap some knuckles on her door to see if she'd like us to make her air tight t'night maybe?" A rowdy guffaw followed another raspy cough. 'Sounds good to me buddy," Dalton shot back. "Yeah, Maynard, just go down there and see if you can get her jumpstarted for us, OK?" With a grin, Dalton playfully punched him in the arm. "And when she's ready for first gear, just give me a holler, why don't ya?'

Dalton gibbered on with his rejuvenated room buddy until his eyes turned woody and his weary mind drifted off. He was flooded with blessed relief when Maynard finally snubbed out his damn cigarette before dropping back down on the floor for some needed rest. Early on, some of the candidates refrained from sleeping on their bunks after they'd painstakingly prepared them in military style for the next morning's inspection. Instead, they slept on the floor on the moldy vinyl-covered mattresses that were "confiscated" nightly from a third floor storage room.

The academy's various classes and study requirements, combined with the demanding physical training and inherent stress, was an amalgam of continuous pressure which many candidates hadn't anticipated. Some military veterans in the class groused about it being worse than basic training, and three times longer, too. Being an army vet, Dalton found it gratifying to see fellow commiserates bond and persevere with each other.

The classroom courses ranged from criminal and traffic investigations, the criminal justice system, police demeanor, first aid, constitutional law, civil rights, report writing, crime scenes preservation, officer safety and much more. Several of the courses, including English and criminal justice, were accredited and were aptly taught by a personable, eternally smiling professor from Baltimore County Community College. At least the pansy-ass typing course had been eliminated; something which didn't faze Dalton's roommate Maynard in the least, since he never could fathom why the typing keys on the keyboard weren't in alphabetical order.

One charismatic MSP instructor, Sergeant Carver, fit the role perfectly. Despite his frequent, melodramatic presentations, the sergeant came across tongue-in-cheek. Broad-shouldered, balding and red-faced when on a roll, Carver had his stuff together. To keep the attention of the trainees, the three-striper laced his classes with on-the-job experiences that were always chaotic and downright hilarious. "*People,*" he said in a ringing voice, his eyes rolling up to the ceiling, "always remember that it is *your* highway out there! If the frickin hose-beaters insist on unnecessarily parking their shiny red fire trucks on both lanes of *your* highway, tell em' to move em' *ASAP*! If they don't, call for a tow truck and tow the damn toys!" he barked at them during a class on traffic direction.

Trouble was, the old sergeant had done exactly that. Yes indeed, he'd gone nose-to-nose with a stubborn, on-scene fire chief several years ago, after he'd escaped from the Westminster barrack for a short break from the desk. That ugly incident badly strained relations with the local Westminster EMS personnel, who temporarily "lost" their big red trucks to the tune of $350.00 in towing costs. It also earned the rambunctious MSP sergeant his lion's share of notoriety when the fiasco hit the front page of the Baltimore Sun next day.

Regrettably, Sergeant Carver had a nasty habit of handing out demerits for minor infractions, and for that dreaded propensity, he was avoided like an empty beer keg. As far as he was concerned, *nobody* could shine the brass knobs of the men's urinals good enough to escape being tagged with at least one demerit.

From day one, and whenever possible, the instructors incorporated the pride, heritage and toughness of the State Police force into their lesson plans. It was drilled into the recruits, that as a State Trooper, you never give up, back down from anyone, or, heaven forbid, lose a fight. The instructors preached to them, in no uncertain terms, that the wearer of the MSP uniform was considered nothing less than sacred. If the uniform was defiled by assault or simply belligerent ridicule, whoever was wearing it was expected to "deck the ass" of anyone displaying such carelessness. Losing was *never* an option.

Dalton felt that the classroom instructors comprised a solid nucleus of experienced cadre who were effective, albeit melodramatic at times. It was also obvious, however, that they were used to instructing all-male candidates, as evidenced by numerous slips and mindless expletives, some directed towards female appendages ("Hey, you split tails...listen up now!"). With the academy now coed, they were ever so reluctantly forced to shelve the normal bag of off-color jokes the guys would have greatly appreciated. Times were changing, and so was the etiquette of the formerly all-male bastion. Classroom courses were one aspect, but the rigorous physical training quite another.

***

Drifting back to Purgatory Ridge, the grinning sergeant flicked the ashes off the rum river crook cigar and drained the last dregs of beer. He belched loudly before tossing the beer can high in the air. Naw, he was never that good, he thought, waiting for the can to land before his Berretta buddy spoke out again. His buddy didn't let him down, and the can immediately jumped out of sight after being rudely kissed by its first and last .40 caliber round. "Time to drain the lizard," he chuckled as he proceeded to do just that. Nestling back down against the tree, he lit another cigar, gave it a few puffs, then blew out a dislocated circle of smoke. He crossed his legs and gazed idly at the bay for a moment before cracking open another warm brewski. Yeah, the PT tended to separate the men from the boys all right, he thought whimsically. The challenge with this unique class and the instructors, however, was if the women could be separated from the girls, if *that* made any sense in the interest of maintaining equality amongst the recruits. Dalton put that aspect on hold and returned to the academy days

#

"Ya walked right into that one, Bragg!" Corporal Simpson, the grinning PT instructor, shouted after Dalton got tagged by a phantom uppercut punch.

Earl Padgett was a one hundred percent beast! Physically impressive at a muscular six foot three, and at a solid two hundred and thirty pounds, the quiet black recruit from Harford County was, like Dalton, just hoping to hang on for the remainder of their three rounds. Up to this point in the three-week boxing course, Dalton had done surprisingly well. A plodder, unlike some natural pugilists like the wiry, steel-eyed Mike Fox, or the hard-hitting, barrel-chested Jim Kerr, Dalton took the fight to the others in his slow, methodical manner. He'd absorbed his share of jarring hits while inflicting some winners on opponents, two days earlier putting a classmate out of service for two weeks with two broken ribs. During other memorable ring moments, Dalton had cornered several others, bombarding them with flurries of jabs and hard rights until the round ended. This time, Dalton was getting his ass kicked.

With his energy waning and his head spinning wildly, the few remaining seconds were turning into dragged out lifetimes, and he was getting dog-ass tired. Trying to ignore the punishment Padgett was wreaking with his jarring roundhouses, Dalton plodded forward again and connected a nice jab to Padgett's unguarded jaw, making him blink. Finally, a decent punch to piss off Godzilla. In doing so, of course, Dalton left himself wide open for a moment not fleeting enough. *Wham!* A leather-coated haymaker from left field connected, jarring his mouthpiece and headgear loose.

"Ya walked into another one, Bragg!" he heard Cpl. Simpson yell over the ringing in his head. Dalton numbly stood up straight, arms hanging at his sides, fighting hard to stiffen his jelly legs. He was sweating as if he were still hooked up to a polygraph, panting like a trailing racehorse ridden by a chubby jockey on a muddy Pimlico track.

Finally, gratefully, the whistle blew to end his misery. He wiped away the snot from his sore nose. Steadying himself, he shot the smiling Cpl. Simpson a lame stare, then shuffled over to his impervious Godzilla opponent. With an unsteady touch of the gloves and a quick, forced smile, Dalton left the ring without kissing the canvas. Damn if his ears weren't ringing like a bitch! *Shit!* Had to be the longest three minutes of his entire life, he brooded to himself before spitting out his saliva-coated mouthpiece. He fought the urge to throw up on an eager-beaver classmate who was trying to hold him steady while peppering him with too many "are you sure you're OK" questions. Yeah sure, I'm *OK,* you dumb shit, my gyroscope just needs re-calibration, that's all, he silently roared in his fuzzy world.

Boxing was a challenging hurdle at the academy, and there were some real knockdown, dragged out bouts between some of the boxers—the competition especially grueling when they vied for test scores. Several classmates suffered a few minor fractures, nosebleeds, and strains, along with some severely shattered egos. Dalton once tore a shoulder muscle throwing a hard right punch that failed to connect with a ducking opponent, a miss which forced him into a light duty status for several days.

They were taught basic boxing 101 techniques before actual ring time, and for the most part the later match-ups were equal and ordinary. There were occasions, however, when a recruit saw red and flew into a rage, pummeling an antagonist into Never Land. Those bouts were usually terminated quickly by the PT instructors, unless they deferred to let swirling gloves pound themselves out on tired bodies. The instructors took sadistic delight in taking their sweet time choosing suitable opponents, adding extra tension to the anxious recruits awaiting their turns. If they discerned that a recruit was timid or holding back, they'd assuredly assign him a Godzilla adversary. There was only one or two in the class, but nonetheless, Dalton was still dismayed when he saw them dance away from others in the ring. And these guys want to be fearless, intrepid Maryland State Troopers? He mused.

Although not of their own volitions, the female recruits weren't required to take the boxing course, a disparity, and a wrench thrown in the gears of the equality cause which undoubtedly festered in the minds of the instructors, Dalton thought.

In addition to boxing, there were endless miles of tiresome running. As a training requirement, a candidate had to finish the infamous five-mile run in under forty-five minutes. There was also the torture of the circuit-training course. A regimen from day one, the circuit training exercises included push-ups, pull-ups, sit-ups, high-bar dips, curls with weights and the hellish rope climbing. As the training progressed, the repetitions in the timed circuit course were increased, pushing the recruits to higher performances. After boxing, the class endured several weeks of judo and restraint-hold training. The judo stretching exercises alone were challenging, but Dalton found that keeping his judo kei outfit from unraveling was even more so. As in boxing, if the fiendish judo instructor perceived a recruit holding back, fearful of being roughed up, he'd select him or her to be the class dummy until the message got through. Ultimately, scores were finalized for the various physical training and classroom performances, which, when tabulated and averaged out, resulted in an overall class rating.

By the fourth academy week, Dalton had formed several friendships founded primarily on the respect he held for several of his fellow commiserates gung-ho spirits and athleticism. On the surface Dalton appeared to be outgoing and a trifle zany at times, but he had a tendency to be more introverted than he let on, much preferring the "lone wolf" role, a characteristic he vainly tried to alter during his academy stay. Nonetheless, he worked around the bothersome trait, helping to develop team spirit and the 'one for all" attitude the academy demanded. To a surprising degree it was working.

After several weeks, the pressure from the instructors subsided, allowing the recruits' true colors to emerge as the comfort levels rose.

One crazy-ass recruit, lanky Wayne Stegman, an Eastern Shore maverick from the sleepy town of Denton, occasionally avoided the early morning run by jumping into the reeking garbage dumpster when the class ran past the MSP cafeteria. Stegman, who favored the nickname "Scrotum" for his frequent habit of scratching his family jewels, was labeled an authentic space cadet after entertaining some of the recruits by gulping down a handful of slimy earthworms one night on yet another dare! Some adamantly believed 'Scrotum" when he boasted in his Eastern Shore drawl that he'd been a drone test pilot in the Air Force a few years before the MSP beckoned. Most simply gave him wide berth when he roamed the halls with that characteristic, loony bird look on his face. Jim Mallard, another batty classmate, was caught Xeroxing his bare foot on a copy machine in the dreaded Executive building. When the flabbergasted captain from Personnel sharply grilled him about what the hell he hoped to prove, the recruit calmly explained that he had a large splinter in the sole of his foot and was merely trying to find its exact location before taking a needle to it. Inexplicably, the red-faced Mallard miraculously escaped from that escapade with no demerits.

Finally, despite weeks of painstaking diligence, Dalton earned himself a dingy weekend at the academy. The much uncelebrated ordeal came when he got involved in a water-hose battle with another classmate after a Red Cross lifesaving class in the "training tank." While they wrestled for the hose, an errant spray splashed against a hot overhead floodlight. With a shrill, echoing *Pop,* it shattered, raining jagged glass into the "tank" depths. Responding post-haste, a leering instructor rewarded them both with three well-deserved demerits.

Dalton received his clinching weekend demerits later that night after homesick Maynard fell asleep right after lights-out, failing miserably in his lookout role when the night duty instructor made his bed-check rounds. Stealthily tip-toeing into their room, Corporal Earhart, a swarthy, rather uncomplicated instructor, got suspicious after spotting light under a closet door. Yanking the door open, he jumped back and dropped his jaw and flashlight while Dalton peered sheepishly from underneath the gray blanket before bursting into a shit-eating grin. By waning flashlight, Dalton had been studying for an upcoming test, a direct violation of an academy "lights-out" commandment! Quickly recovering after realizing Dalton hadn't been caught playing with his personal pocket rocket, Cpl. Earhart tagged him with two demerits and ordered him to bed as Maynard snored on.

Well, at least Dalton and several other intrepid classmates had evaded a sure thing weekend restriction several days before. It was a dubious, brainstorming session culminating with an easy answer to the cleaning of a super-long, black rubber runner in the gym. Simply enough, the bulky runner was tossed into the "training tank." Recovering it, however, was another screwed up matter which was rectified only after nine other candidates were quietly summoned from evening studies to muscle the dripping behemoth from the tank.

Midway through the training, it was musical chair time for new roommates, and Dalton lost his struggling buddy Maynard. His new roommate was Melvin Purvey, a lanky, studious, twenty-five year-old from the dreary; some say borderline Twilight Zone, rural town of Princess Anne in Somerset County at the lower end of the Eastern Shore.

Purvey, who kept his hair in a mini Afro, wore an oversized pair of black-rimmed glasses that made him look even more intelligent than he'd ever chance to imagine. Purvey turned out to be an athletic, determined classmate, and a very meticulous, almost anal-minded, room cleaner too, quite the welcome opposite of Maynard who'd turned into a demerit magnet. Thanks to their teamwork, Dalton and Purvey never received any room demerits, a miraculous feat mainly achieved by Purvey's habit of waking up in the early dawn hours to scour the entire room by shrouded flashlight. Gratified, Dalton eagerly helped Purvey out during the study hours, reviewing material with him that would unfailingly pop up in the daily quizzes and weekly tests.

Dalton was surprised at how soon he and Purvey had bonded, despite his initial perception that Purvey had a tinge of black militancy, an aura Purvey may have acquired after hanging out with militant sympathizers in college. Casual conversation gradually evolved to their personal lives and the places they called home. Unlike Dalton, who'd lived his life in the middle class suburbs, Purvey's lower-class upbringing on the Eastern Shore was quite a contrast.

Melvin Purvey was the oldest of four kids, three strapping brothers and a runt sister, who were raised in a caring, religiously strict, down-home family. To make ends meet and send her kids to college, his mother worked long, nauseating hours on a chicken disassembly line at the Perdue processing plant in Salisbury. Purvey's humble-mannered, stoop shouldered father cut timber and toiled in the soybean fields of their modest family farm. From his preteen years, Melvin cared for his younger siblings as soon as he came home from school and up until the moment his tired parents dragged themselves home from work. His parent's sage guidance and backbreaking efforts were eventually rewarded with the assurance that Melvin and his siblings were afforded college educations, a rarity for most black kids living in the county. They were educations that had enabled them to expand their horizons beyond their parents who'd dropped out of grade school to scratch an existence in one of the state's poorest areas.

Much to his credit, and to his parents' pride, Melvin graduated from the University of Maryland's Eastern Shore College with a degree in economics. When Melvin took his parents aside one evening to tell them that he'd applied to become a Maryland State Trooper, they were stunned. Both parents expressed dire concerns about their son being an idealistic young black man in such a staunchly conservative WASP organization they'd known the State Police to be ever since its inception. Despite their misgivings, Melvin Purvey persevered in his belief that as a minority member of such an esteemed law-enforcement agency, he could strike a blow against inequality by helping others out, regardless of their skin color or personal creeds. Four months later, suitcase in hand, he was staring up at the front entrance of the MSP police academy.

After being roommates for a few weeks, Dalton and Mel threw away cumbersome facades of strained niceties and engaged in intellectually philosophical discussions about basic black vs white disparities.

"You ain't a man till you've split the black oak, hear me, Dalton?" "Hey Mel, ya know why aspirins are white? Cause they work, get it?" "Yo Dalton, for me, the blacker the berry, the sweeter the juice!" "OK, Mister Know-it-all Purvey, what do you call a black chick who's on birth control than? Ha...got ya! Ya call it crime prevention, my black buddy! And yeah, Mel...what the hell is that God-awful shit you brothers put on your face before y'all shave anyhow? Stuff stinks to hell!" "Onlyest thing that stinks worse'n that, Dalton my blond hair, blue-eyed, albino brother from another mother, is that damn Willie Nelson or Johnny Cash twangy crap some of your country-hick white boy pals play too loud when they're doin' them work details every morning!"

For most troopers, such racially dicey subjects were out of bounds, ambiguously taboo for those within the conservative based ranks of the Maryland State Police. But for a genuine, trusting friendship that had transcended racial sensitivities, they served as nothing but comical fodder for camaraderie.

#

Finally, it was time for weapons training, and each candidate was issued the signature Maryland State Police embossed, previously used Colt .38-caliber six-inch revolver. The initial pistol training was conducted in a stuffy, poorly ventilated indoor firing range in the basement beneath the academy. Qualifications were later conducted on the MSP outdoor range next to the picturesque Liberty Reservoir in Baltimore County. In addition to training and qualifying with the long-barrel revolver, the recruits also qualified with the Remington 870 twelve-gauge shotgun using the typical OO buckshot, solid slug loads and the smaller birdshot loads. Annihilating tossed clay pigeons with the skeet rounds was one of Dalton's favorite things.

Familiar with firearms discipline, Dalton quickly became proficient. It wasn't hard to determine who the real shooters were, with most deadeye candidates coming from either the Eastern Shore or Western Maryland. They were naturally talented hunters and expert shots. Dalton was surprised that several of the recruits had never fired a weapon before, with a few having never heard a gunshot. He made it a habit to avoid being near them while on the firing line.

The regimented Liberty Range training turned out to be a welcome respite to the fast-paced academy. The class relished the casual ambience of their week at the firing range, a week which surprisingly concluded with the recruits being treated to a sans-booze barbeque feast. Amazingly, every class member, including all six female candidates, qualified in the weapons training. To the surprise of the firearms instructors, there were neither accidental discharges nor any coincidental bloodletting, either.

Alas, on their last day at the range, the cagey mentors decided it was time to shake up the routine, and the dreaded CS teargas "demonstration" was deemed the appropriate way to do it. Grinning ear to ear, Sergeant Carter popped several canisters of the irritating gas and tossed them out on a grassy field. The fanciful sergeant waited for the billowing white clouds to reach the desired level before ordering the unprotected recruits forward for the assault. Within seconds the entire class was gagging. Foot-long snot bubbles dripped from noses, and burning tears streamed from bloodshot eyes, as they dutifully lurched through the thick wall of CS under the prodding of their gleeful, ever-accommodating academy instructors.

The recruit class eventually moved on to the practical driver training course. Recruits, joined in twos or threes, would receive tutoring by an old-salt trooper who allegedly was selected for his vast skill and experience with road patrol. Dalton and two other classmates (all unarmed for the training) were subsequently delegated to serve under the sage guidance of Trooper First Class Bobby Cantler, a senior trooper from ASED (Automotive Service Enforcement Division).

Known as "Bird-Dog" to his friends, Cantler was a ruddy-face, heavy-set trooper who kept his wavy black hair slicked back like Elvis Presley's. This coiffure was accentuated by thick sideburns extending an inch or so below MSP regulation. With a scowl and a harsh, gravely voice from too many cheap cigars, the old-salt trooper first class at first seemed more of a threat to his apprentices than an instructor. Once they left the headquarters complex, however, Cantler's seemingly gruff manner quickly changed him into a stern but amiable mentor.

The first day on the road was spent practicing the various traffic stops on a closed ramp on the Baltimore beltway. Timing was always paramount, and the high-speed turns and traffic stop exercises were never conducted fast enough to please the badgering instructors. Once these basics were achieved, it was time for the recruits to perfect their traffic stop techniques on live, "Johnny Q" citizens.

During the next few days, Dalton and his two classmates took turns chauffeuring Tfc. Cantler through several counties, stalking hapless motorists and searching for any violations warranting a stop. One evening, to the trainees' surprise, they wound up at Cantler's modest Eastern Shore home in Chester for a country-style dinner before they headed back to the academy. "Bird Dog" Cantler broke out his true colors that evening. Just as he picked up his dinner fork to stab at a slice of baked ham, he heard the raucous squawking of the black birds in the high branches of the cherry tree in the back yard. His eyes rolled, and a contemptuous sneer instantly spread across his face. With an agitated grunt, Cantler sprang from his chair, drew his revolver, and stomped out the back door. Dalton and his two classmates stared slack-jawed at each other when they heard the screen door slam shut.

Blam! Blam! Blam! Blam! (Pause) *Blam! Blam!* Tendrils of grey smoke seeped from the barrel of his empty revolver as the poker-faced Cantler clomped back into the house. Wordlessly, he holstered his gun, returned to the dinner table, and picked up his fork. Cantler's rail-thin, somber wife nonchalantly kept picking through her three-bean salad as if nothing had happened. From across the table, Dalton smiled sheepishly at his two unsettled cohorts, as they sat in awkward silence with lowered heads and fidgety fingers. Yeah, Dalton silently mused, ole Cantler's rambunctious image was rapidly elevating to the veritable-hero status. And the circus of events continued.

En route back to the academy, Dalton slammed on the brakes and jerked the wheel hard to avoid the red 1968 Ford Mustang that had suddenly cut him off as he'd pulled onto Route 50 near Easton. Riding shotgun, Cantler tossed his lit cigar out the window with a loud curse and slammed a fist on the dashboard.

"Jesus H Christ, Bragg!" He sputtered out snarly-like. "Your ass better stop that dumb lil bitch so's we can have us a talk with her! Hear me trooper?" Dalton floored the Torino, but before he could hit the bubble gum light, the Mustang had already pulled off the road. When the cruiser ground to a screeching halt, Dalton and his miffed instructor donned cowboy hats and leaped out.

"I'm *Sooo* sorry if I inconvenienced you in any way, *Sir*," she breathlessly told Dalton as she batted her baby-blues. With a whimsical sigh, she leaned over and gave him a mouth-watering shot of her flawless puppies straining hard against her thin bikini top, begging for release. "Is there anything, I mean *anything* I can do to convince you that I'll never do something stupid like that ever again, huh, trooper Sir?" the twenty year-old lollipop pleaded. "Why me?" Dalton heard the quivering voice in his head squeak as she woefully pouted and gazed into his eyes before breaking into a knee-jerking smile. After discussing the violation with the overly affable, 34B-cup, bikini-clad, long-legged, sandy-blonde vamp, Dalton returned to the cruiser with her license and registration in his shaking hand.

Cantler, who'd been standing close by, scrutinizing Dalton's actions like a mother goose, stayed with the Mustang. With his face in the driver's open window and his hands resting on the roof, he engaged the friendly young tart in animated conversation. When he finally meandered back to the cruiser, Cantler teasingly peppered Dalton with questions about the blonde babe's obvious attributes, what she was barely wearing (an abbreviated two-piece turquoise colored bikini with a gold chain necklace and peace sign medallion necklace), and her availability status.

Dalton focused and gripped his pen tight, scribbling out the written warning while dodging his instructor's questions. Dalton's two backseat buddies were making lewd comments and chuckling with each other, making Dalton vice-grip the pen. While he hadn't overlooked her lusciousness in the slightest way, Dalton was curious about Cantler's relentless barrage of inquiries about her. She *was* a hot number, though. Dalton dismissed his nagging thoughts long enough to scramble from the cruiser and give her the warning.

During the academy study hours later that eve, it hit him. With a laugh, he remembered where he'd seen the blonde's red mustang, and in particular, the small, pink bunny necklace that hung from her rearview mirror! Dalton ran down the hall to enlighten his two driver-training cohorts about the traffic stop setup. They laughed and cajoled each other, agreeing that it was the same red Mustang driven by the blonde bombshell from the Eastern Shore! Yup—the same one which had been parked directly in front of the same room of the Pikesville motel where they'd picked up their lusty driver training instructor the previous two mornings before the days escapades.

They all agreed that Tfc. Cantler's driver-trainer assignment just had to be the most coveted assignment in the MSP. They also acknowledged his great taste in sexy sweethearts too, but more paramount, they conceded to each other that the topic would never leave their lips at any cost. Driver-training instructors could wreak serious havoc on recruits with loose lips, this they were sure of. The driver-training program ended several days later, and Dalton and his two classmates easily passed, the jocular image of "Bird Dog" Cantler never to fade from their memories.

#

When his eyes riveted on the dark-red pool of stale blood on the stainless steel cart, Dalton knew it was going to be a *bad ass,* bummer of a morning. The cart was probably pre-positioned there at the entrance for shock effect by one of the examiner's assistants, he thought, as he followed his classmates down the dimly lit basement hallway of the Maryland Medical Examiner's Office in downtown Baltimore. *Abra Cadaver!* Welcome to the macabre world!

It hit them with stark reality when the pungent, all-invasive, unforgettable scent of death greeted the recruits entering the autopsy room. It was a fetid, copperish, metallic stench that permeated their clothes, an inescapable stink they'd reek of throughout the day. Like several of his cohorts, Dalton breathed through his mouth to avoid the odor. There were six nude bodies lying face up, two white and waxy looking, others shaded in brown and black hues, all of them morosely positioned on stainless steel tables. Two bodies had obvious gunshot wounds, while the others displayed no discernable causes of death. But, they were all very much dead, and the ugliness and reality of death was what the academy wanted you to experience firsthand, as conditioning for the inevitable experiences a trooper would confront.

Wasting no time, a solemn assistant examiner/pathologist, in white frock, motioned for the class to gather around one of the examining tables. Dalton's attention shifted to the pimple-faced, weasel-eyed assistant who was standing bent-over, next to the pathologist. He was

38

casually munching on a glazed donut, as the pathologist picked up the electric scalpel in preparation for a Y cut on the first cadaver. Dalton wondered what kind of a cave *that* greasy-hair troglodyte crawled home to later, or maybe he slept here in one of the vacant body drawers perhaps? The high-pitched whine of the scalpel cutting into dead flesh signaled the start of the first autopsy. Dalton turned his attention back to the event and noticed that several wide-eyed classmates were backing away from the table.

It was fascinatingly mind-boggling! For the first time in his life, and from a bird's eye view, Dalton was witnessing undisputable affirmation of humans being true animals, as internal organs were identified, examined, and removed for analysis. Fascinated, he'd never forget the working of the scalpel as the spinning blade cut neatly through human skull. The busy tool showered tiny blood-speckled, ivory-like bone fragments, a small clump or two of hair, and tiny bits of yellowish dura matter on the floor—and on the shoes, shirts, pants and startled faces of "Scrotum" Stegman and two other stout classmates who'd been standing too close.

From the corner of an eye, Dalton saw the weasel assistant wipe his nose with the back of a hand and yank a half-eaten powdered donut from his grimy, once upon a time, clean white jacket. He opened his mouth and stretched it into one of the ugliest yawns Dalton had ever seen, before cramming the rest of the donut into it. Finishing the stale treat, his weasel-face exploded into a satisfied weasel-smile as spindly fingers flew to his mouth so he could lick up the crumbs. Satisfied, the smiling weasel began picking at one of the many bloated blackheads that decorated his pockmarked forehead. Yeah, buddy!

After the first of the three scheduled autopsies, several members of the class were noticed—particularly for their absence. Dalton thought it was commendable that none of his classmates had puked during the unsavory human disassembly process. Later, they were escorted into the morgue refrigeration room where several nude, Y-cut bodies had been neatly stacked on top of each other after their autopsies. Splendid! Gratefully, they were spared the odoriferous encounter with the decomposition room, where several dissected bodies and parts were stashed. With all senses saturated by the essence of the dead, the class finally left the Medical Examiners Office and the dankness of death for a short walk in the warm sun, and a breath of polluted, but now surprisingly sweet, city air. The "afternoon delight" was up next, and lunch at this point (if desired) was close at hand.

From the Cadaver Cavern to the House of Correction at Jessup, a.k.a. the Human Correctional Corral, the "afternoon delight" of a long, mind-numbing day. It was a dank and dismal place, another conditioning experience factored into the academy training. As expected, the inmate cells were grubby and cramped, and the funk wafting from too many people cooped too close together was pervasive. It was no small wonder to Dalton that the complex had been seen several riots during the last decade. He had a premonition that he and most of his classmates would inevitably find themselves back there again when the humid summer days clashed harshly with the cramped humanity to fuel a sizable disturbance. Not soon enough, the inviting sun once again warmed their spirits as the trooper candidates bid adieu to Jessup and headed back to the academy.

The academy class was winding down, and various ratings were being compiled to determine a final score and class standing for each trooper candidate. Dalton felt confident he'd attain a high rating, and he had an inkling he'd probably wind up amongst the top five in the class.

Finally, the recruits were issued their basic uniforms and equipment by First Sergeant Best, the cigar-chewing, supply officer sage. Rounding off the clothing allowances, they received their much coveted, tailor-made Class A uniform blouses and summer straw "cowboy" Stetsons. It was the unique "cowboy hat" which set the MSP apart from other police agencies. Personnel orders were also issued for assignments, with the candidates usually being assigned to primary or alternate areas they'd selected earlier. Dalton had requested the Annapolis Barrack as his first choice, but his alternate, the Prince Frederick Post in Calvert County, was the assignment he and two other classmates embraced.

"Ya got the Prince Frederick Post?" F/Sgt Best growled at Dalton as he tossed him his blouse. Dalton smiled and nodded. "Ever been down that way, first shirt?" The old mule skinner sergeant shot him a hard glance, chewed on the soggy, unlit cigar stub dangling from his mouth, and rolled his eyes. *"Haw!"* he hooted back, "Who the hell's parade you piss on, eh?" The sage NCO crinkled an eye and smirked. "You'll be doing a lot of bar fightin' with them good ole boys down there in Chesapeake and North Beach, yes sir, you better believe that one for sure, sonny boy," he said with a wave of his cigar. Well at least he'd been assigned to a full service barrack in lieu of being sent to a traffic oriented beltway barrack. Now, if he could only find out where the hell Calvert County, his MSP "proving ground," was.

Although his home was on the lower Eastern Shore, Mel Purvey, Dalton's roommate, was assigned to the Waldorf Barrack in Charles County, and on a good day, Purvey's daily commute would be over three hours one way. It was understood, however, that transfers could eventually put a trooper closer to home after a year or so of seniority. Nevertheless, a transfer to either Western Maryland, or the Eastern Shore, was usually a long wait, according to MSP scuttlebutt. At the time, the new troopers were unaware of the department's pressing need to assign minority members to the more rural areas for high visibility purposes.

On the night before graduation, "Scrotum" Stegman, clad only in a jockstrap, his issued Sam Browne belt, and his felt Stetson, decided to celebrate early by performing a one-man parade down the long dorm halls. To the dismay of the male recruits, their female classmates refrained from joining in. Several other spirited candidates, however, rained on "Scrotum's" parade, spraying him down with streams of liquid teargas (CS) from their newly assigned mace canisters. The ensuing tear gas battle temporarily turned the third floor into an irritable no-man's land, replete with gagging, gasping and swollen eyed combatants. At least the wise powers-to-be had decided not to assign the recruits their "38's" yet, Dalton silently told himself as he ducked wayward CS torrents.

#

The graduation ceremony was held in the gymnasium, where rows of folding chairs replaced the judo mats and all the other torture devices. Dalton gazed at his classmates and reflected on their academy tenure. Physically, they were all in the best shape of their lives. Mentally and emotionally, they were lean, hungry tigers in the law-enforcement realm, each one, male or female, ready for the challenge. All six female classmates had persevered to the end. Dalton especially admired two of his newbie sister troopers for their tenacity and drive— Lithesome, sharp-minded Margot "Da Babe" Trott, and Deanna Cupe, a spunky, street-wise fireplug who'd given her all. The candidates had all persevered to become fledglings in the ranks of "Maryland's Finest," and now it was time to join up with the "big dogs" in the real world out there. En masse, they were given their oaths of office. When their names were called out, each candidate took to the stage amidst applause to receive their graduation diplomas and badges from the beaming MSP Superintendent.

When Dalton's name was announced, he bolted from his chair and bounded to the stage. After he received his badge and diploma, the Superintendent had him pause while he reached for a plaque under the podium. Standing ramrod straight at attention on rubbery legs, Dalton vaguely heard the Superintendent read the commendation before it was presented to him. It was a Superintendent's Commendation for his outstanding performance in being number one in his class.

Amen! Fellow classmates acknowledged his feat with a rousing, standing ovation, and Dalton saluted them and smiled back when he floated back to his seat. *Amen*—to the second power!

(Purgatory Ridge)

A bald eagle, the majestic, regal raptor of the Chesapeake, quietly alighted on the upper limb of a tall oak nearby, grounding the sergeant's mind back to his solitary retirement party. Freezing all movement save for the shifting of his eyes, Dalton watched the large bird use it's curved beak to tear apart the shiny alewife it'd snared from the bay far below. Simple and amazingly natural life, fitting so perfectly well in the scheme of it all, he reflected. Long live Henry David Thoreau and his philosophical perspective on nature's lucidity! The eagle suddenly lifted its head and froze in place. For a long, pregnant moment, the raptor's keen eyes remained fixed on him like a frozen radar beam. Dalton held his breath and locked eyes with it, hoping only that the broad-shouldered bird saw him as no threat. He reluctantly dismissed the rising surge of scrambled vibes, hints of communication perhaps that teased his senses. When he saw the eagle ruffle its tail feathers and casually shift the grip of its golden talons clinging tightly to the branch and its prey, Dalton was relieved. Several minutes after the last few alewife scraps were finished off, the eagle bobbed its bald head in Dalton's direction, let out a satisfied, high-pitched chirp, and launched itself into the air on powerful wings. With an appreciative smile, Dalton watched as the magnificent bird soared higher until the canopy of the tall trees finally blocked it from his sight. 'God Speed, my wise, all-knowing friend," he whispered in the eagle's direction. "In my next life, maybe."

Yeah, the six months of academy training had been pretty rough, but it hadn't been as bad as he had expected. He'd developed a few solid friendships, especially the one with Purvey, and the overall esprit-de-corps of the class had been an incredible experience, one he'd remember with pride—the innocent pride of a naive and quixotic young man who was about to embark on a daring, new adventure on life's proving grounds.

Dalton drained the last dregs from the beer can, raised it in mock salute, and then flung it out in front of him. Deftly switching the Berretta from right hand to left, he quickly shut one eye, gained alignment, and squeezed the trigger. *"Blam!"* Instantly, the can was sent wildly spinning, end over end to careen off the cliff. "To my academy class," he chuckled, taking another rum river crook from his pocket. And than there was the Prince Frederick Post in good-ole-boy Calvert County, the proving ground he'd been assigned to after being hatched from the academy. Now talk about a slow trip down a lazy river at low tide....

Chapter 3

THE PRINCE FREDERICK POST   July-1974

Prepping for his first MSP assignment, Dalton meticulously polished his gun belt and spit shined his black Corframs with melted shoe polish. Damn, how he relished the new leather smell and the leather creaking sound when he slapped the Sam Browne on. Elbow grease and Brasso painstakingly stripped lacquer from ornaments, and a thorough buffing made each piece glitter and beg for inspection. He even polished the round tips of the bullets snugged into the gun belt loops. The Colt .38 revolver was spotless and lightly oiled. Satisfied, Dalton drew the weapon from the new holster and dry-fired it in front of a mirror a few times—mainly to break in the stiff leather, but also to ogle himself a bit. Dalton dressed in his neatly pressed uniform khaki short-sleeve shirt and OD (olive drab) custom-fit trousers. With his hair cut white-wall short, the cop image was enhanced by a new pair of green-tinted aviator sunglasses, a vogue item for most road troopers. After long hours of finicky prep work, he was finally squared away.

Dalton linked up with classmates Al Heister and Tom Rensir, also assigned to the Prince Frederick Post, and on a sweltering day in early July, the three "boot" troopers made the trek south to Calvert County. Heister, a lanky, street-smart former MSP cadet from Baltimore, felt like a duck out of water during the countryside drive. The stocky built, easy-going Rensir, who was slightly more rural than Heister, vainly tried to hide his mounting anticipation with nervous chortling and off-key humming. Dalton sat back and savored the rustic scenery.

"Damn, must be some good ole boys down here for sure," he finally quipped aloud. "Almost every street sign we've passed, has bullet holes in it !" "Yeah buddy," Rensir railed back "Guess when those tipsy hayseeds around here get tired of throwing cow chips at each other, they jump in their pickups and bust off a few caps on the way to their next watering hole," Heister shouted as he playfully roughed up Rensir's neatly combed hairdo. "Sure as shit a long way from Bawl-mur," he added. "And what the hell's that rank-ass smell, anyhow?" Dalton scrunched up his face and held his nose when they passed a pigpen south of Grover's Turn Road in Owings. "*That*, my man, is the odoriferous bouquet of unadulterated pig shit welcoming us to Calvert County," he answered with a laugh.

Entering the parking lot behind the old brick Calvert County courthouse in Prince Frederick, all three boots swapped startled glances in dead silence. Nothing marked their new assignment, save for two MSP marked cruisers on the lot and a plate-glass back door with a Maryland State Police sign next to it. Yeah Buddy!

Although the Maryland State Police has a long history in Calvert County, it wasn't until the mid 1950s that the post was shoehorned into a broom closet sized office. Before that, the county relied on the Waldorf Barrack in Charles County for police assistance. In 1956, the fledgling Prince Frederick Detachment was a power-packed force of two troopers. The Calvert County Sheriff's Office, a sheriff and a handful of deputies, served court papers, handled minor complaints and maintained the squalid county jail. With a slow but steady population growth, the MSP detachment gradually added more troopers. After the courthouse was remodeled in 1971, the pregnant detachment gave birth to an MSP Post comprising *three* rooms serving eighteen assigned troopers! The main room was trooper's room, complete with four surplus desks and a metal pole to which disgruntled prisoners were usually handcuffed while being processed. The county also gave the MSP "squatting rights" to a second-floor bedroom for wayward or divorced troopers.

Centrally located, the Calvert County courthouse complex was the county's political power base, its main activity hub. In addition to the district and circuit court rooms and offices, it also housed the State's Attorney's office, the Emergency control center and a slew of other local government offices. Above the Sheriff's Office was the antiquated, pitifully cramped county jail consisting of three large communal cells, with a squalid cell for female prisoners downstairs. For the early seventies, the centralized services were barely sufficient for the county's twenty thousand citizens. During the next thirty years, and much to the dismay of the old-timers, rural development unexpectedly caught up with the "Charm of the Chesapeake," and the county's population mushroomed.

Greeted by crude jeers from the barred jail windows, Dalton pressed the back door buzzer. Moments later, the three young troopers were met by a thin, balding, blotchy-faced MSP sergeant. Sergeant Jon Bane's neck twitched as he returned their salutes and stuttered through an awkward introduction. They entered directly into the drab troopers' room which served as the multipurpose BS arena. Notified of their arrival, several curious old-salt troopers gathered around, sizing them up, giving the new troopers the hard once-over expected from veterans. One swarthy-looking trooper, his shirt adorned with F/Sgt stripes, had his legs propped on a desk, Stetson cocked back on his head, and an unlit pipe in his hand. His eyes crinkled with amusement as he quietly studied the new troopers shaking hands with the others. Dalton felt a sinking feeling in his gut, sensed an omen that a green French Foreign Legionnaire might have felt when he first reported in to his barren post in the Sahara.

"Hey! Any of you people fish or hunt?" boomed the round-faced first sergeant. The three new troopers glanced at each other. "Well if you do, you're sure as hell gonna like working here, sports," First Sergeant Bill Flyger, the post commander, spouted out to them with a grin. With that welcome revelation, Dalton's sphincter muscle started relaxing.

Flyger, a sharp, sage trooper from Western Maryland, had been stationed in Calvert for several years. Politically savvy to MSP ways, he nevertheless retained his jovial personality and roguishness by not sweating the small stuff that too many others pulled their hair out over. Legendary throughout the force as a consummate raconteur, the colorful first-shirt was also an accomplished outdoors man, "Wild Bill" was well known in the county by most of the farmers, and, unfortunately, by the two state game wardens who were hard-pressed to keep track of his dubious outdoor escapades.

The "boot" troopers would hear many fables about their new commander. The police cruiser hot pursuit of a panicky buck bolting through a muddy cornfield, Flygers' six-gun blazing from the driver's window, was one of the more exalted tales, especially since a tow truck had to be called to pull his steed from the muck before the ill-tempered tenant farmer came home. A stealthy, late evening bass pond poaching by him and a buddy trooper on the ole Morrsett pond in Wallville was only another small adrenalin boost for the complacent top dog. With a leader like Wild Bill setting the tone, Dalton pondered about his new assignment and made a mental note to discuss the merits of bass fishing at the first available moment.

Sergeant Bane waltzed them through a quick tour of the modest post, and then busied them with a slew of required forms. As new road troopers, they'd be assigned to a seasoned trooper as their field instructor during the next four weeks of their break-in. With cramped writing fingers, the boots were ferried to a favored radar site on Route 4 just north of Prince Frederick, where, in the sweltering afternoon their first road-trooper hours were spent working in a radar stopping team

Their first day rounded out, the tired but exuberant trio left for home. Both Rensir and Heister were nearly incredulous about their in-the-sticks assignment. For Dalton, however, his impression of the rustic county was that he'd experienced an overdue, twenty-five year step back into the welcome past.

Kregg Erickson, a tall, thirty year-old, square-jawed, movie star-handsome road trooper, was Dalton's field instructor. Kregg was an easygoing Navy vet with a matchless sense of humor. Since his messy divorce from a clingy wife four years ago, he'd been stationed at PF, and he was well acquainted with the county, its hot spots and local characters. Meticulous in appearance and endowed with an infectious personality, the blond, blue-eyed Kregg cut a stellar image, and Dalton immediately liked him. As his mentor, it would be the senior trooper's responsibility to guide him through a road trooper's myriad of responsibilities.

While not a hustler in either traffic or criminal work by any stretch, Kregg was respected for his steady, levelheaded approach. He also had a silver tongue that was effective in his collaborations with the county's more-alluring females who all knew him on a first-name basis. Kregg, however, was a taken man, as Dalton soon learned after Kregg invited him to lunch at his girlfriend's place. Dalton's jaw dropped when his eyes riveted on the bikini-clad, bronzed blonde sprawled lazily on a pool-side chaise lounge. Jackie was drop-dead gorgeous, a number ten at least—and she knew it. During lunch she sat close to him, teasing him with the scent of her sun-kissed skin and gushy smiles. Dalton steeled himself and feigned complacency, all the while knowing that she was just one bikini short of being the most scrumptious cherry vanilla popsicle he'd ever hope to devour. It was a beastly burden, and he wished someone would shoot him to end his misery, but the allure of a ravishing femme fatale unfailingly turned his head into Silly Putty.

After picking up the PF Post's sole radar unit, Kregg set out to give his trainee a night-shift tour of the county. Posthaste, Dalton got the expected "forget all you learned at the academy" sermon from his earnest mentor. Tired from lecturing, the senior trooper parked the cruiser at his favorite "ambush" spot on Route 4, the county's main highway, at the bottom of a hill in Huntingtown. Setting up the battered old SR-5 radar unit, he aimed the bulbous radar head to the rear, clipped the base to the left rear window, then rolled it up for a snug fit. It was close to the end of the month, and Kregg was in need of a few more traffic stops to attain the minimum ten citations and twenty warnings required to keep supervisors off the road troopers' backs.

Adrenalin pumped, Dalton waited for the inevitable speeders, all the while peppering his trainer with questions. Several cars passed, but Kregg ignored them as mere warnings. Later, when a car rocketed past, Dalton gazed over at the dimly lit radar meter and watched the needle tip over eighty miles an hour. Sparkling with excitement, he turned to find his mentor fast asleep with his chin on his chest.

For the next hour, while Kregg snored on, the dismayed boot trooper monitored the Troop E radio channel, hoping to discern the new, alien-sounding abbreviated jargon of the police ten codes. Being in the same troop, the Prince Frederick post shared the same radio channel with the Annapolis Barrack and the Leonardtown Post in St. Mary's county. During nights shifts and quieter times, there were few overlaps in radio messages. When calls spiraled in the other counties, however, it was a different matter, with garbled radio messages being "walked on" by frustrated troopers and PCOs. With a start, Kregg suddenly snorted himself awake and shot Dalton a sheepish grin. With nary a spoken word, he started up J-12, the Ford Torino cruiser, and bee-lined back to the post for a badly needed coffee.

Dalton soon learned that Kregg had an aversion to two irksome job facets: the night shift and the infernal paperwork. As explained to Dalton, there was some kind of a report required for each daily activity a trooper performed, from dog bites and runaways to crimes against persons, property destructions, motor vehicle accidents, plane crashes, suspicious any things, and anything minutely suspicious! Starting with MSP form 1, the accident report, there were more than one hundred and ninety departmental forms to decipher and abuse accordingly. Dalton thought the MARS (Maryland Accident Reports System) report was a labyrinth of uniquely disjointed codes and blocks, a supreme hindrance for those who loathed paperwork.

The other MSP form of renown was the much-abused MSP form 17 "buck slip" which came in thick pads. The buck slip was an abbreviated multi-purpose form highlighted with ten check-off sections such as, "See me," "For your information," "Approve and return," "As requested," etc, with a space for remarks below. In later years, because of its popularity with lofty superiors aspiring to become creative writers, the form 17 ballooned into a big-brother full-page form 17A. It was said, and devoutly believed, that most troopers could have wallpapered all the rooms in their homes, *and* all their relatives' homes, with the form 17s they'd accrued during their careers.

There were endless forms and reports; monthly performance reports, MSP vehicle reports, bi-weekly pay reports, five different fingerprint cards and even a form to eliminate forms! A criminal or DWI arrest required several reports which would keep the average trooper desk-bound and off the road for hours as he muddled through. And *heaven forbid*, they had to be done the State Police way, using *black* ink only, or a typewriter. A typewriter, yes, if you could navigate it, and were lucky to find one that hadn't been mauled by an irate trooper from the previous shift.

For Dalton, who initially took a stab at creative writing, learning to write in the robotic nuts-and-bolts MSP language was challenging.

Flooded with rejected reports, he acquiesced, realizing any word over eight letters, unless it was a person's name or place, wasn't appreciated or accepted.

Early on, Dalton learned, that other than not having a black ink pen or not wearing your cowboy hat in public, a trooper's paramount duty was to know where he was at all times. In the rural county, timely backup was usually adequate during early and late shifts. During night shift, however, there were no supervisors and only two troopers covered the elongated county. A trooper unsure of his whereabouts during a night shift crisis could jeopardize his buddy and/or find himself in a real world of shit, Kregg admonished him. Requests for emergency assistance from MSP troopers in Calvert's sister counties, or vice versa, were common, and learning to perform a "dog and pony show" while waiting for the cavalry to arrive was essential. Knowing your location in the county in the early seventies wasn't a vexing problem—unless you got entangled in the maze of unmarked roads in the Chesapeake Ranch Club, a convoluted private development on the bay east of Lusby.

Calvert County, or "Culvert" as the locals prefer, is a dagger-shaped thirty-five mile long peninsula with a nine-mile maximum width. The Chesapeake Bay borders the east and the Patuxent River the west. In 1964, construction of a four-lane highway began, and during the next few years Maryland Route 4 was extended eighteen miles south to Prince Frederick. From there, pending dual-lane construction, it remained a single lane road that ended at the county's southern tip in Solomons. MD Route 260 branched off from Route 4 at the northern county line, running east to intersect with Route 261 in the incorporated town of Chesapeake Beach.

In 1974 the intersection was controlled by just one of Calvert County's *two* traffic lights at the time, with the county's other traffic light in Prince Frederick at the intersection of MD Route 231 (Hallowing Point Rd) and Route 2. West on Hallowing Point road eventually brought you to the Benedict Bridge and Charles County. Most of the secondary roads were just minutes away from the main arteries.

Since the MSP had yet to formulate a policy pertaining to secondary weapons, most troopers also carried personal weapons to augment their issued service revolver. Shotguns of varied sizes and gauges were first choices, and were usually kept cased and unsecured on the floorboard against the front seat. Several troopers, the gun buffs, even brought along rifles, one of which was an Army surplus-M-2 .30 caliber carbine with an extended banana clip and an extra clip taped to the stock. Slapjacks were carried, and backup handguns of various types and calibers were stuffed in back pockets, leg holsters or under car seats. The Colt revolver and the backup weapons became a trooper's most intimate "friends" when he patrolled the county's desolate areas.

With "protective" vests still in the planning stage, several troopers wore or carried good luck charms for that added psychic benefit. For that purpose, Dalton carried a 1921 silver dollar, which his father had lent to his older brother who'd dodged bullets and punji sticks in Viet Nam. On his safe return home, his brother had bequeathed it to Dalton, and it remained securely nestled in his wallet throughout his career.

#

More essential then any other phonetic ten code used by the MSP troopers was the prevalent "*SIGNAL 13*," the unsanctioned code the troopers used to call for immediate emergency assistance.

During Dalton's break-in phase, Kregg continuously stressed the code's importance, once even grabbing Dalton's arm to jerk him around and point a finger in his face for emphasis. "If you ever, I mean *ever* hear a trooper call out Signal 13 over the radio," Kregg told him sternly, "I don't give a rat's ass what you're doing or where you're at, you go balls-to-the walls to get to your brother trooper, cause his life depends on it! Nothing on this job is more important than that. *Nothing!*"

Signal 13 was a call rarely heard, one that many troopers never heard during their careers. Those who did, however, never forgot the stunning lightning bolt that shot down their spines when a brother trooper desperately called for help.

During the ensuing weeks, the three new troopers steadily acclimated to the Prince Frederick Post way of life and to their rural proving ground. One of the first painful lessons Dalton learned was that a road flare gets really pissed off when it's kicked. At an accident scene clean-up after the demolished cars were towed off, Kregg told Dalton to extinguish the flares and let traffic through. Dalton jogged over to the first hissing illuminator and kicked it, field goal style. Seconds later he was grimacing and hotfooting toward a drainage ditch after a white-hot glob of magnesium burned through his shoe.

Al Heister, Dalton's Baltimore cocksure classmate, had already developed a nickname for himself after he'd contacted a local farmer who wanted to report a theft. Teeter Harris, a disgruntled, heavy-set, good ole boy Huntingtown farmer, was in the midst of explaining the circumstances surrounding his swiped bush hog. "Well suh," the round-faced farmer mumbled between chews on a wad of Red Man, "I done left that ole bush hawg in that field out thar yonder just yesterday afternoon." He aimed a calloused hand toward the scrubby, overgrown field in front of them. "Fixin' to take it back to the barn later on, but got tied up with some other chores, don't ya know." Teeter paused to hitch up his dirt-stained denim coveralls, and then spit out a stream of foul tobacco juice before continuing. "Come out cheer first thing this mornin' ta find er' gone outta here."

Eyes beaming with confidence, new boot Heister jerked his head up and seized the initiative. Mustering his best convincing face, Heister naively piped up and suggested that the farmer should wait a day or so to see if his bush hog might simply find its way home again after gorging itself on acorns or other nutty things those piggies feed on. Heister's training officer spit out the strand of ryegrass he was chewing on and burst out laughing. He waited a few moments to catch his breath before jumping in to the rescue, agreeing with the wide-eyed, flabbergasted farmer that the bush hog was indeed a piece of farm equipment, very much unlike the imagined farm creature that was rooting around in the new trooper's head. "Got yourself another one of them big city boys here, Trooper Wally, suh?" Teeter barked at the senior trooper, as Heister's face turned ruby-red. Embarrassed but enlightened, "Bush Hog Heister" was the toast of the Post for the next few weeks.

For the new boot troopers, it was odd working in a county that had only one fast-food franchise (Hardee's), two meager strip shopping centers, and no all-night Seven-Elevens. In lieu of those were numerous mom & pop shops or snack bars, and the expected handful of scattered taverns. Excluding the watering holes, the streets rolled up in the county by 10:00 PM. If a vehicle was spotted on the roads of Calvert between the hours of 1:00 AM and 5:00 AM, the occupants were undoubtedly up to no good, and the vehicle was duly stopped and checked out.

#

Early on, Dalton grasped that the job was an adventure fraught with dabs of excitement, jolts of adrenalin, bursts of humor and long stretches of monotony and paperwork. He was impressed with the troopers' teamwork, how they constantly supported and backed each other up whenever possible. Dalton also relished the county's slower pace, and found the laidback residents to be unexpectedly hospitable. Being invited for dinner after investigations was a common occurrence. Dalton always smiled when the good-ole-boy farmers customarily saluted the troopers with the upward flick of a calloused index finger from the steering wheels of their pickup trucks.

In the early seventies, with the ongoing highway construction and the recent completion of the Calvert Cliffs Nuclear Plant and the Cove Point Gas plant in Lusby, the county population steadily increased. Despite the developing bedroom communities, the county was still largely countryside, endowed with many farms and generations of farm families and watermen. Old family names like Bowen, Parran, Mackall, Sewell, Cox, Weems, Buckmaster and Dowell were represented throughout the peninsula. The county's main farm yield was tobacco, but many other farms produced corn, hay and vegetables. While their numbers were dwindling, there was still a sizable group of rugged watermen from enclaves such as Broomes Island, Dowell, Solomons and the northern "twin beaches." The modest watermen were still able to wrest a decent living plying the Chesapeake and

Patuxent for the abundant oysters, crabs, "blues," "croakers," "spot," and the venerable "rockfish," or striped bass. Dalton thought it was no wonder that the troopers serving the county grew to appreciate the local populace and country lifestyle.

#

Dalton's mentor Kregg gave him a condensed heads-up on the local political base, advising him there were two public figures who more or less ran the county. The first was Issac L. Silverman, a renowned Jewish elder statesman, born and raised in Barstow. Forging his way from a family business to local politics, and later to a prominent state government position, Silverman wielded enormous influence in almost all county endeavors. He also owned several hundred acres of choice Calvert land. A warmhearted, gregarious, energetic whirlwind, he was a true country character held in high esteem by his fellow Marylanders. It wasn't coincidental that the local politicos inevitably sought Issac's blessings for electoral aspirations, or before ruminating on any weighty decisions that affected his beloved county. Kregg cautioned Dalton, advising that the easiest way for a trooper to get a hasty transfer from the PF post to the MSP's version of Siberia was to find himself on Issac's dirty laundry list.

The second most formidable Calvert County figure was the honorable Mordeci G. Mackall, the circuit court judge. Towering over six and a half feet, with a husky build and large, powerful, weathered hands, the fifty-five year-old jurist was a self-proclaimed, simple "Culvert" farmer. Farming was his true love. By all accounts, the judge would rather be helping his field hands cut tobacco under a sweltering sun than sit on his court pulpit before the unruly miscreants and young lawyers who, fresh out of law school, were awkwardly cutting their teeth in the field of law. Considered a "hanging judge" and greatly feared by lawbreakers, Judge Mackall was a staunch champion of law and order. It was the judge and his well-earned, common sense, country-tough reputation who made the troopers' jobs a little easier in *his* Calvert County.

Endowed with a jocose wit, Judge Mackall's philosophy of his role wasn't complicated with any frivolous, liberal interpretations. Simply put, you didn't want to find yourself standing in front of him, anxiously waiting for his scarred and weathered face to turn your way to focus that infamous burning glare upon your mortal soul! Woe be it to the unfortunate one about to receive the powerful medicine routinely doled out by Judge Mackall for assaulting one of *his* police officers, breaking into another's home or, heaven forbid, stealing tobacco from a hard-working farmer. There were many abounding rumors that accommodated an imposing legend for "Culvert's" hanging judge. That he frequently wore a large-caliber six-shooter with extra shells in a robe side pocket during major trials, was a favorite.

Several whimsical locals were rumored to have been victims of posterior penetrations, recipients of rock salt from the judge's shotgun, after they'd foolishly taken shortcuts across his precious tobacco fields. And, as far as most local folks knew, Judge Mackall was the *only* sitting judge in the state of Maryland who, on the record, had permanently banished a local sleaze-ball from the county as part of a burglary sentence for looting too many houses in his cherished bailiwick. As with Issac Silverman, Kregg advised Dalton to be sure to stay on the good side of the gun-slinging judge at all costs. "He can read a person quicker than a lightning strike, and sees through BS better than an ole barn owl can see in the dark," Kregg counseled.

#

"When are you gonna learn that you *have* to sign in, Trooper Bragg...and what the *hell* you doing in *my* files anyhow?" The high-pitched shrill voice and eagle-eye glare froze most intrepid troopers in their tracks. Kregg should have included Wanda Gatton, the hefty matron director of the Calvert Control Center, as a runner-up to those who wielded true power at the Post. The control center adjoined the troopers' room, and Wanda's huge wooden desk was planted smack in the middle of the separating hallway as her demarcation line. Her "throne" position aptly provided relentless vigilance and authority over both domains. Wanda, a hands-on-hips, bluntly candid county native, was the grand sentinel of all MSP files, and no troopers or deputies dared incur her wrath by straying into the files or radio room without her supreme blessing. A serene Wanda unfailingly equated to a blissful Post.

Occasionally, Wanda seized the initiative to fill in as an "acting" Post commander when *she* deemed it necessary. Fired up in her piss-and-vinegar mode, she'd vigorously bark orders to the troops, while First Sergeant Flyger and a few of his merry men were out pulling "patrol checks" at some farm pond, hoping to snag a trophy bass or two. While hard-boiled on the outside, the woman with the big hairdo had a heart of gold for *her* boys, those troopers who wore the cowboy hats.

The inevitable day finally arrived for Dalton's mentor to tell his superiors that his new boot was ready to be cut loose. *Yes*, it was time for Dalton, one of Calvert's new centurions, to jump or get pushed into the arena. Before their parting for different shifts, Kregg took Dalton aside for some words of wisdom.

"Common sense and a cool head should always prevail. Coolness under duress would read as quiet confidence by those needing your reassurance during chaotic times. If you don't know what to do, you're at least expected to act like you do when you're out there in public," he drilled into the boot. "There's never a stupid question, and you always ask for advice and for backup when you need it. No room for the John Wayne syndrome here! Bottom line out here Dalton is simply this: don't let your mouth write a check that your ass can't cash. You got it?"

Dalton was impressed with Kregg's steady temperament, an attribute he'd do his best to emulate. He vowed to himself that he'd walk tall and use his head and words before using any force. *If,* however, the line was crossed, and he or any of his brothers-in-arms were ever threatened, it'd be reckoned with like hell hath no fury. Losing was not an option for any Maryland State Trooper under *any* circumstances, an edict drilled into them at the academy.

Now to find a spare cruiser. It'd take many months before the new troopers attained the seniority affording them their own assigned cruisers. During the dragged-out interim, they'd be "jumping" the cars of off-duty troopers.

\#

In the early seventies the Prince Frederick Post "graveyard" night shift covering Calvert County was the responsibility of two road troopers; one on south patrol, the other on north, with the senior trooper as acting supervisor.

The muggy air was heavy and thick, and the putrid odor of rot and decay assaulted his nostrils as soon as Trooper Dalton Bragg rolled the window down. *Not good!* This was going to be really, *really bad*, the anxious voice in his head screamed out. "Now turn your lights off and shut your mouth tight," Tfc. Marty Metzger, senior trooper on the two-man night shift whispered into his mic. Stupefied, but accepting the challenge, Dalton did just that. He slipped the seatbelt/shoulder harness off, gingerly opened the door, then quietly slithered from the cruiser to join his fellow trooper who was braced against the side of his own unit.

Metzger was on full-adrenaline alert, peering intently into the ominous void in front. In the pitch-black night, the tense boot trooper strained to regain his night vision after he heard them moving about. Slowly their numbers grew, and even worse, they were steadily closing in. Soon there were dozens of them out there, more than just the two of them could possibly handle. Dalton's heart pounded like a jackhammer, and his hand instinctively gripped the wooden handle of his Colt revolver. Damn! They should have called for backup from another county, maybe. Naw, why wake up the radio operators at this hour? Marty waited, patiently counting down the seconds until even *he* knew they had to act.

"OK, at the count of three, turn your lights on, then go for 'em, Dalton," he whispered sharply. Dalton sucked in a deep breath and silently unsnapped the leather holster strap. He reached into his cruiser to grab the headlight switch as Marty counted down. At the three count, he pulled the switch and jumped back!

Immediately, the area directly in front of them was bathed with high beams, spotlights and scrambling bodies! Holy shit! They were *everywhere!* Marty started firing first, fast and deliberate, while Dalton picked the closest one to him and let it rip from the hip. A clean miss! Regaining composure, Dalton fired again and again, surprisingly hitting one of them on the run, as attested by the piercing shrieks. Marty had winged one of them also, and, with his revolver now empty, he reached for the twelve-gauge shotgun on the hood of his cruiser. Sighting on a group of three as they frantically skittered up a steep mound on his left, he let loose with a double-O round and an echoing *Blam!* Dalton watched in awe as two of the squealing gray rats were blown over the top of the garbage heap.

"*Hot damn! Holy sweet Jesus!* Well, I'll be hot-friggin damned if that ain't the most I've ever seen bagged at one spotting here!" Marty yelled, his face flushed with excitement. Sporting a major-league shit-eating grin, Dalton shook his head and reloaded his smoking Colt. Once again, he simply couldn't believe it! Another facet of Marty's World: Good ole night shift firearms "training' at the stinky ole Calvert County dump!

"Time for a congratulatory smoke, troop," the senior trooper called out, handing Dalton a small, tightly-wrapped black cigar. "Soaked in rum and better than them piss-ant Tijuana cigars you've been pushing on me, buddy. And they do a better job of keeping the damn flies away too," Marty added.

Both troopers lit up and savored the afterglow of their marksmanship. Sure enough, within minutes as Marty had predicted, their radios crackled with the request for both troopers to check the Barstow dump for a report of shots fired. "Damn nosey neighbors," Marty blurted out. After several minutes' wait, he announced their "official" arrival at the scene. "J-21 Prince Frederick, that'll be negative on the patrol check here. It's a GOA (gone on arrival) and we're clear," he advised after a suitable lapse.

Before they left, Marty handed Dalton a box of .38-caliber ammunition. "Here, my man," Marty said firmly, "put these in your Colt. They're jazzed-up, hard-hittin' blunt-nosed rounds that'll put them piss-poor MSP-issue bitches to shame. Might even save your life some day, don't ya know." Marty took another drag off his sweet cigar and pointed a finger at him. "But remember, you don't know where they came from, right?" he implored with a wink. Dalton nodded in appreciation and loaded up with the new rounds. "And for God's sake, be sure to take em' out before the inspections, hear?"

For the next few minutes, the entire police force guarding the slumbering citizens of Calvert leaned against their cruisers and savored their cigars.

"Come on, I'm gettin' bored," Marty blurted out. "Let's go over to Leitch's Wharf Road and see if we can kick us up some fun." Dalton shrugged his shoulders in acceptance. "Years ago," Marty continued, "at the end of the road down by the river, there used to be an old wharf where they loaded up tobacco hogsheads to take up to Baltimore or beyond." Marty paused to flick off his cigar ashes. "But now, it ain't jack-shit 'cept for daytime fishermen, weekend druggies and some horny fornicators. Yup, real popular place just about this time a night, and if we're lucky, we just might find somebody to mess with, too." They traded smirks then jumped in their cruisers. Dalton barely kept up with the senior trooper as he sped haphazardly down some of the craziest winding roads he'd ever seen. Twice, as he barreled up on them, Marty had to hit his siren to scare a few wild-eyed deer off the road.

After zooming past several cornfields and farmhouses, Marty took a sharp right and immediately doused the cruiser's headlights. He whispered in his radio mic for Dalton to do the same. Both units drifted slowly down the dark road, one close behind the other, until it ended at a partly wooded overlook on the Patuxent River.

Several cars were parked at the end with their lights off. Marty silently maneuvered behind the closest one and stopped. Unannounced, he turned on his siren and red dome light, shined the spotlight on the car and flashed on the high beams. Immediately, Dalton saw the shocked faces pop up from the backseat. Heads suddenly bobbed and arms flailed in a desperate search for strewn clothing. Feeling beside himself with grace, Marty stayed in the cruiser until he thought most of their clothing had been found and essentially readjusted. Satisfied, he signaled to Dalton with his flashlight. After several minutes of checking out ID's belonging to the red-faced, half-clad fornicators, and after dumping beer and sniffing for signs of whacky weed, Marty was done with the roust, and all were sent on their way.

"Damn kids should find a motel or cop a feel down at one of the beaches somewheres," he muttered. "Yeah, me and Donny, our silver-tongued shift buddy, were bored half crazy one night shift not too long ago, so's we did a roust here. Snuck up on this here car without our butts being seen too," he added. "There was a good-size local county boy rockin' in the back seat...think he was a softball player from the rescue squad, matter of fact." Marty broke into a grin and glanced up at the stars overhead. "Man, he was steady knocking the bottom outta that lil thang too. They wuz goin to town on each other, totally oblivious to the world for sure, neither one hearing nothing but just themselves a-panting and a-moaning for all get-out." Marty paused to scratch the side of his head with his flashlight. "Well, we both just decided to watch 'em in the light of the half-moon till they came up for air. Took a while until he popped his cork in her, but if only you could a heard her howl when he did! Hell, me and Donny were so impressed with the performance that we just had to burst out in applause, so we clapped and cheered somethin' fierce. You shoulda seen their faces when we shined the mag lights on 'em!"

Marty smiled when he saw Dalton bent over with laughter. "Yeah, and you should have seen the look on Donny's face when he saw who she was too!" he added. "Turns out that the wild woman in question was Donny's favorite flame from the Frog Pond bar. Whew, it was just about all I could do to prevent all hell from breaking loose, 'cause ole Donny started after the dude lookin' like he was gonna open up a big can of whup-ass on him."

Marty snickered to himself and brought out two more rum-soaked cigars from a pocket of his khaki "Ike" patrol jacket. He popped one into his mouth to wet it, then handed the other one to his grinning sidekick.

Both troopers propped themselves against Marty's cruiser as they lazily puffed up clouds of the pleasant smoke. Marty coughed abruptly, and spit out a few loose tobacco bits. "Yeah," he giggled, "that split-tail ole Donny was sweet on, Lizard Lady, he called her...she was something else, all right. The unfortunate-looking woman had a face on her that could back a starvin' mule out of a feed bin, but damn if she didn't have the awesome ability to touch the tip of her nose with her tongue. Donny was right proud of her talent, too, yes indeed he was! Hell, Dalton, it took him almost the better part of a week to get over the crazy bitch, too!" Dalton smiled and slapped his fellow trooper on the back. Standing shoulder to shoulder in silence, they took long drags from their cigars.

"Look here, my man, we done lost track of what time it was," Marty spouted out in feigned panic after glancing at his watch. Dalton watched curiously as his cohort scrambled back into his car to turn on the AM/FM radio.

He listened as several radio stations flicked by while Marty fumbled with the dial. Finally, he heard the sharp nasal twang of a country-western voice reverberating loudly, and the volume was cranked up. 'This here be Lester Road Hog Moran and His Cadillac Cowboys, coming to you live from the Gene Audrey High School Auditorium," the radio announcer jubilantly exclaimed. Marty closed his eyes and smiled blissfully as he eased back against the front seat. Dalton stifled himself, but was soon chuckling along, as ole Road Hog performed his raucous parody of several old country-western faves, adding wacky ambiance to the night hours of Calvert.

Not content to merely listen, Marty popped the trunk release and retrieved his prized six-string dreadnaught Pearl guitar from its case. After a quick tune-up and a long drag from his cigar, Marty surprised his shift buddy by deftly playing a few passable riffs in accompaniment to Road Hog's hilarious rendition of 'Home on the Range."

After several minutes, Road Hog's AM radio channel started to drift. Soon there was nothing but static, forcing Marty to end his impromptu gig with the Cadillac Cowboys. After thoroughly mutilating a few verses of Willie Nelson's *Blue Eyes Crying in the Rain* with his squeaky, high voice, Marty frowned and gave up.

"Never could do that one too good," he muttered to Dalton. 'Hey! Heard you wuz in some rock-n-roll bands a few years back, buddy. Ummm. If you'd like to strum a tune, she's all yours." Marty held the guitar out to his partner who merely shook his head and smiled. "Not all that great a shake on the six-string, Marty, but on the drums I could beat up a storm," he answered. "Yeah, that's what I heard. So what in the world made you bury the drumsticks to join this outfit, anyhow?" Marty asked, curiosity spreading over his face.

Dalton whimsically stared up at the half-moon and let out a sigh. "Long story there, my friend. Guess after playing the Doors' *Light My Fire* a few hundred thousand times, I just got tired. Maybe someday, over a case of beer or two, I just might have to lay it all out to you,

OK?" The senior trooper broke into a grin and reached into his jacket again. "Sounds good to me, buddy," he said wistfully. "Have yourself another smoke, why don't ya?" Dalton took the cigar and popped it into his mouth. "Hey Marty, you treat all the new boots like this on a first date?" he asked, as they lit their last smoke of the night before returning to the barrack. "Naw, just the ones I feel I can trust, and that just spells *you* at the moment," Marty shot back.

"Hey pard'ner, it's the last night shift, and we secure in a few hours," Marty suddenly exclaimed, his face bursting with excitement. "How's about me and you getting a twelve pack when we get off, and go down to Flag Harbor beach to throw down a few cold ones while we watch the sun pop up o'er the eastern shore again, OK? And hey! My old man went and hickory-smoked a batch of snapper blues he caught off Cove Point just south of the lighthouse yesterday. I'll bring us a few of them bad-boy fillets for some early mornin' 'whore's ovaries,' what ya say to that?" Dalton smiled and gave a thumbs-up. "Hey Dalton, bet I can beat your lame ass back to the post," Marty shouted. Both troopers dove back into their cruisers to start the race.

Trooper First Class Martin Metzger was turning out to be an unexpected surprise, Dalton realized during his first six months on the shift. Twenty-six years old, divorced, and tall and gangly, the red haired, fair-complected, smooth talking, jovial giant was a fun-loving kid at heart. A well-known resident of the county, Marty was also a crack marksman and a skilled driver. During his first week on the shift, Marty helped an appreciative Dalton perfect the art of high-speed pursuit turns, tearing up several median strips in the process.

The bonding with his fellow shift member had even extended to Marty's several failed attempts at hunting deer and geese in the county. Marty bored easily. He'd either wind up falling out of the boat while setting up goose decoys, or he'd cannonade distant, out-of-range, floating rafts of Canadian geese with his favorite artillery piece, his .44 Blackhawk Ruger Magnum! Supreme among his talents, Marty had a third sense for being *the* consummate actor on stage, impatiently waiting forever for the spotlight to shine his way. It seemed to Dalton that police work, while tolerable for the most part, was probably more of a hobby to him than a genuine career. Still, when the fecal matter hit the fan blades, Marty was one of those you wanted to have around you for sure. This he learned soon enough.

The previous night, both he and Marty had responded to a disorderly call at the crowded, all-black Collard Club bar in Huntingtown, a dimly lit, smoke filled, volatile place even on a slow night. Upon entering, Dalton was immediately hit with the overpowering stench of cigarette smoke, stale urine and the warm, funky reek of too many people crammed too close together. In the background he heard a jukebox playing a slow soul song, but with the bar's poor acoustics, it sounded low-pitched and muted. Many pairs of hostile eyes accosted the troopers as they elbowed through the rowdy crowd

Dalton heard glass breaking. It was followed by screams. Suddenly the crowd parted, and both troopers were abruptly confronted by a heavy-set, ready-to-fight, cursing drunk. Obviously fueled from the spirits and hearty encouragement from onlookers, the drunk waved both troopers on, screaming at them to come and get him, if they dared. Marty smirked and shook his head, then casually handed Dalton his Stetson and whispered for him to stay put and be cool. Shuffling his way to the side of the room just out of earshot of the drunk's animated audience, Marty calmly motioned the lush over to him with an index finger.

"Now, you have two choices here, my man," the senior trooper whispered to him, fixing him with steady eyes and a cold stare. "One is to go walking out of here with us, like the big man I think you are." Dalton inched closer to his partner when he saw the drunk's crazed smile. "The other choice isn't a very cool thing, meaning your black ass is gonna be dragged outta here like a baby, kicking and screaming all the way, OK? Either way, you're goin' to Prince Frederick with us," Marty told him with a confident smile.

Wide-eyed, the drunk swayed back and forth in place, trying hard to focus his bloodshot eyes while desperately searching Marty's face for any tell-tale signs of apprehension. Finding none, he hesitated, then broke into a leery grin. "Well sssshit, lezz take a rrride than ossifers," he blurted out. He smiled to his friends, then bowed and waved them goodby before being escorted from the club. Yup, Marty was definitely a cool-hand dude to have around, Dalton realized.

Later, when Dalton rehashed the incident with him, he asked his buddy for his thoughts about what might have happened if the Clint Eastwood routine had been a wash.

"Well, more than likely, we'd a been jumped by a herd of 'em, and might a had a few zingers thrown our way for sure. But we'd a definitely kicked some serious ass, too," Marty added confidently. "Just don't let 'em get you down on the ground, whatever happens, OK?" Marty scratched an earlobe and paused to reflect. "Never tried that line before, 'cause I just didn't think it'd really work, but it's a keeper in my book now," the senior trooper added. "You gotta show them no fear, have to act cool as ice when your insides are shakin' like jelly, or…or, you just go in there balls-to-the walls, acting bold and crazy. Ain't no room in between in those sticky situations. They'll always smell you out otherwise, believe me. Don't worry, Dalton, you'll be back here a lot, so you'll get your chance to work on your delivery style, you can bank on that," Marty added with a laugh.

He was right. Months later, Dalton and Corporal Long responded to yet another disorderly call at the Collard club. Wading through the gauntlet of belligerent taunts, glares and brushed shoulders from the hyped-up crowd, they faced another crazy drunk. This time, it was Ollie Height, a familiar "10-96" (mental subject) mega-loiterer from Huntingtown. To make matters more entertaining during the slow night, Ollie's cohorts had saturated him with several double-shots of cheap gin. The floorshow, however, soon warped out of control, forcing the club's manager to reluctantly call on the police to be the showstoppers.

Weaving side-to-side, eyes staring blankly and foam oozing from his mouth, Ollie was obviously plastered. Yearning to defuse things before they escalated into a runaway shit-fest, Dalton casually approached him. In a calm, low voice, he asked Ollie a simple, thought-provoking question, hoping to cut through his foggy mind enough for a possible connection; anything just to bring down the tension a few notches. In a split-second, Ollie kicked a table over and lunged at Dalton with a shiny-bladed buck knife in his right hand! Instinctively, Dalton jerked his head away as the knife cut through the air inches from his face! In the same heartbeat, Corporal Long painted the drunk's face with a canister of tear gas! Disarmed, cuffed, and ranting about wanting to go back to Crownsville, a state mental hospital, the snotty-nosed Ollie was unceremoniously dragged from the club and taken to the post.

On reflection, Dalton acknowledged the limitations of the power of the tongue. More important, he'd allowed his quarry to get to close to him. It had all happened so damned fast, with no time to draw his revolver, *if he had it with him*, that is. That evening, he also learned that the Colt .38 had a nasty habit of slipping its strap and falling out of the holster on occasion. It was only when he was placing his crazed, vomit-covered prisoner in the cruiser, that he'd found it—AWOL on the front seat.

Hours later, while sitting alone in front of a blank living room TV screen, Dalton gazed down at trembling hands, the first sign that his body was finally catching up with his ragged emotions. An hour and three beers later, the tremors ceased, but from experience he knew there would be no decent sleep this night. Yeah, he'd keep this caper to himself, definitely not for Cindy's ears. It would be the first of too many he'd avoid confiding to her.

#

While Marty Metzger was the gregarious, outgoing member of the group, Dalton thought that Tfc.Donny Roberts, the other member, was the aloof, lone wolf with alternating mood swings, pleasant and outgoing one day, sullen and brooding the next. Like Marty, Kregg, and most other troopers, Donny was divorced. The handsome thirty-five year-old, sandy-haired, green-eyed Eastern Shore specimen was medium built and stood just under six feet. Being from Church Creek, a village south of Cambridge, Roberts was direct in manner and blessed with a distinct "shore" accent, attributes which charmed the "Culvert" honeys to no small end. He also had a slow, feline swagger when he walked on the balls of his feet.

Not one to idly hang around the post, Donny was a true-blue road trooper wholly content on limiting his career to traffic work and the citation book. And he was a kick-ass—the post's top-gun citation writer, which duly earned him a coveted unmarked cruiser. To Donny, criminal work involved too much paperwork, too much costly time away from his beloved road pounding. Donny was also a deadeye marksman. Coolly deliberate on the firing range, he was, indisputably, the best shooter at the post, Dalton heard.

Donny was also a CB radio fanatic who diabolically eavesdropped on the truckers as they searched for the newest "Smokey" hiding places. Calling in false "bear" locations and giving truckers false "green light" info was an essential part of his expertise which resulted in many autographs in the trooper's ticket books. But tricking the truckers wasn't the primary use for his civilian band radio. Early on, Donny also learned that the CB was the perfect mode for contacting a few of the county's more amorous babes, too, and he'd become quite adept at covert assignations, or "afternoon delights" as he termed them, with several appreciative tarts who were instantly enamored with his eastern shore charms.

Bemused after Donny suggested he get a CB, too, Dalton curiously quizzed his playboy partner about his CB-generated conquests. "Hell, Dalton, it's easy when you have the keys to the power line gates," he proudly told him. The nuclear plant's power lines ran north from the Lusby plant to the county line, with several locked-gate access points along the way. Donny's favorite secluded entry point was the gravel access trail just off Calvert Beach Road in St. Leonard. Unless conditions were altered by unforeseeable events, Donny gave the MSP a few solid hours of roadwork during the quasi-busy AM rush hours, before clearing his agenda for the day's afternoon delight.

Except for a stray deer or two, privacy was assured behind the locked gate, leaving the usual young wife, or someone else's ambiguous girlfriend, feeling free from getting caught. "But, you sure's hell better make sure the damn radio mic's outta the way," Donny added with a smile, before telling Dalton how a hapless county deputy had learned *that* lesson. After the deputy had picked up his main squeeze on the side, he parked his patrol car at the rear of a Barstow cornfield, a setting quite suitable for his much-anticipated late shift assignation. In the midst of his front seat display of sexual prowess, his highly vocal strumpet inadvertently keyed the radio mic lying next to her. For several minutes, those on duty throughout the entire troop area monitored the deputy's proficiency as the vixen repeatedly spouted her euphoria while going for the gold. "Oh Sonny...*ohhhh Soneeee! Yes...Oh my God! Give it to me, baby! Yes...YESSSS!*

Donny had even offered to make Dalton an extra set of keys. if he felt inclined toward afternoon delights. While tantalized, Dalton decided to work more at staying married. Being the ladies' man at large, and quite familiar with the county's female talent pool, Donny served as the post's self-appointed love-line conduit for many wayward troopers. Currently, he was also the sole occupant of the post's upstairs wayward troopers' bedroom. Dalton soon developed a growing rapport with Donny, choosing to accept his petulance during his heavy brooding days as a tradeoff for his friendship.

It didn't take long for Dalton to realize the powerful impression a uniformed trooper made on many women, particularly the promiscuous ones, nor was it hard for most of the troops to succumb to their charms either. Some of the more macho troops wildly competed in that regard, trying to score whenever possible with whomever was available. Thanks to Donny's thoughtful efforts, Dalton's classmate Rensir had already strayed and slipped the collar. Married to the only girl he'd ever dated, Rensir was in awe of the once rare, but now daily, attention he received from the trooper 'groupies" he'd recently encountered. He was the wide-eyed, drooling kid in a candy shop, more like a bedazzled moth caught in a spider web as it flew toward the brightest light. Predictably, and within just two years, Rensir was added to the long list of divorced troopers.

Devoted to his favorite rum and coke bracer, Donny was usually found "trolling" after hours with a fellow wayward trooper or two at the hot-spot pickup joint of the county; the Calverton Room Bar and Grill in downtown Prince Frederick, just a two-minute walk from the post.

Initially, Dalton didn't know what to make of the group's supervisor, a shuffling enigma in the form of Corporal Lester "Elzy" Shifflett. Dalton's first impression was that he came straight from an Andy Griffith *Mayberry* special.

Elzy was a hulky, thin haired, mid- thirties, Calvert County hayseed. The stoop-shouldered corporal talked in a unique, low-pitched, pidgin English, lacing his words with pronunciations Dalton hadn't heard before, except for the Cajun mumbo-jumbo of the Louisiana swamps at Fort Polk. As was Elzy's custom, "mutha fucker," seemed to be the usual prerequisite for his declarations. Elzy was the most gifted hustler at the post. In his hard-charging manner, Dalton's zany corporal was relentless in criminal investigations, most of which ended with a timely arrest. Dalton had seen first-hand that his corporal thrived on confrontations, especially fisticuffs, never backing down from anyone. Only his flushed face gave a foolhardy protagonist a fleeting betrayal of his short-fused, incendiary temper.

For several days Dalton respectfully distanced himself from Elzy, trying hard to gauge and acclimate to his corporal's unique quirks, particularly his habit of spitting tobacco juice into a Coke bottle. It took Dalton weeks before he was finally able to penetrate Elzy's tough veneer. He realized that, while lacking finesse in some—no—*most* areas, Elzy was country-fox smart and gifted with a colorful, laidback sense of humor, too. Mocking his own country mannerisms, Elzy elicited chuckles, telling others in a serous tone to: "Be sure to eat a lot of fuckin' bananas, 'cause them yellow bitches have a shit load of *Potato-ism* in them," or he'd complain loudly about the damage all those "*Jap-a-lena* pepper things" were doing to his testy stomach. And Elzy was always worried about that possible "cancer of the *cologne* problem" too! "Elzy-isms" always made the shift pass a wee bit easier on most tiresome days.

Elzy Shifflett was naturally gifted with a "nose," a nigh-faultless ability to read the minds of county-bred deviants. He was an encyclopedia with a keen memory, a walking tall LE (law enforcement) crusader who enjoyed rubbing elbows with the natives. An avid outdoorsman from his early teens, he knew every inch of the county. According to the countless stories that Dalton heard, Elzy was a local legend, known for his humorous exploits and energetic performance in the field and beyond.

During a slow night shift while losing a fight against the dreaded nods, Elzy parked his cruiser in front of the lit-up A&P supermarket in the Prince Frederick Shopping Center. After an earlier afternoon romp with his jaunty brother Chester, swigging beer and dunking worms for the fat bullhead catfish that prowled the deep holes along Hunting Creek, Elzy was hoping to snatch some shuteye before returning to the post to end the shift. Hours later, with a full, early-afternoon sun shining on his face, he woke up on the front seat of the still-idling police cruiser. Squinty-eyed, he meekly raised his head and peered out the window at all the cars parked around him in the packed lot. Nice. Slightly miffed knowing that his shift partner and control center PCOs had compounded his dilemma by not checking on him, Elzy prudently drove home in radio silence.

And Elzy never hesitated to push the envelope to get confessions. According to several who were there on that splendorous day, the corporal was in rare form after he'd arrested a skinny, defiant black kid from Lusby who'd filched some items from a local mom-&-pop store. Tired of the kid's mouthy protests, Elzy sat him down and stared him in the face.

"Look here, boy, I'll let ya go on outta here if you can pass a lie-detection test. Simple test, ya hear? All ya gotta do is tell the truth and lord knows, you be outta here quicker than jack-shit, hear me boy?" The kid briefly studied the veteran trooper's face. Believing he was facing a BS-er who was nowhere near as good as he was, the kid smiled broadly. "Sure will, yup, I sure nuff will be takin' that lie test a yourn, Officer Shifflett," he spouted out in a honed, innocent voice. "Let's do it, let's get it on!"

Fighting to stay poker-faced, Elzy took the kid back to the ID office and sat him in a chair next to a desk. Next, he rummaged around in a file cabinet and brought out a large-spool tape recorder and placed it on the desk, confident that the kid had no clue what it was. Judging from the kid's perplexed look, he was right.

From the desk drawer, Elzy pulled out two long plastic cords and plugged two ends into the machine, leaving the bare wire ends free.

"Here, let me have your hands, boy. I gotta tape these to your fingers so's they can tell me when you lie!" With an anxious look, the boy held out his shaking hands. Stifling a renegade chuckle, Elzy used black tape to tape a bare wire cord to the boy's right index finger. Next, he did the same to the boy's left thumb. "OK, looky here now," Elzy told him, "I gotta adjust me a few things on this here lie-detector box, then we'll be ready." The stern-faced corporal fidgeted with several switches and dials, turning them left and right, clicking them up and down. From the corner of an eye, he saw the boy starting to squirm in the chair. OK. "All right son, this here test is ready to go. You ready?" Wordlessly, the kid stared at the trooper and nodded a weak response.

Peeking around the door, several troopers were trying hard not to ruin it all by breaking into hysterics. Unseen by the boy, Elzy shot them a middle finger behind his back and turned his divided attention back to the job at hand.

"OK now, this is how it goes...but first, do you believe in Jesus, boy?" Elzy shouted at him. 'Hey! Why you axin' me *dat* question?" the boy cried out. "Well never mind then, it don't mean nothin'," Elzy answered, biting his lip to stay serious. "Yeah I do!" the shouted back. "Me and Jesus, yeah... we tight, so don't feed me none of your policeman's jive now, know what I mean?" he added with a smirk. Just beyond the doorway, Elzy saw the troopers bending over in silence, holding their quivering stomachs.

"OK, we'll leave Jesus out of this for now, seein' how's you and him are good buds," Elzy continued "Now, I'm gonna ask you some questions and all's I need from your mouth, is a *yes* or *no* answer. We straight?" "Yeah, damn right we straight, Mister Trooper!" "OK, but listen here good to me now, boy. If you go tellin' this machine a lie, it ain't gonna like it one damn bit!" Elzy coughed a few times to avoid a giveaway grin. "Truth is, if you go lying to it, the machine's gonna shock your ass through them wires, and it's gonna hurt like a bitch!" The kid's eyes went wide as saucers and his mouth dropped. "You tellin' me right?" he gasped, "That thing gonna shock my black ass if'n it don't like what I say?" "Sure's hell will!" Elzy shouted back. The rattled kid slumped in the chair, a resigned look all over his face.

"How's bout you be takin' these here wires off me, fo' that thing accidentally do shock me, OK?" the boy murmured softly.

"I done it, I stole them jars of pickled pig's feet and some smokes too, but I kin pay for em' later if you want me to, and tha's a fact. You jus' take dees here things off me!"

That Dalton's corporal, Elzy was known to be one of the more colorful "good ole boys" at the Prince Frederick Post was an understatement.

Working with his group for the past six months, Dalton realized it was the most aggressive group at the post. Corporal Shifflett was always lending encouragement and backup, setting the pace with his own high performance. It was uncanny how Elzy materialized from nowhere at times to provide that extra measure of support to his confident, but inexperienced, new boot. And Elzy truly had a knack for getting them involved in practically anything, whenever the opportunity presented itself.

Before the end of a recent late shift, Cpl. Elzy had been tipped off by one of his more reliable and surprisingly sober informants that two of the infamous Willet brothers, Lester and Sammy, both well-known thieves, had stolen some yearling pigs from their farmer neighbor in Chaneyville. According to the tipster, the young black vagabonds were smack dab in the middle of rendering the swine at that very moment, too. Smiling ear-to-ear, Elzy waited until the night shift reported in so a decent-size raiding party could be scrambled together. After briefing his makeshift band of marauders, they headed north to surround the Willets' ramshackle tenant house deep in the dismal, swampy woods off Chaneyville Road.

With his team in place, Elzy crouched, took a puff off his cigar stub, and then nudged it against the fuse of a confiscated cherry bomb. Dalton, kneeling beside his renegade corporal, shot him a "what-the-fuck look" and froze in place. With a wry grin, Elzy sprang to his feet and tossed the fizzling cherry bomb in the direction of the shadowy figures out front. "State Police! Freeze, mutha fuckers!" *Kaboom!* Instantly, the six howling troopers charged from the shadowy cornfield!

There were four pig rustlers; two steadily feeding the wood fires under the fifty-five gallon drums of water, the other two pig pilferers dismembering the swine. The shock of the assault registered instantly. Dropping the bloody pig parts, the wide-eyed pig pillagers shrieked and bee-lined toward the murky swamps.

Under different circumstances, Dalton would have joined the chase, but he was bent over in gut-wrenching laughter, close to peeing his pants. He'd lost it after hearing the calamity of bodies crashing blindly through the muddy thickets, each crash or thud accented with a stream of profanities and hysterical shouts. Minutes later, winded and out of breath, Elzy trudged back into the firelight. Red-faced and cursing, he scraped a mass of pig poop off his shoe.

"Almost had me one of them bastards, but the son a bitch made it to the swamp, and I don't do no damn swamps at night," Elzy muttered. Huffing and puffing like spent racehorses, Marty Metzger and the other prisoner-less troopers, all splattered with slimy muck and reeking of wretched swamp stink, broke cover to return from the fruitless pursuit. Marty winced and rubbed the palm of a hand over the red spot on his forehead. "Damn tree limb caught me good," he mumbled. "Muther fuck! Those dudes were hauling some kind of ass, too!" He grinned at Dalton and shook his head.

Still teary-eyed from laughing, Dalton crinkled his face, nearly overcome by the putrid odor from the nearby pots. "What the hell's that wretched smell?" he shouted out, pointing at the simmering pot. "Smells like shit!" "That's exactly what's being cooked out of them hawg innards," Elzy answered with a chuckle. "You ain't never heard of chitlins, boy?" Dalton rolled his eyes and jerked his head back in time to dodge the corporal's flung cigar.

###
(Purgatory Ridge)

Drifting back to his retirement party, the sergeant smiled, remembering the day he'd finally been cut loose to patrol alone. Like all new boots, he'd been leery but confident, ready to show his mettle as a new "Culvert" centurion. Soon enough, challenges and troubles arrived.

"Time for the appetizers," he announced to his pack. Dalton rummaged through a side pocket, looking for the event's victuals. Nothing like a few bites of mesquite-smoked beef jerky and a handful of trail mix and dried apricots, followed by a hearty swig of the brewski. He bit off a large chunk of beef jerky and worked his jaw hard to grind it down into swallow-size pieces. Still gnawing away, he grabbed a low-hanging limb and pulled himself up on his feet for a stretch. Dalton let his eyes roam over the bay again. His attention was drawn to the lone female wind surfer working the powder-blue sail several hundred yards out. Ahhhh, Marlene, the spunky aqua-nymph from Breezy Point! The lissome hottie with the trailing ash-blonde hair was eking out what she could from the light breeze from the east. Dalton shined a smile and blew a longing air kiss at her fading image.

Yeah, damn tootin' he'd fallen hard for the quaint county back then. Such an admiration he'd held for the homespun characters who played hard on her stage. But he also knew that it was a county about to wake up to a population hangover it'd never recover from, too. Lured by the countryside, the urban escapees were scurrying down in droves, hoping to slam the doors behind them, as the inevitable whiffs of development brought more of them, but the doors stayed open.

Dalton finished the jerky and drained the beer can. He stuffed the unopened packs of trail mix and dried fruit back into the knapsack. Suddenly piqued, he crushed the beer can with his hands and threw it beyond the others, eagle-eyeing it as it rolled behind a small sapling. Kneeling, he pulled the Beretta out again. Using the instinct shooting technique sans sights, he smoothly pulled the trigger. *Blam!* The round tore through the sapling and hit the crushed can hiding behind it. He smiled knowingly when the can went spastic. Now why does it take my trusty Italian handgun to jerk me out of a pissy mood, he marveled to himself, gazing wistfully at the weapon gripped in his hand.

He shook his head when he thought back to the old Colt .38 revolver with the six-inch barrel that the academy had issued several lifetimes ago. Back then, running full-tilt after a fleeing dirt ball, with the flopping leather holster slamming against a leg, usually resulted in a nice bruise. He also remembered hearing scuttlebutt about how the underpowered rounds had actually ricocheted off car windshields, too. There were many stories about accidental discharges.

Hank Mitchell, a crusty trooper from the Eastern Shore, watched in horror as the pistol slipped from his holster when he took off his gun belt prior to weighing himself at CMH, the local hospital known as The Calvert Memorial First Aid Station. When the hammer of the gun hit the floor, the firing pin struck the chambered round, which loudly caromed off the floor, embedding itself into a wall next to a nurse station to scare the be-Jesus out of Mitchell, two nurses and a white-faced doctor standing nearby! After hearing about that fiasco, Dalton always kept an empty chamber where the firing pin rested, even if it left him one round short.

Sporting a Cheshire grin, the sergeant settled back against the red oak and gingerly placed the esteemed Beretta on the ground by his leg. "Hmm...This is gonna take at least two of these bad boys," he said aloud as he rolled the cans out of the pack. Closing his eyes again, Dalton drifted back to the memories of his "Cowboy" probationary days, as he called them. And they were that, and so much more!

Chapter 4

PULSATIONS OF A PROBATIONER
(The Cowboy Days)

With the advent of the new, handheld radar Speedguns which had longer range and superior accuracy, the hunt for speed citations kicked in with a vengeance. The portable, black carbon/plastic gadget with its open conical end, vaguely resembled a cut-down blunderbuss, the mini scatter-gun the pirates used to blast their way aboard ships. A trooper simply aimed the stubby blunderbuss at an approaching vehicle, and when in range, a red digital speed indicator popped up in a tiny rear window. Not yet radar qualified, Dalton worked with his shift members as part of a radar stopping team. He also hustled on his own, stopping vehicles for minor infractions like burnt-out headlights or tag lights, hoping to turn equipment violations into citations or even a criminal arrest, if lucky.

Like many scrupulous troopers, Dalton adopted discretion when it involved motor vehicle violations, particularly those involving SEROs (Safety Equipment Repair Orders). For a small windshield chip, he wasn't going to force a poor tobacco-picker to cancel the registration on his dilapidated 1961 Ford station wagon just because he couldn't afford to fix it. If a driver put his ass on his shoulders, however, Dalton, like most troopers, took his time performing 100 percent maximum motor vehicle law enforcement. Mucho citations, a warning and an SERO was the standard when a real flamer was stopped.

On weekends, Dalton usually made a DWI arrest when the loopy driver couldn't keep his car from attacking the guardrails. MADD (Mothers Against Drunk Drivers) and the ensuing push for DWIs hadn't yet evolved, and most troopers merely taxied drunks home. The fiendish troopers made the inebriants park their cars, and when the satiated sot was suitably distracted, they'd chuck the car keys into the woods then split the scene, leaving the simple sot stranded by the roadside.

Soon enough, Dalton learned that a drunk's behavior was wildly unpredictable. Just before he was about to stop a weaving car near Long Beach one evening, the driver suddenly darted down a driveway and accelerated. *Wham!* Dalton watched in amazement as the maroon Buick plowed through the garage door. As he was pulling the dazed driver from his car, Dalton heard unearthly screams. Seconds later, a shrieking, wild-haired woman wearing a black flowing robe and brandishing a heavy-duty push broom came flying out of the house, followed by a howling beagle dog. "Red White! You no good bastard! You stupid son of a bitch!" she screamed as she pummeled her hapless hubby over the head with the push broom. "Get 'im, Blue! Bite 'im real good, boy!" she yelled at the beagle snapping at her hubby's flailing legs. Dalton waited a few moments to afford her a few good licks before jumping in.

After calming the wild woman, Dalton ran a license check to make sure the driver, whose real Calvert County born and bred name was actually Red White, had a valid license. Using the better part of his discretion, Dalton promptly released the browbeaten husband into the custody of his inflamed witchy-wife. Returning to the cruiser, Dalton smiled when he heard more thumps mixed in with a chorus of loud cackling and angry snarls as Red White was pounded with the first blows and nips of round two.

But like the veteran troopers stressed, no drunk was worse than a lady drunk. During his second month on patrol, Dalton stopped a thoroughly plastered young mother who'd been using guardrails for buffers as she tried to aim her way home. As per the norm, he tried to politely persuade her, baby her, to exit her idling car so he could take both her and her upset ten year-old daughter home, a short distance. When he reached in to snatch the ignition key, however, the woman instantly morphed herself into a mega she-bitch, mashing her lit cigarette on his hand while attempting to jam the car into gear. Dalton twisted her offending hand backwards and yanked her from the vehicle. For several minutes he wrestled with the screeching, wildly flailing Jezebel in the slow lane of Route 4, trying hard to avoid the cars barreling past them in the pitch-black night. It didn't add to his joy that she also "accidentally" crapped herself while she was handcuffed to a desk an hour later.

Tom Rensir, a newbie like Dalton, had dragged in a certified humdinger of a drunk several weeks before while patrolling on his own. Responding to the St. Leonard area to check on a suspicious vehicle one otherwise uneventful evening, Rensir was almost run down by a bright red John Deere farm tractor which suddenly shot out from the alley next to Buellman's liquor store. The tractor's single headlight was off, and the big engine growled in loud protest, as the driver swerved along the winding Old Solomons Island Road. Momentarily flabbergasted, Rensir recovered and took off in pursuit of the runaway John Deere. Moments later, he found himself embroiled in a slow speed chase, as the big-wheeled tractor caromed erratically down the road.

As the snail-pace chase continued, the pudgy, red-faced driver kept shooting nervous glances back at the pursuing MSP cruiser hanging back mere inches from his tractor hitch. Finally, after a two-mile gallivant, the dogged quarry tried to shake off his pursuer by going off-road. The tractor plowed through a thicket of thorn bushes and slammed hard into the only tree in sight—a monster, unyielding locust tree.

Cletus Dalrymple, a swarthy tobacco farmer from Port Republic, lost his license a year ago after a third DWI conviction, and, overall, he'd been behaving himself—until that night. Hours earlier, however, the good ole boy farmer had gotten carried away while shooting the bull with a few local "bakker" pickers, guzzling down the last of his Old Crow much sooner then expected. And of course, no one had ever told him that driving a tractor while plastered was contrary to the law, anyhow. Hell, boy!" Cletus blurted out. "You shoulda had me blowing in that there piss ass breath-o-matic contraption of yourn a few hours ago if you wanted to see some real fumes!" he thundered out to Rensir, after the new trooper had congratulated him on his BAC (blood alcohol content) being over twice the DWI level. "Gots to keep the ole pump primed, you know!" So far, no PF trooper had collared a horseback rider DWI arrest in Calvert County, but Dalton wouldn't be fazed at all if it happened soon.

#

Criminal cases came along with the road-pounding, and they ran the gauntlet: dreaded domestics, aggravated assaults, disorderly subjects, B&Es, property destructions (DOPs) and the usual avalanche of routine police calls, most of which amounted to minimal taxpayer lip service only. Death notifications, however, were piteous tasks. While being tutored by his mentor Kregg, Dalton watched intently as the earnest senior trooper gingerly broke the news to the father of a ten year-old girl who had drowned at Lake Lariat in the Ranch Club. Dalton was impressed with Kregg's compassion and later commended him. "It gets a little easier with each notification, but you'll never get used to it Dalton," Kregg told him. "It's all in the delivery...and if you can't act it out, they'll know, trust me, they'll know. But the job dictates muted feelings from us...always."

Sooner then expected, Dalton handled his first death notification. At 0245 hours during a quiet Sunday morning, Dalton left the post with teletype in hand. Unable to locate the post chaplain, and with fellow shift-mate Donny covering the entire county in his absence, things were fine when he arrived at the dirt driveway of the family residence. He spotted the engraved wood sign, "Whispering Pines—The Gotts," on the red oak tree at the driveway entrance and radioed his arrival. It was only after he'd driven several hundred yards down the tree-lined driveway that he noticed his jaw was clenched, his mouth was cotton dry, and he had a white-knuckle grip on the steering wheel.

Dalton donned his Stetson and paused outside the cruiser. How peaceful it was in the solitude of the deep woods, the night air permeated with the scent of the pines that surrounded the modest, two-story clapboard farmhouse. And here he was, Trooper Dalton Bragg, a night-shift novice, an angel of death, ready to forever shatter the tranquility of this peaceful, slumbering family. He wanted to be anywhere else. He took a deep breath when his index finger shot out and pressed the doorbell button. As expected, it took several rings until an upstairs light finally flickered on. Moments later, he heard muffled steps on stairways followed by the brilliance of the porch light. "Who is it?" the high-pitched female voice called out from behind the door.

The door slowly swung open after Dalton identified himself, revealing a gown-clad, pleasant-looking woman in her early forties. Her cordial face suddenly blanched and her mouth dropped, when her probing eyes saw the taunt face of the young trooper in front of her. Instantly, she knew something was dreadfully wrong, realized that her life was going to be changed forever from this day on. "Oh No, Dear God...Nooooo...not Brian!" she cried out as she slumped against the doorframe. Dalton heard someone coming down the steps behind her. Her disheveled husband, his face frozen in a quizzical grimace, joined them to inquire about the somber faced trooper's presence. (I'm sorry, sir, but I see it in your eyes—you know why I'm here.)

Struggling against rising emotions, Dalton quietly guided the parents over to the living room sofa. In a hushed, subdued voice, he told them their beloved seventeen year-old son Brian had been killed in a traffic accident just hours before. Barely whispering, he continued on, telling them that their son had been killed instantly (horribly not correct) when his Mustang struck a tree on a country road near LaPlata in Charles County. The dazed father's lips quivered and he shut his eyes. With a deep sigh, he dropped his head and gently eased an arm around his distraught wife's shoulder. She was bent over and sobbing, swaying back and forth, her face buried in her hands. Dalton bit his lower lip, battling to reign in the emotions running rampant beneath his police officer facade.

He stayed there for over an hour, consoling the brokenhearted parents as they inquired about too many accident details of which he had limited knowledge. Finally, a neighbor arrived for support, a signal for Dalton to leave.

Dalton thought he was doing all right, until the heartbroken wife grabbed one of his hands and pressed it tightly against her heaving chest. With her other hand, she reached out and gently touched the side of his face. Their eyes locked on one another's and he shuddered when he felt hers pierce through to briefly touch his soul in a silent, painful plea for him to undo the horror he'd delivered to them. "Please!" she cried out between sobs. "Some way...somehow. Dear Lord...Please!" And if God would only grant me the power, Dalton silently wished her. Eyes watering, he broke through his professional veneer and hugged her before walking out the front door and back into the fresh air, away from their damaged lives.

He made it back to his cruiser and almost to Route 4, the main corridor that led to the coveted sanctity of the PF post. The Christ Church front parking lot hailed to him, however, and he went no further. With hot tears welling in his eyes, he turned off the ignition and rested his head on the steering wheel. In silence, he acknowledged to himself that he'd absorbed far too much of the anguish he'd delivered to the distraught family an hour before. And his earlier chit-chat with Cindy that evening hadn't made it any easier. Two weeks ago, she'd given him the delightful news that was pregnant. Just seven hours ago they were beaming with joy, fantasizing about his or her future, with countless names being laughingly tossed around like wedding rice. What a contrast it was, from his rapture of an expected child to his announcement of a lifeless one to those parents who'd held so much hope for their only son—until he'd knocked on their door to alter their lives forever.

Half an hour later, Dalton was back at the post. When Donny nonchalantly asked about how he'd handled the death notification, Dalton merely shrugged his shoulders and feigned a disconnected look. Donny paused and searched Dalton's face. Satisfied that nothing seemed amiss, the senior trooper turned to other pressing matters, meaning the next page of the current *Penthouse* magazine he'd been salivating over.

Early on, Dalton realized that amongst his fellow troopers, it was always best to hide any signs of weakness that could lead to his being the victim of gallows humor. Kregg had been right, though. Throughout his career, Dalton would never get used to playing the death-angel role. To some troopers, death notifications were like water falling off a duck's back. Dalton always found that the next of kin knew, they *always* knew, as soon as they opened the door and saw his face, no matter how hard he tried to mask himself behind the uniform.

#

Although F/Sgt. Best, the old muleskinner from the academy, had regaled Dalton with tales of bar fights in the volatile twin beaches, North Beach and Chesapeake Beach, but so far, Dalton had responded to only a handful of calls there. The twin beaches were incorporated, and they still maintained separate five or six-man police departments. Each department handled most calls within their own bailiwick, but the MSP assisted them when the bad stuff splattered the fan. Dalton had heard legends from the PF troopers about the peculiar traits of several twin beach officers. Any perceptions he'd formed, however, had been largely gleaned from their convoluted radio verbiage he'd heard over the shared MSP radio channel.

Idle curiosity, accelerated by nagging boredom, prompted the new troopers occasionally to roam within the twin beach borders. Weather-beaten, semi-dilapidated, seasonal cottages and stick-built houses comprised much of the Chesapeake and North Beach waterfront towns. There were several aging family-owned restaurants in both towns, along with the expected sprinkling of honky-tonk bars, including a few that catered to the gay crowd. The majority of the bars and restaurants were clustered along Bay Avenue, the main road that bisected the municipalities. In the heydays of old, the frequently rowdy towns had attracted their share of bikers and incorrigible types who fortunately contributed to the cash flow and needed revenue. In the late sixties, however, with the loss of the one-armed bandit slot machines, the wild gambling days faded into memories.

The twin beaches in the seventies seemed like depressed ghost towns populated by many who were considered to be down, but not quite out in their lives, Dalton thought. The townsfolk, generations of city migrants mostly from DC or nearby Prince Georges County, were mostly modest, blue-collar, hard working, hard drinking, salt-of-the-earth types. Dalton would develop a certain appreciation, a begrudging affinity for many of the unpretentious, tawdry beach folks he'd eventually meet.

To justify the local constabulary's salaries, there was no small shortage of unsavory, colorful troglodytes in the local populace who seasoned things up during the inevitable slack times. Dalton had recently met North Beach's infamous "General" Morton, supposedly a highly decorated, pseudo Army veteran of many battles in WWII, the "big one." He was also a bedraggled, cadaverous-looking beach sot who was badly losing his ongoing, ill-fought battle of the bottle. In the coming years, the all-knowing General would become a valued beach informant for Dalton, and his payment was usually a fifth of Jim Beam whenever his slurred words resulted in a decent arrest. That commodious arrangement would have lasted indefinitely, if General Morton hadn't been sentenced to a year in the county hoosegow. Blitzed beyond his normal norm, he'd managed to beat a haughty, trash-talking North Beach hussy over the head with a frozen chicken one morning after the frizzy-haired wench had the audacity to butt in line in front of him at the local IGA store.

Several weeks after he was cut loose, Dalton and shift-mate Donny Roberts responded to a North Beach officer's call for MSP assistance after a late night pool-stick party broke out in the Stonehenge, a rowdy bikers' bar. When the MSP cavalry arrived, however, North Beach Officer "Iron Mike" Garber, a grizzled and utterly fearless, thick-necked giant of an ex-marine had the matter well in hand. Iron Mike was standing in front of the club with his meaty hands on his hips and a Parris Island drill sergeant's snarl on his scarred face and his blazing eyes beamed with obvious delight. He howled with laughter as hordes of pissed-off, red-faced "trogs" and Harley biker pirates, some leaking blood from head wounds, all choking, gagging and screaming curses, streamed from the smoke-filled biker's den.

"Told the assholes to break it up," Iron Mike boomed out in a deep gravely voice. "And when they didn't, I lobbed two of them there teargas baseball grenades through the front door for them to play with," he added, bursting into another round of hysterics.

Dalton instantly decided that, while perhaps a bit unorthodox by MSP standards, he liked Garber's style, even if it was partially fueled by an occasional shot or two, probably gratis, of Jack Daniels. Seeing that the situation was under a semblance of control, Dalton and the other troopers wisely decided to vamoose before the trogs and bikers thought to focus on their nametags.

Donny Roberts shot Dalton an adios hand signal when the guffawing North Beach officer yanked the pin on yet another teargas grenade. "Hey State Boys, the bastards got me running low on smoke here. Y'all got a box of flares you don't need?" Garber roared as they saddled up. Returning to his patrol, Dalton shook his head and grinned when the radio crackled with waves of berserk laughter after Iron Mike gleefully advised Calvert Control that, "The sit-chew-way-shun's been rectifiably exterminated, Prince Frederick,..and my ass is clear!

"Yeah, Garber's a tough-ass son-of-a-bitch, and a great one to have around in a tight fix. The man's totally fearless and meaner than a three-legged junkyard dog," Donny later told Dalton. "But watch yourself around him, cause when he gets that crazed look in his eyes, you don't know what's gonna happen, you'll see," he added.

Beach lore had it that while he was on a store roof conducting a dubious one-man stakeout several years ago, Iron Mike stumbled and fell to the sidewalk, three stories below. Holding his broken leg and grimacing in pain, he was discovered by a surprised young couple who were out enjoying an evening walk. When they asked the anguished officer what happened, he shot them a death stare and gritted his teeth. "What the hell's it look like, you dumb assholes! My fuckin' parachute didn't open!" He growled at the retreating pair. The North Beach officer's fearlessness was legendary throughout the area. Most miscreants and other dirt balls walked softly and gave Officer "Iron Mike" Garber extra latitude in their dealings in "his" town. They were crazy not to.

#

Encouraged by Elzy, his inane corporal, Dalton gradually developed a keen interest in the more challenging criminal work. During his first year, he'd surprised himself by closing out numerous thefts, too many assaults and plenty of property destruction cases that ultimately ended with some dirt ball wearing his stainless steel bracelets. The experiences whet his appetite for the cat-and-mouse aspects of sleuthing, and Dalton was developing a penchant for the game. The majority of the minor criminal investigations were conducted by road troopers. Major cases—robberies, sex offenses, burglaries and the infrequent homicides, etc, were handled by the PF post's elite four-criminal investigation section.

As a rule, if Sergeant "Buddy" Hooper, the effervescent, Mountain Dew-swigging ID supervisor, felt the road trooper was capable of not screwing up a felony case, he'd let him roll with it.

Dalton's zeal in criminal investigations hadn't been ignored by Elzy and Buddy Hooper, the wired ID supervisor, and he was selected to attend the coveted two-week MSP criminal investigation course, a rare bequest for a probationary trooper.

Despite his minimum time on the force, Dalton was already well aware of the agency's growing shift toward traffic enforcement, especially now, with the acquisition of the more effective Speedguns. Traffic enforcement competition between the different troops and barracks was heating up into stark reality, as MSP role priorities were once again re-evaluated at the Pikesville puzzle palace. The trickle down effect to the field would take time, but the signs were already there, translating into simple, measurable stats and easy money for state coffers.

Consequently, it became increasingly more difficult to exhaust all investigative leads and sources in the complex criminal cases when there was mounting pressure for traffic citations. As a road trooper at a full-service barrack, a trooper could find himself in the quandary of the "no man's land" gauntlet of traffic versus criminal work. It would be a dilemma of time management and directed priorities that gnawed at the backbone of the MSP, the full-service road trooper, throughout his time in the field.

#

Finally, after six long, weary months of jumping patrol cars, Dalton was assigned to J-12, his first MSP cruiser. He spent almost an hour on the back lot customizing his mobile office, transferring and squaring away his two heavy-duty plastic milk crates stuffed with police paraphernalia. Following the foolhardy advice of other road troopers who ignored the fire hazard, Dalton also reversed the top of the V-8's air filter cover. Like the other troops, Dalton thought the Torino was underpowered and prone to vapor locks, and if it didn't have the desired get-up-and-go power, he'd at least make damn sure it *sounded* like it did.

Everything ship-shape, Dalton drove J-12 to Calvert County's one and only car wash. Before the cruiser was air dry, however, he was directed to respond to a domestic assault in progress call in the Lusby area. *Shit!* Dalton activated the emergency equipment and stomped on the gas pedal, aiming his new cruiser pal south for the high-speed dash down the winding single-lane. To divert his racing mind, he switched on the AM radio and was instantly immersed in Steppenwolf's *Born to Be Wild*. Oh great! That turn of the dial landed him on one of the dynamite rock songs of his pubescent era, a feat that promptly served as the supreme impetus for a swift acceleration that pushed the cruiser into triple digits.

Cresting St. Leonard Hill, Dalton barely rounded a curve on all fours, only to spot a car slowing in the northbound lane just ahead near the Twin Cedar bar. Dalton gasped as the car began an agonizingly slow turn in front of him, the driver obviously searching in vain for a parking space on the parking lot. *Nooo!* In the same split-second, he saw another northbound car passing the turning vehicle on the right shoulder. On his right, there was nothing but the packed parking lot.

He was trapped! It was mere seconds, but it felt like a slow-motion minute. Dalton gripped the steering wheel with both hands and desperately stomped down on the brake pedal. His head inched up toward the ceiling and he jammed his back against the car seat, ignoring the squealing tires which had suddenly drowned out the shrieking siren. Down to eighty miles an hour—seventy—sixty, as the blur of passing trees came into focus. The steering wheel was clutched in a white-knuckle death grip.

"Ohhhh Shhittt! " he yelled, as his barreling J-12 slammed into the right side of the car stopped in his lane. *WHAM!* After the sickening crunch, it was merry-go-round time, with milk crates, clip boards, hat, shotgun and other unsecured gear swirling around in uncontrolled flight while Dalton did his best to hang on to the spinning cruiser's steering wheel.

Finally, the Torino ground to a halt in a cloud of dust, the oscillating red and blues and the shrieking siren signaling an eerie end to the calamity. Strapped in the seatbelt and still sitting upright, Dalton was dazed, but felt no immediate pain when he forced his eyes open. He shook his head, glanced down at his crushed straw Stetson on the floorboard, then wriggled his fingers and toes before he dared to flex his arms and legs. Damn! No pain, so far so good! When he unbuckled the seat belt and shoved the driver's door open, Dalton flopped out and landed hard on the macadam parking lot. After spitting out some blood from a gashed upper lip, the boot trooper grabbed the car door and yanked himself to his feet. Clouds of ugly, black smoke and angry wisps of steam hissed from the front of the crumpled cruiser, and radiator fluid was streaming down on the parking lot. Dalton wiped the blood from his split lip with the back of a hand, and started toward the smoking Plymouth Valiant he'd creamed.

Sure enough, it looked totaled to him! *Son of a bitch!*

The unfazed, wholly unscathed elderly black driver was easing himself from his car. When he saw Dalton approaching, he staggered over to him with a look of relief plastered on his face. "Ossifer! Damn glad you're here, Ossifer!" he blurted out. "Yazz zir, I'd like to report me a hit and runaway axle-dent, by God! Yazz I would! Sums a bitches took off without warnin' me!" shouted the tanked driver with the bloodshot eyes.

Well, at least he'd slammed into a drunk, Dalton realized, as he fought to reign in his mounting anger. Loud drunks and curious onlookers from the bar were forming a circle around them. Dalton snatched the tipsy one by the arm and dragged him back to his steaming cruiser so he could radio in the *departmental* accident.

Elzy, his piqued, but welcome corporal, arrived within minutes to initiate the several pounds of required MSP paperwork for the departmental. After measuring the long trail of skid marks, Elzy frowned, spit out the last remnants of an old Red Man chaw, then tapped Dalton on the shoulder with his Kel-light.

"Hey, hoss, just one question here: were you landing, or trying to take off?" he asked with a smirk. Not waiting for an answer, Elzy turned his attention to the putty-legged drunk who was waving his "Johnson" left to right, pissing all over the hood of a nearby parked car. "Hey! What the hell you doin', you dumb mutha-fucker!" Elzy bellowed out, loud enough to make the drunk piss on himself.

Dalton set a PF Post record by being the first trooper to have a departmental within twenty minutes of being assigned to his first take-home cruiser. Way too soon, he also learned more about the MSP art of detailed report writing as it pertained to his "non-preventable" agency accident. From years of experience, Elzy had become quite the consummate investigator and creative report-writer in such matters. While sometimes pushing the credibility envelope, his accident report endorsements were MSP masterpieces when required. Ever after, *Born to be Wild* had a special, indefatigable meaning to Dalton, serving as the silent background theme for the three other departmental accidents he'd have during his MSP career.

#

When possible during the early shifts, Dalton joined cohorts Marty or Donny for lunch "assignments" at one of the local carry-outs. On occasions when the others were busy, Dalton drove to one of his favorite hideouts to chow down by himself. When he worked his favored south patrol, he'd preferably find himself down on the bay-front beach of the quaintly rustic Scientists' Cliffs community in Port Republic. With a full bay panorama, he'd watch the watermen as they checked their crab pots, or maybe he'd see a majestic "blow-boat" crisscrossing the open waters in search of better wind.

Several miles to the south, the twin reactor domes and the huge grayish-white building which sheltered the turbines of the Calvert Cliffs nuclear power plant were readily seen. To Dalton, the nuclear plant was a misplaced behemoth, an energy-producing aberration plunked rudely along the ageless cliffs overlooking the pristine bay. Unlike some countians who lived close to the nuke plant, Dalton wasn't overly concerned about the possibility of it having any doomsday mishaps. *But*, if the blue crabs started drifting ashore already cooked, *that* would be due cause for reconsideration, he figured.

Lolled by the serenity of the Scientists' Cliffs beach, Dalton lost himself in thought, as the gentle waves caressed the sand and shells along the beach, the melodious, hypnotizing sounds broken only by the random shrill call of a seagull overhead. Chancing upon a bikini-clad sunbather wading shin-deep in the water and searching for sharks teeth was also a delight.

If on north patrol, Dalton would occasionally take "assignment" in his cruiser near the old tobacco wharf in the tranquil, historic "towne" of Lower Marlboro on the upper Patuxent River. There, he watched a few locals fish off the old wooden pier in hopes of snagging a few ugly, sharp-spined catfish or a bottom-sucking carp on the changing tides.

With an occasional swig or two from bottles hidden in brown paper bags, the cajoling black field hands simply enjoyed their day off with each other regardless of the catch.

Except for the occasional night "fire-training" episodes, Dalton thought night shift in the rural area was surrealistic at times. Early on, he'd deferred from taking any meal "assignments" during the graveyard shifts, knowing it'd induce serious nods and the inevitable stomach cramps if he did. Recently, several commercial burglaries had occurred in Southern Maryland, including several in sleepy Calvert County. Patrol checks were stepped up, and the beefed-up night-shift troops were admonished to stay alert, meaning, *awake.*

Led by Leroy "Froggy" Gantt, the notorious Gantt brothers were a determined bunch, undeterred and boldly audacious. For their heists they'd usually steal only high-performance Oldsmobiles or Buicks, their success relying on speed and endurance. Once the car was stolen and safely cached, the back seats were removed to accommodate room to store the stolen goods. Entry to the businesses was simple, efficient, and fast. The driver raced the car right up to the storefront, and, joined by the "shotgun" passenger, they both swung away with axes to quickly chop their way through the front door. Ignoring the blaring alarms, the Gantts loaded up the car with their loot—usually chainsaws, TV sets or guns—and in less then three minutes they'd be racing to a predetermined spot to cache the goods for the next day's trip out of the county after the LE heat lifted.

Despite some drawbacks, Dalton discovered he actually enjoyed working the midnight hours when the "normals" were sleeping in warm beds with warm others. For a new trooper it was a novelty, a time for unique happenings and weird experiences. As the wee-morning hours approached, no matter how many caffeine pills or cups of gut-wrenching, slurried coffee you were able to force down, the nods inevitably arrived to beleaguer the public servants of the dark hours. In the rural county, the twilight hallucinations of a tired mind appeared in many bizarre ways. A newspaper blowing across the road could suddenly turn into a scurrying cat, dog or possum. The sound of rolling tires on road-shoulder gravel jarred you awake with a gasp, sometimes before your head dropped to the steering wheel, and normally familiar roads turned into confusing uncharted routes in foreign countries.

Extraneous sounds heard over the MSP radio during the slow, boorish, mid-week nights were all encompassing, and mostly engrossing. They'd inevitably include random belches or a renegade tooting of flatulence (Dalton was always amazed how some troopers were gifted with the art of on-demand flatulence), followed by various animal squawks, short plays of popular song lyrics, and radio-check squelch battles. On those rare and treasured occasions, atmospheric conditions also played havoc with radio frequencies, allowing them to skip hundreds of miles beyond. It was always a pleasure hearing some good ole cowpoke deputy in Mineral Wells, Texas yapping about how he'd untangled a cow from a barbed wire fence or the like. Dalton grew to appreciate the graveyard shift's warped humor, and he eagerly contributed to it whenever the mood hit.

Inevitably, with the onset of the nods, Dalton, adhering to his lone-wolf habit, drove to his favorite night refuge, a place where he knew he wouldn't be hassled when he grabbed a few winks. Balancing the power of the lord and the fearful mystique surrounding the departed ones, no one would bother him here, he mused to himself when he parked his cruiser on another slow night.

He thumbed up the radio's squelch knob until he heard static, thumbed it back a tab, then set the radio mic in his lap, carefully positioning it so the transmit button wouldn't accidentally activate. Didn't need to wake up and see the glaring red transmit light staring at him. With few exceptions, particularly during most night shifts, a trooper inadvertently keyed the mic, creating loud static (or worse) on the troop radio frequency, and soon the scramble was on to find out which unit messed up.

Assured that things were in order for his catnap, Dalton stretched out his legs, leaned back against the vinyl seat and closed his tired, woody eyes. *His* coveted refuge of the dark during those slow hours was the cemetery behind Christ Church in tranquil Port Republic. No chance anybody would ever bother him there, especially because of the witch, who, according to a county legend, had been re-interred there a few hundred years or so ago. As a matter of fact, Rebecca Fowler, circa 1650s, had been the only woman who'd ever been tried, convicted and hanged on Maryland's soil for being a witch. Her body was refused burial at all of the county's church cemeteries after she'd been executed for the spells she'd cast against prying neighbors. It was a long-held belief that her distraught husband had taken her witchy remains from the family farm in Barstow several nights later to bury her, sans headstone, somewhere amongst the eternal ones doing their dirt naps in Christ Church cemetery.

Yes indeedy, Dalton felt surer than jack-shit, that he'd be safe there, except of course on that one lone occasion when he'd experienced an eerie sense of the presence of others lurking amongst the graves. It'd jarred him out of a decent nod-attack to instantly raise the hair on the back of his neck. Eyes open wide, jaw clenched and heart thumping, he eased the revolver from its holster and drew it across his lap. Easing his head to the left, his peripheral vision picked up the three apparitions huddled together in the dark, just several yards away. Turning his head further, he saw them gaping directly at him. A grin soon replaced his petrified expression. Standing their ground, the three curious deer canted their heads then jerked them up and down. When they heard the MSP radio crackle out a time check, they snorted with indignation, flashed their white tails and bounded off. Greatly relieved but with his heart in his throat, Dalton fired up the cruiser and headed back to the post. Sometimes the coffee there wasn't all *that* bad.

Ever the gregarious one, Marty, Dalton's shift buddy, usually worked off his night-shift blahs at the post, keeping the PCOs awake with corny jokes and iffy guitar strumming. Every too often, however, crippling boredom sank in, and he'd talk Dalton or some other weary trooper into practicing high-speed pursuit turns as part of their OJT (On-the-Job Training). Undoubtedly, Tfc. Marty Metzger was the post's premier pursuit driver, and thanks to him, Dalton and many other post troopers acquired valuable hands-on driver tutoring. The night-shift lessons might have continued indefinitely, if one of the new troopers hadn't royally screwed things up.

Denny Miranda, the boot trooper from Philadelphia, was sadistically sent south to the rural Prince Frederick assignment after his academy graduation. As a young, horribly-gullible trooper, Miranda faithfully followed Marty Metzger's sage advice about needing to "burn off the carbon buildup" in the cruiser's carburetor, along with the need to practice power turns during slow nights.

In true MSP balls-to-the-walls fashion, probationer Miranda proudly maxed out the borrowed cruiser to 122 miles per hour on the Route 4 flats just south of Prince Frederick. Standing beside his cruiser parked along the shoulder, Marty smiled proudly as Miranda rocketed past him. He watched with great expectation as the brakes lights flashed, signaling the expected power turn. Marty's smile instantly vaporized when the cruiser swerved wildly off the shoulder to careen into several mail and newspaper boxes. In a cloud of dirt and dust, the cruiser finally slammed into the guardrail, creating an awesome shower of white sparks until it came to an abrupt, neck-wrenching stop.

"Jesus H Christ! A damn departmental!" Marty uttered as he dashed to his unit.

Shaken, but not the least bit injured except for his pride, the disheveled young trooper gawked at the mangled cruiser. He readily agreed with the senior trooper that it'd be a good thing for all to tell the investigating supervisor that he'd swerved to avoid a deer, while his shift buddy Marty was duly performing building checks miles away in his assigned patrol area.

The hastily contrived plan would have probably succeeded, had the right supervisor showed up. Instead, Sergeant Ira Craig (a.k.a. Mr. Personality), who'd been rudely awakened a half-hour before, had responded to handle the departmental. Filling in for another sergeant, he was visibly piqued. One menacing stare from old-salt Craig when he slammed his car door shut was all it took. Miranda's face turned ghost-white. Marty shot the boot trooper a quick glance and groaned. He'd seen that panic-stricken look before, indicative of a hapless boot just about ready to shit himself.

It all fell apart quickly when Miranda messed up the phantom deer story. "Ssssarge, one of them mule deers, ummm, maybe it was one of them white-legged deers, or, or, whatever y'all call em...yeah, one of them critters lying in the road here, umm, and I had to swerve to avoid hitting it too," Miranda spouted out. "Yeah, and it was one of them girl does, and you should have seen all them big tusks that were stickin out of her head, Sarge!" Standing within spitting distance, Marty winced and kicked lamely at some loose gravel.

With a somber grimace chiseled on his leathery face, Sgt.Craig paused briefly and let out a low sigh. Deep in thought, he slowly rubbed the back of his head with the end of his flashlight. "Deer my ass, Miranda! Strike One"! he rasped at the trooper quivering in front of him. "In *my* game you only get *two* strikes, stud, so try for the other one, why don't you?"

Petrified, Miranda gaped into the supervisor's steely eyes. "Sergeant Craig...sir, are you gonna make me think before I have to talk?" he asked in a shaky voice. Without waiting for the answer, Miranda promptly recanted his first story and coughed it all up. Sheepishly pointing his finger at Marty, the boot trooper told the sergeant that the senior trooper had indeed been teaching him some handy evasion maneuvers during their current graveyard shift. "Nice way to take it on the chin, boot asshole," Marty muttered under his breath when Sgt. Craig glared over at him, well aware that his driver training days were over.

Unruffled to any large extent, Marty later took the ten-minute ass chewing from the first sergeant after the mountain of departmental paperwork was done. At least there hadn't been any mention about his rat shootouts at the dump.

"Hey Marty, now that we're straight about *not* teaching the boots how to wreck their cars, ya know where I can scrounge up a bushel of number-one jimmy crabs, cheap?" the pipe-smoking top-kick inquired. "Be back in about an hour with 'em steamed for ya, Boss," Marty spouted back. "Ole man Scooter Denton down at the packing house on the island owes me a favor, big time." Wild Bill Flyger chuckled as he set his pipe down on the desk. "And Marty, *no* lights or number twos mixed in with em, OK?" Marty, upbeat again, saluted and shot a thumbs-up to the grinning first shirt. Marty's expertise as the post's top scrounger and pack rat was highly valued by many, especially Wild Bill, who was quite an accomplished colleague in such matters.

Marty's attributes were valued just high enough to dampen more than a few hot issues surrounding his rambunctious, wayward endeavors.

When Dalton worked night shift with Donny Roberts, he encountered some problems, the major dilemma being Donny's occasional failure to respond to calls on his assigned patrol. Too often, Dalton had to leave his own patrol to find his "missing" cohort, who'd lost the nods battle to some serious Z-time. To his credit, Donny was usually found parked at his favorite "nod zone," the All Saints Church parking lot in Sunderland.

To his *discredit*, when Dalton went to rouse Donny a second time during a recent night shift for a call, he found his fellow trooper's cruiser with its windows all fogged up. Dalton bathed it with blinding high beams, reds and blues and a gleaming spotlight, prompting spastic movements in the back seat. Sure enough, Donny was deeply immersed in the throes of passion with yet another Calvert damsel, a spirited, whimsically married waitress from the Honey Suckle Café, Dalton found out later! Damn if this job didn't hamper a man's amorous intentions. Dalton tapped car bumpers for emphasis. Two blanched faces and a respectable pair of pale, strawberry-tipped boobies materialized in the foggy rear window. Satisfied, Dalton jammed the gear shift into reverse and split the scene.

Moments later, the slightly winded Donny radioed the control center for a time check, signaling to those in the know his belated return to duty. Dalton's shift mate would be available of course, but only after he'd dropped his strumpet back off near her house, praying that her husband was diligently hibernating for the night after throwing down too many double shots of Wild Turkey.

#

Night shift in rustic Calvert was prime time for some horrendous "road pizza" accidents, especially after the not-so-golden bar-closing hour. Dalton's first fatal accident arrived just four months after he was cut loose.

"Prince Frederick J-12 and all units!" Not Good! The voice of Bill "Pop" Howland, the senior night shift PCO, was really shrill. Pop Howard, a retired PG County fireman, was an old salt who didn't sweat much about nearly anything. Dalton had a gut feeling this one was gonna be bad-ass ugly, and he quickly answered up. Moments later, Elzy, his corporal, and Donny Roberts radioed their acknowledgments. "J-12 and all units, you've got a 10-50 PI...a head-on...on Route 2 just south of St. Leonard's Creek!" Pop rasped. "Company Four from the rescue squad and Company Five in Solomons are en route! " "10-76 (enroute) from Lusby!" Dalton edgily advised, kicking the cruiser into a power turn to start north.

Until now, it'd been almost too quiet for a cold, early-morning Sunday in February. Pop Howland's anxious voice came back on, advising them to step it up! Dalton played it safe and flipped on the siren and the emergency lights, hoping to keep any wayward deer skittish enough to stay off the road. On such clear moonlit nights, the county corridors were dotted with the glittery-eyed critters.

Elzy was first on the scene. Seconds later, he excitedly requested Calvert Control to call for an MSP helicopter. *Damn!* This one's gonna be a bitch, another repugnant glimpse of the macabre. Dalton measured his breathing and tried to reign in his racing mind, steeling himself for what lay ahead on the dark, winding road. Cresting a hill, he saw an eerie cloud of steam and smoke spiraling up into the night sky. Moments later, what remained of both wrecked cars came into view. Elzy's cruiser, dome light swirling and outside radio speaker crackling, was on the shoulder just before the ghastly mess, its headlights illuminating the foggy scene.

Dalton set his cruiser behind the mangled gray Cutlass Supreme station wagon pointed north in the southbound lane. Black smoke and clouds of steam billowed up from the vehicle as fluids streaked down on the macadam and streamed across the road like roving liquid snakes. The noxious odor of hot antifreeze and spilled battery acid assaulted his nostrils. Farther ahead, he saw Elzy frantically waving his flashlight, shouting for him not to light any road flares. Dalton bolted over and joined him at the smoking mess of what remained of a small white import. "Don't bother with the guy in the station wagon! His ass is dead!" the corporal yelled. "This guy needs help!"

Amidst the scattered bits of fiberglass and other debris from the explosive head-on collision, Elzy was pointing his flashlight at one of the larger chunks. In the dim light, all Dalton could see was a bundle of wet, multicolored clothing in what appeared to be the detached rear end of the car. On the ground nearby, there were magazines, toiletry items, a broken tennis racket, and a pair of sneakers strewn beside the wreckage. Peering closer, Dalton was startled to see movement in the pile of clothes. A bloody, horribly mangled, human face ever so slowly came into focus. Dalton's immediate attention riveted to the empty eye-socket, then down to the broken, offset lower jaw. The jaw barely moved, the mouth opening slightly, as the young man struggled to speak. Nothing came out, except loose teeth, a rivulet of blood, and a hoarse cough. Elzy put his hand on the driver's chest, and then ran his fingers up to the bloody neck, checking for a decent pulse. There were rasping sounds mixed with moans, and the victim's chest moved steadily as his lungs worked hard to suck in needed air. Good! He was breathing. "Hold on, man...you're gonna make it! Hear me? Hold on!" Elzy shouted, imploring him to fight for his life.

Dalton gazed at the jagged end of the shiny white thighbone protruding from the man's blue jeans, and then gaped at Elzy who merely shook his head. Both troopers were relieved to hear sirens screaming in the distance, heralding the approach of the rescue squad meat wagons and fire trucks. It'd seemed like hours, but they'd arrived within minutes of the call. The mangled driver was thoroughly saturated with spilled gasoline, and as the volunteers sprung into action, Dalton alerted them so they didn't set out flares or park their meat wagons too close. Already, he could see firefighters setting up portable lights while others began hosing down the roadway. Dalton gingerly made his way back through the haze of steam and choking smoke. Although the Cutlass wagon had extensive front-end damage, the passenger compartment looked relatively intact.

Dalton peered into the driver's window at the teenager still poised behind the steering wheel with his head cocked back against the headrest. His mouth was open, a perfect O, and his unseeing, gaping eyes had a languid, "thousand mile stare," that dead fish washed-up-on-shore look. While the driver's injuries didn't look that bad, his bruised sunken temple hinted otherwise. He wasn't wearing a seatbelt, a fateful error, and his head had smashed against the top of the windshield frame.

Dalton reached in with two fingers to test for a pulse. The driver's skin was clammy and cold, and there wasn't one. The young man's waxy pallor told him the story before he'd even checked, but now he was dead certain that the corpse was exactly that. Dalton took his Stetson off and wiped his brow. There was lots of work to do, and he had to focus, couldn't allow himself to reflect on the horror. *That* would come later, as it usually did.

As he crossed the Chesapeake Bay Bridge en route to his new home on Kent Island, Dalton was momentarily dazzled by the sparkling late afternoon sunrays reflecting off the bay's expanse. It was bright and awesomely-clear, a rare gem of a day, and he could see for several miles. His attention drifted down to several freighters churning north through calm waters to Baltimore Harbor. As he sped on, he admired the peacefulness of the watchful seagulls perched delicately on the bridge railings. What a stark contrast to the ugly tragedy he'd left behind in that sleepy little county some forty miles south.

Emotionally spent, Dalton swung the cruiser into his driveway. First, he peered in the other bedroom to check on the snoozing baby, touched her lightly on the back for reassurance. He quickly slipped out of the room after she stirred. He tossed his black clip-on tie on an easy chair, detached the thin metal collar stay, and then undid the top buttons of his uniform shirt. The Sam Browne belt he sloughed off, leaving it where it fell, and the grimy Corfams were nimbly kicked off. Dalton rubbed his jaded eyes with the heels of his palms and massaged his throbbing temples with tight fingers. Moments later, he was sitting at the kitchen table, draining the first bottle of beer he'd rescued from the fridge. Damn! He still reeked of gas and radiator fluid. He could only tell a groggy, probing Cindy that it'd been a kick ass night, before he collapsed on the bed and passed out.

#

Part of the night-shift norm was the infernal mail run with other MSP installations. In the tiresome hours of a crisp June morning, it was Dalton's turn to meet a Barrack "H" Waldorf car at Benedict just across the bridge in Charles County for the exchange. Minutes after leaving the post, he pulled up next to a Barrack "H" unit and broke into a wide grin. "Mel, you son of a bitch! How the hell ya doing, my man?" he shouted to the trooper whose hand was frozen in the middle of a salute. Seconds later, he was bear-hugging and shoulder-slapping his beaming academy roommate. Neither had seen each other since graduation, and now, eight months later, they were finally able to catch up with each other and trade war stories.

The experience had been tough for Purvey, one of the few black troopers in "good ole boy" Southern Maryland. Dalton could only imagine how difficult it was for his friend, who was out of his Eastern Shore element, despised here by many only because of his skin color. "Things are pretty innate with these crazy people down here Dalton, just no gettin' around it. Been in lots a bar fights, and Lord...way too many domestics with them Cracker Jacks." Purvey sighed and shook his head. "But overall, I'm hanging in there just waiting for that transfer back to the shore. Trouble is, I'm a just an Uncle Remus cop to the more extreme white folk down here, and an Uncle Tom cop to many of the blacks who grill me about which side I'm on. Yeah, people around these parts expect white police officers like you to be *the man*, but for me, there's little respect I get from either side, believe me, my friend," Mel told him from the heart.

Ill-at-ease about bigotry, the BS session moved to other matters, Purvey finally chiding Dalton for not following up on the dinner invitation he'd offered months before. With a pending July promotion and transfer list, the former classmates agreed to make it a date later that month.

As Dalton took the mailbags from his fellow trooper, a swerving pick-up truck streaked across the Benedict Bridge and whisked past them. Purvey took off in pursuit with Dalton close behind. After making contact with the red-faced, obviously tanked driver, Purvey had him perform several sobriety tests while Dalton observed close by. The beefy drunk was overly polite and quite intent on proving to the troopers how drunk he wasn't, which, of course, proved how drunk he truly was. His walk and turn demonstration was almost passable too, until he peed himself while turning. The drunk's demeanor changed quickly when Purvey told him he was under arrest for DWI.

"Ain't no goddamn nigger cop gonna put his filthy black hands on me, boy!" he yelled in Purvey's face, pulling away from his grip. Dalton suddenly felt a hot wave of anger. Incensed, he dashed over and threw the drunk across the hood of his truck, making sure his head bounced off the hood a few times for good measure. With a powerful arm-lock, Dalton forced him up on his toes, and Purvey slapped the cuffs on. It had been purely reactive and surprisingly effortless, Dalton realized.

He stuck his face close to the man's head then jerked him up on his toes again. "Hayseed, I don't see any niggers around here, and you better think twice about using that word when you take a ride to Waldorf with my trooper buddy," he growled into the drunk's ear. The lush snorted and glared at him beady-like through bloodshot eyes, but wisely kept silent. Mel shrugged his shoulders and gave his former classmate a wane smile.

"No big thing, my man, just another typical SMIB (Southern Maryland In-Breed), that's all. See you in July, Trooper!" 'It's a deal, my man," Dalton shouted back Chocked full of prim and pride, the boot troopers saluted each other smartly. Dalton kept his pledge to visit his classmate; however, it was sooner then expected and not as he'd anticipated.

The last set of bench presses almost forced Dalton to dump the weights off the unsecured bar until a final burst of energy pushed the bar high enough to set it back in place. Months prior to the academy, and ever since, he'd pushed himself hard to stay in top physical condition, alternating daily between the weights and running. Today had been another exhausting workout with the weights, and he was drenched with sweat. He sat up on the bench and stretched, eyeballing his garage workout area for the dumbbells needed for his biceps curls. Needing their own nest, Dalton and wife Cindy eventually found a house in Cove View, a quiet community on Kent Island. It was a modest two-bedroom, stick-built frame house on a small corner lot, a cozy starter home where they'd enjoy the delights of a newborn.

'Hey, honey, there's a phone call for you from the post," Cindy chirped from the kitchen doorway. Dalton bounded from the garage, slapped her playfully on her firm butt and kissed her on the forehead before snatching the phone from her outstretched hand. As he'd heard from someone—maybe his mom—women who were young, happy and very pregnant seemed to glow. Cindy beamed!

She watched with raised eyebrows when Dalton's face turned serious and pale, his words turning into somber whispers. When he sighed and slumped against the kitchen wall, she grew apprehensive. Dalton hung up the phone and slumped down on the kitchen table with his head in his hands. "It's Mel...it's Melvin Purvey, my academy roommate," he muttered in disbelief. "Cindy, he was in a departmental a few hours ago, and...and he's dead!" Seeing her husband's pained face, Cindy rushed over and clasped her arms around him. Dalton trembled and held her tight for a few moments, his chin resting on her shoulder. Leaving her in the kitchen, he dashed to their bedroom and shut the door.

Stupefied, Dalton sat on the edge of the bed. Tears welled in his eyes, and a knot formed in his stomach. His mind raced in overdrive. *"Damn! DAMN!!"* He yelled at his anguished reflection in the dresser mirror as he tried to put it all together.

While en route to the Waldorf Barrack, twenty-three year-old Trooper Melvin Purvey had apparently swerved off the road to avoid hitting a dog. Only weeks away from completing his first year on the force, Dalton's soul-brother friend died when his cruiser struck a tree outside of Mardela Springs on the Eastern Shore.

Minutes later, with beer in hand, Dalton was woefully perched at the end of the Matapeake pier overlooking the Chesapeake. He stayed there, restlessly contemplating for nearly an hour and a six-pack. As the crimson sun sank below the western horizon, the blinking red lights of the majestic bay bridge to the north grew more prominent. The warm, comforting breeze gave off wafts of bay scents he'd always savored: the pungent, oily smell of the abundant alewives the rockfish fed on, occasional whiffs of drifting seaweed mixed with the faint, salty tang of brackish water. Whenever a personal loss occurred, Dalton held true to his penchant for seeking the solace of the outdoors, a hallowed refuge realized years before. Now, as then, nature's setting aptly served to ease the painful loss of another close friend.

Ten years ago, his best friend canceled himself just months after their high school graduation. For months adding up to several years, Dalton remained uncharacteristically melancholy, pained from the loss of his beloved pseudo-brother. Ricky Yinger, his best, forever friend, warily opened up his heart and gave it to his first and last girlfriend. She ravaged it and threw it aside, abandoning him just weeks after she vowed to stay with him for eternity. And on that brisk November day in the woods near his home, Ricky lost his mind too. Unable to hang on, he put an end to his spiraling pain, his crumbling life, with one round from a Winchester single shot .22 rifle, Dalton's gift to his friend on his final birthday.

It took years before Dalton eventually worked past his sentiments to revisit their favorite Nirvana, Fosters Pond, nestled deep in the woods near Severna Park. It was there, bonding in the foibles of early youth that they learned much about nature, especially how to snag the elusive largemouth bass the pond ever-so-reluctantly granted them. Girls were frilly, budding enigmas for the future. True life was being with your best Huckleberry Finn pal, sharing innermost, adolescent musings about the fickle meaning of one's very existence, all the while cradled in the wondrous realm of the imperceptible creator himself. It was during that lonely visit to the pond, awash with comforting memories, that Dalton finally came to terms with his loss.

"But what swirled through your mind as your finger tightened on the trigger, Ricky? And tell me why you couldn't let me know how bad it was for you, my forever friend?"

The funeral of Maryland State Trooper Melvin Purvey was a showcase for the MSP and the affiliated police departments paying tribute to their fallen brother. Dalton traveled to Purvey's hometown of Princess Anne with fellow classmates Heiser and Rensir. In front of the rural church, the troopers and more than three hundred allied law enforcement personnel formed ranks to give last respects to one of their own. Dalton proudly stood in the front rank, as the funeral detail accompanied Purvey's casket to the hearse. He felt a lump in his throat as he watched Purvey's distraught mother reach out to touch the Maryland flag draped over her son's coffin. She nodded, then turned and smiled a weak acknowledgment to the contingent of somber officers standing before her.

Fighting back rising emotions, Dalton concentrated his thoughts on the color guard next to the hearse. "Troopers! A-ten-hut!" Barked the MSP Captain in charge of the column. The loud, echoing command forced Dalton to click his heels together and stand ramrod straight at attention. The order to "present arms" was given as Purvey's casket was loaded onto the hearse, the white-gloved salute held until the vehicle left for the cemetery. The grave site service was thankfully brief.

The Maryland State Police was quite capable of performing many duties and ceremonies in its usual, exemplary fashion, and Dalton thought the agency truly excelled when it came to putting their own to rest. Unfortunately, throughout his MSP career, he would attend several funerals of fellow troopers. One was always one too many.

Two months after Trooper Melvin Purvey's funeral, on a stifling hot and humid August evening, three young shiftless lowlifes waited quietly in a stolen van parked at Patterson's Spirits, a popular Eastern Shore liquor store just off Rt. 50 in Stevensville. Desperate for drug money, they waited anxiously for a few more customers to leave before they robbed the place. All three suddenly went numb when MSP Sergeant Randall Branham's stern face appeared at the driver's window. Branham, a topnotch supervisor at the Centreville barrack, was on his way home after ending his uneventful shift. As per habit, he'd stopped at the store to pick up a few random breakfast items for his wife and three kids. The sight of the rusty, beat-up van angled across two parking spaces near the storefront, along with the two scruffy types that were in it, gave off a gut feeling that didn't quite fit the picture.

As he'd done so many times before when the alarm bells sounded, the sergeant radioed his location and the suspicious vehicle info to the barrack before exiting his cruiser. From their panicked faces, he knew that he'd interrupted something—maybe some drug deal going down.

What the sergeant didn't see, however, was the ugly snout of a sawed-off shotgun thrust suddenly over the driver's shoulder.

No time to call out a desperate *SIGNAL 13*!

The weapon fired with a horrific roar! At pointblank range, nine double OO pellets tore into Sergeant Branham's neck and upper chest, leaving him mortally wounded on the parking lot.

The subsequent manhunt for the killers ended in their captures, and later, their convictions for the murder. The state of Maryland, however, had once again lost one of her very finest.

Although Dalton knew Sergeant Branham only from several minor calls that the NCO had backed him up on, Dalton was quite familiar with his sterling reputation in the agency and amongst the locals. Desolating to Dalton, the cold-blooded murder had occurred less than a half mile from both Branham's home and his own. His classmate Purvey's accidental death was tough enough. The senseless death of this stellar MSP sergeant, the waste of such a promising life, which had somehow been allowed to occur, left Dalton empty and incensed.

"Where are the Guardian Angels who keep watch over the sentinels?" the voice in his mind pleaded, to no avail.

(Purgatory Ridge)

Shaking the distant glaze from his eyes, the veteran sergeant drifted away from the painful memories of the early-years loss of his two fellow troopers. He snatched another cigar from the knapsack, popped the tapered end into his mouth to wet it, then lit the blunt end to savor another fine draw. Nice. The death of his academy roommate had numbed him, and he'd lost a piece of his MSP innocence early on. Purvey had certainly garnered his respect, was always driven and diligent, qualities Dalton had admired. He also hoped that, with his limited time in the field, Purvey hadn't experienced much of the subtle racism that prevailed within the MSP, a traditionally conservative force still in the early throes of attracting more minorities into its ranks.

Growing pains galore. Hell, as a black trooper back then, it was bad enough just to deal with the racism of those outside of the ranks, let alone from those within who wore the same Stetsons. It would take years before Dalton discerned how pervasive the problem was in the agency, how, as a matter of custom in certain barracks across the state, subtle discrimination flourished with feigned impunity behind closed doors. When he reported to the Prince Frederick Post, there were no black troopers, a thorny circumstance that soon changed with the times. And there were very few supervisors who'd commanded more respect from their peers like Sergeant Branham had during his short, ill-fated MSP tenure.

"Enough," Dalton muttered aloud, drifting back to the more congenial thoughts of earlier years. Yeah, those two probationary years, when the agency could fire you for minuscule infractions as it pleased, were tough. But damn if they didn't add up to two years of some serious challenges, a menagerie of heart-pounding experiences and myriads of encounters, some coming at high speed, most in slow, but all adding up to being priceless on the job-learning scale. Undeniably, in those forming years, he loved his job. Some of the situations he'd managed to blunder and bluff his way through were incredible. It was impromptu acting "extraordinaire," during those times when he didn't have a clue as to what he was supposed to do, or how the hell it was exactly supposed to be done.

Sure, the academy training, the regulation books and the break-in periods with the seasoned troopers gave invaluable guidance to the new boots. Still, nothing, but *nothing,* could circumvent the need for good ole OJT, a crucial factor that didn't have its own fast-forward button.

Some of the new troopers found their comfortable grooves sooner than others. Some never did, and a few eventually quit from the frustrating apathy of what they perceived police work was, as compared to its reality. The scary ones were the slackers and pretenders, with which the Prince Frederick Post hadn't been infected—to any dire extent. Such personas were ominous to their fellow troopers in many ways. The chicken-hearted slackers dependably shied away from confrontations, did the turtle waltz responding to risky calls, or had predictable radio problems whenever the shit hit the fan. In contrast, the "Super Trooper" pretenders got overly involved, twisting petty encounters into runaway cluster-fucks in bursts of unnecessary machismo as dictated by TV depictions of endorphin-charged super cops.

Overall, Dalton had been impressed with the majority of the hard-charging troopers at Prince Frederick. Like many other troopers, he frequently stayed hours beyond shifts on his own time to help out on busy-days-gone-wild, fearful that he'd miss out on bragging rights if something big erupted in his absence. It was the bonding, the glue of camaraderie he'd admired more than anything else about being a Maryland State Trooper in those early, heady days. As Dalton eventually learned, however, his gung-ho attitude would be the cause of undue consternation, causing serious distress for his young wife who remained at home with their newborn during too many terribly long hours.

The sergeant tried blowing a smoke ring, failed miserably, then took another swig of warm beer. Yeah, those barrack parties were something else, weren't they? His initiation was the annual summer hoopla held at Williams Wharf on the Patuxent River, which long ago was an embarkation site for tobacco hogsheads headed for Baltimore. Softball and horseshoe matches were played with combined teams chosen from the MSP, the sheriff's department, and the Calvert Control members, while the wives and kids frolicked in the swimming pool. Centerpiece was the mountain of steamed blue crabs and the sumptuous crab soup prepared on the spot by the gregarious PCO Bo Grady, a round-faced, beer-bellied, good ole county boy. Burgers and dogs nicely complimented the various homemade dishes each family brought along.

Twin kegs of beer packed in tubs of ice equated to ample revelry amongst the troops, who, far removed from the druthers of police work, let loose to blow off some steam. Dalton smiled, remembering Elzy, his erstwhile corporal, being at least four sheets to the wind when he regaled them by singing a few painfully grating verses of *Old Shep*. Elzy's luminous performance ended abruptly when he staggered and fell backward onto a picnic table piled high with hot steamed crabs, an unfortunate happenstance that provoked his wife to drag him home before he could butcher an encore of *Danny Boy*, his all-time favorite.

The most esteemed affair was the annual Prince Frederick Post banquet and awards ceremony normally held in late January. The coat-and-tie gala was usually held in one of the fire department halls, local restaurants or at the Elks Club. The customary buffet dinner was followed by the awards ceremony, where troopers garnered honors for the previous years' feats. The coveted Trooper of the Year award, a tribute determined by the post supervisors, was the evenings crowning event. After too many impromptu speeches and scads of plaques and trophies, it was time to dance to the DJ tunes, a long-awaited romping where Dalton, the free-spirited air-guitar player, shined like a rock star.

After attending their first awards banquet, Dalton and Cindy spent the night at Marty Metzger's place. Soon enough, Slumber Land blind-sided both wives like a rogue tidal wave. Shortly thereafter, the trooper cohorts were standing precariously in front of Marty's ancient Wurlitzer jukebox. Wobbling, with bloodshot eyes lolling aimlessly, they drunkenly pushed buttons on the cherished machine for the 45-rpm record plays, totally mesmerized by the steady streams of rainbow colors swirling in front of their noses.

Marty did a bullfrog belch to catch Dalton's divided attention. He snorted, and then passed Dalton the fifth of half-empty tequila. "This here bbbbitch...she'll play zzzall night...ifff she wants to, an' zzats a damn fact, don't ya knows!" Dalton shot him a shit-eating grin and back around to mash more jukebox buttons. When the last drop of José Cuervo dribbled from the bottle, Marty yanked the jukebox plug so they could have a go at some live music.

In the wee early-morning hours, tired of wailing through too many off-key country songs to the accompaniment of Marty's untuned guitar, both troopers suddenly found themselves mired in a tequila-fueled stupor, and dog-ass hungry. Minutes later, in the icy mid-January air, they were staggering onto a weathered pier over a small cove that emptied into the Patuxent River. As one, they stopped midway down and turned to face the water. Marty belched and set the glowing

Coleman lantern down on the pier, and, side-by-side on rubbery legs, they anointed the glassy-smooth water with arcing jets of warm, sterilized pee. Seeing tendrils of steam wafting up from their efforts, Dalton laughed. Marty hummed aimlessly and his body shook, signaling he was almost done. Business taken care of, they sheathed themselves and tottered on.

At the end of the pier they tussled with a set of oyster tongs Marty filched from a neighbor's boat. After a few bumbling attempts at scraping the bottom with the long-handled grippers, they surprised themselves by hauling in several foul-smelling clumps of thick, black muck. As they plied through the sloppy conglomeration with stiff fingers, they found several hefty "breakfast" oysters. Laughing like hyenas, they swished the craggy oysters through the water to rid them of the muck. Marty was ecstatic, while dumbstruck Dalton stood back in silence, admiring their feat. "Nuff'n like a fffew shotzz a tee-quilla and, and, ssssome r-r-raaaw arsters ta ssstart za day withhh!" Marty spouted. "Makess a reeeal *man* outta yaaa...know what I means, Jelly Bean?"

Dalton broke through his numbed stupor and gave a nod. "Dddamn ssstraight, ole bbbuddy," he answered weakly. "Lezzz zzzopen em bbbitches up!" Marty magically produced a folding buck knife and slapped it in Dalton's hand. He then pulled out a confiscated switchblade from a jeans pocket and held it out at arm's length. Chuckling, he pressed a button, and the shiny blade snapped into position. "Tttt-touche' mutha fuckers!" he yelled at the night sky. Heads hanging low in shaky concentration, they staggered and bumped into each other while feverishly working the knives to pry open the shells and lay bare the tasty morsels.

Sober or slammed, Marty knew his way around oysters, and he cautioned Dalton about the fine art of oyster shuckin'. "Day's got lips and day's got a butt too," he slurred out to his shift buddy. "Gots ta wwwork da knife up under da lips zen ya should be fine, hhhooky-doky? Tryin' ta shove da knife in their butts, don't gets ya no wheres! A few nasty nicks aside, the drunken duo miraculously avoided filleting their fingers with the mini-scimitars. They were hungry, and the raw, slimy mollusks went down easily enough.

Minutes later, however, they came swirling back with a vengeance. Dalton would vaguely remember being pleased with himself when senior trooper Marty lost his cookies first. Guess I muss-ta ssswalloed da damn worm!' Marty uttered, bowing his head again for another "encore" performance. For the next hour at least, both shift buddies called out for their favorite Saints of Overindulgence, '*RAAALPH* and *EAARRRLL*,'' while tightly gripping the wood pilings to avoid falling off the pier. Never again would they share such an awesome Tequila Sunrise.

The soon to be retired sergeant crushed the soggy cigar butt and leaned his head back against the rough bark tree. That first year, he'd been invited by "Wild Bill" Flyger and the others to hunt on McKinsey Mackall's farm near Wallville. Wild Bill's main concern was where he'd be scrounging up the oysters for the fried oyster sandwiches. Realizing early on that Dalton was a devout fisherman, Wild Bill shared his hoarded secrets about certain big mouth bass haunts down at ole judge Mackall's pond near Bowens. Taking advantage of his commander's sage advice, Dalton landed some nice-sized keepers, even if the ever-elusive Bubba kept spurning every Jacques Herter lure he tossed his way. What a scamp Wild Bill was, and what a great job he'd done setting the tone for troopers who'd come down to cut their teeth in his wondrous bailiwick.

Over the next fifteen years, Dalton spent much loads of time in the woods and waterways of Calvert, particularly on the farm ponds scattered throughout the largely unspoiled county. His interest eventually waned when the incoming hordes made the woods shrink, the ponds to be over-fished and trashed with litter.

The sergeant took another swig of beer, emptied the can, then raised it high above his head. "I salute you Mel, ole buddy, and you too, Sergeant Branham...though I wish I'd known you better, my friend. And bottoms up Bragg, for making it past probation too, you dumb ass!" He hurled the can in front of him and within seconds, it was neatly perforated with the last .40 caliber round in the gun. Nice, real nice, he mused silently before jettisoning the empty clip on the ground.

A full clip was quickly slapped in. Using the Berretta's slide release lever, he flicked it to slam the slide forward—exactly like he'd been taught not to.

There would be worse and better years ahead, *that* was certain. With the birth of his daughter Anne Marie during his earlier MSP years, he and Cindy had become closer, elated with their newborn who radiated so much happiness, so much hope for their family. Just being in the same room with her, hearing her soft, rhythmic breathing, gazing at her complete innocence, was pure jubilation, he remembered. Hell, he'd even curbed his tendency to linger beyond his normal shift hours, just so he could beeline home to bask in his golden child's presence. Many cherished days of easy smiles and laughs....

Dalton shook his head and broke away from the caught-up moment. Yeah buddy! This was the best retirement party ever. With a brilliant noon sun overhead, and a warm breeze caressing the cliff, it was picture perfect. He foraged in his pack for another beer before drifting back to those early, revered MSP years, his "glory days'.

Chapter 5

GLORY DAYS-PART ONE

Dalton's two-year probation ended auspiciously. Recently-promoted First Sergeant Bane congratulated him on becoming a merited state employee, and shortly after, Elzy presented him with a sound half year appraisal. Dalton was gratified by the superior rating, felt assured he'd become a true-blue PF post stalwart. Promptly after signing his appraisal, however, Dalton was offhandedly told he was losing his cruiser to a senior trooper who'd just transferred in. Instantly, his sprouting ego and skyrocketing aspirations plummeted to dismal reality. Once again it was back to jumping cars. *Whoa!* And a hardy Zippity-do-da from the seniority ogre!

Kregg Erickson, Dalton's silver-tongue mentor, had been transferred out, and three new troopers arrived to boost the post's manpower. Kregg was finally getting the plum job he'd salivated over: the Governor's glorified limo driver and newspaper-fetcher in the politically elite Executive Security Unit.

Well, at least the trooper who filched Dalton's cruiser did a passable job feigning how upset he was about it. Small comfort there, but regardless, Tfc Colby Merson was a hard one not to like.

Dalton had seen him before in the county when he'd worked narcotics while undercover. For whatever reasons, Merson had escaped (or was pushed) from the covert world, surfacing back in the MSP patrol realm again. Colby, a mid-twenties transplant from bluegrass Kentucky, was gifted with an effervescent, easygoing personality, always ready to break into a grin. Heavy-set and a few inches shorter then most troopers, he had an innate physical strength that surprised many who underestimated the gregarious officer. Colby had a ruddy complexion on a rounded face and an always-lit cigarette hanging from the corner of his mouth. With his droopy eyelids and glazed-over sky-blue eyes, he had the premature look of an old-salt road trooper. Colby's head was topped with shocks of unkempt, wavy black hair, which topped out the always-disheveled appearance he presented in uniform.

Colby had a large gap between his two front teeth, and he was a fanatic country music fan, which belayed his cannier side, a role he agreeably took advantage of when sparring with the criminal elements who dismissed him as a simpleminded country hick. A red, white and blue, all-American son who had little tolerance for those who preyed on decent folks, Colby was also a robust party-hardy guy who'd fit in easily with the post's sundry collection of troopers. After their first awkward meeting, Dalton begrudgingly admitted to himself that he liked Colby's savoir-faire and his unique perspective on life's roller coaster. For better or for worse, destiny turned them into buddies sooner then anticipated.

"Hey Dalton, any need for this damn thing?" Colby asked, holding up his new protective vest the MSP had recently issued to the rank and file. Dalton was removing the last of his personal gear from his cruiser, the coveted chariot he was losing to his newfound trooper bud. "Naw, no need to bother with 'em down here, Colby," Dalton shouted back. "Hell, I haven't ever worn mine. Just toss it in the trunk." "Right on, chief," Colby yelled back, "got ya loud and clear on that one."

They were working the late shift together, and Colby, eager to check out his assigned south patrol, burned rubber and fishtailed from the parking lot to head south. Nearing 2200 hours, with the end of a lackadaisical late shift close at hand, the Calvert Control Center directed all units to respond to the Twin Cedar Bar in Lusby for a "shots fired" call.

Kermit Weems, a young, low-level PCP dealer, had finally reached the end of his humiliation. Rodney Gantt, one of the county's infamous Gantt brothers, an archrival drug dealer, had butted his way into the next pool game to shoulder Kermit aside for the last time. Weems, very much wasted after hours of smoking PCP, knew he had to act for the sake of what little honor he still had. Shouts led to pushes, and Rodney, fueled by too many vodka tonics, whacked Kermit in the head with a pool stick, leaving him dazed and sprawled on the pool table in front of his brother and his shocked girlfriend, a cardinal sin violation of drunken bravado. Enraged, Kermit dashed from the bar and sped to his nearby pad.

Kermit returned with his "Saturday Night Special," a corroded .25-caliber automatic with an obliterated serial number on the frame. Approaching the front door, he was accosted by a burly, pokerfaced bouncer who barred him from entering the dingy, smoked-filled bar. Sensing trouble, the bouncer told Kermit that he'd already called "Prince Frederick," equating to *The Man,* as known by the bar's shady clientele. Unfortunately, one of Rodney's lame friends witnessed Kermit's tirades, and he promptly alerted Rodney about Kermit's return, and how he was threatening to kick his black ass if he dared come outside. Pool stick gripped tight in both hands, Rodney barged out from the bar to confront the fool who dared to provoke him again.

Kermit was cat-scratch quick, and for him, abnormally bold. When his antagonist drew back the pool stick, he jammed the little gun into Rodney's chest, shut his eyes, and yanked the trigger. The muffled shot stunned them both. For several shocked moments, Rodney's eyes and mouth hung wide-open and he stood paralyzed in numbed silence. As his panicky shooter dashed into the shadows, Rodney grabbed his chest and slumped to the ground.

Colby radioed he was out at the scene. Minutes later, shrieking rubber announced Dalton's arrival. Searching for his fellow trooper, Dalton elbowed through the mingling crowd on the dark parking lot. Colby was kneeling next to a shirtless black male who was prone on his back, and Dalton saw a thin stream of blood spurting out from a small chest wound. Colby slapped a trauma pad on the wound while Dalton shouted at the victim, hoping to keep him from going into shock. "Mutha-fuckin' cheap-ass bitch shot me! The bitch shot me!" the perforated victim shouted in his face.

Dalton gave Colby a grim look when the victim's shoulders started shaking. A hand flew up to grab one of Colby's wrists, and the man cried out for his mother. *Ohh shit!* A trickle of blood oozed from the corner of a trembling mouth. *Not good!* The victim's violent shaking suddenly stopped, and his body went limp. Dalton heard a grotesque, metallic sound escape from the open mouth below the vacant eyes—a "death rattle," his first encounter with a dying man's final gasp.

Both troopers hurriedly performed CPR. Dalton pushed down several times on the victim's chest with his palms, while Colby wiped blood from the victim's mouth and performed the more unsavory part. They kept it up for several minutes before realizing it was hopeless. The young black drug dealer was stone dead. "Un-fuckin' believable!" Colby murmured, staring down at the still body. He wiped his mouth off with the back of his hand then turned to spit. Dalton shook his head and got back on his feet to direct the gaping bystanders away from the crime scene. An easy death over a simple matter, and once again, nobody saw anything.

After they cleared the hospital, Colby confronted his partner on the post parking lot. "Don't need to wear a vest, my ass, you son of a bitch...I owe you one big time!" Colby yelled at him in feigned anger. Dalton grinned as Colby anxiously popped a cigarette into his mouth and saluted him with a raised middle finger.

"Ya know, I worked that rat's nest when I was a narc down here a few months back, and the damn crack-heads there tonight didn't even recognize me in this costume," Colby told him. Dalton shrugged his shoulders and fixed him with a blank stare, noticing that somehow after they'd left the hospital, Colby had slipped on his white protective vest. He grinned and shook his head when he saw the vest had been tugged over his Colby's uniform shirt, leaving the lower tails hanging absurdly below his belt. Colby acknowledged by blowing a lazy smoke ring at him. Smirking, Dalton took Colby aside and casually draped an arm over his shoulder. "Nice job on the mouth-to-mouth, Colby. Can't say that most of the others would have done what you did back there, my friend." Colby shirked it off. "It's like this, Dalton; ya just gotta remember that he was some mother's son, her pride and joy once upon a time. I was just doing it for her, that's all. His life dead-ended long ago." From then on, Dalton knew he'd found a friend who'd remain cool-headed and unruffled no matter what fate tossed their way.

Dalton was also impressed with Gary Rephan and Craig Harmel, the other new PF troopers. Harmel, transferred from the Rockville Barrack, was the post's first black trooper, a twenty-four year-old, towering giant. Calm and soft-spoken, he exuded the confidence and maturity of a trooper who'd been on the job much longer then most thought, an asset in his southern Maryland assignment, Dalton figured.

Gary Rephan, a youthful, two-year MSP veteran, lived on the outskirts of Randles Cliff near the twin beaches, and he was super ecstatic about parting ways with the Forestville Barrack. Fresh from the academy, Rephan worked the lower Prince Georges County area, and he salivated over his dream to leave the chaotic beltway behind. A good-looking, charismatic type, Gary was tall and wiry, with penetrating hazel eyes and a full crop of dirty blond hair.

Dalton was struck with Gary's self-assurance, which occasionally lent credence to those who thought him to be rather egotistical. That he'd also graduated at the top of his academy class, didn't surprise anyone. Obviously bright and daringly outspoken, Gary Rephan was perceived as a possible threat by some of the seasoned country-boy troopers who vainly tried to keep the heady, college educated trooper in his place. Despite his limited time on the force, Gary was a forthright, intuitive sort—the savior-faire type who could walk into any barrack and be immediately judged as a natural leader. He was also highly competitive, a true fitness nut and sports fanatic who thrived on rivalry at work and on the softball fields, and he reveled in the company of his fellow troopers. They'd yet to brew a beer that Gary wouldn't hesitate pouring into his prized Redskin mug.

Like Dalton, the three new troopers were young, sagacious and motivated, all welcome additions to the post's complement of stalwart officers. And, praise the Lord, they'd also arrived just in time for the annual MSP Superintendent's Inspection and the PF post stag party which immediately followed.

A SUPERINTENDENT'S INSPECTION

The Maryland State Police was born as a quasi-military organization patterned along the lines of the US Army. Adhering to such traditional standards, military-type inspections were part of the overall plan, and exemplary appearance was an absolute in the fabled prestige of the proud force. The Superintendent's annual inspection included a review of the installation, and an in-depth evaluation of troopers and their assigned equipment. Installation commanders regarded such inspections highly, and as a matter of personal pride.

Whipped up to shipshape status by the unflappable Lt. "Wild Bill" Flyger and his peachy-keen supervisors, everything MSP and each MSP everybody was standing tall, awaiting the arrival of Colonel Schmidt and his Pikesville entourage. The Pikesville head honchos were first escorted through the immaculate post by Captain Riggs the troop commander, who was followed by Wild Bill and F/Sgt Bane. Under the direction of Elzy, his corporal, and with guidance from Marty Metzger, Dalton had turned his cruiser into a shimmering work of art, after spending many off-duty hours prepping it.

As mandated by the MSP Patrol bible, each trooper ensured that his cruiser had all required equipment—and nothing else—and of course the layout of the equipment display was strictly uniform. Dalton was amused by some of the official gear they'd been issued, particularly the first-aid "kit." The assorted bandages, dressings and tape were crammed into a small, metal olive drab Army-surplus .50-caliber machine-gun ammo can, which was left clearly marked as such.

For the inspection, the troopers meticulously lined up their resplendent vehicles in two rows on the parking lot. With trunks open for display, several fidgety troopers scooted around making last minute adjustments, while the more seasoned troopers snickered at their feverish antics. Notified that the Superintendent was en route, the troopers quickly formed two long ranks and stood at-ease. As the seconds ticked down, supervisors checked out their edgy group members, assuring that badges and ornaments were properly centered, and that their thoroughly-cleaned and lightly oiled revolvers were *unloaded* for the inspection.

Gazing down the ranks, Dalton felt proud of his fellow troopers standing ramrod-tall and looking razor-sharp. He didn't notice Elzy slipping from the second rank to make hasty checks on some cruisers parked behind them. Colonel Schmidt and his Pikesville Princes graciously arrived. Standing in front of the formation, F/Sgt. Bane anxiously saluted the Colonel and nervously stuttered out the order for the front rank to come to attention. Dalton could see Bane's face turn red after he screwed up the order for the rear rank to remain at parade rest. Sweet Hallelujah! The Superintendent's annual inspection was underway.

Hands clenched behind his back, and bird-dogged by two prissy looking Pikesville Princes, Colonel Schmidt strode behind the troop commander before the impressive troops. Now and then, the Colonel stopped to make a comment or ask a trooper a question, got a clipped reply, and then proceeded on. Standing at parade rest in the second rank, Dalton felt a nervous tinge as the front rank inspection ended. He bit down hard on his lower lip to keep from bursting out in laughter when the somber-faced Colby, standing next to him, managed to coax out a muffled fart. "Musta stepped on a damn frog," Colby muttered. The second rank was called to attention, and Dalton suddenly felt as if he were standing on a sliding board. Damn! Rather endure a dozen ugly-ass domestics than stand for this annual MSP enema any day, he thought, as Captain Riggs turned to face him.

After the troops were inspected, they were ordered to stand at parade rest behind their cruisers. Each cruiser was thoroughly scrutinized by the commanders while Colonel Schmidt's main interest seemed to focus on the trunk displays. As he eagle-eyed each display, the MSP leader made several muted comments to aides, who furiously scribbled them on notepads.

From the corner of an eye, Dalton watched Colonel Schmidt confer quietly with Captain Riggs, as they stood next to Tpr. Larry Wilson's cruiser. He saw the Colonel reach into the trunk, then heard a loud commotion after he removed an item and held it high in the air. Immediately a large pinup unfolded from the *Penthouse* magazine to display a young, big-breasted sweet thang. Dalton watched as the high-ranking, head-shaking officers formed a semicircle around the flabbergasted, red-faced young trooper. Ignoring the trooper's innocent exclamations, the non-regulation item was appropriately seized. Pens jotted frantically, as the visibly peeved Colonel tromped over to the next vehicle. Dalton was aghast, could only imagine the amount of hot water Wilson had fallen into, the dumb ass!

A lifetime later, the Colonel had worked himself up the line and was standing with folded arms at Dalton's cruiser. Dalton saw nothing but subdued anger in the stone-cold face. The Colonel gazed at his MSP tag and rummaged through the trunk. The loud metallic click told Dalton that his first-aid kit had been opened. He flinched when he heard the lid slam shut with a loud curse. "Captain Riggs! *Son of a bitch!* I need an immediate explanation for this!" boomed the agitated MSP head. "What in God's name are these rubbers doing in this trooper's first-aid kit?"

Dalton felt the hot flush over his face, felt the sweat forming on his brows, as he watched the Colonel drop several packs of condoms into Captain Riggs' hand. Captain Riggs' eyes burned deep holes into Dalton's crumbling thought process, and Dalton merely shook his head, knowing he was dead meat on a stick. Seconds dragged ungodly slow, as the bigwigs clustered around him—the Captain in utter disbelief, and Wild Bill muttering under his breath.

Just before he pitched himself headfirst off the sliding board, Dalton saw the Colonel give Captain Riggs a wink. The troop commander's face crinkled and he broke into hysterics which quickly spread to the inspection team and Dalton's fellow troopers. "Nice work, Elzy," Captain Riggs shouted to Corporal Shifflett with a shit-eating grin. "Ya caught both those boys with their pants down!" Scarlet-faced, Dalton sighed relief, as Colonel Schmidt smiled broadly and patted him on the shoulder.

On that note, the Colonel wrapped up the inspection, having nothing but the usual praise and accolades for the PF post and its intrepid members. With all seemingly happy and dancing to the same beat, the troopers were summarily dismissed. The much-revered party would begin as soon as they shed their trooper costumes and boogied on down the road to Camp Canoy.

THE PARTY AT CAMP CANOY

Camp Canoy was a wooded recreation site at Lusby, several miles from Route 2 and the nearest residents. *Hooray!*

Under an early afternoon sun, they meandered in, parking their souped-up cars, "bikes," and pickups on the grass next to the cabins and picnic tables where the foodstuffs were arrayed. A keg of

Budweiser chilled in an ice-filled tub, a backup keg awaiting its turn alongside. The victuals were the standard fare of barbequed venison (confiscated road kill), barbequed pit beef, hot dogs, baked beans, potato salads and munchies. Several troops, the self-professed card players, brought bottles of Wild Turkey and Jack Daniels. Dalton's shift buddy, the guitar-playing Marty Metzger, brought a radio and two humongous speakers, along with his six-string. Soon, ole Willie Nelson's craggy voice crooning *You were always on my mind* echoed amongst the trees.

At fifteen dollars a head, the troops were in hawg heaven! Dalton and his new cohort Gary Rephan arrived early for the crucial tapping and testing of the keg. With eyes closed, both of them could tap a keg quicker than they could unhinge a bra strap, and soon enough, their foamy shit-eating grins gave silent testimony to the keg's excellent quality.

In essence, the party became a back slapping brotherly event, a time to cement camaraderie, and a chance to corral and BS each other with their ever ballooning war stories. It was time to expound on their outlandish encounters with wild babes who, without mercy, pursued them throughout the county. All of the strumpets, of course, desired nothing from them but raw, adulterated sex in untried, unimaginable positions, which had to be repeated, over and over, until the hapless troopers finally got it right. It was also a chance for the ballplayers to air their inflated fantasies of prowess on the fields, time to drink mash, talk trash, and get home fast, to avoid getting thrashed.

The turnout was better then ever. Several troopers from the "sister" barracks attended, and Almos Jett, Calvert's laidback sheriff, brought some deputies. A few local attorneys, including Warren Blackstone, the State's Attorney himself, were also present. Sergeant "call-me-by-my-first-name Bobby, but-only-when-I'm-off-duty" Long, brought his usual retinue of police-buff pals, who worked wonders preparing the food.

In the main log cabin, the old-timers, led by Wild Bill Flyger, sauntered over to a table and broke out the cards. In the time it took for Wild Bill to fill his pipe and scrounge for a match, the table overflowed with serious poker players. Tipsy onlookers drifted in and ringed

themselves around the card sharks. Grinning and holding a half empty
Jack Daniels bottle, Donny Roberts plopped down on the picnic bench.
Signaling he was in the game, Donny passed the Jack Daniels around.
Elzy easily won the first pot, prompting State's Attorney Blackstone to
call facetiously for a forthright examination of the cards.

"Lady Luck, don't turn your pretty lil butt on me now!" Elzy
whooped, gleefully corralling the winnings. "You can only keep that
horseshoe up your ass for so long, Elzy," Wild Bill guffawed,
completely oblivious to Attorney Blackstone's left hand shooting out to
dump chopped-up pieces of rubber band into the bowl of his
smoldering pipe.

Outside around the beer keg, troopers vied to impress each other
with their anonymous "inside" sources, getting the skinny on the latest
Pikesville rumors, while Marty and other country-music junkies were
slurring through Lynyrd Skynyrd's *Sweet Home Alabama*. Dalton
watched with amusement as they strained like constipated cows to
harmonize. Fueled by libations and machismo, the hours drifted by
slowly.

Every PF trooper knew that Sherwood T. Smith, the new boot
trooper mired down in field training, was cranially-shortchanged, or as
some elderly Broomes Islanders would say, "Dumber than a shucked
female arster!" It'd been quite a while since the post had embraced
such a mental dud, one of many who followed their father's footsteps
and coat tails to join the MSP. Like Sherwood's father, many of them
pulled their accrued "owe-me cards" to assure their kids an inside track
to become a trooper like them. Fortunately, most proud sons fit
smoothly into the mold. Some fell horribly short.

It would take divine diligence, endless frustration and reams of
detailed reports to Pikesville to justify Sherwood T. Smith's
termination during his break-in period. With his stream of idiotic
mishaps, however, Sherwood T. Smith was well on his way out. To his
genetic credit, Sherwood was strong and built like an ox.

As Colby told several at the party, "The ignoramus couldn't even
go out and get himself a decent tattoo! No, not Sherwood! Most guys
got their girlfriend's name, an old military patch, a tiger, or something

cool branded somewhere on them, but nope, not Sherwood! The big ape went out and got his chest branded with a huge *Sturn and Ruger Gun Company* tattoo! Even had the company's red eagle! The goof-ball said the dealer promised him a nice discount on his next off-duty gun, if he'd get himself tattooed with the company's name. Good publicity, he reckoned. Ya know, that boy just ain't right."

Amongst his other defects, Sherwood T. Smith also had an overriding, abnormal attachment to his "wheels." Hours before the inspection, he'd even found time to wash and wax his cherry-red 1975 Ford Mustang for the third time in a week, beaming like a peacock when the troops commented favorably on the object of his toils. Therefore, he was incredulous, no, *dumbstruck,* when tipsy Larry Wilson, a fellow trooper, dumped a cup of beer on the hood. Basking in the admiring ooohs and ahhhs of those salivating to see Sherwood's red-faced reaction, Larry unwisely opted for an encore. A workhorse as a road trooper when sober, Larry was known for bizarre stunts when soused. During last year's summer party, his fellows nearly drowned him in a pool after he dumped a bottle of ketchup over the heads of two startled trooper's wives. Predictably, and in short order, the hops and malt had once again turned him into a berserker.

Today, for a change-up, Wilson had chugged down shots of Wild Turkey on top of the beers. With a hearty *Yee-Haw,* Larry leaped onto the hood of Sherwood's Mustang and started dancing! Sherwood went Neanderthal! Nostrils flared and death in his eyes, he roared at Larry to get off his car! Larry smiled broadly and continued, flapping his arms, one leg kicking out after the other, each step putting a sizable crease on the metal hood of his improvised stage. "You're dead meat, asshole!" screamed the enraged Neanderthal.

Totally oblivious, Larry closed his eyes, cocked his head back, and danced on. "Aagghhh!" Like a crazed Brahma bull exploding from a rodeo pen, Sherwood charged over to his wounded pride and joy, grabbed Larry by the belt and his scrawny neck, and raised him over his head. Roaring loudly, he effortlessly tossed the flailing nitwit up and over the Mustang. *"THUNK!"* Witnesses later agreed that when Larry crash-landed on the ground, he executed one of the best dead-cat bounces they'd ever seen.

Dalton and several others scurried over to settle things down, as the moaning Sherwood collapsed over the hood of his beloved Mustang. Lying in a heap yards beyond, Larry groaned, wondering how the hell his tap dance had ended so painfully. No more encores for those ungrateful sots, he groggily told himself. Dalton rushed over to check him out, but Larry brushed them all off, dragged himself into the bushes, and passed out.

Viewed from the peanut gallery, Sherwood had turned into The Man of the Moment. Paying homage to his hurling feat, Colby brought him a beer. Heart-struck and teary-eyed, Sherwood backhanded the beer from Colby's outstretched hand, splashing its foamy contents into Colby's shocked face. Uttering a few Neanderthal grunts, Sherwood slowly evil-eyed them all before diving into his Mustang chariot. In a raging exit with rpms revving wildly, he spun tires and showered clods of dirt and grass on his audience, as the Mustang fish-tailed toward the dirt road to civilization. "Can't beat that one with a stick," Colby snickered to no one in particular.

Things gradually settled to a low roar until.........

"*I'll kill you, you dumb bastard! You're mine!*" Dalton, Colby and Gary, turned their heads when they heard the shrill bellow. Sonny Tarbuckle, a barrel-chested, bald-headed corporal from the Leonardtown post, was seething and in full pursuit of Trooper Pat James.

An MSP aviation division helicopter pilot, James was a rambunctious daredevil even when sober. Either drunk or sober, the tall, lanky Air Force veteran had never mastered the game of darts. He'd also grown weary from listening to Tarbuckle's inflated MSP war stories. And besides, the cantankerous James was already feeling that the party was becoming more humdrum then necessary, bolstering his urge to play tag with the sharp pointed mini-spears in his hand.

Later he'd claim that he was only aiming at Tarbuckle's beer mug. With a hyena grin, James launched the dart, sailing it in a high arc over the heads of Wild Bill Flyger and his merry band of blitzed card players. "*Thwap!*" The dart embedded itself deep into

Tarbuckle's leather loafer, and a horrific shriek punctuated the air. Grimacing and hopping on one leg, Tarbuckle yanked the dart out of his foot. Narrow, angry eyes wildly searched the room for the fool who'd missed the phantom dartboard. Staring wide-eyed and slack-jawed, James was a dead giveaway.

"Oh *Shittt!*" he muttered, when Tarbuckle growled and yanked out his snob-nose .38. The room fell deathly silent after Tarbuckle cocked the gun, an action which inherently has a sobering effect on most cops.

Curious about the animal screams, several troopers blocked the corporal's way after his second orbit around the cabin, pinioning the enraged supervisor until he surrendered his hand cannon. "James! Your number's up! Hear me, scumbag?" Tarbuckle roared at the woods where James had wisely fled.

Two shots of Old Crow later, the flustered corporal still wanted to blast away at the tires of James' new Ford pickup, thought to be parked in the field below. James, however, had already made a speedy exit for greener pastures, meaning his ditzy girlfriend-on-the-side. Several hours later, for reasons unknown, James' truck suddenly went berserk to attack a guardrail in the median of Route 2 in Huntingtown. *Damn!* He was only two miles from home, just minutes away from his embittered wife who was fighting the nods battle, hoping to stay awake long enough to greet her drunken hubby with one of his treasured softball bats.

Several beers later, Dalton stumbled into Colby staggering out of the woods from another nature call. Colby was doing his best to stuff down another stacked plate of barbequed venison and a mound of cold, leathery baked beans. "So what do you think?" Dalton asked him, nodding in the direction of Larry's earlier crash-landing site. "Think this shit tastes just like chicken," Colby chuckled back while fingering a spicy deer rib. "You think everything tastes like chicken, you dick-head," Dalton retorted. "Naw, there's somethin' I know that's some damn fine eatin', and it sure as shit don't taste like chicken either, but you probably never been there yet, I suppose, right, dip-shit?" Colby hooted back, jamming an elbow in Dalton's side before resuming his feast.

121

Colby focused his beady eyes in an effort to aim the dripping morsel toward his gaping mouth. The slimy rib slipped between his fingers, and when he spastically grabbed at it in mid air, the plate of food flipped over and landed in the dirt with a *splat!* Colby shook his head and let out a worthy belch. "Some of the best damn Bambi meat I never got to pass between my lips," he added mournfully. In the receding daylight they traipsed through the woods, searching for Larry Wilson, who, an hour before, had dared to provoke the wrath of Sherwood. They found him lying on his side, moaning in pain.

Half an hour later, Dalton and Colby guided their agonized cohort into the emergency room of CMH (a.k.a. The Calvert Memorial First Aid Station). While waiting for their buddy to be patched up, both hapless troopers meandered over to the nearby nurse station. Dalton's face flushed, and he suddenly felt warm all over. Jamie Cox, his favorite, chatty-friendly, candy-striper cutie, waved and blew an air-kiss at him after he'd "shot" her with an extended index finger. In the past year, during his many trips to the ER to interview victims, Dalton had struck up a playfully innocent acquaintance with Jamie which had evolved into a chummy familiarity of sorts over the last few months.

Dalton grinned at her, and Jamie countered with an impish smile. Dalton and Colby teased with Jamie and her candy striper pal for a while, and things were going smoothly—until Colby snatched the lily-white nurse cap off Jamie's head and slapped it on his noggin. Grinning, he darted behind the counter, snatched a white lab coat off a hook and slipped it on. Spying an unattended stethoscope, he picked it up and draped it around his neck so he could play doctor—again. "OK boysss and girlssss, uhhh...what am I?" Colby slurred as he plugged the stethoscope earpieces into both ears. "An albino *Tyrannosaurus rex* with a hearing problem," Dalton quipped back. "A horny drunk cop," Jamie's nurse-buddy piped up. "Yeah baby!" Jamie shouted gleefully. Colby placed the scope against his chest and sneered at them. "Noooo, you daaamn d-d-dingbats! I'm a Quack, Quack, Quack! Get it?" he quacked back at them.

Jamie's dog-ugly nurse supervisor, who'd untimely drifted by, failed to see the humor in Colby's antics. Ears bent back in anger and eyes burning, she threw a major hissy-fit to abruptly end his performance, and both troopers were unceremoniously ushered out to the waiting room.

An hour later, still reeking of beer-breath, a smiling Larry was wheeled out. Dalton and Colby exchanged wary glances when they noticed that Larry's right arm was in a sling. Ole Doc Bowen, Calvert County's crusty head physician and part-time medical examiner, rubbed the top of his bald head and narrowed his beady eyes. In his country drawl, the sage doctor placidly declared that their trooper cohort had been treated for numerous abrasions—along with a broken collarbone and a separated shoulder.

"You boys playin' a little rough with each other this afternoon, ain't ya?" he asked with a smirk. Larry hopped from the wheelchair and patted the doctor on the shoulder with his free hand. 'Aw, it ain't nuthin', Doc, just a broken wing, 'tis all." He grinned and turned to his cohorts. "OK, you meatheads! Time to get back to the party so's we can finish off them kegs!" Dalton shrugged, and Colby innocently turned away when Doc Bowen canted his head down and gazed at them over the top of his glasses. With a weary sigh, the doctor threw up his hands and shuffled back into the emergency room.

In a record seventeen minutes, they were back at Camp Canoy. Most of the sensible, more seasoned troops had already left for safer places. Even the stalwart poker players had folded their cards and called it a night. In the dark, with the ground beneath them turning into Jell-O, and slurred words mutating into scrambled thoughts, Dalton, Colby, and Gary Rephan started thinking along the same lines. All three were relieved when told that Sergeant "call-me-by-my-first-name-Bobby, but-only-when-I'm-off-duty" Long, was taking the broken-winged Larry home.

Unencumbered by a walking-wounded, it was Gary who piped up first. Dalton and Colby promptly agreed that if Gary was intent on having a last-call quaff at the Calverton Room on the way home, he'd certainly need two bodyguards to assure his safe departure afterward. Dalton sprinted to his Ford Pinto as Gary and Colby scrambled into Gary's Volkswagen for the race to Prince Frederick.

S. Eric Briggs

It was a weekday evening, and the Calverton Room was slow, meaning too few barflies for too many bare stools. When the trio entered the smoke-filled lounge, they quickly spotted Donny Roberts and Jack Nimitz, the post's cracker-jack investigator, perched at the bar. Cigarette dangling from his fingers and a coy smile tattooed on his face, Donny was absorbed in animated conversation with a foxy, long-legged babe whose shiny, jet-black hair cascaded beautifully below her bare shoulders. She sat comfortably close to him, and she wore a delectably tight, rainbow flowered sundress which showed off her perfectly-tanned legs and arms. Donny's Eastern Shore accent was doing the trick again, and the babe's brown bedroom-eyes sparkled as she leaned over and edged her pretty face closer to his.

That's who she is, Dalton told himself when he finally recognized her. Damn! If it wasn't Dawn, the voluptuous clerk from District Court! Yes, *Dawn*, the one so many drooled over, the siren they whispered lewd guy-thing thoughts about during court session lulls. Yes indeedy, it was she, the flat-chested wannabe-babe who recently went away for a weekend to visit a sick aunt and came back with a set of bolt-ons that would make a grown man's knees shake. And Dalton, now half snockered, thought she looked simply ravishing, a Calvert County angel well worth salivating over for sure.

Glad to share his lucky-streak poker winnings with fellow troopers, Donny bought them a round of drafts. Saluting their friendship, they clinked bottles and gulped the brewskies down with gusto. "Just don't get no better then this, guys," Colby spouted out, bracing him-self against the bar in time to avoid a nasty spill. Grinning broadly, Gary put both arms around his buddy's shoulders and let out a nasty belch. "All for one, and one for all," he gushed. "Yeah, that's us all right, we're the three original mutha-fuckin amigos!" Dalton shouted after another gulp.

Edging closer to the bar, Dalton nudged Gary, and they watched with curiosity as Donny unleashed his highly-perfected midnight-hour moves on the wholly entranced Dawn. She was a picture of contentment, sipping on a double rum and coke, the third liquid panty remover Donny had plied her with. Dawn smiled and shook with glee as he lightly grazed the back of her forearm with sure fingers which spawned a rash of goose bumps. She returned the gesture, pressing a bare, supple leg against his knee, smiling mischievously when she spotted what that feat spawned.

"Oh holy *hell!*" Dawn muttered nervously, her eyes suddenly dropping to the floor. What appeared to be at *least* a three hundred and fifty pound, lean-machine, Washington Redskins linebacker swaggered over to stand directly behind her. Through the smoky haze, all eyes riveted on the Godzilla towering overhead. He was wearing a frayed cowboy hat, black biker boots, and dirty jeans held in place by a thick belt and a huge steer-head buckle. The short sleeves of his grease-stained denim shirt were rolled up high, displaying a monstrous pair of biceps. The veins in his beefy neck bulged, and his square jaw was clamped tight, as he stared them down with a jittery pair of pig-eyes. The not-so-golly giant actually seemed slightly more piqued than bleary-eyed Colby, who, in his typical timely manner, had just bumped a passing waitress to knock the drinks off her tray.

With a low growl, the Redskin-Godzilla-behemoth snatched his wife by the elbow and effortlessly plucked her off the bar stool. His nostrils flared like an enraged bull's as he gave Donny's reflection in the bar mirror a death-glare. Donny hunkered down on the stool and stared straight ahead at his own blank likeness. With a trembling hand and a quivering Adam's apple, he eased the beer bottle to his mouth for another sip. The Redskin-Godzilla behemoth snorted with contempt. "Come along home with me, lil woman, before you get these here trooper boys in trouble," he bellowed. "Ain't no use in me workin' up a sweat in here if I don't have to!" Gary and Dalton silently nodded in agreement, while Jack Nimitz, in his customary aloofness, casually sized the giant up. Colby weaved back and forth on his feet, beaming like a drunken aborigine. With his frenzy-eyed wife in tow, Buster Hardesty tromped from the Calverton Room, slamming the door hard on his way out.

"Whew! Never knew her hubby was *that* frickin' big!" Donny sputtered with relief. "That son of a bitch could a kicked all our asses big-time." "Yezzz indeedy," Colby added with a loud belch. "Wonder who stuck a ffffrozen hotdog up hisss ass?" Donny delicately unfolded the napkin she'd slipped under his beer bottle earlier and waved it under his nose for a few blissful moments, savoring of her perfume. Already aware of the message scribbled on it, he smiled and tucked it into his shirt pocket. Donny ordered another nerve soothing double-shot of rum and coke before hitting the road. Dalton and his buddies thought about joining him for the nightcap, but the Budweiser beer clock over the mirror silently declared it was time for the three pickled amigos to vamoose.

The fresh air felt good as Dalton led the way out to the parking lot. He smiled and gave an exaggerated salute to a pair of CMH nurses he recognized as they headed toward the Calverton Room. Following his buddies, Colby caterwauled through a verse of Willie Nelson's famous ballad about not wanting to be alone. Dalton smiled. What a trip Colby was turning out to be. After fumbling in his pocket for his key chain, Dalton surprised himself by jamming the right key into the door lock on his first try.

Blam! Instinctively, Dalton dropped and hugged the cold asphalt with a passion. Both nurses screamed and flung themselves down on the parking lot. In an instant, he knew without a doubt that her husband—*Dawn's* husband—had returned and waited for them to come out so he could ambush them. Dalton glanced at Gary, who was pancaking himself on the asphalt. Gary's face was lily-white, and his bloodshot eyes bulged with panic. *Not* a good thing—especially since both of them were gun-less.

Blam! Blam! More shots, one round zinging through the air after glancing off a light pole. Dalton winced and dragged himself behind one of the Pinto's wheels for better cover. When he heard Colby's voice warbling on with that insidious, "I don't want to be alone tune," he shot Gary a queer look. Dalton cautiously peeked around the tire in the direction of the Calverton Room. Sporting a Cheshire-cat grin for all who dared to see, the wild-eyed Colby was swaying side-to-side on the sidewalk. In his right hand was a smoking pistol held high over his head.

'Yee-Hawwww!" *Blam!* And another echoing shot. "Gimmie that, you dumb son a bitch!" Jack Nimitz yelled at Colby when he sprang from the shadows to wrestle the .357 Ruger magnum from him.

Several bar patrons at the front door saw what was happening and wisely ducked back inside. The nurses froze where they were, their cheeks kissing the pavement. Prematurely relieved of his gun and entertainment, Colby sneered at Nimitz. Growling out a curse, he staggered toward the detective, hoping to recapture his Ruger for another shot at the light pole that wouldn't stay still. One way or the other, he'd get his six-shooter back from the obstinate, ID dick-head for sure!

As one, Dalton and Gary sprinted over and wrestled their swearing cohort to the ground before he accosted the piqued detective who wasn't backing off. Kicking and screaming, Colby was dragged over to Gary's VW and was crammed into the back seat. "Y'all are nothing but *crazy,*" one of the nurses shrieked, as Dalton darted back to his Pinto. He chuckled when he saw Colby's head pop up from the back window of Gary's departing Volkswagen. "Douse the lights...my party's over!" Colby sang out in a maniacal voice. "Damn if that boy ain't wrapped too tight," Dalton muttered as he jammed the Pinto into gear.

Like a bad dream that never happened, and with gun smoke still hanging in the air, they left the scene at a high rate. The Prince Frederick Post was only a short block away, and Dalton knew that if any lingering troopers had heard Colby blasting away, the response would be swift. Thoroughly and appropriately pissed off, Nimitz tucked Colby's warm Ruger under his belt and tromped back to the post. *Mum* would usually be *the* word for whatever transpired after the trooper parties, but this one would be rough for a guy like Nimitz to swallow.

It took a while, but after all, Captain Riggs, the troop commander, *did* live in the county, and his wife Melinda, *was* a well-known member of the local chamber of commerce. A small county like Calvert did have its disadvantages, with everyone knowing just about everything about everybody else's business. In the after-party twilight three troopers had managed to wreck their pickups on their way home. Pat James, the first, sat on the guardrail next to his crippled truck, waiting hopefully for someone to drive by. As luck wouldn't have it, he'd picked a grandstand seat for the next trooper's fiasco. Swatting mosquitoes for close to an hour, he perked up when he heard the sound of an approaching vehicle. Soon there were headlights, but moments later the headlights careened wildly off the road and veered for the trees. *CRASH!* Cursing up a storm, a figure stumbled from the woods rubbing his head. A minute later, there were two commiserating troopers sitting side-by-side, doing their best to keep the guardrails warm.

The all-discerning Captain Riggs later feigned ignorance, and there was never any official inquiry concerning the crackups, nor did any details filter down about the crazy trooper who was target practicing in the Prince Frederick Shopping Center that night. Nary was a peep heard about the two troopers' wives who decided early the next morning that their marriages were doomed beyond repair, nor would it ever be known that Dalton was almost creamed by a tractor-trailer after he'd stopped his Pinto on the Bay Bridge while on his way home to urgently relieve his bladder. No, the locals simply rationalized that the boys who wore the cowboy hats were just blowing off the dust, 'twas all. Captain Riggs, ever so reluctantly, *did* pass the word around that, henceforth, the party-hearty troops had to ramp down the volume of their revelry to a low roar.

Sadly and perhaps most appropriately, there would never be another MSP party at Camp Canoy. In the memory of those who attended, the "Party in the Woods" remained unsurpassed as the most-fabled Prince Frederick Post party ever, bar none.

#

The next eight hours of a trooper's shift, with its potpourri of obscurities, was predictably unpredictable. Homeward bound, there were always the expected traffic stops and disabled motorists, but occasionally things dicey in a heartbeat. Like most troopers, Dalton accepted those hairy times in exchange for the gratis state transportation, and for that sporadic adrenalin rush which most troopers craved and lived for.

It'd been a long and hectic Thursday late shift, a dog day when you knew you'd have been a whole lot better off calling in sick, lame or lazy. A good day to fish. Those days normally started when the cruiser left the driveway, and there wasn't a damned thing you could do but grit it out.

It was an hour drive to home base, and Dalton was already salivating about the cold brews in the fridge screaming his name. And maybe, just maybe, Cindy was waiting up for him too, perhaps feeling randy again—and, maybe the beers could wait a while, maybe. Intense musings of unbridled sex saturated his pondering head, causing a stir in his loins. *Agghh!* He reached over and punched another button on the AM/FM radio, searching for a moldy-oldie he could drift away with.

Suddenly, the MSP radio crackled alive. "Pikesville to all units on Channel One...we have a 10-3 (do not transmit) due to a 10-80 (chase) on the Baltimore Beltway!" Dalton quickly jacked up the police radio volume. It was always captivating to monitor the other barracks frequencies as they coordinated emergency responses. Visions of the chase surfaced in his mind, when the Glen Burnie barrack duty officer came on the air. *Good frickin' luck!*

From the radio chatter, the chase started when a trooper tried to pull a car over for a simple equipment violation. At his southern Anne Arundel County location forty miles away, however, Dalton couldn't hear any of the MSP vehicles involved in the pursuit, due to the limited radio range. He listened closely as the chase unfolded. "Glen Burnie to all units! Be advised that the 10-80 involving the stolen white van is now southbound on Ritchie Highway approaching Severna Park! We have several MSP and AA County units in pursuit at this time!" the radio crackled. "Be advised...the MSP helicopter is not available!" Having been in several high-speed chases already, Dalton could well imagine what was racing through the minds of his fellow troopers. He wasn't involved in this baby, but already he was feeling the surging twangs of adrenaline, the familiar dampness of his hands. "Get the bastard, guys, but watch your asses," he muttered out loud. He was passing through the sleepy junction of Lothian now, finally getting within radio range of the pursuing troopers.

The Annapolis barrack duty officer came up on the air to direct several "J" units to start toward the Severn River Bridge, hoping they'd arrive in time to set up a roadblock. Still plowing recklessly ahead at high-speed, the van miraculously navigated the sharply curved ramp leading to westbound Rt. 50. No time to set up a roadblock there. Dalton heard the car-to-car chatter clearly now, the radio buzzing alive as the troopers attempted to set up a rolling roadblock on the van, a dangerous move, extremely difficult at high speeds. "Ok J-23, I'm moving in now!" a shrill voice called out. "Go! Go! Go! Watch yourself...he's coming your way, P-37! Box 'em in! Step on it, J-23!" shouted another trooper.

Numbing silence, then: "J-12 Annapolis...*J-12 Annapolis!*" a trooper screamed over the radio. His piercing voice shot shivers down Dalton's spine! "Subject's rammed an MSP unit! I repeat, subject has rammed an MSP unit! We're still proceeding west on route fifty...approaching Ridgely Road, Annapolis!"

Zipping through Harwood, Dalton gritted his teeth and mashed the gas pedal. "Come on, guys...get the bastard!" he yelled at the windshield, praying that his fellow troopers hadn't been injured. Feeling helpless, Dalton felt his gut churning. They were his brothers, and he wasn't there for them.

"AV-21 (MSP aviation unit) Annapolis...we've got shots fired from the van! I repeat... *shots fired!* Ok, the van is turning onto route two now! Continuing south at a high rate, Annapolis!" the radio blared. Frenzied messages flooded the air, some walking over others. "We're passing West Street now, Annapolis!" "He's all over the road...he's running people off the road! Passing Parole Plaza!" "Back off, J-3...*back off*! He just sideswiped the Chevy in front of me! Got another 10-50, Annapolis. Looks like a PI!" another trooper barked. "I'll get it, J-12! You stay with him, OK?" "J-12 Annapolis...request permission to take him out!"

Streaking through Edgewater, Dalton's mind raced wildly when he realized the lethal chase was coming his way. *Holy Shit*! He flipped on the emergency lights and siren. "It's show time," he shouted. "Annapolis to any unit in the southern end!" rang out the calm, familiar voice of PCO Annie Black. Dalton grabbed the mic. "U-17...Annapolis, I'm northbound on route two approaching the South River bridge at this time!" he answered sharply. "U-17 Annapolis, I'm gonna try to set up this unit at the north end of the bridge to block it, 10-4?" Seconds passed slowly. "Annapolis direct! U-17...Go for it!"

came the curt reply. "Move! *Move people!*" Dalton yelled at the cars ahead which were moving in super-slow speed, taking their time pulling over to let him pass. He jerked the steering wheel to the left, crossed over the double-lane for a quick pass, then zigged back just in time to avoid creaming an oncoming pickup. Close! Dalton jammed the pedal to the floorboard, and the cruiser barreled across the old concrete drawbridge, startling the living hell out of two fishermen on the bridge's sidewalk just inches from the road. Flying by them, Dalton glanced over to see eyes as big as saucers, mouths frozen open in fear, as they crouched down by their fishing rods against the railing. With tires shrieking amidst a cloud of burning rubber, the cruiser skidded to a shuddering stop at the end of the bridge.

"Annapolis...we're passing Gingerville now!" a pursuit vehicle radioed. Dalton quickly positioned the cruiser sideways across the bridge to block both lanes, fully aware that his unit would be rammed, probably totaled, too. "Screw it," he muttered. The sacrifice of the State of Maryland's two thousand pounds of metal, rubber and plastic wasn't worth a second thought. Leaving the emergency lights on, he flipped on the PA speaker switch, snatched up his flashlight and scrambled from his cruiser.

Running hard, Dalton met several southbound vehicles as they slowly approached the bridge. Half-winded, he filled his lungs and shouted at the motorists while frantically directing them to the shoulder with the flashlight beam. "AV-21 Annapolis...we're approaching the South River bridge! Still doing over ninety!" blared U-17's outside speaker. Annoyed, Dalton glanced hard at his cruiser after hearing the Annapolis duty officer's last message. "Annapolis to U-17...make sure you get out of that vehicle, young man!"

Standing in the roadside shadows, he heard the shrieking sirens first. They were oscillating wildly, piercing the still air and reverberating off nearby buildings as they came closer. Soon he spotted the streaming kaleidoscope of flashing and swirling reds and blues which heightened the intensity. Scores of police cruisers trailed in this one, a Christmas Parade gone spastic! His eyes focused on the white van leading the way. Its headlights were off, but the vehicle was still zooming ahead at a high rate. Goodbye U-17!

The van hurtled on, but at the last second it swerved to the left, tires squealing harshly as it attempted to avoid the police car. *Caarrump!* The van slammed into the concrete end of the bridge and careened into a copse of trees for a jarring stop. Dalton pulled his revolver and dashed over to the passenger door as a phalanx of bellowing police officers stormed the van. Quickly scanning the van's interior for weapons, he yanked the door open and shoved the gun in the driver's face. "State Police! Freeze!" he thundered at the man centered in the iron sights. The heavy-set, sweaty-faced black man curled up his lip and glared crazily at him, all the while keeping both hands tight on the steering wheel. The look in his eyes told Dalton that the imbecile was higher than a kite, probably strung out on some badass PCP or crystal meth. Officers screamed commands at the driver, and several pairs of hands shot in to grab the man's arms and neck. Kicking and cursing, the googly-eyed junkie was dragged from the van and bulldogged to the ground. Dalton jumped into the van to give it a decent search.

Wham! The exploding rear window rained bits of broken glass all over him. Dalton gasped and scrambled out, as streams of teargas mace shot through the window opening. *Damn!* Way to go, guys. He shook his head and wiped his stinging eyes before rushing over to the tangled bodies on the ground. Under the mass of flailing arms and legs, five of his fellow officers struggled to handcuff the drug-crazed dimwit. Too many in the pile. Avoiding the "feeding frenzy," Dalton leaned in and shined his flashlight beam on the dirt ball's contorted face.

Coming up for air, a highly pissed-off, red-faced, balding A.A. County sergeant stuck his hand out and politely asked Dalton for his flashlight. "No problem, trooper...this ain't my first rodeo," he uttered. Dalton handed the Kel-light to the three-striper, who quickly straddled the wild man. With a loud *thunk*, the heavy flashlight scored a bull's eye on the man's head, and like an over-ripe tomato dropped on a kitchen floor, blood flew everywhere. With a muffled groan, the man went rag doll limp. "Thanks, troop, much appreciated," the smiling sergeant said, handing back the blood-specked flashlight.

Dalton whisked the Kel-light through the grass to rid the blood traces, and then casually walked back to his cruiser still guarding the bridge. "U-17 Annapolis...everything's Ocean King (OK) here. 10-95 (prisoner) in custody," he advised. "Annapolis U-17 ...10-4...and thanks for your assistance. Much appreciated!" the duty officer piped up. Knowing those who'd been involved in the chase would probably stick around and swap war stories, Dalton hit the road. Most compelling was his lingering hope that if the planets were in exact alignment, and if Mister Moonlight hadn't committed hari-kari yet, he still might get lucky at home, reason enough to stow his share of bravado for the moment.

Except for the dim light over the kitchen stove, he returned home to a dark, gloomy house. He deliberated in silence, staring mindlessly at the blank TV screen in the unlit den, all the while sipping beer and tapping restless fingers on the easy-chair armrest. Predictably, the trembling began right after he pulled the tab on his third beer can. Some time later, after his body won the battle over mind, the shakes faded away, and he dozed off

Donny was bulgy-eyed incredulous when he showed Dalton the jagged tear in his uniform trousers. His winced his ashen face and rolled the right pant-leg up until the swollen, bloody puncture wounds were visible. "Thought I was kidding you, didn't ya?" Donny blurted out. "*Man...*I can't believe this shit, either," he added with a grimace.

The trooper first class had almost filled out his citation book that morning, when the call of nature direly begged his attention. Too far from the post, Roberts drove down a service road beneath the BG&E power lines to facilitate his urgent need. "There I was with my Johnson hanging out, and damn...outta nowhere, the snarling lil' mutha runs up and latches onto my leg! You believe that shit?" He paused and shook his head. "Pretty damn hard to draw the Colt when you're peeing and shaking a damn fox off your leg, but I did get a shot at 'em when he took off for the woods. Missed the furry lil bastard, though. Little low on the aim I guess," his piqued shift partner added.

While rare, Dalton had heard about rabid raccoons in other counties, but he hadn't heard much about foxes being afflicted with rabies, especially in Southern Maryland. In the troopers' room, they sat shoulder-to-shoulder, examining the bite marks. Still not sure if they should mash the panic button yet, the matter was decided for them in the form of Wanda Gatton, the ever-vigilant Calvert Control head honcho who'd been eavesdropping from her nearby hallway "throne.' Unknown to them, Wanda had already informed the first sergeant about the crazy fox calamity.

The CMH emergency room doc left it up to him, but Roberts was strongly urged to get a series of rabies shots over a four-week period, just in case. After too much deliberation, he opted for the treatment. The first excruciating shot pierced his stomach that day, with five more to follow. Although he could have taken sick leave for a few days, the fox-bitten trooper merely chose to take the rest of the day off. The next day, none the worse for wear, Donny reported for duty as usual. Two weeks later, however, after receiving the third rabies shot, Dalton's sidekick grew nauseous and complained about severe headaches. The headaches got worse, and soon he was forced to go out on indefinite sick leave, while his condition was evaluated.

Test after tests, a lifetime of wretched medical tests, were conducted, but the origin of his malady couldn't be determined. In time, the possibility that he was having severe adverse reactions to the rabies shots became an unfortunate reality, and it was apparent to his fellow troopers that Roberts was a long way from returning to duty.

Dalton checked up on his shift mate several times at his rented cabin in the woods, and unfortunately, his last visit was hellish. No, this wasn't the same Donny Roberts he'd worked with during the last two years, he was certain of that. Standing in the compact kitchen, Dalton watched anxiously as Donny paced the floors, talking gibberish. He railed incessantly, quite incoherently, about the treatment he'd gotten from the clueless doctors and the MSP higher-ups. They were all conspiring against him—*all of them*—to keep him drugged and in that constant, sleep-deprived pain, and now they wanted his badge too. They were all screwing around with him, and he was getting tired of it, almost ready to explode, and maybe soon, he warned.

Dalton had seen at least five prescription bottles on the kitchen table. At one point, Donny stopped talking and had simply stared out the kitchen window for a few minutes, his tortured mind fixed on the troubling enigma. With a thundering curse, he suddenly ran back to his bedroom and returned with a black-powder six-shot revolver. (MSP had retained custody of his issued weapon weeks before). With a blood-curdling scream, Roberts swung the barrel of the antiquated firearm in the air and smashed it through the kitchen window, spraying glass shards into the sink. Cackling to himself, he thrust the gun out the window and fired it in the air a few times. Satisfied that he'd scared away his fleeting demons, he tossed the smoking gun onto the floor and quietly shuffled over to turn on the TV.

When he left, Dalton was shaken, realizing that his presence merely served as a provocation to his friend now. Other troopers felt the same, and even Donny's girlfriend admitted they were having more frequent quarrels in their souring relationship. Dalton knew that there was little he could do for his hapless colleague. The optimistic doctors and therapists thought Donny was doing all right, but they were the only ones who thought he'd recover. Time, however, would eventually run out as his accumulated state-employee sick leave ended. It took more than two years until Donny, unable to return to work and tired of fighting the bureaucracy paper battle, was finally granted a medical-disability retirement.

Most who stayed in touch with Roberts realized that he'd never be the same, and close friends remained perplexed by his sporadic temper flare-ups and mood swings. Like them, Dalton worried about the omens they'd been trying hard to ignore. Twice during the previous months, fellow troopers had responded to Roberts' cabin after his distraught girlfriend had been eerily threatened by him. Dalton hoped things would eventually smooth for him, but deep inside he felt a foreboding about his former cohort.

#

Dalton and Colby Merson were busy tallying up their traffic stops from the radar-stopping team they'd worked earlier with their corporal. They couldn't help laughing at Elzy every time they gawked at his cherry-red, balding pate. Endeavoring to keep his group ahead in patrol stats, Elzy met them on Route 4 at the northern end, just within the county line. On a near blinding, sun-kissed Sunday morning, they set up the radar team to fish for wayward weekend revelers. This time

Elzy went stealth mode, unfolding a lawn chair and setting up his ambush spot in a row of waist high bushes, smack-dab in the middle of the median strip just fifty yards south of the roadside sign welcoming all to the "Charm of the Chesapeake." Suitably camouflaged from both directions, Elzy stowed his Stetson under the chair and plugged the cord of the handheld Speedgun into the battery pack.

While rampant rumors abounded early on that the Speedgun, or "lil black-ass blunderbuss," as Dalton labeled it, was suspected of causing cancer via its microwaves, most troopers weren't obsessed with such hearsay. Elzy nevertheless made sure to protect his crown jewels during lulls in traffic by not resting the energized unit between his legs.

After popping a jumbo wad of chaw into his mouth, Elzy picked up the walkie-talkie and radioed his already quasi-delirious, two-man stopping team. Colby and Dalton's cruisers were forty yards south, parked on the shoulder and diligently shielded from any telltale northbound traffic. Colby set their citation books beside the walkie-talkie on the hot hood of Dalton's Torino and hitched up his Sam Browne belt.

"This is gonna be like shooting fish in a barrel, huh, buddy?" "Yeah, well, it *is* the end of the month, and our stats *are* a bit low," Dalton quipped with a smirk. Elzy wasn't in much of a good mood today, so he'd dropped his usual tolerance for speed "arrests" down to ten miles an hour over the limit. "Time of the month again for the old lady," he'd told them earlier.

Soon enough, the fish arrived. "Arrest at seventy-two on the lil white Fiat with the number one driver," the walkie-talkie crackled. "Warning on the ugly yellow Ford pickup with the fatso number two driver," Elzy called out. "Arrest! Arrest on the green Malibu with the sleazy-looking number two female driver...seventy-six!" And on it went, Colby and Dalton doing their best to avoid getting splattered while they did jumping jacks in the lanes signaling the errant speedsters who'd been snared by the ole Doppler radar system. "Arrest on the blue Mustang with the number two female driver at eighty-five! Ummm...10-22 (disregard), I repeat, 10-22 on that one, copy?" Dalton jabbed Colby in the side, as the buxom, dark-haired vamp with the oversized sunglasses beeped her horn and blew them a kiss in passing.

"Yeah, that's the one Elzy left the Calverton Room with last Wednesday evening. She owes the state one, ole buddy," Dalton blurted out.

After two hours, they'd reaped a bounty of violators, most of them dumbfounded when apprized of Elzy's wily radar perch, and the shits and giggles could have lasted for hours—had it not been for the agitated elderly driver who'd circled back after being cited. Pulling over on the shoulder next to Elzy's spot, he dragged himself out of his car and limped over to the edge of the road. Above the clamor of traffic, he reamed out their baffled, tobacco-chewing sergeant. Shouts and expletives were fired back and forth as tempers flared. "Ain't no goddamn fair you assholes being sneaky like that," the fossil shouted over the traffic. "And besides, you ain't even wearing your damn trooper hat, baldy...and I know that's illegal as hell, too!" "Hey! Get your lame self back in your car, you ole fart, before you get your dumb ass run over," the fuming Elzy spat back.

Finally, Elzy had enough. From the distance, Colby and Dalton saw him shoot up from the bushes and throw the lawn chair at the startled relic. "Oh shit, here we go...Elzy's working on his people skills again!" Dalton shouted, both of them suddenly wishing they were elsewhere. Elzy stomped toward the old man, who quickly hobbled back to his car and split the scene post haste. As he passed both troopers, the red-faced ignoramus stuck out his warty tongue and shook his feeble fists. Colby smiled and presented him with a perfectly executed Hawaiian Good Luck sign. Ahhh, another satisfied customer, courtesy of the MSP!

Thoroughly pissed, Elzy broke the radar team down. By the time they arrived at the post, Elzy's face no longer matched the top of his sunburned head. "Just about to open up a can of whup-ass on that ole fart, but I guess he saw the light...dumb son a bitch," Elzy muttered, as they totaled their stops. "Had to quit anyhow," he added. "The damn Speedgun was startin' to pick up some weird-ass phantom readings, and besides, my damn head was gettin toasted like a mutha! Damn if we didn't go fishing in the right place today, boys." Elzy whistled a few off-key notes and delicately touched his smarting head. "Yeah, we tore them suckers up big time, Corp," Colby cheerfully answered as Dalton nodded in agreement.

"Oh, by the way, Dalton, Sergeant Hooper dropped by. He wants to see ya back there," Elzy said, pointing toward the ID room. Elzy placed a hand on his shoulder and looked him in the eyes. "Congratulations, my man, for better or for worse, ya got what ya wanted. You're going into ID." "Well, I'll be damned!" Colby announced. "Looks like that's cause for a few cold ones at the Calverton Room, if you ask me."

Chapter 6

CRIMINAL INVESTIGATION
(A Slice of Sleuthing)

During his first year as a criminal investigator, Dalton was busier than a beaver on Ritalin. Being the new man at the end of the slippery ID totem pole was tough, and cases flew his way like he was stuck at the end of a wind tunnel. Each case had been a learning experience, however, and skullduggery was more his style—much more challenging than pounding the road, and he was always elated when he could slap cuffs on punks. Being an elite ID member was also a rung further up the MSP ladder. Still, it was tedious work, and unlike road patrol, Dalton developed a nagging mental tendency to bring cases home with him. Slack moments on the home front were suddenly filled with new ideas and perceivable clues, resulting in family inattentiveness.

Dalton had been promoted to trooper first class, an automatic promotion and a badly-needed raise for keeping one's nose clean during the first three MSP years. At home there was great news as well. Cindy was pregnant again, and soon Anne Marie, their feisty toddler, would have a sibling to compete with. Cindy was delighted with Dalton's re-assignment as an investigator, knowing it'd eliminate those dreadful revolving shifts she'd loathed for months. No longer would she be forced to endure that cold and lonely bed when her soul mate worked those interminable grave yard shifts in that backwards county. Maybe now they'd have a normal life after all, she hoped.

Unlike most, Dalton wasn't obsessed about keeping up with any fashion sense, preferring year round to wear blue jeans and modest sport shirts if he could. With the investigator's clothing allowance, however, he rounded out a passable medley of polyester pants, button-down shirts, several sports coats, two pairs of gum-sole casual shoes, and a handful of patterned clip-on ties. Dalton despised ties, shunned them like bad breath—until Sgt. Hooper finally ordered him to wear the damn things. Against regulations, he stuck his snob-nose .38 in a non-issue suede-leather clip-on holster which he wore snugged under his belt at the small of his back. Extra non-issue hollow-point rounds were kept in a pants pocket.

Dalton disdained the "Dirty Harry" shoulder harness holsters, although ole Harry was indeed *da man* out there in Tinsel-Town. The reason was that the shoulder contraption had to be concealed under a sports coat, something he fastidiously avoided wearing. To Dalton, Calvert was still country, a blast from the past where fashion sense in the midst of tobacco fields, farmlands, and grungy tenant houses, was pure nonsense.

The covert car Dalton inherited from Jack Nimitz, the other mongrel, low-ranking ID trooper, was a gigantic enigma, and Nimitz was in ecstacy about losing it. Having more seniority than Dalton, Nimitz was finally getting a plum ID car worthy of his emerging super-star status. After endlessly jumping cars, Nimitz's persistent begging, pissing and moaning finally netted him a confiscated covert car, courtesy of the badgered head honchos at the Waterloo Motor Vehicle Division. To placate the bull-headed pain-ass, Nimitz was awarded a clunker—a beat-up, aqua-blue 1968 Ford Mustang. After more wrangling, he finagled a peeved mechanic into installing an antiquated siren in it, and with a plug-in red bubble-light, Nimitz had himself an official state police ID car. A month later, however, the Mustang's wheezing engine gasped and had a fatal seizure, forcing the determined investigator to wheedle a rebuilt engine from a Prince Frederick car dealer who owed him too many favors.

Naturally, Dalton found the retooled Mustang made-to-order for his impetuous persona. Sure, every time he topped sixty miles an hour, the frame shuddered like an epileptic trapped in a snow drift, and when he hit the siren, the car sputtered and slowed and its spastic headlights flickered on and off. And it was hard to ignore the shower of sparks which frequently shot out from under the dashboard to dance around the accelerator pedal whenever he plugged the red "fireball" light in the cigarette lighter. Still, the clunker did have an MSP radio and intermittent heat, *and* Dalton wasn't paying for the gas or hitch-hiking anymore. Yes indeedy, the Mustang sufficed supremely, although there were several hairy times when he wished it had an ejection seat. Dalton renamed the Mustang "Wonder Bitch," a more fitting name than "Ass Wipe," the title Nimitz had bestowed on her.

#

Sergeant "Buddy" Hooper, the square-jawed ID sergeant, was a perpetual whirlwind. No doubt the caffeine in the countless Mountain Dews he daily guzzled fired up his raging metabolism, Dalton figured. Flittering about as if ravenous fire ants were feasting on his family jewels, Buddy Hooper wasn't a desk-sitter. Also from the Eastern Shore, Hooper was a homegrown boy from Centreville, the oldest son of a chicken farmer. The sandy-haired, compactly built supervisor had a wicked, explosive temper that wreaked havoc on those who pierced his thin patience. Buddy was a tack-sharp, take-charge guy who disdained BS'ers, and Dalton respected him immensely.

Corporal Lester Murphy, Hooper's right-hand man, however, was quite the contrast. It wasn't that the thirty-eight year-old Lester didn't have the capacity to be an effective investigator. No, the balding Western Marylander with the early paunch and Roman nose was savvy and quite knowledgeable in criminal work, and few doubted his accrued expertise. And he did have a penchant for fomenting nebulous BS and scuttlebutt amongst the troops—and for making kick-ass strong coffee.

No, Lester was simply, prematurely, afflicted with a debilitating case of the slows, an innate procrastination compounded with unadulterated laziness. Being an avid fisherman and hunter certainly worked to his advantage, though, and he'd been riding on Wild Bill Flyger's stretched out coat tails for a long time. Surprisingly, the ride had been smoother then anticipated, so he happily stayed aboard. Since his arrival at the fledgling PF post years before, Lester had shared many a bass boat, deer-hunting escapade and BS session with both Buddy Hooper and Wild Bill.

Dalton, nonetheless, grew to like the easygoing corporal. Lester just never seemed to get fazed about anything. Anything except for a bass slipping off a hook, or a ten-point buck being just beyond the kill range. And Lester had also taken Dalton into his confidence, coughing up a plethora of tips which rewarded him with several nice bass from ole Judge Mackall's pond. Still, Lester riled Dalton with his uncanny ability to sniff out and avoid new criminal cases when they dribbled in. One second, he'd be leaning back in his vinyl chair, feet propped up on his desk and slurping hours-old coffee, cheerfully expounding on a new bass plug that would undoubtedly lure ole Bubba out from his shallow lair at the end of the pond for sure. Next second, he'd simply vanished, nowhere to be found, when Sgt. Hooper tromped into the ID room to assign the next case. Dalton, the new guy, would normally be the recipient, while Lester breathed a sigh of relief as he perched silently on the throne in his men's room refuge.

There was another characteristic, Lester's most repugnant one, that couldn't be easily ignored. At his whim, the man had the ability to vent some seriously foul gas. It was Lester, slowly shifting his lard-butt on the chair, then, *barooom*—followed by his "Heh-heh-heh"cackling and an instantly ruined room. It was so pervasive some days that Dalton wondered if something had crawled up his ass to die a thousand ugly deaths. *Barooom!* "Heh-heh-heh!" Suffering through a heavy gassing one morning, Dalton succumbed to his better judgment and decided to even things up, hoping that Lester could honestly declare himself purged for once in his life.

Catching a break in Lester's endless war stories, Dalton sneaked out to the troopers' room to fix the next pot of coffee. He felt proud of himself after he had dropped a few chunks of Ex-Lax into the coffee pot without being detected. Dalton waited until Lester had slurped down two cups before dumping out the rest of the pot. Prior to the feat, he'd also removed the single roll of toilet paper from Lester's men's' room refuge. In innocent silence he waited, as Lester's growling stomach rebelled. Minutes later, after Lester made a wild dash to his refuge, Dalton broke out into hysterics. After several dashes to the odorous haven, the unsuspecting corporal hurriedly called it a day and left to take care of some "urgent business."

Lester's aversion to intricate criminal cases, and Sgt. Hooper's tacit recognition of it, enabled Lester to be the willing recipient of most of the administrative cases: trooper applicant investigations, handgun permit applications and other such mundane-ness that most detectives disdained anyhow.

The prima donna of the ID section just had to be someone like Jack Nimitz. Nimitz was another Eastern Shore son, born and raised on wind-swept Taylor's Island, a debatable chunk of Dorchester County on the mighty Chesapeake. Conceivably, that's where he'd become so hardnosed and deliberate, many thought. Nimitz was a tall and slim, blue-eyed blond, quite Aryan looking in fact. Adding to his character, he sported a flattop military haircut, but it was the scarlet-welted scar that made him look fearsome. Starting just below the corner of his left eye, the ugly scar extended horizontally several inches. Jack Nimitz was proud of it, claiming that it came from the bayonet of an NVA soldier he'd killed with his bare hands in Hue while he was a marine during the '68 Tet Offensive. What couldn't be misunderstood, however, was the small US Navy Seabee tattoo on his upper right arm, the one few ever saw.

True to his strict Irish upbringing, Jack was resolute, which, for one raised on Taylor's Island, was frequently defined as being hardcore obstinate. Dalton thought that maybe it *was* true what they said about those web-footed guys—you could tell a man from the Eastern Shore, but you couldn't tell him much! Except for being a tad prejudice, Jack was the kind of investigator most people wanted around when it came to solving their cases. He was a relentless, get-in-your-face cop with a stellar reputation, feared and hated by those he hunted down and collared.

Dalton respected Nimitz who'd shown him the ropes and shortcuts of criminal work. A year later, however, it was still irksome being the section's whipping boy as compared to Nimitz, the shining star! With Sergeant Hooper's unfailing acquiescence, Jack was allowed to pick and choose almost any criminal case *he* deemed worthy of his talents. Weary of humdrum cases, he preferred the higher-profile homicides and robberies, cases he could build a reputation on, cases that got his name in print and could earn him another rank sooner. In his mind, Nimitz was certainly beyond the whipping-boy phase, and with Dalton now on board, he'd make every effort to keep it that way.

Dalton appreciated Sgt. Hooper starting him off slowly, allowing him to "cut his teeth" on the petty, "who-struck-John" cases. Still unpolished, Dalton nonetheless felt confident and competent, and already he could fling fingerprint powder with the best of them. As his style evolved, his efforts produced positive results with solid arrests.

When Dalton's investigative baptism ended, Sergeant Hooper tossed more complex cases his way, and soon the trickle of cases turned into a flood. Dalton put his head down and dogged on, realizing he'd have to pay his dues. But it still gnawed at him, knowing that the egotistical Nimitz got the nod over him whenever a newsworthy case filtered in.

#

As the smallest county in Maryland, Calvert's crime rate was low when compared to the more populated counties to the north. With Calvert's recent influx of "outsiders," however, calls for service skyrocketed in the late seventies. Most of the crimes were thefts, B&Es, assaults, property destructions, minor drug possessions and bad checks. There were occasional homicides, mostly domestic, armed robberies and sporadic sex offenses. The Prince Frederick Post was full-service and multi-dimensional, and its troopers handled everything: traffic enforcement, criminal calls, and the burgeoning myriad of police-related calls.

With thirty-plus troopers, the post provided the primary law-enforcement for the county. The Calvert County Sheriff's Office, officially formed in 1654, mustered less than a dozen deputies, and while they occasionally handled minor calls, their primary role was handling prisoners and serving court papers. Any major crime reported to the Sheriff's Office would usually be punted over to the MSP.

Before the rapidly changing seventies, the fight against crime was considered paramount, and the majority of the road troopers preferred working criminal cases. With the recent proliferation of the new Speedguns, however, Dalton saw the change. Speed arrests were easily harvested in great numbers with minimal efforts. As many of the old-salts gloomily predicted, MSP readily ensnared itself in the race for traffic-enforcement stats, and competition between barracks and regional troops soon flourished. Troopers who once had adequate time to conduct thorough criminal investigations, now felt the pressure to produce more traffic stats. For the troopers in the field, it became a balancing act between the runaway race for traffic citations versus quality criminal investigations, with many disgruntled troopers feeling they were caught in a vise. Feeling the heat, some troopers merely reported crimes, rather than waste precious time away from the road investigating them. Overall, it was a precarious balancing act which would continuously plague most-full service MSP units for the foreseeable future.

#

Occasionally after late shifts, Dalton sauntered over to the Calverton Room with fellow troopers to maintain his contacts with "confidential sources." Bellied up to the bar, he'd throw down drafts and get embroiled in heavy police jargon with Nimitz, Colby, Marty Metzger or anyone else who set another frosted mug in front of him. Damn, why the hell not, since he knew that Cindy was already doing serious zzzs at home.

While nursing brews there, Dalton had bumped into his old MSP pal Donny Roberts a few times. The first time they connected, Dalton thought Roberts was doing OK with his life off the force: still undergoing medical care, but things seemed better. The second encounter was portentous. Both he and Nimitz agreed that Donny looked haggard, his mood somber, almost dark. He was sitting by himself, hunched over the bar and unwilling to acknowledge his former friends until they forced the issue.

Donny rambled on and on, with colliding thoughts that barely made sense. "I've found a new friend they call *Jesus*, and he's molding me to his call," Donny rasped at them. "Like my long-lost uncle, I never wanted to be anything but a Maryland State Trooper, but the piss-ants at Pikesville screwed me up Shit Creek big-time! Well, let me tell ya somethin', my friends...The sun don't shine on the same dog's ass every day, believe me! Screw them bastards!" It was the look in his eyes that made Dalton uneasy. As Donny drank and rambled on, his eyes blazed open, the dark pupils intense fixed beams of smoldering animosity. He'd seen such eyes before, and Charles Manson owned them.

Dalton or Nimitz couldn't fathom where their former cohort was coming from, as he bounced off the bar walls that night. When Roberts squeezed a shot glass with both hands hard enough to shatter it, Dalton and Nimitz paid their tab and left. "He's not our problem anymore, but sure's I'm talking to you, Dalton, it's only a matter of time before he is," Jack told him as they walked back to the post. "Yeah, you probably got that one right, friend," Dalton drearily added. "Things don't bode well with me, either. Think he's beyond our reach now, Jack?" Nimitz looked over at Dalton, pursed his lips and nodded. They walked the rest of the way in silence, each thinking the same thoughts, but neither wanting to air them.

While Dalton hadn't been the lead investigator in a homicide yet, he had, amongst numerous other cases, investigated several unattended deaths and suicides. Over time, he'd become fairly de-sensitized when working with the dead. The circumstances leading up to one's death, however, always affected him, but he held back the deluge of mental images that often toyed with his emotions. The suicides were depressing, especially the three involving young adolescents who'd finally, irrevocably, lost their ways and had given up. All three lives were wasted with a pull of a trigger, easy enough.

There was the teenager high school dropout from Dunkirk whose girlfriend had just dumped him for another sweetheart. He left her a terse, unforgiving note, wedged a shotgun against a pillow, then gloomily waited for his nerves to build so he could pull the trigger. When Dalton entered the murky bedroom, he was instantly engulfed in the lingering cloud of shotgun smoke—nearly choked on the stench of cordite. Through the haze, the TV displayed a blaring car commercial, the pinhead announcer gleefully raving about how low the dealer's prices were—but for the next day only. Several feet away, the young man was sitting propped up against the headboard, looking very much alive with his bulging eyes fixed eerily on the screen, almost as if he was in sticker shock over the rock-bottom prices.

And there was the young mother from Port Republic who could no longer endure her crippling depression. She'd waited patiently until her husband and son had finally left for the store. Immediately afterward, she locked the cottage front door and raced to her bedroom, where she'd hidden the single-shot .22 rifle. After arranging several family pictures in front of her, she adjusted her nightgown and lay down on the bed. Barely able to handle the unwieldy rifle, she placed the end of the barrel against her head and pulled the trigger with her extended index finger. She was remarkably beautiful, almost angelic, Dalton thought when he saw her. Such a sad waste of a promising life. Dalton could only imagine how her abrupt departure would echo forever in the lives of those who'd loved her during her short life.

The twenty-two year-old apprentice carpenter from Wayson's Corner hadn't been able to hold his recent demon at arm's length, either. Dalton had arrested him after he'd exposed himself to the startled female clerk behind the counter of a Chaneyville mom & pop store, and after an hour of patient probing, Dalton had elicited a full confession from the cooperative but visibly distraught young man. Perceiving his quandary, Dalton convinced the court commissioner to release the father of two toddlers on his own recognizance, since he didn't have a record.

When Dalton returned after several days' leave, he found the man's arrest disposition sheet on his desk. It was stamped *Closed* in bold, red ink. Sergeant Hooper apathetically broke the news, telling Dalton that the guy had apparently been so overwrought with guilt that after he'd returned home, he had shot himself in the barn behind his house, just minutes after hugging his unknowing wife and kids. Dalton wanted to pound Lester Murphy's face into hamburger after he chided him that day, jostled him endlessly about how he should have busted the guy's balls to make him confess. Instead, Dalton angrily tossed Lester's typewriter into his lap. Lester yelped in pain, confirmation of a direct hit on his family jewels, and Dalton stormed from the barrack, hoping the cramp in his gut would dissipate soon—but knowing full well it wouldn't.

What dark, desperate tunnels were they slogging through when they ultimately realized their very lives were utterly barren, totally beyond despair?

The old sage forest ranger was different though, and Dalton had actually admired him for the way he played things out in his world. Suitably, for this type of call, it was a chilly, overcast April day. Dalton double-checked his notebook before turning into the dirt driveway leading to a rustic log cabin in the tranquil woods of Flag

Ponds just south of Prince Frederick. Surrounded by towering oaks and poplars and teeming with wildlife, Flag Ponds was Dalton's favorite haven in Calvert.

The forest ranger's son approached him as he parked the Mustang, and Dalton saw an anguished mask of pain on his face when they shook hands. "I should have never done it...should have known better than to leave him alone today! I'm Tom's son, Eric...I'm a US Park Police Officer, and...D*amn!*" Teary-eyed, he looked at the somber detective's face, searching hard for an answer he'd never get.

Dalton followed him to the rear of the cabin, where his father lay slumped against the cinder block wall. He'd remember later that the peaceful backyard seemed almost surreal for the moment. From the bordering woods two mourning doves called each other, their soft, plaintive death-knolls soothing, subdued. There was also the gentle whooshing of the breeze in tall loblolly pines—rueful sentinels. And the hardy scent of the pine needles was pervasive and too pleasant, a sharp contrast to what lay at his feet.

Initially, what he saw didn't fit. An old model twelve-gauge pump shotgun, chamber open, was propped against the wall, and a spent shell lay on the ground next to it. Both items were fifteen feet from the body of Thomas Lozier, the well-known, retired forest ranger. "I know it was a wrong move, but I just had to move it away from him. It was too ugly...he...he...!"

Dalton heard the son's rambling voice in the background, but his attention was riveted on the death scene details, virtually oblivious to what was being said. There were blood spatters in the shotgun barrel. *OK!* The gaping chest wound had been efficiently directed, precisely at the heart, and there were powder burns mixed with blood streaks on the old man's pajamas which indicated a close contact wound. But it was the fresh abrasion on his right thumb, the thumb he'd pulled the trigger with, which tied it all together. Dalton eased up and started listening more, all the while studying the old ranger's body. With his chin resting serenely on his chest and his lifeless, half-shut eyes gazing down at the ground in front, the ranger's gaunt face looked peaceful. Dalton scrutinized the drag marks in the dirt leading from the side of the house. What excruciating pain the man must have been in when he pulled himself forward to where he had to go.

Dalton followed Eric into the cabin. Passing through the kitchen on the way to the old man's bedroom, Dalton noticed the unopened plastic quart bottle of milk perspiring on the kitchen table. There were several loose rounds of twelve-gauge rifled slug rounds scattered on the bedroom floor, and on the bedside night table were three prescription pill containers still partly filled with pills—presumed pain meds. Dalton slipped them into an evidence packet and directed his attention to the son.

He learned that the seventy-four year-old ranger had been diagnosed with liver cancer last year. Early chemotherapy treatments proved futile, and later examination indicated that the cancer had spread rapidly throughout his body. It was terminal. Pain-medication doses were increased several times, but the misery spiraled. It had been an ordeal, living alone in the cabin and mostly bedridden since his wife had recently passed away. Today, Eric had planned to take him to Johns Hopkins Hospital for a scheduled exploratory operation, hoping beyond hope that the specialists could come up with something—*anything*—that would alleviate at least some of the pain. Surprisingly, for once, the father acquiesced to his son's nagging pleas. Yes, he'd get dressed and would go, however, he needed a favor in return.

"Son, while I'm getting myself ready, why don't you put a smile on your old man's face and drive up to O'Dells store on the corner? I could surely use some milk for the ride," he told him.

As soon as Eric left, his father crawled from the bed. Stooped over in agony, he shuffled over to the closet where he'd hidden the venerable shotgun, his companion of many years' good hunting. He dropped a few shells before chambering one into his trusty weapon. Slowly, painfully, he dragged himself from the bedroom to the side door that led outside. Too weak to stand, he slumped to the ground and caught his breath. Summoning what little strength remained, he groveled his way over to the rear basement wall. No, for whatever reasons that made no sense to anyone else but him, he damn sure wasn't going up the road again. There would be no return this time. It would be ended here, with his friends—the birds, squirrels, deer, and other wildlife amongst the tall pines surrounding his beloved cabin in the woods. With time he hoped his son would understand, but being a staunch catholic himself, he knew the almighty wouldn't. He'd deal with that reckoning soon enough.

Thomas Lozier, the West Point grad who'd fought in two wars, the highly decorated, infinitely respected colonel who'd left the Army and its haunting nightmares of untold horrors—the tormented soul who'd finally found peace as a ranger in nature's realm—was finally making his eternal truce. He waited until he heard his son's car pull into the driveway again, and with a wistful smile he got the job done.

Dalton stayed with Eric while his father's body was taken from the scene. He remained at the cabin for more than an hour, while Eric recounted several touching stories about his father, eventually learning that the ex-colonel and forest ranger was a man whose company he would have greatly enjoyed.

"Yeah, Dad was a disciplinarian, a harsh taskmaster in my early years, but even then I understood why. West Point instilled certain values in him...honorable ones he wanted to impart to me," Eric said. "We camped together, did a lot of fishing and hunting too, and I was always in awe of him, fascinated by his knowledge and his wisdom of nature's ways. That's when I could truly feel the father and son bond between us...the love he couldn't admit to me, directly at least." Eric looked up at the overcast sky, his eyes red and glassy. "He was always a changed man when we were enjoying the outdoors together, always at peace. Guess this was the way he wanted it to end, probably made up his mind weeks ago, too."

Dalton dwelled on the suicide during his long ride home, pondering whether or not he would have had the guts to make the same decision under the circumstances. No matter what, he knew he couldn't fault the man at all. The old Army veteran's fight with his demons was finally over.

#

The New Year brought welcome news to Dalton and Cindy: the birth of Charlene, their second daughter. Anne Marie, their bright-eyed toddler, now had competition for attention, someone to share all the smiles and giggles with. Cindy had grown into the young mother role better than even she'd anticipated, and now she had two tykes to dote over. Dalton felt that things were all right on the home front, even if the quality time between him and Cindy had waned. It'd get better with time; he knew it would.

Still, something sorrowful plagued his wife, making her melancholy and distant. Dalton couldn't fathom it, but every so often she'd be immersed in a place that drowned her with sadness, despite the showering love her young family gave her. Dalton only hoped that her dour mood swings would fade with time. He didn't want the "divorce devil" to have one smidgeon of a reason to cast a look his way, to throw the pitchfork at him, as he'd done to some of the other troopers.

Tom Rensir, his academy mate, had recently been pricked and was already in the throes of divorce after his wife discovered his extracurricular assignations with a certain comely vamp from Juvenile Services. The uniform had given Rensir an unexpected boost with more then just a few county tarts, and in due time he salaciously turned into sweet-toothed kid in the candy shop. During the last three years, five other post troopers had either been divorced or were teetering on the downside slope leading to it, eventually joining the majority of troopers—a whooping eighty percent—who couldn't contend with married life. No, Dalton didn't plan on being the "divorce devil's" next pitchfork victim.

#

Things were rockin' in Dalton's MSP world—simply *Supercalifragilistic-Fuckin-A-Adocious!* At year's end, speculation mounted as to which worthy trooper would snag the Prince Frederick Post's 1978 Trooper of the Year award. While he had a rock-solid year in ID, Dalton felt there were other troopers equally deserving. The Trooper of the Year award was the last one presented during the post's winter party held that February night at the Chesapeake Beach Elks Club. Dalton and Cindy were genuinely surprised when Dalton's name was called out for it. After chugging down a few beers with Colby Merson and Marty Metzger, Dalton was flabbergasted that he hadn't fallen off the stage when the plaque was handed to him. Colby tried hard to bite his tongue, but after the applause tapered off, Colby couldn't help being Colby.

"Speech! You blond-haired Pecker-head!" he bellowed from his table. "Yeah, that's right," Marty joined in, "Let's hear from the Dickless Tracy of Calvert County himself!" Great having your buds around for needed levity, the blushing Dalton thought as he traipsed off the stage.

Being selected Trooper of the Year, however, also equated to mandatory attendance as an "honored" guest at slews of award celebrations thrown by Calvert's various civic groups. That droll aspect, along with his mug being plastered in the local papers, was barely palatable to Dalton, who shunned center stages. While Cindy championed his achievement, she opted out as his dinner date on the fried chicken supper circuit. Perhaps all those ungodly long hours away from her and the kids hadn't really been for naught, she thought ruefully.

Coinciding with his early year exploits, Dalton received what he thought was a competitive yearly evaluation which amounted to fifty-five percent of the overall promotional rating, the remaining being the written exam. For the evaluation, the post supervisors bumped elbows in a "round robin" meeting, with each supervisor providing rough scores for troopers in his work group. During those occasionally explosive meetings, a final evaluation score for each trooper was somehow hammered out, leaving many disgruntled troopers swearing later that the scores were undoubtedly determined by a whimsical toss of loaded dice. In essence, it was a subjective, nigh-workable system, but barely. Being a good-ole-boy member of that certain clique of insiders did indeed have its advantages. Dalton was gratified when Sergeant Hooper told him he'd received a ninety-four (out of one hundred) evaluation rating. Elation instantly crashed to deflation, however, when he learned that other post Trooper First Class types, the senior more cliqueish ones, were gifted with much higher evaluations.

Dalton was flabbergasted when fellow crime warrior Jack Nimitz appealed his grossly bloated rating of ninety-nine point seven! Nimitz, however, knew the game well, and through a dragged-out buzz-saw presentation of his prior year's work, he was amazingly granted a revised score of ninety-nine point nine by the appeal board! Dalton realized that Nimitz *knew* he walked on water, but he never believed the higher echelons would so blatantly confirm it for him. Bah!

Over the next three months, Dalton pored over the mind-numbing mélange of MSP study material related to the corporal's exam. Two weeks after the test, he learned he'd achieved the third highest, state-wide score. *Sweet Hallelujah!* When his written test and evaluation rating were compiled, Dalton's name was riding high on the promo list—much higher than he'd ever dreamed.

The massive MSP promotion /transfer list was spit out by teletype the second week of June. Effective July 1, Wild Bill Flyger was the new commander at the Westminster Barrack, superseded at the PF post by a newbie lieutenant from the Eastern Shore. Sgt. Hooper got the nod to the Detective Sergeant rank, and Dalton, Jack Nimitz and, surprisingly, Colby Merson were all spanking-new corporals. Wild Bill, Sgt. Hooper, and Dalton, were sent to other barracks while "Jesus" Nimitz and crazy Colby lucked out and stayed at Prince Frederick. .

Dalton was ranked sixteenth on the corporals' promotion list amongst a total of thirty-two. All the promotions were effective on July 1—except for Dalton's which, inexplicably, took effect a month later, a loss of one month's seniority to the other new two-stripers. Moreover, instead of Dalton being sent to the Annapolis Barrack as an ID supervisor, as a certain, sober-minded FOB colonel had told him by phone the day before, he was now shipping out to Barrack "Q" Greenbelt as a uniform road corporal.

Dalton merely chalked it up to the infamous Pikesville Promotional Wizard of Oz who hid behind curtains, haphazardly yanking the wrong assignment levers again—the lil bastard! Hell, he'd even heard of the MSP Wizard screwing up once before by promoting the wrong brother. The promoted brother hadn't even taken the next rank's test, but to save somebody's ass, the puzzle palace princes thought it best to let the infallible Wizard have his way. While the deserving brother fumed, his brother's asinine promotion was set in stone.

.   No, Dalton thought, Colonel Edwards himself personally assured him beyond a doubt he was going to the Annapolis Barrack as an ID supervisor, and he was confident the Barrack "Q" faux pas would be swiftly rectified—another MSP lesson to be learned. With or without the cranky Wizard's "help," Dalton pledged to himself to grit it out and do his best, nothing less.

Chapter 7

GLORY DAYS- PART TWO
(Barrack "Q" And The Merry Go Round)

Corporal Dalton Bragg's first day at the MSP Greenbelt Barrack was enlightening. Marty Metzger, his ole shift buddy, spirited him up the road to his new Prince George's County assignment, and Marty couldn't wait to aim his cruiser south and scat back to the sanctity of his beloved Calvert County. Hopping out of Marty's cruiser to the blare of an ole Willie Nelson favorite, Dalton was greeted sharply by the incessant droning of the Washington beltway traffic. Coming from Calvert, he was vexed by the heavy traffic volume on the "Merry-Go-Round," as he later termed the beltway.

Dalton donned his straw Stetson, smiled subtly at Marty, and jokingly patted the new corporal stripes on his short sleeve shirt. Marty rolled his eyes and gave him a thumbs-up, then shot him a middle finger to wish him good luck. With a shit-eating grin, he stomped on the gas pedal and cut rubber on the hot asphalt. Standing nearby, two troopers gawked at the fleeing cruiser, then at the approaching corporal who was shaking his head. *Yeah buddy !*

Barrack "Q" Greenbelt equated to five very cramped and decrepit looking rooms at the State Highway building on Kenilworth Avenue, just a stone throw from the beltway. Standing tall, Dalton paraded into the mini lobby and introduced himself to the cute PCO hunkered down behind the radio console. While he chatted with her, Sergeant Charlie Wykowski, the duty officer and his new supervisor, traipsed into the radio room to greet him. A swarthy, wavy haired, "old school" sort who seemed cheerful enough, Dalton's new sarge promptly told him he was just months away from retiring. Super!

After swapping pleasantries, the chipper sergeant introduced Dalton to Lieutenant Ted Harrell, the barrack commander, and his assistant, 2nd Lieutenant Tilden Kurtz. Harrell was a lean and tall, gray-haired, matronly-looking man in his late forties. Dalton's immediate impression of 2nd Lt Kurtz was that the pot-bellied, double-chinned, puffy-cheeked man with the bushy eyebrows looked like Captain Kangaroo on steroids, someone who needed to push away from the kitchen table more often, and one of those rare people whom many would have an immediate aversion to—like a dull needle ripping across a vinyl record. Kurtz's perceived cockiness flashed instant warning signs on Dalton's fine-tuned radar. He saluted both lieutenants and shook hands. Sure enough, Kurtz gripped his hand harder than necessary before releasing it with a satisfied sneer. *I'll get your cocksure, fat-ass next time*, Dalton's inner voice called out. Sergeant Wykowski rolled his eyes and shot Dalton a quick wink before traipsing from the room.

His commanders exchanged niceties and expounded on the merits of their barrack with their new, slack-faced corporal. "One of the finest barracks you'll ever find," Harrell proudly chortled. "One of the busiest in the state too," Kurtz added in a clipped, nasal voice. "You're definitely gonna like working here Corp, trust me. Plenty of room to make rank here, if you get my drift." For several minutes, both lieutenants continued on with flowing accolades.

Finally, Dalton had to square things out. Clearing his throat, he put his hands on his knees and leaned forward. "With all due respect sirs, there's been a misunderstanding which should be corrected soon. According to Colonel Edwards, you're looking at an Annapolis ID corporal, not a road corporal here."

Dalton promptly pulled out his typed transfer request from his briefcase and reached across the desk to hand it to Lt. Harrell. Taken aback, Harrell stared at it as if it had herpes. Dalton hesitated before he placed the form on his desk. His perplexed new commander gaped at Kurtz who glared back at Dalton with a perfect New York City-cultivated sneer. Nothing but dead silence as the welcome band stopped in mid-verse. Instant persona non-gratis! Dalton felt the Big Chill while Lieutenant Harrell twitted his thumbs.

Harrell abruptly cleared his throat and shot up from his chair. "Well my young corporal," he growled, "looks like we really don't have much to discuss than, do we? Just do a decent job while you're here. *Am I clear?*" Dalton nodded his head. "Yes sir" he answered in a detached voice. Obviously piqued, Lieutenant Harrell folded his arms. 'That's all, Corporal Bragg...you're dismissed!" "Oh, and by the way, Bragg," Kurtz bellowed," submit this through the *proper* chain of command, meaning Sergeant Wykowski, your supervisor. You understand me?" Shaking his head, the sneering Kurtz threw the transfer request across the desk.

Dalton felt the daggers flying his way when he turned to leave. If he'd stayed as a fly on the wall, he would have heard Lt. Harrell, in more colorful words, give his second-in-command marching orders to "get on that new corporal's ass, *ASAP!*

The Greenbelt Barrack was considered a transient assignment. Many troopers assigned there after the academy, normally transferred out within a year. Unlike Dalton, who was painfully naive of MSP etiquette in such matters, most troopers refrained from waltzing into their new assignment with a transfer request in hand. No points scored in the first round, and Dalton instantly became a huge bull's eye to his new commanders, an unenviable status that plagued him the entire year he was there. Once again, it was back to round the clock shift-work, something he knew would bring tears of joy to Cindy. And as a bonus, he'd be driving another canary-colored cruiser; the one's the joking truckers called the "Tijuana Taxis". Life was good, and the shits and giggles were getting better each passing day.

The awkward Barrack "Q" initiation aside, sage Sergeant Wykowski, or "Sloth," as he was nicknamed, did his best leading interference for Dalton during his waning days on the force. "Sloth," however, was daintily walking on eggshells, having been involuntarily sentenced to the beltway barrack because of a month-long dalliance with another trooper's not-so-estranged wife, Dalton learned. He couldn't blame his sarge for not wanting to screw up his retirement after surviving twenty-nine taxing years in the MSP.

Dalton immediately liked First Sergeant Vince Petty, the amiable supervisor of the NCOs and the Big Kahuna of the master schedule and sick leave program. Petty had been around a while, had seen more than his share of barrack brass too, from the shining best to the dog-ass worst, and he much preferred the company of his supervisors and troopers to those who wore the glitter bars on their collars. Petty was unflappable, never intimidated, and, most important, he could retire at whim. Levelheaded and forthright, the towering top kick with the peppery gray hair was armed with a zany sense of humor.

In place of the customary salute, Petty's daily greeting to Dalton and others he liked normally arrived in the form of a stealthy, solid knuckle punch to the shoulder, followed by raucous snickering. Dalton's esteem for him swelled when he learned that Petty had little regard for butter-bar Kurtz and his brash, "old school" style of confrontational leadership. He cautioned Dalton to cover his ass, every 'i," and slash every "t,' since word around the barrack already had him at the top of Kurtz's shit list. Dalton always depended on Petty's hard punches to remind him of that.

Feeling like a constipated duck out of water, Dalton would have nearly been lost in his new role if Trooper First Class Nate Odom hadn't taken him under his wing. Odom was the senior trooper in his six-man group, and with eight years of road-pounding experience, he'd already had his share of breaking in "cherry" road corporals. Alas, he'd inherited another one. Sergeant "Sloth's" suggestion that Dalton accompany his senior trooper on patrol during the first week was right on target.

On just his third day at Barrack "Q," one of Dalton's overzealous rookie troopers somehow managed to smash his cruiser into the rear of a VW while responding to a petty call. Other than for the young trooper's wounded pride ("Corporal Bragg, I swear I never saw the damn *Bug* stopped at that light"), there were no injuries. Welcome aboard. Dalton had his first *departmental* to investigate, one of seven he'd eventually handle during his stay at the beltway barrack. Taking pity on his green corporal, Nate bird-dogged him through the sweeping investigation and shit-load of reports.

Dalton strongly admired the professionalism displayed by his sandy haired, quick-to-smile, twenty-nine year-old road trooper. As reflected by his being assigned an unmarked cruiser, Nate was an aggressive "high writer" in traffic enforcement. Soft-spoken and self-assured, he carried a confidence years beyond the cockiness flaunted by many senior troopers. Dalton readily took him into his confidence, and Nate reciprocated, spending hours filling him in on the intricacies of the barrack policies and nuances. He also let Dalton know about those troopers who could be trusted, along with those who were headaches, the proverbial screw-ups who inevitably plagued every MSP unit.

As characterized by Nate, the barrack had just about the right jambalaya of characters and personalities one would expect to find at any MSP installation. The mix normally ranged from several super-macho types, one or two cheese-eater screw-ups, and some antsy clock watcher barrack rats, then finally to the largest compliment each barrack predictably had; the proud, hard working, walking-tall types. Typically, there were also those special few who thrived in an exclusive clique, Nate added. Few outsiders rarely found their way into those tight cliques, and Dalton's character made it verboten for him to dare try.

"Seein' as how you're married, you best be careful about the trooper groupies we have around here, Corp," Nate suggested early on. "They can't leave a uniform alone, and lord knows there's enough of them, you'll see. Hell, some of the troops, especially those who seem like the straight-arrow types, go ape shit over the attention they get from 'em. *Whamo!* Next thing you know after that first bout of horizontal aerobics, they convince themselves they've found true bliss, that instant-love stuff. No time at all, they wanna leave their heads and their wives and kids to shack up with the bitches."

Nate paused, wondering if his message was getting through. Satisfied it was, he continued. "Yeah, I'm sure you'll be meeting Ms "Juicy Lucy" soon, you bet ya. She'll make a point of it, matter of fact. She's definitely a looker...think she's even double-jointed, and she owns a set of high beams that'll blind you in a heartbeat! Yup, she'll give ya a class-A attack of the rubber knees big-time after she's done with ya." Nate rolled his eyes and let out a high whistle.

"One fine sexy thing she is, sort of like the barrack mascot, our own one-babe welcome wagon, matter a fact. Lord, if she gets her claws in you, she'll turn you any which way but loose...until she makes a move on the next new trooper, that is," Nate added with a laugh.

Dalton smiled knowingly. Seemed like an innate MSP problem no matter where you went.

"Ever been there Nate...with Juicy Lucy ?" Nate broke into a Cheshire grin and his head sunk back against the headrest. "Man's gotta do what a man's gotta do, Corp." Dalton laughed and nodded. "Yup, maybe so, Nate. Hey, while we're on the subject, what's the real deal with Terri, that perky lil cutie-pie PCO ? She seems, well, pretty friendly, to me at least."

Nate studied him for a moment. "Ahh, sweet Terri! Mmm, ya interested there by chance, Corp?" Unless one was faithfully married, who the hell wouldn't be, Dalton thought, as he shook his head otherwise. "Terri's a fox all right, but she recently had her pretty lil heart banged up real bad by a stud-puppy trooper who forgot he was married," Nate said. "She's a nice girl though, and most of the conscientious troops hold back from hitting on her. Yeah, ole Sloth has his hands full trying to keep the troops out of the radio room when she's working. Kurtz gets all over his ass about that. She's damn sure a surge for the libido, yes sir." Dalton nodded and eased away from the topic before Nate sensed any undue interest on his part.

Since it was his first experience working at a barrack with them, Dalton was curious about the barrack's two female troopers, and how they were holding up. Nate told him that of the two, one "sister" trooper was surprisingly sharp and quite capable of holding own amongst the male troopers. Diane Colson, the promising one, was a young military brat who was one deceptively tough and independent young woman. Easy on the eyes and disarmingly quiet, with short blond hair and fair blue eyes, her looks betrayed her rugged, spirited manner. At five foot eight, and just one hundred and twenty pounds on a lanky frame, Diane appeared to be no match for the average dirt ball. According to Nate, however, she'd already gained the respect of her group members who'd seen her in action several times.

"Damn! Her corporal told me that she kicked some serious ass last Friday night during a DWI arrest when the jerk resisted," Nate told him, "said the dude was almost twice as big as she was too, but she flipped him on the asphalt and had him stuffed and cuffed before he knew what the hell hit him."

Nate also said that Trooper Colson readily handled the male locker-room talk and the sexual innuendos which were endlessly tossed her way by her testosterone-laden fellow troopers. Nice, Dalton thought, a take-names and kick-ass female trooper who can handle herself.

According to Nate, Samantha Biddle, the other female trooper, was a short, slightly built, quiet mousey type who had trouble expressing herself. She also had a nagging tendency to hang back when things went south, and tears usually flowed more then adrenalin, whenever she found herself under stress. Unlike stoic Diane, she continuously whined and over rationalized her assortment of screw-ups.

Both female troopers had been at the "Q" Barrack for less then a year, however, and only time would tell if they'd be able to pour themselves into the road trooper mold. Nate thought that most of the troopers felt neutral about their "sister" troopers being on the macho job. Others, including many supervisors, considered them as novelties, or accidents waiting to happen. There was a natural tendency to be overprotective of them at times, a nagging aspect which caused some troopers undue concern for their safety, and on risky calls other troopers were genuinely wary when they realized their only available backup was a female trooper. For now, Dalton reserved passing judgment on them.

"Hey Nate,"any of the horn dogs messin' around with them yet?" he asked in jest. Nate rolled his eyes and chewed on his lower lip for a moment. "No names from my mouth Corp, but does a stuff dick on this job have any real conscience?" Yeah, Dalton mused, there were very few barriers that a normal, testosterone crammed trooper couldn't scale when it came to his raging hormones.

#

In the seventies, the MSP shared dual law-enforcement responsibilities with the Prince Georges County Police Department. The Geenbelt Barrack handled all MSP calls in PG County from north of Rt. 50, while the Forestville "L" Barrack handled MSP calls in the county south of the heavily traveled corridor. While both MSP installations normally had a combined total of perhaps ten road troopers working at any given shift on a good day, the Prince George's County PD, on the other hand, probably had forty plus officers available. As the predominant force, the county police handled the vast majority of calls.

Over the years, the tough, street-wise police force acquired a fierce reputation for hard-knuckle law enforcement. On the street level, it was commonly known that if you turned rabbit on a PG officer, and got caught, you'd win a sure ticket to the hospital afterward, a done deal for "resisting arrest." Being adjacent to crime-ridden DC, the officers hunkered down in the front-line trenches, straining to hold the thin blue line against the growing crime spilling over on their turf. They also had the assurance of expedient backup, a luxury not afforded to the troopers in rural Calvert County.

Soon enough, the new corporal got to observe a few of PG County's gendarmes in action. While most experiences were positive, others were just plain ugly. His first encounter was borderline farcical.

Dalton, with backup from Nate Odom, stopped a speeding car on the outer loop of the beltway one otherwise-uneventful evening. The driver, a young black man with straggly cornrows falling from his head, got agitated with both troopers after receiving a speed citation. Standing in front of his car with ticket in hand, he shook his fist, kicked gravel, and hurled streams of heated, uncharitable words their way. Shrugging it off as trivial grandstanding, both troopers started back towards their cruisers.

Suddenly, a PG County police cruiser, lights flashing, screeched to a skidding stop behind them. Moments later, an obviously piqued PG officer who was built like an ox, waved a hand at them before turning his glaring attention to the ranting black man who was still doing his roadside floor show. With his walkie-talkie clutched in hand, the officer hitched up his pants, squinted his eyes, and marched over to the clown. Dalton's eyebrows shot up when the beefy officer stepped hard on the man's jogging shoes with his boots to pin him firmly to the asphalt. "*Dip Shit!* Don't you ever talk to a Maryland State Trooper like that again! he screamed in his face.

The county Mounty slapped the startled man's face with the walkie-talkie's rubber antennae, emphasizing every other word with a stinging whack. After receiving a suitable number of "Yez suh's" from the panic-stricken punk, the officer released his right foothold clamp and calmly hooked his radio back on his gun belt. He smiled, crazy-like, then jerked his right leg up to knee the unsuspecting man squarely in the balls. With his breath gone and his manhood embracing throbbing pain, he gagged and bent over. When he raised his head, Dalton spotted the big snot bubble dripping from flared nostrils. Smirking like a renegade choirboy, the officer ordered the shaking black dude to apologize to the troopers for his detestable behavior. Right after he was allowed to leave, the grinning officer sauntered over to Dalton and Nate.

"Sorry to butt in here troops, but that's the way ya gotta handle them ass-holes! Can't take no shit from them jive heads round here, if you know what I mean." Chuckling to himself, the county Mounty departed, spinning tires and kicking up loose gravel in his wake. Flabbergasted, Dalton turned to Nate. "Nate...what the hell was *that?'* Nate merely shrugged his shoulders. "Aww, that wasn't nothing. They do that kind of shit out here all the time, Corp," he answered. "Wait til you see 'em break out the night-sticks some time. Things just go ape-shit crazy!"

In sharp contrast to the way the MSP handled such matters, citizen complaints really didn't hinder the P.G. county police in the early seventies. Realistically, the county had more than its share of badlands infested with the hardcore, cold-blooded types who, more than likely, deserved to be kept on the tight leash of police intimidation, Dalton inevitably learned. .

#

While it'd take a few years to earn a seasoned supervisor's stature, Dalton was slipping easily into the role. As exhibited by their monthly performance, he supervised a solid, productive group, and early on, he did his best to keep them that way by avoiding any unnecessary nitpicking or hassling. *That* unsavory chore was left to the second lieutenants, the assistant barrack commanders, who always had too much time on their hands. Much to the chagrin of many road troops, it'd take another decade before the superfluous 2nd lieutenant rank was phased out of the MSP rank structure. Although Dalton knew the rules and regulations like the back of his hand, he'd never be the type who strictly adhered to the exact lettering in the MSP bibles. There were more than enough robots like that in the agency already.

#

Damn the wrecks, though, the god-forsaken accidents. The shear volume of metro traffic dictated it, but coming from Calvert, Dalton found them hard to fathom. Granted, the vast majority were simple fender-benders, but one or two caused tremendous havoc and instant, massive backups, especially on the merry-go-round beltway. The Route One corridor and the treacherous Route 95 horseshoe curve were also accident prone, but the merry-go-round won top prize for being *the* collision magnet. Traffic problems spiraled drastically during the rush hours when the work-beetles madly dashed to and from their work sites. Work-beetles zipped on and off the ramps with the finesse of drunken maniacs warping out in a Chinese fire drill. Naturally, all this was exacerbated when the weather turned dog-ass ugly.

On those wretched days when Dalton was en route to his barrack from his Eastern Shore home, he developed the restless habit of switching the radio to the "Q" barrack's channel. Listening to the endless calls for troopers to respond to the 10-50s that sprouted up like pimples, was foreboding, an affirmation, that in their never-ending haste, many drivers were simply not concerned about each other's longevity.

On those days, troopers leapfrogged from one accident to the next. The rubbernecking motorists, particularly those on the opposite loop of the merry-go-round, caused even more wrecks. Innately curious about the possible glimpse of ghoulish carnage as they approached accidents scenes, many gawked as their cars rolled on, the drivers totally oblivious to the shouting troopers frantically waving hot, magnesium-dripping flares at them seconds before they creamed the vehicle in front. Dalton's group tallied up five unrelated rear-end collisions alone near one forgettable accident scene after an MSP helicopter landed on a cordoned-off stretch of the outer loop during a medevac mission.

164

And there were the motorcyclists, particularly the sporadic kamikaze hotshots who mindlessly zoomed their crotch-rockets in and out of heavy beltway traffic. Dashing wildly between eighteen-wheelers, buses and cars, they were nothing but road pizzas in the making. Crotch-rocket accidents were never pretty pictures.

Nate Odom had recently witnessed one on the beltway near Route 50. "Never seen anything like it, Corporal Bragg! There I was, in hot pursuit of a speeder in the inner loop fast lane, approaching Rt. 50, when all of the sudden...right in front of me, I see this guy wearing a helmet go fuckin' airborne! I kid you not Corp, he must a been hurled over a hundred feet in the air before he dropped like a rock," Nate told him excitedly. "Poor sucker was run over by two other cars and an eighteen-wheeler before things came to a screeching halt. Found his bike wedged under the damn big-rig too. Splatter City, blood and guts all over the place! Just about lost my cookies on that one!" There were very few barrack "Q" troopers whose guts didn't churn when a beltway 10-50 involving a motorcycle was broadcast over their radios.

While traffic enforcement at the Greenbelt Barrack was a priority, troopers also handled minor criminal cases, along with a scattering of the usual police-related calls. Most of the troopers, however, preferred playing in the traffic rather than writing up a stolen bike report or handling a domestic at the Pumpkin Hill Apartment complex near Laurel.

Ahhh, Pumpkin Hill! Undoubtedly, for the troopers and the county Mounties, Pumpkin Hill was indeed a deflating experience—a sprawling, low income, drug-infested, war zone of a substandard apartment complex inhabited largely by an indigent black populace which had little regard for those wearing badges. If one unknowing law officer entered the complex alone, it was usually a guaranteed ticket for a thorough butt stomping. It'd take a squad of officers, with one assigned to guard the cruisers, to assure minimum safety.

In his first months at the barrack, Dalton visited the unruly Pumpkin several times, and arrests were made on each occasion. The first responding officer to the complaint, usually a drunken-domestic call, duly waited for requested back-up on the road leading into the

165

shabby complex. The half-dozen officers or more proceeded to the call, mumbling to themselves as they passed piles of old, moldy furniture, discarded house wares and personal effects heaped along the sidewalks and curbs, evidence of recent evictions. Cruisers maneuvered past groups of leering adolescents mingling along the curbs, waiting to resume their open-market drug trade once the cops left. If the drug traffic was slow, they'd be there, waiting for something to get agitated about, in their lamentable existence in the woeful Pumpkin.

For the LE brothers and sisters, the norm was a quick dash up a flight or two of trash-strewn stairs, loud knocks on a door, and a thunderous greeting of: "Who the fuck called the po-leece?" shouted by a drunken boyfriend, husband, or an out-of-control hoochie-momma. The parties were separated, with the woman victim suddenly finding her voice and anger when she found herself surrounded by the police. Predictably, the flames of the domestic squabble rekindled, and like clockwork, the bored and rowdy, young toughs started gathering outside, waiting for an opportunity to join in.

Seasoned cops knew that getting people in handcuffs and out of the area post haste was always the underlined name of the game. If they lingered, taunts and bottles were thrown, officers got fired up, more back-up units were requested, and people ultimately started leaking serious blood. Still, despite the calamities, some troopers, and probably ninety percent of the PG County PD, appreciated the frequent adrenaline boosts the Pumpkin afforded them.

In addition to the Pumpkin Hill fiascos, there were also fun times on the late weekends for the troopers patrolling the Route One bar strip in the Laurel area. Drunken bravado and machismo amid the luring bar queens predictably deteriorated into fisticuffs and flying chairs at the Gatehouse or Turf-land bars. There was never any shortage of inebriated bar warriors who were hell-bent to put their asses on their shoulders. Ten-ten fight call broadcasts resonated from cruiser radios, jarring troopers awake. Adrenaline surged and blood pressures soared, as the troopers visioned what lay ahead of them. It was always entertaining to see the fight suddenly melt away from bar-warriors who unexpectedly came face to face with a snarling, snapping, German

Shepard K-9. Throwing competition to the wind, the fun was greatly enhanced if the PG County officers got on the scene first and gravitated into their renowned "shark feeding frenzy" before the troops arrived. Yup, there was nothing better than a good ole fight call, a chance for some serious night-stick time, or a few well aimed punches, to enhance camaraderie within the LE ranks.

#

Barrack "Q" also handled several "special assignments," along with its usual calls. Directing traffic at the Bowie Racetrack during the horseracing season was a mundane task. On the days the horses ran, the early shift was held over for several hours of overtime for the sole purpose of traffic direction. Depending on the mood of the crowd and the weather, things normally flowed well. Aside from the sporadic taunts or the rare flying beer can thrown by some dipsomaniac car passenger, the troopers on the tedious assignments suffered mostly from boredom.

A coveted assignment was the University of Maryland's home football games at College Park. The crowd-control and traffic assignments were high profile, showcase affairs for the twenty-plus troopers working them. In addition to a slew of MSP higher-ups, the news media and local politicians, Governor Mandel and entourage usually attended the spirited Terp games. So did an abundance of young and peppy female students.

Accordingly, troopers assigned to the Terp games had to look pretty, and the ceremonial Class A blouse with all its trappings was pretty enough. For normal police work, however, the blouses were too constrictive. The Sam Brown gun belt was positioned too high on the blouse keepers, making it difficult for a trooper to easily access his revolver or handcuffs, and the awkwardness was compounded when the protective vest was worn underneath. Although "Maryland's Finest" may have looked like proud peacocks, they felt more like stuffed turkeys. But on those stirringly crisp fall football days surrounded by hordes of titillating, babe-a-luscious eye-candy, the Class A uniform was nothing but perfect.

During Dalton's first assignment to a Terp football game, he'd been captivated by the spirit of the young college students. Both teams' marching bands, their banners swirling to rumbling drumbeats and brassy horns, competed with the delirious cheering of the Terp fans as Jerry Claiborne's crew, led by premier running back Lemuel Atwell, powered down field for an eventual win over hapless Duke. Except for minor disturbances among student fans, or a few testy motorists stuck in traffic jams, the football game assignments were relatively uneventful.

For Dalton, being back on the College Park campus brought back strong memories from his awkward pubescence years. Thirteen years before, he'd spent the better part of his weekend evenings with Theresa, his first full-time, cute-as-a-button, free-spirited sweetheart who was attending the university that fall in the tumultuous mid-sixties. Dalton remembered when he and Theresa, for good luck's sake, rubbed the bronze beak of Testudo (a.k.a. Myrtle the Fertile Turtle), the terrapin statue that basked eternally in front of the McKeldin library eclipsing the campus green. Right then and there, they vowed to always be there for each other, forever and ever, till the end of time itself. ("Gotta be with my Gingerbread Girl, chasing the moonbeams and living out dreams ...")

They also shared quality time at other campus spots too, like the dimly lit parking lot behind the Engineering Hall, on the cramped back seat of his dad's 1961 Renault, or on a blanket after dark on the mosquito-plagued golf course across the boulevard from Denton Hall. Dalton was heartbroken when their indefatigable, "for all eternity" love flickered out and died that fall. The breakup had been *the* reason for his immediate plunge into Uncle Sam's Army, too.

Hell, if they'd stayed together a year or so more, he'd probably have joined Theresa and all those other radical students she hung out with. Yeah, he could have stood shoulder-to-shoulder with them all, coughing in blossoming teargas clouds as they tore up Route 1 for ammunition. Macadam chunks were the ammo of choice that rained down upon the ranks of his future Maryland State Police comrades during the campus protests against the Viet Nam war. And if he'd been arrested, he would have missed out on the free Terrapin football and the press box chili too.

Months after the Terps football season, on a quiet midnight shift several days before his pending transfer back to Prince Frederick, Dalton parked his cruiser near the McKeldin library. Minutes later, he stood under dim light in front of Testudo, the university's mascot. He glanced around, making sure there were no witnesses. This would look ridiculous, but—hesitantly, he reached out with a hand. The bronze beak was stone cold when he rubbed it for the last time, willing the transfer of his aching, torn sentiments back into its possession where he knew they belonged, forever and ever. "They were right, *they're always right,'* he confided to the silent terrapin. "You can never go back."

#

Dalton inherited a new sergeant after "Sloth" Wykowski's retirement. In true form, on his last day while being driven home, Sloth grabbed the radio mic. "Q-31 Greenbelt," he gleefully shouted, "Sergeant Charlie E Wykowski, ID number 2713, is 10-42 (ending tour of duty)...*forever!* Sloth's sign-off message elicited a barrage of congratulations and keyed mic squelches from troopers who'd heard his final farewell.

With his flattop haircut, piercing brown eyes, and trim, athletic build, Sergeant Bill Bowman, Dalton's new supervisor, looked damned hardcore. His stern, impressive demeanor, however, belied his down-to-earth, common sense approach. Dalton found the eighteen-year MSP veteran to be an unpretentious, positive-minded supervisor who demanded an eight-hour a day, dedicated performance. His respect for Bowman grew immeasurably when Dalton also learned that he steadfastly avoided doing things exactly "by the book."

If things were calm during night shifts, Sgt. Bowman occasionally called Dalton in from patrol around 0200 hrs to relieve him as duty officer for a few hours. Rampant speculation running amuck in the barrack's rumormill had it that the married sergeant was visiting a sweetie who lived close by. Dalton never probed into Bowman's business, and besides, Bowman's night shift absences gave Dalton more quality time spent with Terri, the shift's cute and effervescent, super-efficient PCO. With her strawberry-blonde hair, pert nose, and a scattering of freckles dotting her high boned cheeks, working with the waif PCO was, admittedly, captivating. Dalton sensed something electric in the air between them whenever they worked together. They both, however, were totally certain that *he* was indeed married, a status which thwarted the exploration of the subtle overtures which teased them too often. Maybe in his next life on another planet, perhaps.

#

On the home front, Dalton finally persuaded Cindy that a bigger house was needed for their growing family, and Calvert County beckoned loudly to him as the place to live. Eventually, they found a charming three-bedroom split-level in bucolic Long Beach, a close-knit, bay-front community east of St. Leonard. With community beaches, wooded lots, and dozens of families with kids, Long Beach was ideal. Dalton felt that Cindy was genuinely pleased with the move, and despite his detestable shift work, he was hoping things would get better for them now. It was the insufferable shift work, the dark, lonely nights and the long evenings away from her and the kids that she'd grown to loathe so much. It was an ordeal she kept mostly to herself, but with each passing day, she was being numbingly drained from it.

Unbeknown to her husband, Cindy was feeling trapped in a life style she wasn't so sure she wanted to live in much longer. Dalton hoped she'd allow herself the opportunity to meet neighbors and make new friendships within the extended trooper 'family,' an aspect that wasn't readily available to her back on the Eastern Shore. He was almost oblivious about how much she truly resented the lack of support from others—friends and relatives all, while she stayed at home alone with their infant daughters.

When Dalton was home with them, things were lovey-dovey good. It was his job, the nature of the job itself that was the looming problem, and to her it seemed to be changing him, making him drift further away from them. She picked it up sometimes, when she'd catch him biting his lip, staring endlessly out the living room window, dazed or unfocused. There were also times when she'd find him sitting on the back porch with his head in his hands, rocking silently back and forth. Sometimes, she wished she could brush away some of her growing resentment just long enough to reach out to connect with him, to find out what was really going on deep inside his unsettled mind. For reasons known only to herself, she couldn't force herself to do it—nor would she ever urge her husband to leave the state police, *the job,* either.

And even though it bothered her deeply, she wouldn't dare pester him about spending less time with his close MSP buddies. Faithfully staying in touch with his Prince Frederick colleagues was an obsession with him, she realized. If he wasn't hunting or fishing with them, he'd be out spending hours away from home, gallivanting and clinking beer bottles with Marty Metzger, Gary, the irascible Colby Merson and others. For now, she resigned herself to hold on to where she was in her life, but for how much longer, she wasn't quite sure.

#

Dalton's first winter at the "Q" barrack was a tough one, with several heavy snowstorms wreaking tremendous havoc throughout the Washington metro area. Dalton was working the night shift filling in as the duty officer, when a wretched snowstorm battered the area. As the inevitable deluge of phone calls and radio traffic surged, he and Terri strained to keep up. Phone buttons burst alive with orange flashes until all incoming lines were blazing. Press the button and another strained voice—and one more problem to be dealt with by too few troopers.

Suddenly, the MSP radio crackled: "Q-27, College Park! Q-Queen 27...I've been involved in a departmental 10-50...minor PI, on the inner loop near route ninety-five! Need a supervisor to respond ASAP!" *SHIT* ! Dalton matched his PCO's shocked look. He quickly dialed a number, and within minutes Sergeant Bowman was back at the barrack and Dalton was en route to investigate his fifth departmental.

At 0215 hrs, on a lightly traveled beltway in the middle of a snowstorm, it was simply a fluke. Trooper Scott Davidson, a quiet, dependable junior road-pounder, had responded to the scene of a minor property damage accident involving two cars. Blinded by heavy snowfall, a motorist had drifted onto the beltway shoulder to crash into an abandoned car. Trooper Davidson arrived minutes later and parked his cruiser in back of both vehicles that were now on the grassy area next to the shoulder. Later, while filling out the accident report, a wayward car rear-ended the cruiser, slamming it into the two vehicles

171

in front, resulting in a four car departmental accident! While the motorist sitting beside him escaped injury, Trooper Davidson's back had been wrenched hard and he was in pain.

The driver of the car that struck the cruiser, an off-duty DC fireman, sustained only minor injuries. He'd become mesmerized by the cruiser's rotating dome light, the only thing he could see through the falling snow, and his car followed his eyes. Of course it hadn't helped that he was also stone drunk and later charged with DWI, either. Under the circumstances, the departmental accident was a sure-fire cluster-fuck. It was late afternoon before Dalton finally broke free to return home for some badly needed sleep.

When he dragged himself down the barrack stairs to leave, F/Sgt. Petty ambushed him with a solid sucker punch to the shoulder before telling him his group had done a great job during the snow emergency. Relieved, Dalton thanked him, but immediately noticed the disgruntled look on the top kick's face. *Not Good.* Petty scowled and shook his head. "Hate to piss on your parade, Corp, but watch yourself around that ass-hole Kurtz, OK? Guess I don't have to tell ya he's been riding your ass hard ever since you got here, chaffing at the bit with every little piss-ant problem you or your shift run into. Just do yourself a favor and just let things slide off your back whatever happens, hear?" A parting punch painfully reinforced Petty's advice.

Dalton had been the recipient too many times of Kurtz's demeaning tirades over petty problems. Kurtz had become his relentless tormentor, and while Kurtz's acidic tongue-lashings were duly absorbed with a stiff upper lip, Dalton was hard-pressed to keep his cool with him.

During the last two night shifts Sergeant Bowman took sick leave, and Dalton filled in as the duty officer. Adverse winter weather continued, and conditions were hectic on both nights, leaving Dalton scant time to work on the departmental accident paperwork. To the chagrin of those within the MSP tiers who held the mentality that, "every report about anything, should have been turned in the day before it happened," the departmental paperwork was still far from being finished.

Early the next morning, during the last hour of the night shift, Dalton was in the duty officer's pit discussing a case with Nate Odom when Lieutenant Kurtz hastily waddled into the barrack lobby. Dalton saluted him sharply before hitting the buzzer to the side door to let him in. With his disheveled uniform, tousled hair, and bulging, bloodshot eyes, Kurtz looked as if he'd fallen off the wrong side of bed. His rare presence at the barrack at that hour was ominous, and Dalton sensed trouble. Continuing his discussion with Nate, Dalton anxiously shot glances at Kurtz who was vigorously poring over the barrack phone logs and activity sheets in the radio room. After scrutinizing the records, Kurtz disappeared into his office. Minutes later, on the rampaging warpath, the 2nd Lt suddenly rounded the corner and strode into the duty officer's pit.

"Uhhh...Corporal Bragg, I want to know where the *hell* the reports for Q-27's departmental are!" Kurtz demanded in a shrill voice. Taken off guard, and in the midst of a discussion with his senior trooper, Dalton paused to collect his thoughts. Looking Kurtz squarely in the eyes, he quietly told him that the paperwork hadn't been done yet, due to his shift being swamped with calls during the previous two nights. Without a word, Kurtz whirled around. In a loud, booming voice, he asked Terri, the PCO, if the night shift had *really* been busy the last two nights. Taken aback, Terri squeaked out a barely audible "Yes," and nodded her head. Kurtz shot her a hard look, gnashed his teeth, and then glared at the corporal.

With a guttural "Heh," he brushed by Dalton and sat down at the duty officer's desk to thumb through the control cards marking the group's activities for the last two nights. After several long, unsettling minutes, he shoved the cards back into the file box and flew up from the desk with a sneer. Crossing his arms, Kurtz strutted over to Dalton and planted his jowly mug inches from his face.

"*Corporal Bragg...*I can't see where you and your group were so damn busy at all! Need a better excuse than that, pal," he blared at him. "And another thing, I don't like the idea that a Corporal on this job thinks he can outright *lie* to me either!"

It hit him like a thunderbolt! Dalton saw Kurtz's lips moving, knew he was shouting at him too, but for some weird reason he was oblivious to what was being said as internal sirens blared. What he *did* realize was that his fists were balled, his right leg was starting to shake, and he felt a warm flush of blood in his cheeks. Nobody—*Nobody* in the Maryland State Police had ever impugned his truthfulness, had ever dared to call him a liar before, and he was stunned! To emphasize whatever he was ranting about, Kurtz jerked up his stubby index finger and started shaking it in Dalton's face.

Dalton felt tiny drops of spittle sprinkle his face and he smelled sour breath. He fixated on the large black mole under Kurtz's bulbous nose, lining it up for a ready reference point to land a balled fist on. From somewhere far away, he heard a loud, demanding voice. "Lieutenant! Get your *damn* finger out of my face, or I'm going to ram it up your *ass* and beat the shit out of you!" Dalton glared at the finger that had suddenly stopped waving in mid-air, then reverted his eyes to the ugly mole. The voice repeated itself, this time the warning issued through a clenched jaw. (One, two, three, ready or not, here it comes, you ass wipe!)

Kurtz's finger slowly dropped, and Dalton sensed the 2nd Lt's growing apprehension, just as Nate forced himself between them to shoulder them apart. "Get in my Office! *Now!*" Kurtz bellowed at him before turning to leave. "*Screw you Kurtz* ...I'm not your damn dog!" Dalton heard the strange voice thunder back as the door to Kurtz's office slammed shut. Fighting hard to control his mounting rage, Dalton turned and started in that direction.

Realizing that his corporal was just about to cross the line and commit an ultimate MSP taboo, Nate grabbed Dalton by the shoulders. In a quiet voice, the senior trooper slowly talked him down until Dalton could almost hear what he was saying. "Go home Corp, you just go home, man. I'll handle this...I'll talk with Kurtz later after things settle down some. It ain't nothing man...ain't nothing to lose your job over." Still livid, Dalton took a few deep breaths and shook his head in disbelief, trying hard to calm down while his all-knowing senior trooper stood by. 'Thanks Nate, I owe you big-time," he finally muttered before leaving the duty officer's pit.

Only when he hit the Calvert County line, did Dalton start to feel better. Needed time had elapsed, and for the moment, Kurtz was fading from his archenemy status. It took more than an hour working with the heavy weights, followed by two beers and a half tab of Sominex, before the image of Kurtz's ugly black mole finally faded away to be replaced with blessed sleep.

Early the next morning, and much to Dalton's surprise, the 2nd Lieutenant, coffee in hand, cordially invited him into his office before the shift change. Kurtz forced a smile, pointed to the fabric chair next to his desk, and politely asked Dalton to have a seat..."if you don't mind." After several awkward, conversational gambits, Kurtz coughed and cleared his throat. "Yesterday we had us a ticklish situation. Umm...maybe too early in the morning, and both of us were tired, and,...uhh...*we* really shouldn't have been talking to each other like that, OK?"

Dalton thought it was a small, uncharacteristic gesture, almost apologetic in fact. His eyes involuntarily shifted to the black mole under Kurtz's nose again. I'd still like to beat the shit out of your sorry ass, the silent "id" voice in Dalton's head screamed at the 2nd Lt—over the whispered pleas of his outmatched superego voice. After playing nice with each other for a while, Dalton left Kurtz's office feeling somewhat placated. From that point on, Dalton thought Kurtz was diffident to him, almost too polite at times. Consequently, there were no more confrontations.

Word of the incident spread like wild fire through the barrack, of course, and several troopers and fellow supervisors privately commended Dalton for standing up to the brashly contentious 2nd Lt who thrived on making their jobs so miserable. Dalton refrained from discussing the incident, hoping that, with time, the unpalatable affair would drift away to become a vague memory some bright, sunny day.

#

Several months later, on his last day at the "Q" barrack, Dalton was summoned to Lieutenant Kurtz's office. In the presence of the smug-looking 2nd Lt and Lt Harrell, the departing corporal was given his half-year evaluation score. Dalton forced himself to stay cool as his eyes browsed through the scores of adverse comments. With a blank expression, he signed the form. He'd been expecting retribution from Kurtz, and now that he'd received it, he was unfazed. Dalton's rating was extremely low—the lowest rated corporal in the entire Washington Metro troop. Poker-faced, he saluted the black mole on Kurtz's face first, and then gave a final salute to Lt. Harrell. When the smirking Kurtz stood up and reached out for a parting handshake, Dalton vise-gripped his hand and smiled inwardly when Kurtz's eyes widened and a faint grimace stole his smirk. When he left the office, all Dalton realized was that his long year at the merry-go-round barrack was over. The instant wave of relief nearly drowned him.

Dalton had just turned the corner after signing out for the last time, when it hit him once again, harder then ever before. "Best one yet, Corp. Didn't even see it coming did you?" shouted F/Sgt. Petty. Eyes watering, Dalton rubbed his shoulder where Petty had just stiff knuckled him, trying hard to eke out a smile. "Yeah, First Shirt, I knew I probably wouldn't make it out of here without you punching my ass good-by. Much appreciated," he shot back with a lame smile.

Like a supportive big brother, Petty smiled, put an arm over Dalton's shoulder and walked him to the door. "Don't really give a rat's ass what the idiots with the bars on their collars might think, but for a green corporal, you did pretty damn good in my book, son," he told him. "Just don't let anybody on this job get to you, no matter how hard things get. Ain't worth it, hear?" Signaling his appreciation, Dalton smiled back at Petty and snapped an exaggerated salute. Damn good man, he thought to himself. They don't come much better than him on this job.

Petty looked over his shoulder, diligently searching for any loose pairs of ears that might be around. Satisfied, his eyes lit up and a devious smile crossed his face as he leaned in closer to Dalton. "Psst...but I gotta know something, Corp...it's been killing me. Now that you're leaving, you gotta tell me, just between us," he whispered coyly. "I know you got some mud for your turtle while you were here, sure's I'm standing in front of you. But, but, I just gotta know, OK? Did you and sexy babe Terri ever get it on with each other?"

(Purgatory Ridge)

The veteran sergeant stood up and duly awarded himself with a seventh inning, retirement party stretch. He flexed his hands and stomped the ground to chase away some of the numbness. His blood moving again, Dalton lit the cigar that had died an hour before, then dumped out the stale dregs of his last beer. Didn't matter if it was ice-cold or even warm sometimes, he savored the taste of almost any beer. Those flat, metallic dregs, however, were the pits. He puffed twice on the rum river crook, allowing the familiar smoke aroma to coax his memory back to where it'd abruptly strayed from. He started to smile, then chuckled out loud again when a drifting remembrance appeared.

Like most troopers, Dalton found that special solitary haven in a barrack's area where, however briefly, he could catch his breath, sip a coffee, and maybe puff on a cheap cigar. His "Q" barrack refuge was a closed ramp of the outer loop near northbound Interstate 95. Several hundred feet down the ramp, a bridge spanned a deep ravine and a small, trickling stream. It was there, parked on the bridge and ringed by tall trees, away from the barrack and the clamorous traffic, where he'd usually grasp a few blessed moments of solace.

During his third week at the "Q" barrack, on a slow, Sunday early shift, Dalton was up on the bridge in the warm sun, propped against the cruiser with a cigar in hand, his mind adrift in reflections. From the corner of an eye, he spotted the station wagon barreling out of the curve on the ramp behind him. So much for cherished serenity. Dalton was stumped when the station wagon slowed down and stopped next to him. Out of the car bounced a tall, slim-built, longhaired brunette with a big smile on her pretty face. She was barefoot, and she wore a skimpy pair of old cutoff topped by a sparkling white, skin-tight T-shirt that barely obscured her ample cleavage. For a woman he judged to be in her early thirties, she was nothing short of tongue-hanging tantalizing. Too much serenity is toxic.

"Hi! You must be the barrack's new corporal, right?" She chirped. "Nice seein' ya...I'm Lucy. One of your buddies told me I'd probably bump into you here sometime, and today it is, sure as shootin'."

Dalton let out a nervous cough and stooped down to retrieve the cigar that had just fallen through his fingers. He felt his face flush instantly, a dead giveaway! Hips swaying magnificently, Lucy sashayed over and planted herself in front of him. She raised her elbows up high, allowing her fingers to push loose strands of hair behind her ears, a teasing move that accentuated her cleavage to the high-beam level. Damn if she didn't have this act down pat, Dalton realized. *Agghh!* And Nate was right, she was one hot-looking number. His eyes searched desperately, hoping to spot someone, anyone, who'd shoot him to end his misery. Lucy slowly chewed her gum and beamed at him as she swayed back and forth in a well-rehearsed manner.

Conversation with her staring at him was awkward at first, but Dalton warmed up quickly. Lucy made sure to rest her hand lightly on his forearm every time she laughed at one of his harebrained jokes. Somehow, during their animated chatter, he'd been able to muster just enough functional control over the weaker side of his brain. Except for her soft brown, alluring eyes, he'd been able to partially deflect her sensuality. Dalton only prayed that she hadn't yet noticed how his weak side, the infatuated side, had already caused an involuntary reflex below his gun belt.

With a major attack of vacillation on his part, he eventually, *regrettably*, told her that he was one of those rare, authentic, MSP "married-guy types." Lucy smiled mischievously and embraced him in a comfortably long hug before she strutted back to her car. Before leaving, she playfully snatched the pen from his shirt pocket and scribbled her phone number on the inside of a matchbook. With a spirited laugh, she shoved the pack of matches down his shirt, allowing her fingers to roam teasingly across his upper chest for a lingering moment.

"Just in case you ever want to join me for a beer...or maybe more," she purred with a foxy wink. "By the way, new corporal-guy, looks like you got some nice altitude workin' down there, don't ya?" she asked, confirming what was obviously a swelling problem under his belt. Immediately after she left, Dalton retrieved the matches, and nervously lit up another cigar. For some reason, it didn't taste quite right at the moment, so he flipped it over the railing and watched it splash into the stream below. With a deep sigh, he lit another match and stuck it under the match-pack to cremate Lucy's phone number. This just *had* to be a set-up!

He never told anyone at the barrack about it, preferring to wait it out to see who'd be the first trooper to give it up. Either they were all superb actors, or they didn't know zilch about the encounter, but Dalton was never able to discover if the troops were aware of his intoxicating introduction to the barrack's favorite mascot.

"Yeah you dumb ass, she was *hot*. Guess most of the guys would say you really screwed that one up big-time," Sgt. Bragg muttered to himself. 'No doubt about it, if you'd a been a tad bit more heathen, you'd a been on her case in a New York minute!" He blew out another mutilated smoke ring, casually wondering what ole Juicy Lucy was doing with her life now. Probably been married through a few troopers and has a dozen or so kids by now, he thought. He slowly meandered over to the edge of the cliff to catch the warm breeze from the east, which had picked up enough to nudge a few dusky clouds his way.

"Damn! Kurtz was a real ball-breaker though, wasn't he?" the sergeant groused to the osprey lazily drifting back and forth on the air currents high above. He cleared his throat and saluted his memory with a good spit. Too bad he'd experienced Kurtz's wrath when he'd been a green corporal. If the simple 2nd Lt had ragged him out like that years later when he was a sergeant, he'd have probably pulled out his gun and chased him around the barrack—exactly what an infuriated, half burnt-out sergeant did to his asinine, ball-busting first sergeant at the Glen Burnie barrack, once upon a long time ago.

Naw, fatso Kurtz hadn't been all that bad. Just one obtrusive actor amongst several who performed dubiously on the MSP center stage, that's all. "Catch this one Kurtz!" he yelled out, whirling to sight the Beretta on the beer can he'd just tossed out. *"Blam!"* The perforated Kurtz memorial beer spun end over end to drop off the edge of the cliff and out of his memory forever.

The retiring sergeant holstered his smoking Beretta. He rummaged through his pack, brought out another beer, and ceremoniously popped the top. "This one's for you, Nate. Just wish I could have been there for you man...just wish I'd known," he announced to the blue sky above. He held the can up high over his head before taking another a hearty swig of the lukewarm brew. Trooper First Class Odom's death, coming several years after Dalton's Greenbelt barrack debut, troubled him, since he hadn't been aware of Nate's being diagnosed with terminal lung cancer. For reasons deep within his guarded entity, Dalton hadn't attended his funeral, preferring a long reflective hike in the woods instead.

The sergeant took another sip of beer and rubbed his glazed eyes. "Damn cigar smoke," he quipped facetiously. With his eyes fixed on the faraway shoreline across the bay, he steeled himself and returned to his retirement party mood again. "Shit Sarge, Nate would have laughed his butt off at your simple-ass self cryin' tears in your beer. Knock it off troop!" He took another stogie out, decided not to light it, but shoved it in his mouth anyhow before easing himself back down against the tree trunk. Returning to his fraternal Prince Frederick Post and rustic, tranquil Calvert County was like Christmas in August that year. Things would inevitably get better, in his personal life and in the MSP for sure. Dalton's return was cause for celebration, and the impetuous Colby Merson, the epitome of eternal effervescence, was destined to play the starring role in it.

#

With an elated Gary Rephan rounding out the trio, the musketeers sloshed down draft beers at the Calverton Room before Colby adamantly insisted on a quick jaunt down the road to the Frog Pond in St. Leonard for a nightcap. Ten minutes later, they were there, perched on bar stools with their hands wrapped around frosted mugs. While Dalton and Gary were feeling pretty mellow, it was obvious that the beaming Colby, cigarette drooping from his mouth, was merely getting primed for his party mode.

It was a slow night with few customers, and Tony Mattingly, the rail-thin, cock-sure bartender, was downright bored—until he recognized the threesome straggling through the front door. A master of jive, Tony filled their ears while they slurped his beers. With his two favorite cohorts on one side, and two decent looking, off-duty nurses seated on his other side, Colby was feeling like a pig rooting in a mountain of truffles. To ramp things up, Colby switched from beer to double-shot vodka tonics, his favorite late-night bracers. Soon, he was serenading them all, wailing his way through the verses of Kenny Roger's *The Gambler*. Squinty-eyed, and with a cigarette dangling from the corner of his mouth, Colby sang a horrendous rendition, which made his cohorts grimace, and brought tears to the eyes of the hysterically laughing nurses.

To clam him up, Tony waved his hands in Colby's face and shouted out a challenge, stopping him in mid-verse. "Hey Kenny, you country troubadour, you...wanna go shot-to-shot with me partner? Mano-a-mano...on the house? I choose the medicine?" he beckoned. Colby tilted his head and shot him a queer look, then broke out in a shit-faced grin. "Youzzz jjjust git dem lil glasesss zzout, my man...I can drrrink yo scrrraaawny asss zzzunder a taaable yenny ole day. Brrrring it on bitchhh!"

Knowing from experience that Colby was now beyond reasoning, Dalton and Gary just sipped their beers and watched. It reminded Dalton of a Mexican cantina scene in a Clint Eastwood spaghetti western. Tony poured a shot from a long-necked whiskey bottle, then slapped both drinks down on the bar. With a nod of his head, he locked bloodshot eyes with Colby's for a moment before they threw back their heads and gulped down the liquor. After draining the shot glasses, they slammed them back down on the bar. *Whap!* The last round, probably round five or six, Gary figured, was a humdinger. With both contestants' heads rolling side-to-side, Tony clumsily poured a clear liquor concoction into and around the shot glasses. After several attempts with a lighter, he managed to set the drinks, and a section of the bar top afire.

Dalton and Gary gaped at each other, as Colby and the leering bartender picked up the flaming toasts. "Thisss shhhiits tooo gggood furrr *meee*," Colby blurted out, "but I'll drrink itt anywaaazz!" Tony blew out the flame and downed his shot. Colby closed his eyes and lifted the flaming tumbler towards his gaping mouth. Alerted, the amused nurse sitting next to him pursed her lips and quickly leaned over to blow the flame out just before Colby guzzled it. "Damn nice blow-job," Gary whispered to Dalton, nudging him with an elbow.

Tony shattered his shot glass when he slammed it back down. Shaking his head, he staggered back and crashed into the cash register behind him. "Looksss like yoouzz can hhhoold your sssttufff pprettty good," he spouted out to Colby with a maniacal smirk. Pounding the bar top with his fists, Colby hooted and bounced up and down on the bar stool. Suddenly, he stopped, deep in thought. With a sly grin, he reached into his pants pocket and brought out a small aluminum-foil packet.

"Neeed ussss sssome ba..ba...balooonzzzz to cellbrate," he blurted out, slowly pulling a yellow condom from the packet. He puckered his lips and blew into the condom's open end, turning it into an oblong "balloon.' Satisfied, he knotted it, and then slapped the inflated rubber up in the air in the direction of the two nurses who were bent over laughing. The makeshift balloon was gaily bounced back and forth between them until one of the nurses finally popped it with her lit cigarette. With a loud grunt, Colby hoisted himself up to a standing position on top of the bar.

As the background music blared from the jukebox, Colby positioned himself directly in front of the nurses and started gyrating his hips in a horribly exaggerated version of the twist. Going for the gold, Tony revived himself and made a wild dash toward the albino version of a lame Chubby Checker. In a surprisingly deft move, he grabbed Colby's waist belt and yanked down hard. Flabbergasted, with his mouth frozen open and his pants and underwear down at his ankles, Colby gaped down at himself with hazed eyes to see his flaccid man-of-war beckoning vainly to the wide-eyed nurses seated below.

"Jeezzuusss!" he wailed, reaching down to grab his pants. Colby teetered back and forth, arms thrust in front of him, in a vain balancing attempt. "Ahhh...shhiiit!" With an ugly, bone-jarring *Splat*, Colby fell off the bar and landed in a heap on the dirty tile floor.

In a low animal voice, he moaned and rolled around in true agony. Dalton and Gary shot off their barstools to help him, but Colby pushed them away when they tried to yank up his pants. "Colby!" Gary shouted out, "You OK, man? Where's it hurt, huh Colby?" Looking duly concerned, Gary knelt down next to him. Colby belched in his face. "Where's zzzzt hurt, Garreeee? I'mzz hurtin all over, b-b-but I think I really sssscrewed up the ffront of my baaack or sumpin like ttthat," Colby answered with a shit-eating grin. Gary grabbed Colby's right elbow while Dalton latched onto the other one, and, at the three-count, they hoisted him to his wobbly feet. Colby swayed back and fourth, and his head lolled on his chest as he slipped both arms over his buddies' shoulders.

Before Dalton and Gary could lug their star performer pal to the door, Tony yelled at them. "Howzzzz bout one furrr da rrrroad, *saaaay trroopzz?*" Tony's nightcap summons sent a shock wave through Colby, giving him a second wind. With a loud whoop, he flexed his strong arms and broke free to scramble back to the bar. Dalton and Gary traded shrugs then joined him. They'd seen the wild glint in Colby's eyes, and wisely decided to put off the inevitable confrontation that would come soon enough. After they'd finished off several more one-for-the-road beers, Tony, feeling pangs of nausea fast approaching, turned on the bright overhead lights and hustled everyone out into the night.

Dalton and Gary herded Colby in the direction of their cars parked across the street. In the middle of the one-lane country road, Colby abruptly stopped and turned around. Spotting the neon moon hanging low in the southern sky, he dropped down to the road on all fours, jerked his head back, and howled like a coyote at the glowing sphere. Grinning ear to ear, he forced himself up on shaky legs and stood up straight on his tippy toes to blow a few sloppy kisses at the two nurses passing by. "Y'all gggit hhhome sssaafely...hhhear!" Colby cried out to them, gyrating his hips for emphasis.

"Come on, Colby, you dumb ass! We're taking ya home to your wife," Gary yelled at him, fully aware that Colby intended to drive himself home. "Ssscreww tthat sssshhit, uuu's basssturds! Colby roared. Gary grabbed Colby's car keys as he tried to force them into the driver's door lock. Colby bellowed loud in drunken protest and struggled to wrest them back. Moments later, there were three off-duty troopers wrestling in a pile, smack dab in the middle of Route 2, the main road bisecting sleepy St. Leonard. Colby fought hard, hitting and kicking his fellow troopers as they dragged him off the road and tried to stuff him into the back seat of Gary's VW. Eventually, the battle was won, after Colby slipped and his head struck the doorframe. Slightly battered, with a thin trickle of blood oozing down his face, Colby was wrestled into the back seat where he promptly puked and passed out.

Dalton followed Gary down the road to Colby's place, a bungalow nestled in the woods near Drum Point. They quietly carried their passed-out pal into his house, leaving him slumped against the downstairs bathroom toilet, facedown, ready for action. Colby was a total mess. Blood from the minor head cut and several other road-rash abrasions, was smeared all over his face and clothes, and the front of his polo shirt was coated with a thick layer of coagulated vomit. Gary and Dalton felt confident they were almost home free as they started tiptoeing their way out.

Colby's wife almost knocked them down in her haste to get at them. "What the hell have you two dumb asses done to him?" she shrieked. In shocked silence, they could answer only with sheepish grins. "RRRRachelle, there's more to this story than what you see, woman...b-but we'll let Colby tell you how he...uhh...won the fight later, OK?" Gary uttered shakily. Ever so slowly, the two musketeers backed toward the patio side door.

Colby's wife squinted her eyes and gnashed her teeth at them. "Yeah, you should see the other guy," Dalton croaked hoarsely, making a grab for the doorknob. As they dashed out, she went ballistic, shrieking and cursing at the hapless musketeer they'd left behind. "Son a bitch is evil as a banshee with an in-grown toenail, and stronger than shit when he gets all screwed up like that," Gary muttered on their way up the road. "Yeah, and I'm just tickled shitless he's our best bud too," Dalton grumbled back, rubbing his aching shoulder with his bruised hand.

Chapter 8

DENTS IN THE ARMOR

On another bone-chilling, mid-February morning in Calvert, Corporal Dalton Bragg was minutes away from starting his early shift. It'd been almost a year since his transfer back to the re-designated Prince Frederick *Barrack*, and while the rough-idling cruiser struggled to warm up, Dalton reflected back on the surprisingly smooth transition. His year at the metro Greenbelt Barrack had been tough, but it had also afforded him experience and time to scramble his supervisory act together. Around his PF colleagues, Dalton's climb to the corporal rank, not just one of the guys anymore, was readily accepted.

Yes Sir, both on the job and presumably at home, things were running A-OK. That he could radio in a 10-41 (beginning tour of service) message from his driveway, and be at the barrack minutes later, was true bliss itself. He smiled and took a sip of hot coffee, then tuned the radio to catch the WTOP news.

While Dalton savored the last dregs of strong coffee, six miles away, in the bedroom of a modest brick in the tranquil woods near Adelina, lives were drastically unraveling. Finally, inevitably, after months of wavering, Missy Parran was leaving her boyfriend. Against the persistent advice of her distressed family and friends, Missy had nonetheless persevered and stayed with him. During the last few months, however, it had all turned dark and ugly. Fiery quarrels evolved into beatings, and she found it hard to make up excuses about her frequently swollen black eyes or the occasional split lip.

Still, she'd hung on, hoping and praying for him to get better, for her love to make it so. This very morning, she'd startled herself awake, shaken by the stark reality that her boundless prayers hadn't been enough. Despite her steadfast support and love, all she could possibly give of herself, he'd steadily mutated into a deranged, unknown entity reeking of cold malevolence.

After the last beating, which left her with a gouged cheek and a badly bruised arm, she knew it was hopeless. Despite the fear, she had to save herself and her son, had to leave now—and forever. Yes, she'd take Matt, her six year-old son, and stay with an aunt in PG. County until she could shuffle her act together again. Last night, after breaching the subject with her boyfriend, he once again broke down and begged her to stay, sobbed to her through a river of tears. It'd be different this time, he'd prove it to her, she'd see. When he threatened to shoot himself in front of her, she got rattled enough to acquiesce yet one more time. Tossing aside strident pleas from relatives, Missy caved in and spent her last night with him.

They got up together, and while he was in the kitchen making a pot of coffee, she dashed to her son's bedroom. Together, they hastily jammed clothes and some overnight items in a suitcase. From the kitchen, however, her vigilant boyfriend had overheard her talking in a strange hushed voice. Alerted, he peered into Matt's bedroom and saw them packing clothes. And in that irrevocable instant, he knew it was all over.

The final link in his wretched life, the last stable factor he still clung to in his plummeting insanity, his last hope of hopes, and now she was heartlessly deserting him, forcing him to face his ultimate horror of aloneness and total alienation? No, he'd never go that end route alone. She'd go too! He screamed out a blood-curdling "N*ooo!*" and stomped down the hall toward the living room. She trembled violently, but steeled herself enough to quietly urge her terrified son to stay calm. Slamming the crammed suitcase shut, she yanked it off the bed. Tightly gripping Matt's hand, Missy started down the hallway.

By then, her boyfriend was frantically pushing buckshot and rifled slug rounds into the magazine of a twelve-gauge shotgun. After loading it to capacity, he stuffed a pocket with shells and slowly pivoted toward the kitchen. His contorted face was an ugly mask; cold black eyes drawn to slits, his jaw clenched tight with bared teeth.

Yes, Donny Roberts, the former Prince Frederick Barrack trooper, had finally slipped over the edge.

The caffeine was just kicking in when Dalton arrived at the barrack. After autographing the sign-in log, he saluted and exchanged greetings with F/Sgt. Bane and a yawning Sgt. Long, the day shift duty officer. In the trooper's room, several goggle-eyed night-shift troopers were bent over desks, straining to finish up loathed paperwork. He drifted over to the Calvert Control Center and comically saluted the PCO's manning the radios. After greeting the bunch with his usual goofball gibes, he rummaged through his crammed mailbox. Amazing how much infernal paperwork he'd find jammed in the box after a few days leave.

He poured some lukewarm, black-as-tar coffee into a Styrofoam cup and took the mountain of paperwork back to the lieutenant's vacant office. When he passed Pearl's office, Dalton made sure he smiled and wished the barrack's cantankerous secretary a good day. Although Pearl was annoyingly meddlesome when she got herself embroiled in matters beyond her secretarial tasks, most knew the outspoken, easy-on-the-eyes, young at heart scribe, had a heart of gold. Apparently today was starting out A-OK for her, since she gave Dalton a cheery smile. Nice. No trademark curses—yet.

Dalton was reviewing reams of accumulated forms when he heard shouting from the control center. From the shrill tone of PCO Bo Grady's voice, he knew instantly that something big was going down. *Great!* The wall radio monitor spat out the familiar emergency tone alert, immediately followed by the broadcast:

"We have a reported shooting at the Roberts place off Mac's Hollow road in Adelina! I repeat, a shooting at the Roberts place in Adelina. Information available is that one person is down! All units acknowledge!"

His pulse rocketing, Dalton dashed out to his cruiser. Premonition told him who the shooter was, but he only hoped he was wrong. Additional frenzied broadcasts had all but confirmed it was Donny Roberts, his friend and former MSP shift mate.

(Follow-up investigation determined that a next-door neighbor had heard loud screams coming from Roberts' place. Badly shaken, she peered nervously from her kitchen window to see Missy, Robert's girlfriend, run screaming from his house. Roberts was running furiously behind her with the shotgun. Suddenly, he stopped, aimed the long gun, and fired. The blast knocked the young woman down. Missy rolled over, tried to get up, and then collapsed. As the horrified witness watched, Roberts calmly strolled over and stood next to his girlfriend. Sensing burning eyes, Roberts slowly swiveled his head and stared eerily at the shocked face in the kitchen window. Zombie-like, he smiled crazily at her, before turning back to shoot Missy again—at pointblank range. Laughing hysterically, he stood over her until the death throes ceased. Satisfied, Roberts turned and calmly walked back to his house. Moments later, the horrified witness found her voice and called the control center.)

Dalton monitored the bust radio chatter as he sped toward Adelina. He heard clipped, nervous dialogue against a shrill background of wailing sirens whenever radio mics were keyed. If his fellow troopers and deputies shared what was going through his racing mind, that the familiar ex-trooper had finally gone berserk, he could well imagine their trepidations. His soared already!

Trooper Larry Wilson excitedly radioed he was on the scene. Seconds later, Dalton heard Wilson's high-strung voice advised that he'd located a female subject DOA from gunshot wounds. After arriving, Dalton glimpsed the young woman's body. Although she was blood-splattered and awkwardly sprawled, she still had a peaceful look on her pretty face.

The crime scene was secured pending the arrival of ID personnel, and F/Sgt. Bane and Lt. Black, the new barrack commander, soon arrived to set up a command post. Several troopers and deputies were directed to set up a safe perimeter around Robert's house, while others evacuated nearby residents. According to one distraught witness, Roberts was last seen walking toward deeper woods, and stumbling beside him was a young boy who tightly held his hand. In his other arm, Roberts lazily cradled a shotgun.

In those early MSP days without SWAT teams, several old-salt troopers performed the nerve-wracking search of Roberts' house. A coordinated search of the dense woods and surrounding farmlands was soon being prepared.

Since they had a sizable area to cover, Dalton directed his two assigned troopers to take up roving patrols along meandering Sheridan Point road, the first hardtop road south of where Roberts had entered the woods. They'd also make contact with those living on neighboring farms to alert them of the danger. Both troopers were familiar with Roberts, and they feared that he'd kill or be killed, rather than give up.

After they left, Dalton snatched his protective vest from the trunk and quickly strapped it on. No doubt, this one was a real badass scenario with pangs of anxiety, a rarity. An ex-cop, former colleague and friend gone crazy! Bad doo-doo! Dalton vividly recalled that Donny Roberts, the former firearms instructor, was an excellent marksman. And now, he'd lost his mind, had killed and fled to the woods with nothing to lose, yet something to gain perhaps by killing others who dared get in his way. Too many disturbing images.

Dalton visioned his crazed former colleague bursting from the woods, screaming like a maniac with shotgun blazing. No, he couldn't give him the chance. He pulled his personal twelve-gauge shotgun from its canvas scabbard, thumbed three more .00 rounds into the magazine, then snugged it next to him on the front seat. Shifting the cruiser into drive, he continued down Sheridan Point Road until he came to the first of several dirt driveways.

Slow, tense minutes passed while radios crackled with messages, but no sightings of the suspect. Low overhead, an MSP Bell Jet Ranger helicopter; a vigilant, giant drone bee, framed against a sullen gray sky, flew widening circles. Those aboard felt confident that with most trees leafless this time of year, they'd be able to detect anything remotely suspicious in the woods below. Just the shrill buzzing of an approaching chopper usually froze the hunted in their tracks. A phalanx of heavily armed, adrenaline-pumped troopers and deputies had already entered the woods to the north. Slowly, methodically, they pushed on, searching in a general southern direction. Dalton knew it was only a matter of time before they pressured Roberts into making a wrong move, and with each passing minute, the determined law officers grew more edgy.

Dalton had already contacted several families, the salt-of-the-earth farmers who'd reacted as he'd expected. All took the news calmly; a few were almost too nonchalant. With silent nods, they brought out their hunting rifles or shotguns and had their children, many still awaiting school buses, ushered back inside their homes. Dalton knew from experience that Calvert's dwindling population of "good ole boys," the farmers, field laborers and watermen, were a tough breed. When warranted, they damned sure wouldn't hesitate to take care of business themselves, a trait they also fancied to keep to themselves, too.

After another hour, good news from an excited team member finally crackled over the radios. They had found Matt, Missy's son, as he was meandering in the woods. The boy was unharmed, though shaken up. It was later discovered that Roberts had convinced the protesting boy to go back toward his house after several heated demands. Such was his closeness, still, to the man who'd brutally snuffed out his mother hours before. Wary and wired, Dalton and his two troopers continued their roving patrols, checking and re-checking the driveways, logging trails, fields and wood lines bordering Sheridan Point Road.

#

Crazed and on the run, Donny Roberts fought through the tangled briars and burst onto a grassy, windswept field almost two miles from his house. Dashing through the woods, he'd heard the faint, echoing sirens of responding police cars. Now, in the area not far behind, he vaguely picked up the familiar whine of the MSP chopper. He fumbled through a pocket and brought out a rifled slug and jacked it into the shotgun. If the damned thing flew near and too low, he'd give the fool pilot something to think about.

He crouched low and scurried over to a hedgerow that cut through the field, following it until it came to a wooden shed behind the white clapboard farmhouse he'd spotted earlier. Several thick, low-cut bushes bordered the shed, and Roberts crawled behind them to catch his breath.

He'd lain there for only a few minutes when he spotted the yellow MSP cruiser easing up the dirt driveway. His muscles tensed when the cruiser stopped beside the farmhouse, some thirty yards from his makeshift hiding place. A dark rage boiled up in his head when he saw the trooper cautiously exit the cruiser with shotgun in hand. Easy pickings now. Trembling violently and battling for control, Roberts eased the shotgun around, bringing the sights in perfect alignment with the trooper's chest. Holding his breath, he settled the sights just below the gold badge on the trooper's brown patrol jacket.

Suddenly, with a loud, grating creak, the side door to the farmhouse swung open! Eyes narrowed, Roberts watched in dead silence as the crippled old black man gingerly limped over to the trooper. He silently cursed when the old man stepped in front of the trooper to block his aim. Roberts was too far away to make out the trooper's face, but he heard the officer's voice echoing in the clear, thin air. Something familiar nagged at him, but he wasn't quite sure why. Roberts studied the two men as they stood there talking, the obviously tense trooper all the while scanning the area around the house and the backfields.

The officer was now the hunted, and the hunter was close enough to his scorned prey. The trooper finally made a parting gesture, and the old man turned and shuffled back to his house. Roberts squinted his left eye and zeroed in on the trooper's back as he returned to the cruiser. With perfect alignment, he let out his breath and slowly tightened his finger on the trigger.

Loud, familiar echoes suddenly whirled up from deep in his brain to cut through the demented fog. With a gasp, he lowered the shotgun. The voice *did* belong to someone he'd once known, someone from his vaunted trooper days. Yes, *he* was one of the few he genuinely liked back then, a colleague he had no quarrel with, even if he was one of *them*. *No*, he could never gun down Dalton Bragg, this day or ever.

Shaking in silence, Roberts watched his former shift mate back the cruiser down the driveway to Sheridan Point road. Almost immediately, another MSP unit zoomed up and stopped alongside. Damned cops were everywhere! No way he'd make it to the Patuxent River now, no hopeful escape by a pilfered boat. He'd have to backtrack and follow the hedgerow and fence line to the east instead.

Stooped over low, Roberts took off. The sudden harsh buzzing of the pesky helicopter startled him. The noose was tightening, and they were getting closer now, too damned close. From several directions he heard more sirens wailing in the distance—more cops joining the hunt. In a flash, it all came together. *He was trapped!*

His frenzied mind raced as he spiraled further down the abyss of his deranged finale. At the edge of the field, just steps away from the woods, he stopped. In a stupor, Roberts shuffled his moccasin-clad feet in a ragged, abbreviated circle. The sun had fought through the clouds, casting a surrealistic glow all around him. His mouth dropped open, and he craned his neck to fix his vacant eyes on the golden orb overhead. The overwhelming brilliance immediately forced him to close them. With a low moan, he forced them back open, but when they rolled up until just the whites showed, he slammed them shut again. Roberts dropped his head and rested his chin on his chest. Shifting his weight from one unsteady leg to the other, he clumsily rubbed his burning eyes with the back of a dirty, scratched hand. Irritation nearly gone, his eyes still flickered with a strange haziness. He opened them wide and gazed down at the distant ryegrass fields and the vine-covered hedgerows, then over to the fuzzy dirt road meandering down to the river where windblown waves churned wildly. On wobbly legs, Roberts turned around to face the tall, muted stands of leafless hardwood trees—his final audience.

The unearthly shrieking returned, reverberating and rambling through what remained of his lingering sanity. When he realized the screams were his, Roberts gouged at his face, tearing out tufts of beard and ripping tight flesh with fingernails until rivulets of blood streamed from his eyes, nose and cheeks. He bit down hard on his tongue, almost severing it when the screams turned deafening. The ground beneath him trembled, and he started to wail. Suddenly, he stopped tearing at his face and stood still, his head canted down in mute resignation. Grabbing the barrel of the shotgun, Roberts folded his shoulders and slumped down on the hard packed clay.

The radio barked to life as the distinct, clipped voice of Captain Riggs came on the air to ask if any units south of his command post had heard a gunshot. Dalton waited, then radioed a negative. Once again, he turned onto the winding dirt road next to the double oak tree marking the passage to the black farmer's clapboard house he'd checked out minutes before. He passed the farmhouse and drove the cruiser down the bumpy trail parallel to the first field.

Suddenly the hair on the back of his neck tingled, and he slammed on the brakes! He wasn't sure, but he thought he spotted something in the field near the distant tree line, something he hadn't noticed before. It was maybe a hundred yards away, and from the distance, it looked like a lumpy pile of clothes, maybe a fallen scarecrow. *No,* he it wasn't a scarecrow, and he hadn't missed it before, either. He grabbed for the mic, but the cord caught on the metal console, and it fell from his hand. Dalton's pulse raced when he picked it up from the floorboard.

"U-17 to command post!" he snapped into the mic, "I've got something suspicious in a field at the end of the third dirt driveway off of Sheridan Point Road. You copy? Request back up, 10-18 (immediately) at this location!"

Jumping from the cruiser, Dalton heard the radio burst alive with acknowledgments. He double-checked the shotgun to make sure a round was chambered before starting out on his guarded walk across the field. Shotgun pointed ahead, he stopped after half the distance. It was definitely a body now—*no shit!* A chill ran down his back, and icy fingers seized the shotgun stock in a white-knuckle grip.

Dalton glanced up and nodded at the chopper that had suddenly materialized low overhead. Rotors biting the air, the chopper banked sharply before swooping in for a bumpy landing forty yards away. As the skids kissed dirt, a trooper-medic wearing an olive-drab jumpsuit bounded out with his snub-nosed service revolver in a two-fisted grip. He was an older trooper, and Dalton was instantly reassured by his confident look. They gestured to each other, and then riveted their attention back to the body on the ground. Unspoken and on cue, both troopers started forward, Dalton approaching from the left, the medic from the right. As they edged closer, Dalton jammed the shotgun butt into his shoulder and clicked the safety off, keeping the front sight bead centered on the prone figure. Closing in, he saw that the pajama-clad body lay face down with the head facing away from him.

Warning signs flashed in his head when he didn't spot a weapon. Instantly his pulse shot up, and his mouth went dry. He had a premonition, a hideous gut feeling. Roberts was hiding the gun under him, cagily playing dead, just waiting for them to get close enough so he could roll over and blow their shit away. They were only a few yards away when Dalton stopped and signaled the medic to continue. He kept the shotgun pointed at the body's center mass, covering his fellow trooper who gingerly angled in from the other side.

(*"Don't Move Donny! Don't you fuckin' dare move!)*

The medic crept to within a few feet of the body, and then paused. He waited a few seconds before nodding to Dalton. Dalton nodded back, tightened his grip on the shotgun, and watched as the medic squatted down and cocked his head, straining hard to take it all in. Satisfied, the medic stood up and quickly gave a thumbs-down signal to his colleague.

"Sucker's deader than dirt, Corp!" he yelled over the din of the chopper's rotors. "You know him?" Dalton nodded and mouthed a silent yes. He brought the shotgun barrel up, flicked the safety back on and walked over to his former colleague's body.

The bloody shotgun was lying partly under the body, the muzzle just below what once was the handsome face of the trooper he'd known so well. The self-inflicted blast had obliterated the left side of his bearded face and a large part of his head. The crimson explosion made a repugnant, glistening smorgasbord of stark yellow, marmalade-like brain matter; sinewy purples and white bone shards splattered with coagulating globs of red blood. White vaporous tendrils slowly wafted from the massive wound. A twelve-gauge rifled slug makes a very ugly mess of a human head.

Dalton shifted his gaze slightly and was immediately stunned when he stared directly into Robert's undamaged right eye. The glazed eye was wide-open, frozen in death and unfathomed horror. Dalton sensed a chilling recognition, a macabre, haunting insanity that beckoned him. Electrified, he bolted upright and gasped for air. When he felt the hand on his shoulder, he flinched and spun around. Open-mouthed, he stared into the welcome face of Elzy Shifflett, his former sergeant.

194

"You doin OK, hoss?" Elzy muttered softly. With a pained, perplexed look, Dalton stood in silence, his eyes boring deep into Elzy's in a mute plea for an answer he knew he'd never get. Elzy had worked with Donny Roberts years before Dalton's arrival at the barrack, and Dalton saw dismay on his face, too. Chatting uncomfortably as they tried to make sense of the horror, they stared at the corpse of their former buddy.

Elzy pointed to the numerous cuts and scratches on Robert's bare legs and ankles before turning to spit out a glob of tobacco juice. He ran the back of a hand over his pursed lips and turned to Dalton. "Crazy son a bitch ran hard out here, didn't he? We all knew he'd probable wind up doin' himself in, sure as shit, but damn shame he had to go and take her with him, too," the sergeant muttered. "Yeah Elzy," Dalton added, "Poor girl must have gone through hell before he snuffed her out like that. Tell me, Sarge...Tell me how this makes any sense at all, can you?"

Elzy rubbed the back of his leathery neck in thought for a moment while he cleared his throat. "Sometimes the volume just gets turned up in this crazy life, and things happen when they don't have to. Know what I mean, Dalton?" he asked, fairly sure that Dalton's attention was elsewhere. Elzy looked up at the sun and winced before continuing. "When you're born under a bad sign, this shit's gonna come your way, and there just ain't a whole bunch you can do about it, either. You can take that one all the way to the bank. He'll get no sympathy from the devil, that one won't."

On his way back to the barrack, just before leaving Adelina Road, Dalton tasted a harsh copper tang in his mouth, felt the palms of his hands suddenly became damp with sweat again, as the rising flush of blood warmed his face. He pulled off and drove a short distance down the dirt road leading to Judge Mackall's pond. Satisfied he was alone, he stopped the cruiser. Gritting his teeth in anguish, he balled both fists and pounded on the steering wheel. Feeling queasy, close to vomiting, Dalton dashed from the cruiser and bent over, gasping deeply to fill his lungs with fresh air. For the most part, he'd been OK with it all. Eventually, most troopers learned to deal with it and go on. Like sloughing off the effects of the abominations he'd experienced already, he thought he'd be able to steel himself behind his buffered, calloused wall that normally shielded him so well.

But a former good friend, a fellow trooper, made it too personal, so painfully different. It was his eye, the semblance of some supernatural recognition he perceived in Donny Robert's eye that had pierced through to play havoc with his psyche. Yes, *that* was it, a message signaling something—but what? Dalton waited for his head to clear enough so he could function around his fellow troopers without drawing undue attention. He plopped himself behind the steering wheel and adjusted the rearview mirror so he could practice putting on a mask of indifference. When he had it nailed down to a credible semblance, he started the cruiser and drove back to the barrack. As the remaining shift hours dragged by, Dalton grew more pensive. He couldn't put it into perspective right then, but he knew he'd lost another part of himself that day, another dent in his psychological armor.

The tragic news spread fast throughout the close-knit county, and Dalton wasn't surprised when he learned that Cindy had already heard about it when he finally came home. Dalton related a few details to her, but shied away from unveiling the tumultuous emotions exploding deep within. Unlike those who wore the badges, he knew that his wife wasn't able to fathom the reality of it through mere words, and he was glad when she finally excused herself to fix dinner. When she left, his stomach cramped into knots, and for a moment he thought he was suffocating.

He dashed to the bedroom, stripped off the uniform and gun belt, and then donned running sweats. Minutes later, on the sandy Flag Harbor beach, he was running briskly in the chilly air and waning sunlight. It was low tide with plenty of firm sand to run on, and with the sun setting on the calm bay, Dalton felt he could run forever.

Later that night, after Cindy and both daughters were asleep, Dalton hustled down to the basement and returned to the rec room with a cached six-pack. He stuffed several slats of seasoned oak into the woodstove and stoked it, leaving the stove door open for the radiant heat. After he cracked open a beer, he dragged the dilapidated easy-back chair over to the stove and collapsed into it. Aimlessly, he stared into the glowing, reassuring flames. It would come, he knew it would, sure as shit. When the tremors hit this time, however, he'd be ready. Hell, he was almost accustomed to the bouts, could almost count on them. It was the increase in the once-sporadic nightmares that was plaguing him now. With time, he was hoping they'd subside—the tremors were so much easier to endure.

#

The influential powers to be, particularly the county commissioners, were pleased with the State Police handling the predominant law enforcement in the burgeoning county. Like the politicos, the law-abiding countians appreciated the troopers' professionalism. And, as far as "Culvert's" good-ole-boy Sheriff Almos Jett was concerned, the State Police playing the big-cheese role was fine and dandy with him. He had politicking to do, meaning he'd be running dozens of fishing trips out on the bay off Solomons with the county's more influential citizens. If one could ever catch the sheriff in his cramped office under the antiquated jail cells, he'd be luckier than most.

During the late seventies, the county's swelling population screamed for more police presence, as emergency calls steadily mounted. Acknowledging the Sheriff's Department's limited resources, the commissioners huddled to make a surprisingly quick (for them) decision. Voting to put a sizable band-aid on the growing law-enforcement demands, they embraced the Calvert County Resident Trooper Program. In addition to the allotted PF barrack troopers, there would be, at its peak, a dozen additional troopers assigned to Calvert. The county assumed seventy-four percent of the pro-rated cost for the contracted manpower, while the State picked up the remainder. In return, the county acquired a well-trained group of fully equipped troopers who tailored their enforcement activities toward the community, a novel concept that earned valuable PR for the MSP.

Many of the seasoned barrack troopers hastily volunteered for the program. As resident troopers, they'd be assigned to one of three districts in the county, but more important, they'd be working fewer late shifts and *no* graveyard shifts. While the resident troopers wouldn't be pressured to write tickets, they were expected to handle most criminal calls, and they'd also perform basic PR roles such as crime prevention and safety courses.

The consummate barrack-rat Marty Metzger, along with his academy mate Al Heister and the stoic Tfc. Craig Harmel, gleefully left road-pounding behind to join the enticing program. Dalton's intimate crony, the ever-smiling Colby Merson, surprised him, though. Ogling a gift horse in the mouth, Colby clambered aboard with aspirations of greener promotional pastures. As a corporal, Colby was the first official supervisor of the resident trooper program. With his friendly, upbeat personality and enthusiasm, Colby was a perfect head honcho pick, and Dalton was pleased his buddy snagged it. The resident trooper contract mandated a fully staffed barrack, and within weeks, Prince Frederick was buttressed with an infusion of new troopers.

Dalton couldn't help notice one new trooper from the Annapolis Barrack who really glittered. Three years on the job, Jim Buckler, the twenty-six year-old Calvert County native was a dynamo. Towering at six feet-three, and tipping the scales at two hundred and thirty beefy pounds, Buckler had the physique of a linebacker—his position at Salisbury State College after two years serving as a Marine. Known as "Junebug" by his friends and fellow troopers, Buckler was the consummate man's man. He was a true competitor in every sport he played. More than any other sport, he had a divine mad-dog obsession, for slow-pitch softball. Excluding cow-chip tossing, softball was *the* official Calvert County sport. Losing wasn't an option in *anything* Junebug undertook.

Initially, Buckler displayed a cockiness, but Dalton soon learned he was the rare, fearless type who backed up his words with a vengeance of action. In the never-ending battle to prove himself, Junebug never conceded, nor did he ever back down from anybody, even when prudence dictated otherwise. No one that is, but his sage father. Ed Buckler, his callous, tough-as-nails father, was not only a hard taskmaster still capable of kicking his boy's butt, but also a high-ranking, highly respected US Park Police officer. From his toddler days, Junebug held an innate fear of his heavy-handed father, and come hell or high water, he strived to keep out of his ever-critical spotlight.

Junebug, however, did have one peculiarity quite disconcerting to those who worked with him. Too frequently, Junebug's wired brain had a propensity to warp out far ahead of his slower tongue. In essence, he usually talked so fast that only a chosen few could fathom his falsetto stammering. Bursting out in his signature machinegun staccato, Junebug's verbal micro-bursts got worse when things turned dicey. As Sergeant Long put it one day, "The boy's wound up tighter than a drum, and fearlessly foolhardy to boot!"

In Dalton's opinion, Junebug Buckler was like a racehorse hooked up to a baby carriage, and to play nice with others, he just needed to be attached to an intravenous codeine drip-bag. And Junebug's uniform was always rumpled, giving him the appearance of having just emerged from a nap in a cocoon. Regardless, Dalton admired the young-buck trooper's positive spirit and gung-ho attitude, knowing that Buckler was one he'd be relying on whenever things turned ugly. And as a bonus, Dalton had a new buddy to play with! It wasn't long before the two were lifting weights and clinking beer bottles together.

With recent promotions, the PF barrack now had a respectable cadre gung-ho road corporals serving under tempered sergeants. Like Dalton, several of the new corporals made their rank after only four or five years on the job. Corporals such as rock hard Ben Wiley, or the gruff, practical-minded Dan Collison, were Dalton's age. Eventually, and with some certainty, one could accurately gauge which supervisor a trooper worked under, based on the way the trooper performed. Dalton was comfortable with his own style of calm, respectful supervision. When conditions were ripe (no brass around), however, he readily liberated his madcap humor in an attempt to loosen things up. More than any other MSP idiosyncrasies, Dalton detested the pointless, by-the-book nit-picking that frustrated the troops and led to needless personality issues. The very nature of the job left little room for those not-so-rare, anal-minded commanders who thrived on total "hands-on" control regardless of adverse consequences.

#

"Dancin' With The Devil Under The Crescent Moon—"

Dalton was relieved when he saw fellow corporal Dick McNulty sign in to begin his night shift on that warm September evening. It had been a long five days of late shift for Dalton's group, and tonight, his last, had been hectic.

"How's it goin out there, big D?" McNulty chirped. "Just trying to keep our heads above water at high tide, Dick-ee," Dalton spouted back. They grinned and exchanged mock salutes. McNulty was a trooper at the barrack when Dalton had first arrived, and Dalton had gleaned much from his insight and experience. Branded a whiner by some supervisors, the amiable doughboy corporal also had a plaguing tendency to get infected with a case of the slows when the bad stuff splattered the fan, meaning he was never the first one to rush out the door. Never. Regardless, Dalton appreciated McNulty's sense of humor and upbeat mood.

Soon enough, Dalton was asking McNulty which night-shift troopers he wanted to send to an ominous domestic call at Kenwood Beach, a quiet, bay-front community several miles south of Prince Frederick. The woman caller sounded terrified when she told the PCO that her husband was threatening to shoot her with a gun he'd recently acquired just for that purpose. McNulty hesitantly chose two troopers for the call. Dalton was off in a few minutes, but he also knew, as did McNulty, that Kenwood Beach was close to his home just south of there. Silence turned awkward, with Dalton perceiving that his friend wasn't overly inclined to head out to the scene.

Aw, screw it, he silently told himself. "Hey Dick, no problem. I'll back em' up on my way home," Dalton shouted as he dashed out the back door. "Thanks, big D, and...uhh...just let me know if you need anything, OK?" the relieved McNulty yelled at the swinging door.

Seconds later, Dalton was barreling south on Route 4 again. Just a small delay from the beers chilling in the home fridge, that's all. He heard one, then the other trooper radio their arrivals at the scene. Umm—another damn domestic to heap on the shit-load of others he'd handled over the years. Like most troopers, he'd learned early on that when responding to the ominous-sounding calls, the sphincter-tighteners, you had to force yourself *not* to vision the worst-case scenario. Instead, you just forced yourself to concentrate on getting there without wrecking the cruiser. Hell, most calls never came close to being exciting, let alone dangerous. Yeah, right.

Dalton was dwelling on his welcome-home beers, when the radio barked alive: "U-18 Prince Frederick! We have shots fired! Request assistance and a supervisor *ASAP!* " *Shit!* Dalton stared straight ahead for a moment before flipping on the lights and siren. "U-17 to U-18...10-77 (ETA) two minutes," he calmly answered. "U-17, Prince Frederick...Put out a 10-3 (do not transmit) on this channel!" Yeah, he thought, no matter *what* happens out here, your guys have to at least *think* they have a cool head taking charge.

The road corporal took a sharp right off Governor's Run road, flipped the siren switch off and stayed on Kenwood Beach Road, following it up a steep hill. He turned right, then left, and immediately spotted the two MSP cruisers parked close to a small frame house surrounded by several large trees. Dalton came to a skidding halt in back of the cruisers.

"U-17, Prince Frederick, I'll be out with 'em!" Springing from the cruiser, he saw two troopers crouched behind a thick tree, and another knelt beside a cruiser. All three troopers had their revolvers aimed straight ahead at the man frozen in the high-beam headlights.

As he scrambled over to the two troopers behind the tree, Dalton's eyes stayed riveted on the scraggly-haired man. He was probably in his early thirties, medium built, red-faced and wobbly—and very pissed off! Dalton's attention was drawn to the semiautomatic handgun he held at arms length, its barrel pointed at the ground between them. Great, this isn't as bad as he thought it'd be, it's a whole helluva lot worse!

"Corp! Boy, am I glad to see you," Tfc. Leonard whispered anxiously. "This guy's one crazy muther fucker!" Dalton patted Leonard on the back, then turned and nodded at the husky young black trooper crouched next to him. Oh super, it just got better—a new boot! It was boot-trooper Ronny Kern's first day at the barrack, and Leonard was his field-training instructor. Kern was wide-eyed apprehensive, but like a good boot, he stayed quiet and hung tight to his mentor. All eyes were on the ranting man out front, as Tfc. Leonard filled Dalton in on the situation.

It was another ugly quarrel between husband and wife, after the jobless husband had once again returned home drunk and piss-ass angry. After the usual shouting and shoving, the irate hubby eventually got tired of playing Frisbee with her cherished china, so he smashed a few kitchen windows out instead. Standing in the shattered rubble, his fuming wife threatened to call the cops, and of course, he dared her to. When she reached for the phone, he pulled out a .380 Browning automatic from a pocket of his urine-soaked jeans. Terrified, she ducked, as two hollow point rounds slammed into the kitchen wall where her head was seconds before.

"Tell 'em to bring what they got, bitch, that's right! Tell 'em to bring every swingin' dick cop they can find! I'll kill 'em all, 'fore I take out your sorry ass, too!" He snarled, before ripping the phone wires from the wall. Shaken and in tears, she cowered and slumped to the floor after her enraged husband kicked the front door open and stormed out.

Tfc. Leonard told Dalton that he saw the wife come to the front door a few times since their arrival, and, from what he observed she seemed all right. "His name is Vince, Vince Morgan. Never heard of 'im either, but his wife told us to be careful with the crazy son a bitch. He's got lots of serious issues that keep messing him up real bad, and when he gets to drinking, she said, he goes bonkers," Leonard warned the corporal. Dalton studied the man, as Leonard vainly called out to him again. Weaving back and forth, he kept ranting and raving, threatening to return to the house to take care of unfinished business— his wife. Several times he brought the handgun up and pointed it in the general direction of the troopers, but so far he hadn't fired a shot. Good, but not good enough.

Dalton turned to Leonard. "You got a barrack shotgun, Barry?" he asked. Leonard gestured to his boot-trooper who'd overheard them. Slouched over, Trooper Kern scrambled back to a cruiser, quickly returning with a Remington 870 pump-action, twelve-gauge. "It's in car-safe mode (no chambered round), Corporal, sir," Kern murmured, gingerly handing it to Dalton. Good man, the new boot, Dalton thought.

He eyed Tfc. Heslip, who was still kneeling beside his cruiser. "Jack...You OK?" Dalton whispered. He held the shotgun up so Heslip could see it and wouldn't be surprised when he heard it. Heslip smiled knowingly and signaled thumbs-up. Dalton had already made up his mind—the screwball wasn't getting the chance to make it back to his house again, couldn't allow him to harm the woman. If he bolted for the house, the first 00 buckshot round would be aimed at his legs, to bring him down. Dalton took a deep breath and braced his left shoulder against the tree, as he canted his body to the right. Keeping the barrel pointed down, he wedged the butt of the shotgun into his right shoulder. Dalton's eyes narrowed, as the cursing Morgan brought the pistol up and pointed it in their direction again.

Training, training, training—usually comes down to just that. Adrenalin flowing and revved up to full alert, Dalton remembered what the firearms instructors had preached about the psychological use of a shotgun, and he prayed it'd work now.

"Hey Morgan!" he thundered at the man in the glaring headlights. For a split second, Morgan stood still and silent. Dalton jacked a shell into the chamber. *Cha-chunk!* Slowly, methodically, he swung the barrel up and pointed the bead at his target's chest. Tfc. Leonard later told Dalton that the shell being pumped into the chamber was the loudest, nerve-wracking sound he'd ever heard.

The specter of looming tragedy hit strong. Dalton was too focused, unable to pay much attention to it, but the target had. "Go ahead mutha fucker! Shoot! Shoot me, mutha fucker...shoot me, then!' Morgan screamed back at him.

Well, *that* sure's hell didn't work, Dalton thought to himself with a silent *Aw, shit*. He kept the shotgun leveled on his target. The man's obviously screwed up on some heavy juice, maybe even on PCP or some other mindblowers, and because of it, he's found himself a real pair of balls, the corporal decided. "Come on, you chicken-shit mutha fucker...*shoot!*" Dalton saw Morgan's arm come up with the handgun again, and his finger tightened on the shotgun trigger.

Blam! Blam! Blam! Three shots rang out when Morgan fired rounds into the ground separating himself and the troopers. Dalton flinched when one of the ricocheting rounds zipped past and struck a limb behind them. "Shoot, you bunch a pansy-ass pussies!" The corporal kept his finger on the trigger, waiting for Morgan to bring his gun up just a tad more. (Don't do it—no, go ahead, fool! Do it!) If he raised the gun any higher (Go ahead, fool), he was gonna cap the bastard, end of story!

Dalton knew he had ample grounds to take the guy out right now. No doubt, others would have done it already. But deep in his gut, he was feeling this fiasco was looking like a police suicide in the making, and he held back. Yes, he'd gamble with the idea that maybe Morgan really didn't want to kill anyone this night. No, this guy just wanted to end his dance with his demons, whatever they were, and he, or another hapless trooper was supposed to do the dirty work for him? Amazing how the adrenaline quickly brings it all together. But was his gut right this time?

Dalton exhaled, lowered the shotgun from his shoulder and held it by his waist, keeping the barrel pointed at his target. "Hey, Vince, ya need some smokes?" he asked nonchalantly. A moment of anxious silence passed. "Fuckin'-A, man, I could use a cig, if ya got one." (Whew, we're talking) Dalton signaled to Heslip, who eagerly tossed a half-pack of Marlboros in Morgan's direction. "Beau-coup thanks, man," Morgan spouted when he picked up the cigs. Morgan shook the pack and snatched a cigarette out with his mouth. Using the fingers of one hand, he bent a match over and flicked it hard across the bottom strip several times until it flared. He cocked his head back slightly, took a long drag and stared hard at the troopers.

Dalton hadn't seen anyone do a one hand match light up since his stint in the military. It registered—*Nam* vet maybe? "Looks like we got one of them Mexican stand-offs here, huh, storm troopers?" Morgan slurred to them after puffing out a stream of smoke. Dalton kept his voice low, hoping to persuade Morgan to end things where they were. While he was talking man-to-man, Dalton caught Morgan's eyes nervously darting back to the house. He was pensive, wavering from one foot to the other, obviously trying to make up his mind for the next move. After a brief interval of chilled silence, Morgan snapped his head up. "Tell ya what I'm gonna do right now," he told them offhand. "I'm gonna take me a walk down to the pier, and if one of you muther fuckers tries to stop me, I swear, I'm gonna blow your shit away! Ain't afraid to shoot nobody. Lord knows I've killed a few when I had to," he blurted out with finality.

Enough said, Morgan dropped the gun by his side and reeled toward the driveway. Intent on making it to the road to the beach, he walked in an extended half circle, an attempt at distancing himself from the four troopers just ahead. As he approached, Dalton cautioned them to let him pass, knowing any attempt to stop him now would probably lead to unnecessary bloodshed. After he passed, Dalton, hoping that Morgan wouldn't alter his route, told his troopers to follow him at a healthy distance as he made his way down to the beach. He watched them turn their cruisers around and follow Morgan as he pitched down the road on unsteady feet. Dalton waited until they passed the first intersection, then dove into his cruiser to speed down an adjacent street.

Two quick turns took him back to Kenwood Beach Road, and from there he zoomed down to the beach entrance. The cruiser came to a shuddering halt, blocking both lanes. Morgan wasn't going any farther than this point now, and Dalton sure as hell didn't need any late-evening traffic to botch it all up. He switched on the emergency lights and flipped up the outside speaker knob before radioing the barrack an update. He was advised that additional assistance, a sergeant, was at least fifteen minutes away. Dalton grabbed his shotgun and flashlight, threw his hat on the back seat and scrambled from the unit.

Standing in the shadows just off the road, the corporal took stock of himself, surprised he felt little fear so far. Sure, he was tense, but his confidence prevailed. Typically, he was more concerned about his guys than himself, and he knew with certainty he wouldn't let them down. Dalton's eyes drifted to the nearby beach, then far beyond to the long wooden community pier stretching out a hundred yards from shore. There were several lights beaming from tall poles at intervals along the pier, and he noticed there wasn't any light at the end.

A crescent moon hung low in the southeast sky, its pale, dusky light almost reassuring. He gazed at the flickering lights of houses along the bay on the Eastern Shore. The gentle rippling sound of the compact waves on the beach signaled the receding high tide, and the bay seemed unusually calm for a typical September night. The distinct smell of the brackish water and the sweet aroma of honeysuckle bushes wafted together. No doubt about it, this was too nice a night for this kind of chaos. Chirping crickets, joined by a lone cicada, lent a false sense of security to the scene, but the static popping from the radio's outside speaker quickly grounded Dalton back to reality.

Several blocks away a dog started barking, and Dalton promptly turned in that direction. He saw the headlights first, then spotted the shadowy figure of the man in front of them. Morgan was stumbling and staggering down the hill, just ahead of the MSP units. Morgan glared icily at Dalton as he rambled toward the pier. Dalton studied him when he stopped at the stairs to catch his breath. Tfc. Heslip pulled his cruiser to block off the other side of the road, and Tfc. Leonard parked his unit at the bottom of the hill, moves which boxed Morgan in. So far, so good.

Morgan started up the stairs, but suddenly stumbled, and the gun flew from his hand to land on the sand. He was so close, and for a split-second Dalton fought the urge to throw caution to the wind and sprint over in a race for the gun. Surprisingly, Morgan was swift, diving from the steps and snatching it up in a flash. (Ok, Ok, nothing lost—Keep cool, keep *real* cool) Morgan blew the sand off the gun, then coughed and spat a few times to clear the grit from his mouth. "Y'all better just leave me the fuck alone, ya hear me?" he gasped. "Any one of you fools follow me out on the pier, he's gonna be one dead son a bitch, and I ain't foolin' around, understand?" he spouted as he ambled back to the pier.

Dalton kept an eye on Morgan as he staggered toward the last functioning pier light. Moments later he was swallowed up in darkness. It was nothing but a gut feeling, but it gnawed at him and Dalton knew he had to play it out. *No*, he wasn't going to let Morgan do it, not on his watch! He handed Heslip the shotgun and his flashlight, then motioned for the three troopers to gather round. "OK, here's how this is goin' down. First and foremost, you guys are staying here," he told them, pausing to make sure they heard him. "I'm going out there by myself, simply 'cause I think I can get through to 'im. Think a one-on-one stands a better chance with him, trust me. Gonna play it low-key on this one guys. If I walk out there with that shotgun, a flashlight, or even if I wore my hat, I don't, think he'd hesitate to blow my ass away, so that stuff stays behind, too."

Heslip, the senior trooper, pursed his lips and shook his head. "Corporal Bragg...I don't think that's a good..." Dalton quickly cut him off. "But I know one thing, if I *don't* go out there, I'm sure as shit he'll kill himself, and *we're* not gonna let that happen," Dalton heard himself tell them. Deliberating, the corporal shot a quick glance at the crescent moon. Yeah, it's show time—reason why we make those megabucks for being the ringmasters out here, he silently chided himself. He'd much rather be home listening to the soft, reassuring breathing of his infant daughters as they slept soundly; knew that he'd rather be cuddling spoon-style in warmth with Cindy. To hell with the after-shift beers, to hell with a long walk on a pier that might lead to Nowhere Land.

"Well, here goes nothing," Dalton edgily chuckled to Heslip as he unsnapped his holster strap and started toward the pier. He took a few steps, then stopped and turned back around. "Regardless of whatever happens out there, Jack, don't let the son of a bitch get off the pier unless he's in handcuffs. Or...or...Just do what you gotta do, OK, Jack?"

#

(Hey *Dad...R*emember when your toe-head sons were pre-pubes? Remember challenging us with all those Brave Tests you concocted? You know, like the one where we had to lie perfectly still with our arms at our sides on our metal army-surplus beds, while you whacked away—within inches, mind ya, with that razor-sharp Japanese samurai sword souvenir you kept from WWII? "Don't move...Don't move an inch, I'm tellin ya, I'm not kiddin!" *No?* How's bout the time you had us brothers stand outside in the dark shadows while you hid a certain pair of shoes in an upstairs closet of the unlit house...just to see which son persevered against the goblins and his fears to fetch that exact pair of shoes? Remember who freaked out, Dad? Remember who won? Dad? *Dad?* Guess I don't remember that stuff much any more either, 'cause I'm still doing some crazy-ass shit out here, Pop)

#

It was a long pier that grew a lot longer when he set foot on it. Dalton experienced a momentary tunnel vision when his anxious eyes strained to pierce the shadows. He slowly walked down the pier, but before passing the last glowing pole light, he paused. It was coal-black, sinister and foreboding at the end of the pier, and while he couldn't spot Morgan's form, he sensed his presence just ahead. Dalton gazed down at the water where the comforting glow from the overhead light glittered off the water. It was almost dead calm. He saw several small blue crabs skitter back and forth, searching for prey. A school of tiny silverside bait-fish swam lazily into the circle of light.

Suddenly two snapper-size bluefish exploded furiously into their midst. The sleek marauders devoured several of their quarry before darting back into the shadows. Evidence of the feeding frenzy; a crippled bait-fish spiraling wildly in its death throes, loose scales mixed with a strand of entrails in a diluted crimson mist—the plundered remnants of life just seconds before, slowly dissipated and sank. Too soon, it was still again, with no sign of what had just occurred. A chilly omen?

Dalton dismissed the thought and focused on his own pressing reality. Instant chills shot down his spine when he heard someone calling him from close behind. It was a matronly woman's voice speaking softly in a foreign tongue. He whirled around and saw no one, but felt an unsettling presence he'd never known before. For an unsure moment, the corporal felt close to panic, thought about dashing off the pier post-haste. Her echoing voice drifted away with his panicky sensations, instantly replaced by an embracing sense of calm. He was blanketed with an ethereal righteousness that convinced him he wasn't alone, that he now had a backup from somewhere far beyond his understanding of the world as he knew it.

Dalton wasn't the religious type, but he knew it must have been a guardian of sorts, a sacred presence which assured him that he'd been put in the right place, at the right moment, for the right reason. Or, as Gary told him a few nights later at the Gold Dust Inn, "You were blessed with a visionary certainty my friend, something few in this life will ever experience." Providence, or whatever, for the first time in his life Dalton Bragg almost felt invincible.

Dalton knew his silhouette would be clearly seen by Morgan, and he wanted to take advantage of it by displaying a calm demeanor. He stuck his left hand in his trouser pocket, dropped his right arm down at his side and purposely slumped his shoulders before resuming his casual walk forward. Through his body language, Dalton appeared unthreatening, but with each step it got harder to ignore the thumping in his chest and the cotton dryness in his mouth.

Canting his eyes up slightly for better night vision, he made out a human form several yards ahead. Vince Morgan was sitting up with his back pressed against a pier railing. Dalton managed to find his voice. 'Vince...Vince?" No answer, and worse, no movement. He took a deep breath and continued. "That's far enough, mutha fucker! One more step will be your last! So help me God...I'll shoot!" Morgan hissed at him. Dalton froze. "Think you wuz just gonna bad-ass walk your way out here, John Wayne style, chief?" the man pointing the gun at him rasped. 'Think you're too damn tired of living or something, super trooper?" Now close enough to see Morgan's features, Dalton spotted the gun aimed at his chest.

"Vince, no doubt in my mind you could have taken me out by now if you'd wanted to," he said calmly, "but I just came out here to rap with you some, man." Dalton heard the blood pulsing wildly in his ear. "Don't like you being out here alone by yourself, that's all. No tricks in my play book, Vince...And you can keep that gun on me, if you feel you have to, but mine's staying in the holster, OK?" Dalton paused, his mind racing to come up with something, anything, while Morgan sat like a statue. If only he could see his eyes, the gateway to his soul....

"Vince, I'm going over to the railing while we talk, OK with you?" Dalton implored, sauntering over to a side railing. When he reached it, he turned his sideways, his right side canted for a lesser profile. He draped his left arm on the handrail and rested his left foot on the bottom railing, then casually slouched over and swiveled his head back toward Morgan. To Morgan, it looked like the trooper had probably just propped his right arm against his right hip, but the palm of Dalton's right hand was now resting comfortably on his revolver's wooden handle. He'd already made up his mind that if Morgan did shoot at him, he'd get a quick shot off in return, before vaulting over the railing and plunging into the murky water below. (Hello darkness my old pal)

It took several awkward starts, but Dalton was finally able to elicit a few terse responses from the troubled man. A surge of relief flooded over him when Morgan lowered his gun and set it down on his leg. After exchanging some aimless prattle, Dalton notched things up. "Vince, why don't we just drop things where they are now, and call it a night?' he ventured. "*Every* night's been a bad fuckin' night since I've been back, man," Morgan cried out. "Just feel like I can't go on anymore, feel like I don't fit anywhere. Can't hold a damn job, can't deal with the old lady any more, everything's closing in on me man...Nothing fits anymore, Goddamn it!" Morgan's shoulders started shaking, and he broke into sobs. (*Whew*, keep talking, Morgan, keep talking) Morgan lifted his tear-streaked face.

"Nam, man...Nam messed my whole fuckin' life up, and I don't see no way out!" For several pregnant minutes, they shared an ugly silence. "What service you in, Vince?" Dalton finally asked. He'd already sized him up as a possible infantry grunt from a combat unit, but he wasn't sure. "Ninth Division in the Mekong Delta, man, 2nd of the 60th Infantry. Beating the rice paddies and bush near Tay Ninh in 1970," Morgan cried out. "Saw beaucoup bad shit, and lost a few buds. Killed my share of gooks, too. Good, bad, or in between, it didn't matter no more, we killed 'em all. Nothin' really mattered over there, man. I was just trying to make it back to the world again, that's all. Hated the whole fuckin' mess!"

Dalton paused. "Where'd you do basic training, Vince? Did mine at Fort Puke, Louisiana, in '67. What a hole." Morgan's head jerked up. "No shit, man? I did basic there in May '69! Most fucked-up Army post I ever saw. Hot, stink-ass swamps and slimy muck in the bayous. Damn place crawling with snakes, gators, scorpions, them wild pigs and some of the craziest drill sergeants there ever was. Yeah, got my sorry ass sent to Tiger Land for AIT (Advanced Infantry

Training) right afterwards, then to Nam after thirty days' leave. Where'd *you* wind up, man?" Dalton coughed and cleared his throat. "Well, buddy, I wound up in the "Tropic Lightning" 25th Division's home base back at Schofield in Pineapple Land. My brother was already humping the highlands in Nam with the Fighting Fourth Division, those dudes who wore the Ivy Patches, and I never got there." "No shit." Morgan stammered.

For a while, they swapped Army stories ("Ever do any of them skanky-bitch whores there in Leesville? How many of them two-percent PX piss-beers you had to guzzle down before you started feeling anything?"). As they jabbered on, Dalton was feeling that the whole affair could possibly be rolled up and bundled nicely into a smooth ending. After a few more exchanges, he took a stab at it. "Come on with me, Vince. Give me your gun and trust me here, brother. Let's walk off this damned pier together, OK?" The corporal paused to let his words sink in. "You need some help, my friend, and maybe, just maybe, it'll all change for you, Vince. I'm askin' ya, please...Let's call it a night and end things where they are. Waddya say?"

The tense silence was punctured by Morgan's loud sobs. "No, man, I appreciate you talking with me, appreciate it a whole lot, but I can't do this shit no more," he cried out.

Dalton suddenly found himself in a captive-audience paralysis, a witness to the finale of a horror movie, when he saw Morgan yank the gun up and place the barrel tip against his head. Teary-eyed, Morgan stared vacantly into Dalton's eyes. "Don't do it, Vince...Listen to me, please. Don't do it, brother," he whispered to him. "Think about the guys who didn't come back with you, man. Think about what they'd say to you if they were here now. Put the gun down, Vince. It's over now, time to move on!"

Seconds eked by, while they locked eyes. Morgan's shoulders heaved, and his head dropped down on his chest, only to jerk back up, catching Dalton off-guard. "You want the gun, trooper? OK, I'll give it to you," he growled. Morgan yanked the barrel from his head and swung it in Dalton's direction.

Blam! Dalton flinched as the thunder and concussion assaulted him. When the stream of blazing orange flame streaked from the barrel, he was momentarily blinded—but still quite alive. Maybe the old-timers weren't jiving when they said, "You'll never hear the shot that kills you!" Instinctively, Dalton pulled his revolver and cradled it under his left arm, pointing it waist level at Morgan's torso. (*Wait! Not yet...wait!*) With an anguished groan, Morgan swung the gun around and pointed it down at the water between them. *Blam! Blam! Blam!* Blinded by the bright flashes, Dalton heard the rounds ricochet off the water, zipping off into the night air like angry bees. He blinked his eyes and strained to see. Suddenly, there was a clumping sound several feet from where he stood. Bending down in the shadows, he spotted the handgun on the deck. The slide was locked back—an empty weapon. Dalton walked over and picked it up, then stuffed it into his waist belt. He looked over at Morgan and nodded. "Come on, man. Let's get off this damn pier," he told him.

Morgan grabbed the wooden railing and slowly pulled himself to his feet. After hearing the excited shouts from the troopers onshore, Dalton called back and reassured them. He holstered his revolver, then walked over to Morgan and draped an arm over his shoulder. "Hang with me here, Vince," he told him, before patting him down. Dalton found a small buck knife in Morgan's pants pockets, jammed it in his own back pocket, and then started down the pair with his prisoner.

When they approached the light at the middle of the pier, Sergeant Long emerged from the shadows. Morgan spotted him, jammed a hand into a shirt pocket, and suddenly pulled away. When Morgan crammed the contents of his hand into his mouth, Dalton grabbed him around his neck in a headlock and drove him head first down to the pier.

"Spit 'em out, man! Spit 'em out, or I'm gonna choke you out!" Dalton yelled, tightening his hold. Morgan coughed and gagged, and the pills spewed out. Dalton kept the chokehold on him until he was satisfied nothing was left in his mouth. Morgan's chest heaved, and he gasped for air. Minutes later, the corporal was en route to the PF barrack with his prisoner, signaling the climactic end to the Kenwood Beach episode.

When Dalton left the barrack, Tfc. Heslip was waiting for him on the parking lot. "Just wanted to tell you that you did a great job out there, Corporal Bragg. Been on the job a while now, and I've never seen anything like that before. Took some balls! Just wanted you to know that, Corp," Heslip added with a smile. "Thanks, Jack, much appreciated," Dalton replied as they meandered over to their cruisers. "We *all* made it work right tonight, Jack, and I'm damned proud of all three of you. You guys held back and used your heads, and nobody got hurt. Hard to believe, huh?"

Driving south on Route 4, Dalton felt a huge weight lifted off his shoulders. Approaching St. Leonard, he suddenly pulled off onto the shoulder and stopped. He pushed his sore back against the seat, rested his head against the headrest and rubbed his aching eyes. No, he couldn't go home just yet, not yet. Minutes later, he was barreling down Kenwood Beach Road. He soon found himself standing alone on the pier he'd left behind several hours ago.

The wind had picked up some, coming from the south now, and the slit moon had dropped lower to the west. Dalton walked anxiously to the second pier light. When he looked down at the glow on the water, he didn't see any bay creatures as before. He continued on until the end of the pier. Night-vision acclimated; he spotted the three expended brass shells on the deck. Dalton whisked them off the pier with his foot, plopping them in the water. OK, he was back again, but alone with no witnesses.

He had to give himself another shot at this, another chance to experience what he thought, *No*, what he *knew* he'd encountered here. He had to hear her consoling voice again. He leaned back against the railing and pulled out a thin, rum-soaked cigar, lit it and drew in a mouthful of the savory smoke. Several minutes passed without a hint of surrealism. Other than the splash of a breaking fish, far out of sight, or the crackly "Awkkk" of a blue heron, he heard nothing from the night. Still, no matter how it all added up, it was the waning part of a very special night.

Dalton tossed the cigar butt in the water and turned to leave. Down on the pier, just about where Morgan had hunkered down hours before, he spotted something fluttering in the breeze. It was wedged tight in a crack between two deck planks. Curious, he picked it up. It was a thick piece of paper, folded over several times, and he stuffed it into his shirt pocket.

When he reached the light at mid-pier, Dalton took it out, unfolded it, and began reading. It was addressed: "To Jon Boy, Pig Man, Slick Dude, and Figgy...my Delta buds of the 2nd of the 60th, the best of the 9th," and it started with, "I'm Sorry, my brothers...!" His mind racing with anticipation, Dalton read the front page. When he turned it over to read the scribbling on the back, a sudden breeze blew the paper from his hand. He dropped to the pier on all fours and scrambled after it, but he was too late. The note sailed off the pier and down to the choppy water below, and within seconds it was gone, outbound on the tide.

Except for the dim overhead stove light, Dalton came home to a dark tomb. Just a note from Cindy, just a simple, caring "Hi, honey, thinking of you," scrawled-out thought would have sufficed, but as usual, nothing. He unbuckled the gun belt and slipped it on the top shelf of the broom cabinet. Shuffling over to the fridge, he liberated several beers and toted them over to the living room coffee table.

No, he had to see them—had to check on the daughters first. He smiled as he climbed the stairs and tiptoed into Charlene's room. In the dark, she was lying on her tummy, a Cabbage Patch doll embraced by a bare arm, and he could hear her soft, shallow breathing. He adjusted a blanket, and gently put his hand on her warm back, letting it linger for a while. Satisfied, he sneaked into Anne Marie's room. Typically, she was lying on her side, and when he touched her, she rolled over with a soft moan and opened her sleepy eyes. Always, this always happens with her, Dalton knew. He smiled and brushed back her silky blonde hair with his fingertips, then pursed his lips to blow her an air kiss. Half asleep, she smiled and tried to return it, but sleep quickly returned, and she rolled back over with a sigh.

Relieved, Dalton crept from her bedroom and eased the door shut. He gazed over at the closed door of the master bedroom, paused for a moment, then shuffled down the hall to the unlit bathroom. Quietly, he rummaged through the medicine cabinet until he found the half-empty pack of Unisoms. He took out two sleep capsules and swallowed them, chasing them with several gulps of beer. Dalton could vision Morgan now, sitting in the corner of a dank cell on suicide watch, head in hands, picturing his life as nothing but a meaningless abyss. He could only imagine what Morgan had lived through, all he had seen and done in the hellish quagmire of Viet Nam—all the close friends who'd been ripped out of his life, lost forever.

Dalton finished his second beer, closed his eyes and settled back on the couch. "Yeah, trooper, you really got yourself into some hairy shit, didn't ya?" he muttered. The ticking of the kitchen clock over the sink resonated louder than usual, and already he was feeling the familiar signs of an expected headache. He brought a hand up to his temple, and as he did, his fingers started trembling. With a silent curse, he pulled his hand away and held it in front of his blanched face. The trembling traveled to his arms and legs and quickly spread through his entire body, making him groan and shake violently from the incessant spasms. When his teeth started chattering, he clenched his jaw and fought for control. It was bad this time, real bad. It was all he could do to hold on, as wave after wave of sharp, intense tremors wracked him.

Later, when the first light of dawn crept in, Dalton woke up to find himself sprawled on the living room floor. He rubbed his eyes and eased himself to his feet. His arms and legs were stiff, and he could taste blood in his mouth from a bitten lower lip. Ignoring it, he steeled himself, hoping to pierce the fog in his head for a sluggish attempt at climbing the stairs.

#

"Hey Dalton, you douche-bag, my lame ass is out and about after another knucklehead Long Beach Community meeting," Colby rasped in the phone. "How's about joining me for a few cold ones at the ole Hole in The Wall in Lusby?"

It was 10:30 PM, and Dalton was near the end of another lackluster late shift. "Come on, man! Your old lady's gonna be doin' major zzzzs when you get home, wanna bet? Sure be nice to quaff a few with my bud." Dalton shot an idle glance at his watch. Hell, why not? "Sure, Colby, you whacko, no problemo, be there soon's I can. Warm up a bar stool for me, hear? Hey, uh, ya think Gary can squirm out tonight, maybe?" Dalton asked. "Naw, he's got himself all pussy-whipped again," Colby replied, "so it's you and me tonight, bud!" Dalton winced when Colby shrieked *Yee-haw* and cut the connection. Crazy damned bastard. Just might do us both some good to drink a little mash and talk a little trash, Dalton mused.

Forty-five minutes later, after racing home and throwing on a pair of jeans and a tattered sweat shirt, Dalton sauntered into the Hole in The Wall bar. From the blaring jukebox, Credence Clearwater's gravelly *Born on the Bayou* assaulted his ears. Dalton smiled, remembering how that Cajun ditty was one of his favorites back in his frenzied band days of yesteryears. The tune added a proper down-home flavor to the Hall in the Wall's gritty ambience. Even the hooded ghosts of those gentry' sons of Calvert lore, the white night-riders, who many years ago attended the hushed-up weekly KKK meetings in the musty cellar below, would be hard-pressed not to slap their thighs to that tune, he reckoned.

Peering through the veil of cigarette smoke, Dalton saw only a handful of patrons cemented to bar stools. There were several other motley types in side booths away from the bar's tacky glitter, and he scoped them out carefully, searching for dirt-ball faces that might set off warning bells. Satisfied, he plunked himself down on the stool next to his renegade friend.

Colby stubbed out his cigarette, shot him a shit-faced grin and slapped him on the back. Snapping his fingers, he ordered up two drafts from Mary Lou, the Hole-in the Wall's perky, mentally challenged bartender. Tonight, Mary Lou was sporting a bleach-blonde rat's nest hairdo, complemented by heavy makeup she'd sloppily dusted all over her pockmarked face. Dalton watched in feigned amusement when Colby lowered his face to the wood bar top. Colby sniffed and snorted, then jerked his head up with a grin. "Had to smell the hops to get the ole pump primed," he chortled, nudging Dalton with an elbow.

Two older, painted-up women sat next to Colby. Probably county cougars on their way home from a bowling league outing, Dalton figured. On this slow weekday evening in greater Lusby's premier tavern, they were basking in Colby's divided attention. "I attract the bitches wherever I go, my friend," Colby whispered between beer gulps. "Yup, nothin' but a chick magnet I am, but I won't hold that against 'em, 'cause it's out of their control." Dalton laughed as they clunked their marred plastic mugs together. It was true, through and through: Colby's effervescent, happy-go-lucky, piped-piper persona lured people to him wherever he went.

"God, how I love my job, Dalton," Colby said gleefully. "Get to rub elbows with the county's bigwigs, do the fried-chicken dinner circuits and schmooze meetings, do my own schedule, and get to meet all sorts of wanton hussies, too...all on the MSP clock. Quite a deserving reward, if I don't say so myself!" Dalton rolled his eyes and feigned a yawn. "Yeah, the lieutenant is happier than a stuffed hog about how the program's catchin' on," Colby said with a wink. "Pinch me, dude, my ass is in heaven!"

It was true, Dalton realized. In the resident trooper program, Colby was well known, liked and respected countywide. In some endeavors, however, particularly his extracurricular escapades with loose women, he was becoming *too* well known.

"Yeah, Colby, while I'm still out there riding herd and doing road-pounder shift-work, you've managed to turn yourself into the consummate MSP politician with your smile and silver tongue, that's for sure," Dalton told his schmoozer friend. Colby shirked and took a long drag on his cigarette before answering.

"Think I got this gift horse figured out, ole buddy," he spouted in a cloud of smoke. Dalton wrinkled his forehead and shot Colby a hollow stare. "No, serious, man! Listen to me. Think I'm good for two ranks at least in this here Residual Trooper Program," Colby added with a grin. "Then, with a little luck, and some serious brown-nosing, and I'm talking vacuum-tight deep here, my friend, I just might be able to wrangle my way up to be the MSP coordinator for the entire statewide program!" Colby paused and smiled at his reflection in the stained glass mirror above the bar.

"Yeah, rubbing elbows with the Pikesville brass for a spell should get me in striking distance of maybe a captain's spot somewhere, no? Who knows, ya just might be looking at the lovely face of a future MSP "Super" right now! Wanna job driving my ass around when I'm wearin' those chicken wings on my collar, ole buddy?" "Sure you don't have some whacky-weed in them cigs you been puffing on, partner?" Dalton asked half seriously. "Screw you, bitch face," Colby blurted back. Dalton was about to gush out a few beer-fueled philosophical MSP musings, but Colby's attention had already been drawn to the big-haired, heavy-set woman sitting beside him. Sporting an overblown, borderline-ugly, Cheshire grin over a flabby double chin, she was tugging on Colby's elbow. Dalton raised his eyebrows to signal Mary Lou for another round, while Colby and Ms Cheshire slobbered endearingly in each other's ears.

After several minutes, the flush-faced Colby turned his attention back to Dalton. "Yeah, buddy!" he panted, "It just don't get no better than this, my man, ya know?" Straight-faced, Dalton studied Colby's reflection in the mirror. "Pssst, I think she wants me, she wants me bad...*and* her bored girlfriend's with her too," Colby spouted. "Go on...Take a look at that bitch, why don't ya, and tell me if you don't feel lucky tonight?" Dalton gave Ms Cheshire's friend a quick side-glance, rolled his eyes at Colby, then took a swig of beer. Yeah, sure enough. He'd seen her effervescent, glitzy-eyed friend trolling the bars before, sending out "I'm available *now*" vibes, hopelessly foraging for someone to do the nasty with, before she snuck home to her tiresome lawyer hubby sawing the zzzs in the spare bedroom of their mini-mansion in White Sands.

"Hey, this is the only merry-go-round we get to ride in this life," Colby preached, "and you gotta lean out pretty far to get that brass-ass ring sometimes, get my drift?" "Yeah, sure Colby, but right now would probably be a good time to pull the plug and get your brass ass down the road, so you can ride that merry-go-round with your ole lady, maybe, no? Besides, her friend looks like a nasty bitch-bulldog, anyhow!" Colby snorted, pulled out another cigarette and ordered a rum and coke from fickle-headed Mary Lou, signaling his intent to warm the bar stool longer.

"You hear that ole song playing on the jukebox, Dalton? The one about dust in the wind?" Colby asked. Dalton nodded and stared at him with warm eyes. "That's it, my friend," Colby added. "All in a nutshell out here in this life. We're simply just dust in the wind, when it comes down to it, savvy? That's the bottom line, and we might as well live it up while we can, brother, before the wind blows it all away."

Colby squinted his eyes and gave Dalton a satisfied look before he took another puff on his cigarette. Dalton smiled and nudged an elbow into his zany friend's side, then pulled out several bills and slapped them on the bar. "See ya when I get back from leave, my friend! I'm outta here!" He'd almost made it to the door when Colby's booming voice thundered out. "Hey, *Trooper!*"

Dalton turned and gazed back at his grinning friend, who was holding his hand steady over an eyebrow in a frozen salute. With a cigarette drooping from his mouth, Colby did his best to ignore Ms Cheshire's fleshy arm draped over his shoulder. Yeah buddy! Dress her up and it'd be like putting earrings on a pig. Dalton slammed the heels of his Reeboks together and jerked himself up tall to stand at mock-attention. With a lame smile, he returned an exaggerated salute, following it with a half-hearted bow. A quick about-face, and moments later he was out in the brisk, star-filled night.

Yeah, maybe if Colby could keep both ends of the candle from blazing too long, he just might make it up the ranks, despite himself, Dalton silently mused. Not soon enough, he was quietly snuggling up, spoon-like, against Cindy's warm, welcome body.

#

The Dodge Charger's super-charged engine screamed as the powerful black car barreled down Rousby Hall Road, the driver going balls-to-the-walls in an attempt to shake off the MSP cruiser hanging on his tail. The panicky driver abruptly turned off Route 2 onto the first paved road he saw. The trooper knew the road dead-ended, and from experience, he knew that whoever was in the car would probably bail out when it did.

It was night shift, and Dalton was making patrol checks in the Solomons area. He'd just passed Bunky Dow's Tackle Shop near the tip of the sleepy island, when he saw a red flash in his rearview mirror. The Charger's headlights were off as it shot out from a side alley, but the driver had accidentally tapped the brakes as he exited. Dalton floored the gas pedal and did a tire-squealing power turn. A quick glance down the alley—a side door smashed in, a cash register on its side, confirmed the burglary. Dalton quickly closed the distance. Super! It was a DC tag, stolen no doubt. Galvanized with adrenaline, he barked into the radio mic, but the red transmit light didn't come on. He cursed, balled his free hand into a fist and whacked the side of the radio console a few times, hoping to jolt it back to life. No deal. Once again it was dead, leaving him totally incommunicado. *NO!* That wasn't going to stop him now—*screw that!*

On the long, straightaway section of the unlit road, Dalton tried several times to pull the cruiser alongside the streaking vehicle. Each time, the driver swerved at him, forcing him to back off. Suddenly, he saw a hand pop up from the passenger window. There was a flash, and a sharp report! Instinctively, Dalton ducked below the steering wheel as the bullet ricocheted off the hood of his cruiser and smashed into the windshield! Instant gaping hole and a huge spider web fracture! *Shit*! Blasted into the self-preservation mode, the corporal hung back, hoping they'd make a stupid mistake, one that didn't include slinging any more lead his way.

When the Charger fish-tailed coming out of a tight curve, he knew the end was near. All he had to do now was just hang tight with it until the dead end. Dalton's chest tightened, as gravel kicked up from the car and pelted the cruiser's hood and windshield like a hailstorm. The brake lights suddenly blazed red, and smoke poured from the screeching, skidding tires as the Charger came to a jolting stop. Immediately the car headlights were doused.

In a thick cloud of smoke and hanging dust, Dalton skidded to a head jarring stop yards behind the suspect vehicle. He flicked his high beams on and swiveled the spotlight around to bathe the Charger in a sea of light. Along with the swirling reds-and-blues, Dalton left the wailing siren on, not only for the unnerving effect, but also in the vain hope that a nearby resident might be concerned enough to call the control center after hearing the ruckus. Dalton quickly unbuckled his shoulder harness and took a deep breath. His heart was pounding like a jackhammer when he snatched the shotgun from the floorboard and grabbed his Kel-light flashlight. He exited the cruiser on cat feet, leaving the car door open.

So far, he hadn't spotted any movement in the car, but from where he was, he saw that the Charger had mirror tinting on its windows, making visibility zilch, something he always dreaded on traffic stops. *Not Good*! Taking a position several yards behind the car, Dalton gingerly cranked a shell into the shotgun, placed the flashlight under the stock to illuminate his alignment, and then leveled the weapon at the rear window. Seconds passed way too slow as he stood crouched over his shotgun, waiting for something, *anything,* to break the impasse. The need to take action roared at him, each second thundering louder. Ignoring the surging adrenaline and his trembling legs, he found a suitable warrior voice. Loud demands for the driver and whoever to exit the vehicle were met with dead silence. Without the radio and with no backup, Dalton realized that he'd just slipped into a world of some really bad shit.

Maneuvering closer, he kicked the car's rear bumper and jumped back. *Nothing.* Damn, *damn*! For a moment he felt like calling it a bad night, felt like slinking back to the cruiser to speed away unscathed. Who'd ever know? He answered his own question.

Blam! Blam! The thought hit him quick, and he instinctively let loose with it. Ignoring textbook MSP policy, he blew out the Charger's rear tires with two rifled slug blasts from his twelve-gauge patrol buddy. Troopers can't, No—they *don't*—back down from anything or anyone. They take action!

He paused to collect his thoughts before slowly inching over to the driver's door. He drew the shotgun back, poised to smash it into the ugly tinted window. *Wham!* Suddenly, the window blew up in his face! Dalton felt the heat and concussion of the searing blast, followed instantly by unbearable pain. It felt like he'd been hit with a sledgehammer, when the .357 magnum hollow-point struck him in the upper chest, sending him sprawling to the cold macadam.

His swirling mind fought for control, but he was aware of little but the agonizing pain and the loud ringing in his ears. No, dear lord, no...*not now!* He heard someone screaming, realized it was himself, and he never felt more helpless in his young life. Nothing worked right—couldn't move his arms or legs, couldn't raise his head, couldn't do anything with the excruciating pain wracking his body. But he was still miraculously conscious, could still hear and see. He felt something warm spreading across his chest, realized that it was his own blood leeching from the horrific wound. *(Don't panic...Don't you dare let yourself panic!)* He could hear the screaming siren, could see the wildly oscillating lights casting their eerie red-and-blue glows all around him, foggy-like. Dalton fought hard as waves of numbness washed over him. Spasms shook his body, and everything started turning dark and blurry. He was vaguely aware of a car door being slammed shut, could almost discern the shadow of a human figure slowly shuffling over to where he lay. In a last effort, he tried to ignore the pain and the loud ringing in his head enough to concentrate.

Slowly emerging from the darkness, the blurry, leering mask stared down at him. He saw the beaming eye first! When what was left of the mangled face finally cleared the shadows, he gasped for the last time. *Donny Roberts!* Helplessly paralyzed, with the last dregs of consciousness ebbing away, Dalton felt the cold, steel barrel of the .357 magnum being jammed against his head. He opened his mouth to scream, tried to move his lips, but nothing came out!

Dalton woke up with a start, gasping for air, his heart beating wildly and his hands clutching at his sweat-soaked pillow. Once again, another nightmare, but the ringing remained. He blinked his eyes and grazed Cindy's back with trembling fingertips for a reality check. The ringing continued. Yes, of course! It was the phone ringing in the hall, that was it. He glanced at the illuminated hands of the nightstand clock, saw that it was only 5:45 AM. *Damn!* Dalton pushed himself from the bed and dashed out to the hall.

It was a very somber Cpl. Buddy English on the line. Dalton heard his fellow corporal's measured words, but he couldn't put them all together at first. What he gradually absorbed was impossible, and he felt like someone had knocked the wind out of him with a baseball bat. *No!* This was the wrong movie; this couldn't be right, could it? Minutes later, after throwing on a pair of jeans and a jacket, Dalton sped to the barrack to join his fellow troopers.

Just days after celebrating his twenty-seventh year of immortality, Colby Merson was dead.

The investigation determined that Colby Merson was traveling on the notoriously-winding Sixes Road when his treasured lime-green Ford Mustang swerved off the road and careened into muddy Cypress Creek, just yards from the small wooden bridge. The Mustang flipped, throwing him out and trapping him underneath when it rolled over. No one at the scene realized there was a body underneath the Mustang, until the tow-truck operator managed to wrench it upright.

Corporal English was surprised when he saw the body. He was totally stunned, however, once he recognized who he was gawking at. It was ugly. Countless photos were taken at the scene, but they were grotesque and were sealed and censored on the authority of the barrack commander.

As usual, rumors about possible causes of the accident ran rampant in the county. Those few in the know, however, refrained from divulging Colby's high post-mortem BAC (blood alcohol content). Most assuredly, they'd never disclose the identity of the woman Colby had been with minutes before his mishap—the least they could do to protect the reputation of their lost colleague. In that regard, Dalton had already learned that the activities of fellow officers could be warped to extend way beyond the norm.

One such "courtesy" had been performed on behalf of a deceased deputy sheriff from a sister county a few years back. He was an older deputy, married with kids, but he was also a known, hardcore philanderer anchored to a shrewish wallflower wife. Engaged in a particularly strenuous bout of frothy jungle sex with one of his babes during a slow night shift, the deputy keeled over and died from a heart attack. His country-gal, grits-and-scrapple girlfriend was clearheaded enough to call another deputy she knew. Minutes later, he and several officers arrived to rectify the situation.

It'd been a struggle, but they eventually manhandled the defunct one back into his uniform, before carrying him out to his patrol car which was driven to a lower parking area behind the county courthouse. There, next to a reeking, rat-infested dumpster, they left him propped up behind the steering wheel to be "found" by a fellow deputy a half-hour later. Along with the paperback copy of Joseph Wambaugh's *New Centurions* found on his lap, there was a hint of a smile on the dead deputy's pale mug. Scuttlebutt and legend eventually entwined to give the incident a comical, albeit morbid aura of truth. What *was* horribly too true was that Colby Merson, Dalton's close friend and future MSP superintendent, was dead, many years before his time.

#

At Colby's wife's request, Dalton and Gary Rephan, both immaculately clad in the MSP Class A uniform with badges cloaked in black, stood the casket watch during Colby's viewing at the Barstow funeral home.

Dalton had a strong aversion to funeral homes. The strong, almost sickening sweet fragrance of flowers barely masked the musty, vacuum cleaner bag odor he typically smelled in every funeral home he'd been in. The piped-in melancholy organ music didn't help, either. And, like each one he'd been in before, he couldn't help notice that those who worked there never failed to have that pasty, odd, robotic look to them as they performed their duties. He couldn't imagine having such a job. "Hi, honey, I'm home! You won't believe how screwed-up ole man Garner's embalmment went today! Talk about collapsed veins! We had to ratchet up the pump so high that I thought he was gonna have a damned blow-out!"

Nonetheless, Dalton felt strangely comforted being near his departed friend during the casket watch, and this time the funeral home encounter was tolerable. He and Gary stood rigid in parade-rest at both ends of the open casket, and now and then Dalton's gaze drifted over to Colby. From the mutilated mess they'd worked with, the morticians had done a remarkable job reconstructing Colby's face. In final repose, decked out in his class A uniform, Dalton almost discerned a smile on his dead friend's rebuilt face, but it was so out of place not to see a cigarette dangling from the corner of his mouth.

Every so often, Dalton gazed over at the glazed and vacant eyes of Rachael, Colby's new widow, who was tightly holding her toddler daughter's hand. At those awkward moments, flashes of guilt passed over him, and he wondered what she knew about her enraptured husband's affairs. Fellow troopers reached out to embrace her, touch her shoulder or hold her hand as they whispered comforting words.

Dalton felt himself choking up once when he saw her composure start to melt, so he quickly diverted his eyes back to Colby. Maybe, yes maybe, if he just leaned over and reached down into that glitzy, sterile-looking fiberglass coffin, he could grab his waxy-faced friend's stiff body by the shoulders and shake him, tell him to cut this shit out. Yes, maybe Colby would open his eyes and break out in that infectious, toothy smile of his, followed by waves of his usual high-pitched laughter. Most assuredly, he'd demand a smoke and another frosty beer to put an end to this bad dream trapped in a horrid B-movie. And each time he forced himself to break away from the tear-laden gaze of his friend's wife, the bad dream gravitated back to somber reality.

Dalton saw the girl hesitate at first, unsure of herself, but after pausing, she lifted her head and approached him. Marsha Trott, the cute, promiscuous secretary in the public defender's office, gingerly reached out and put her hand on his arm. Teary eyed, the wavy-haired blonde looked at the casket, and then turned her emerald eyes back to Dalton. She opened her other hand, revealing a gold braided necklace with a heart-shaped charm.

"Dalton, you know me. I'm pretty straight up, and I usually don't ask for favors, but a good friend of mine would like to return this to him, to Colby," she said in a wavering voice. She paused for a moment and bit down on her lower lip. "Would you indulge in her wishes, and try to find a place for it next to him, if at all possible...for me, Dalton?" she whispered, her fingers tightening on his sleeve. For a moment, he thought he should accommodate her, and in a knowing way he wanted to—but he knew he couldn't. When he took the easy way out and told her that he'd have to ask permission from Colby's wife, a tear ran down her face, and she pursed her lips and nodded sadly. She glanced at the casket again, made a brave attempt to smile, and then turned to leave.

Dalton's head swirled with imagined scenarios stemming from his brief exchange with her. No doubt Gary had sensed something amiss in her demeanor too, but Dalton knew Gary wouldn't ask about it.

At the family's request, Colby's short funeral service was held at the packed funeral home in lieu of a church. It was biting cold and breezy earlier, overcast, with an ugly gray, sullen sky. As the MSP pallbearers brought the casket to the waiting hearse, the sun burned through the clouds, saluting those below with rays of warmth. Dalton and Gary, along with fellow corporals Ben Wiley, and Dick McNulty, were four of the six chosen to be Colby' pallbearers. Somber and silent, all four rode together, several cars back from the hearse.

Finally, after minutes of ungodly silence, Ben Wiley leaned over in the front passenger seat, yelled out, "Anal alert!" and emitted a long, squishy-sounding fart. Instantly, the trumpeting from his buttocks shattered their sullen moods and putrefied the cruiser's already-stale air. All three gassed victims burst into shoulder-jerking laughter, while windows were quickly rolled down. As McNulty wiped tears from his eyes and concentrated on driving, Dalton and Gary both bent over low in their seats, trying to hide their grins from those in the car behind them. "Jesus Christ, Wiley," McNulty cried out between gasps, "Smells like something crawled up your silly ass and died again. You better check your damn self after that one!"

"Hey, y'all, were getting too damn serious for me, guys. I just had to break up the mood some, know what I mean?" quipped fartster Wiley. "Aunt Penny's early-bird breakfast special, that scrapple and green pepper omelet of hers, is just tearing my ass up. And besides that, you know damn well ole Colby would a done the same thing by now, if he'd been sittin' in my place!"

Wiley turned the radio on and fumbled with the dial until it landed on DC 96.9, the Diesel Dude's station, Colby's favorite. More laughter reigned in the cruiser as the Diesel Dude broke into another one of his testosterone-packed, maniacal monologues. This time, it was Sergeant Rock telling his squad of macho killer-marines how kosher it was for him to choke his chicken while dodging a horde of enemy bullets. The awkward silence had been duly extinguished.

"Ya know," Dalton said to no one in particular, "I never figured that Colby would be in the big picture for the long run, but I thought he'd at least hang around for a couple more years with us." Gary snapped his head up and winced. "Who the hell you kiddin', Dalton?" he rasped. "You, me, and all of us for that matter, we all knew he was playing around in the fast lane too long. Sometimes you just gotta ease over to life's slow lane, but that wasn't him. No, ole Colby lit the candle on both ends, he did, and stuck a blazing flare under the middle of it too, just to see what would happen!" Gary paused to let his words sink in. "Yup, you gotta move over to let others pass you by every now and then, know what I mean?" Both McNulty and Wiley nodded in unison. Dalton just turned and stared out the window. Yeah, you could almost predict the limited longevity of those Colby types, the live-for-today shooting stars, he thought to himself.

When they carried Colby's casket to the burial site, Dalton shot quick side-glances at his fellow troopers and the large crowd of waiting mourners. Many were standing under or next to the crowded canopy which marked the newly-dug hole in the ground—Colby's final resting place. On the outskirts of the crowd, Dalton spotted Cindy. With her long blonde hair blowing in the wind, Cindy stood alone. She'd always liked Colby, especially his distorted sense of humor, and Dalton knew she'd never before experienced the death and loss of someone close to her. She was frozen in place, immersed in deep thought, far away in her own protective world.

#

Four days later, as the sun sank below the trees at twilight, Dalton stood in front of Colby Merson's headstone in the serene Asbury Cemetery. It was windy and brisk, but he had no problem hearing the distinct mooing of a lone cow in a distant field. Along the tree-line, several deer emerged, ghost-like, to browse in the grassy field next to the cemetery. You sure got yourself a nice place to take a dirt nap, Colby, he thought to himself, gazing down at the fresh sod marking the cemetery's newest addition.

Flower arrangements, most wilted but some fresh, adorned the area around the granite headstone bearing Colby's full name (middle name "Franklin?" You gotta be shitting me Colby.) Under his name were the dates marking the beginning and end of his twenty-seven short years.

As he'd vowed earlier, Dalton took two miniature bottles of dark Bacardi rum from his jacket. On his way to the cemetery, he'd already scarfed down two lukewarm brewskis to calm the mounting anticipation. "You first, my friend...our toast," he said. Dalton twisted the cap off the miniature and poured the dark liquor on the sod in front of the headstone. Satisfied, he snapped to attention, lifted the other miniature high over his head for a moment, then downed it in Colby's honor. With the rum warming his stomach, he set the empty bottles against the headstone. When he did, something shiny to the right of the marker caught his eye. It lay under an arrangement of wilted red roses, and at first, it didn't register. But when he gingerly picked it up and turned it in his fingers, he knew. Sure enough, it was the gold braided necklace chain and heart locket that Marsha Trott, Colby's premier paramour, had shown him four days before at the funeral home. Awash with mixed sentiments, Dalton fumbled with the tiny latch and finally managed to open the locket. The words leaped out at him: "Marsha, Forever Is Always"—Colby. Dalton stood up and stuffed the necklace into his shirt pocket.

"Well ole buddy, this confirms that you had at least one devoted flame in your abbreviated life," Dalton told his friend in a hushed voice. "Can't chance your wife finding this one, though, Colby...The poor woman's been through enough." Dalton bowed his head, silently cursing Colby for leaving him, for cheating him of his friendship. Finally, his emotional dam burst and a stream of hot tears flowed down his cheeks.

"Now look what you made me do, Colby, you dumb ass," he muttered. Dalton rubbed tired, bloodshot eyes with his fingers and struggled for composure. (Damn you, Colby, you know troopers don't cry!) He picked up a small dry clod of dirt at the edge of the fresh sod, held it at arm's length, then slowly crumbled it in his hands. He watched passively as the dust was quickly blown away in the breeze. "You had that one right, what you said at the Hole in the Wall, my friend. All we're ever meant to be, is dust in the wind." Dalton brought himself up to attention and smartly saluted Colby's shiny new granite headstone before turning to leave.

On the way home, Dalton pulled off Route 4 and stopped alongside the bridge at the bottom of Hall's Creek Hill. He jumped from the car and walked over to the steel railing. Leaning over the railing, he took the gold chain and locket from his pocket and studied it for a moment before he tossed it into the silted creek. He got as far as Huntingtown before the urge hit strong enough to detour him from his homeward route. Cindy would be fast asleep by now, anyhow. Yeah, and besides, he was in that rare mood for some doleful country music right about now. Minutes later, he was elbow-to-elbow, puffing on a cheroot and quaffing a few "gratis" beers with the local hayseeds in the clamorous, smoke-filled, Aunt Penny's restaurant.

Chapter 9

EXIT THE WHITE KNIGHT

With seven years of faithful service, Corporal Dalton Bragg was in full-blown gung-ho status with the MSP. It was becoming painfully obvious, however, that the situation on the family home front was slip-sliding away. Whereas it once served as a warm, embracing shelter from the stressful job's stark realities, life at home had become more unstable and distant to him.

Dalton knew it didn't stem just from the pressures of raising the kids, either. They loved them infinitely, and under Cindy's devoted maternal care, they thrived. Sure, he realized the constant revolving shift work made it difficult for normal, everyday interaction with them, and it was also true that with only one and a half weekends off a month, their social activities with relatives and friends were sharply restricted. With time and rank advancements, however, Dalton repeatedly assured Cindy, shift work would eventually be a thing of the past.

During the last year, the walls separating Dalton and his wife had grown undeniably higher, leaving little room for those special moments they both relished so much in the earlier years. Where once they shared open intimacy in their heart-pounding lovemaking during those elusive quality times, now they were sharing virtually nothing, both seemingly content to surf alone on the cascading waves of remoteness. While Dalton knew he couldn't arbitrarily point his fingers at her for most of their problems, he knew he'd at least tried to reach out and communicate with her.

And most emphatically, he *did* blame her for allowing herself to shut down, to withdraw to someplace deep within her self, somewhere safe behind a protective shield, to avoid going through the motions of communicating with him. And *that* iciness was also becoming very, very frustrating, marked by a total sex void during the last few months. Dalton was beginning to resent her for the constant rebuffs and chilled indifference, and since she refused to open up to him, he, in turn, clammed up to her. He'd tried to contain his discontent, avoiding the inevitable confrontations she so much deplored, preferring to let things continue indefinitely, hoping for magical changes to arrive.

Eventually the festering emerged—vented anger and lashing frustration. One night, just before she dozed off in the core of another new book, a Carl Sagan cosmic navel-contemplator, Dalton, exasperated and buoyed up by a few beers, surfaced for a yank on her chain again. After he'd massaged her shoulders and teasingly stroked her back with wandering fingertips, hoping for a response, she acknowledged his efforts with an annoyed sigh and another page turn of her interstellar guidebook. Stymied, Dalton pointedly asked her if it'd be within the realm of possibility to reserve an intimacy appointment with her some time within the next few months, perhaps.

Cindy lifted her eyebrows quizzically, allowing the shell-shocked look to eke across her face. Carefully placing a bookmark between pages, she stared at the book cover while she gathered her thoughts. She sighed again, then slowly turned her head his way and gave an answer he didn't want to hear.

"I'm really not happy with my life, hon," she blurted out. "Too many complications, too many heavy issues to go into right now...or maybe ever. I know what you're going to say, you've said it many times over, so maybe I'll let you save your breath this time," she added coolly. "With all honesty though, I wouldn't blame you if you went out and found a girlfriend who treated you right, and that's all I want to say about it."

They stared at each other in wounded silence, searching each other's eyes for any signs of empathy, any shards of understanding—until Cindy slid the book onto the night table, turned out the nightlight, and rolled away to the other side of the bed. Thunderstruck, Dalton merely sunk his head on the pillow, allowing the dark room to silently absorb his drubbed sentiments. Still, when her body trembled and she began to cry, he put his arm around her and wordlessly drew her in close, immediately regretting the pain he'd caused. God, he hated it when he hurt her. Thankfully, this time she didn't pull away. Undeniably, Dalton knew he loved her, and the mere thought of him ever leaving her and the kids had never crossed his mind.

He'd never do it. Gary Rephan, his close compatriot and fellow trooper, was already separated and immersed in the beginning throes of a messy divorce. The effect it was having on Gary was clearly devastating, no matter whose fault the breakup was. He'd refrain from following that path if at all possible. Dalton even suspected that despite her cool indifference toward him, Cindy was probably still in love with him, too. Nevertheless, her detachment had become unbearable, cutting through his very core to play havoc with his now-brittle self-esteem.

Her crying that night eventually tapered off, and she fell asleep, or so he'd assumed, but he couldn't sleep—no, not now. Cindy's eyes were wide open too, however, staring unfocused in hazy gloom as she tried to sort through her myriad of torn feelings. She wasn't sure how she felt about him any more, couldn't readily define her confused feelings for him as love, or whatever that was supposed to be. And if she dared to be honest with herself, her feelings about the multitude of other unsettling dilemmas in her life were a mind-numbing fog.

There were far too many long nights alone in a cold, unforgiving bed, too many distressingly empty hours after she'd finally put the kids to bed when he worked those horrid shifts. And she could never make decent plans for family weekends, when his rotating shifts gave him only one full weekend a month off. Added to that, of course, was the burden of taking care of the girls with limited support from him, something she'd grown to detest. She especially resented it when he allowed himself the freedom to gallivant with his trooper buddies, when she felt he should have been spending more quality time with her and the kids. Inevitably, sadly, she turned her resentment toward him in the only way she knew—cold, bitter indifference.

And if Cindy had really been even more honest with herself, she might have also seen his personality change drastically during the last few years. In her eyes, he'd become more withdrawn, his quick laugh and smiles more frequently replaced by somber, brooding detachment. It had been ages since he'd shared any semblance of in-depth conversation with her about his work experiences, although she was probably better off not knowing about most of them. There were several perplexing times at home when she'd caught him staring blankly at the walls or at an empty TV screen, deep in thought, somewhere in another happenstance far removed from her and the family.

His increasingly frequent nightmares alone, the chilling ones where his moans and stifled wailing frightened her awake, were revealing enough. He ceased telling her about them some time ago, but when they first started, when he was more open to her, she'd been alarmed by the horrific images of violence running amok in all of them. Those nightmares indicated he was constantly in some violent, state of conflict within himself, and they were getting worse. Yes, and his growing penchant for the salving effect of too many beers had soared. All told, it wasn't a pretty picture to her anymore.

Really, she never had envisioned herself as the wife of a law-enforcement hubby, a cop's wife, in the first place. She certainly hadn't signed up for that gig and he'd never asked her opinion about it, either. No, she'd merely drifted along with *his* decisions, simple enough, and now she was passionately regretting it. For reasons known only to herself, she'd avoided confrontations and other trouble whenever possible, simply because that was her way. And now, partly because of her reclusive nature, she felt trapped in an unfulfilled life-maze with no discernable way out.

That night, when she thought he'd drifted off to sleep, Cindy took his arm from her shoulder and rolled over to her side of the bed to sift through her simmering feelings. Within minutes she was sound asleep. It would take another hour of staring through the darkness, searching for answers to too many imponderables, before Dalton finally shut his eyes, too.

#

It took only six weeks after that night, the night of the foreboding impasse, for Dalton to shed his knight-in-white armor image, and like most infidelity liaisons, it was unexpected.

It was a typical, muggy Maryland day in July, a hot and clingy, humid Saturday, and Cindy and the girls were at her parent's place in Deale. Shortly after arriving home from a grinding day shift, Dalton received a distraught phone call. Half an hour later, he was hunkered down on a bar stool in a run-down watermen's bar in North Beach with

Gary Rephan, his haggard-looking cohort. After several hours of soul-searching deliberations fueled by many drafts, Dalton drove his soused friend home to the beachfront cottage he shared with another trooper. Characteristically, Gary had a tendency to be coolly reserved about his personal problems. The beer and camaraderie had loosened his stoic veneer, however, and Dalton was able to gauge the extent of Gary's distress, as his marriage slid down the tubes. Hearing the minute details had gnawed at him with a ringing familiarity.

Dalton was passing through Prince Frederick, homeward bound, when he remembered Junebug Buckler's earlier pleas to join him at the Frog Pond in St. Leonard later that evening. The Frog Pond was having its first-ever Beach Party at the down-home country bar on the Route 2 thoroughfare, miles from the bay. The thought cheered him up, although he still had qualms about the last fiasco there with the dynamic Junebug a few months ago.

It was one fiasco too far, which had firmly grounded his cohort to his home base for several months afterward. As usual, it was close to closing time after a long and hectic late shift, and he and Junebug were the only barstool warmers left to talk trash with Tony, the cocky, slightly plastered bartender. After several "ones for the road," Junebug and Tony managed to put their asses squarely on their shoulders.

"Yo, Junebug...Wanna play Shoot the Goose with me tonight?" Tony taunted. The grinning, red-eyed bartender pointed to the shabby stuffed Canadian goose hanging on a wall across the room. Dalton slipped from the stool, squinted his eyes, and sauntered over to the goose. He noticed that the inert fowl didn't have a left wing, and it was also missing both webbed feet and half of its black beak too. Stumbling closer, Dalton spotted the bullet holes in the wooden mount. "Yeah," Tony piped up, "Van Tassel, one of your trooper buddies, won a few drinks from me last week. Son a bitch hit the damn thing every time, feathers flying and all that good shit! All's I hit was wood," he spouted out before downing another shot of Jack Daniels.

Dalton and Junebug knew that Van Tassel, a young trooper who lived in a bottle when he was off duty, was an overdue accident waiting to happen. They eyed Tony with amusement as he rummaged through a cash register drawer. With a triumphant shout, he tossed the small chrome-plated .38 caliber revolver on the bar. Dalton and Junebug stared wide-eyed at each other for an awkward moment, before Dalton squinted back at Tony. Grunting indignantly, Tony grabbed the gun and slid it under the counter. "Guess y'all ain't in much of a shooting mood tonight, huh? Well then, have another beer on me, boys," he shouted, setting two chilled bottles of Coors Light on the bar top.

Soon enough, bravado turned to open dares, and before Dalton had polished off his fourth "one for the road," Tony had hotly challenged Junebug to a slap-boxing match. Shaking with glee, Junebug cleared chairs away to make an impromptu boxing ring, while Tony bolted over the bar top and locked the front door. Feeling mellow and loose, Dalton was still slightly taken aback when Junebug took off his watch and shoved it into his hand, designating him the official timekeeper for the one-minute rounds to follow.

Despite being much smaller than Junebug, Tony, the tipsy gamecock, was raring to go. Dalton thought the lopsided match-up equated to a one-round blowout. And besides, Dalton thought they were kidding anyhow, so he took another swig of beer, peeked at the watch in his hand and yelled "*Go*" to call their bluff.

What ensued was nothing but pissy-pants delirium. To Dalton's amazement, they slap-boxed their way through the agreed six rounds, and both were still upright. When Dalton signaled the end of each earlier round, the red-faced, gasping combatants staggered back to the bar for gulps of brew and a half-minute's rest before continuing. Dalton had to admire the hapless Tony for his drunken tenacity. Time after time, Junebug connected with hard, open-hand slaps to the bartender's face, sending him sprawling into tables and chairs. Amazingly, Tony staggered up from the floor each time, shaking his head and wiping the blood from his nose, to jump back into the fray. Incredibly, Tony even landed a few choice slaps on Junebug's exasperated mug, an affront that spurred on Junebug in his relentless quest to floor the pesky twerp for good. After Dalton yelled out the end of the last round, they kept pummeling each other, oblivious to their official timekeeper, and it was only when Dalton shook up a beer and sprayed them with foam that they finally broke it off.

Junebug was huffing and puffing, and blood oozed from a split lip. With a weary smile, he staggered to the bar and drained his bottle. Winded and sporting a bloody nose, split lip, and a limp, Tony still managed to hurl himself over the bar to fetch a few more "last calls." "Hey Junebug, you big puss," Tony blurted out between gasps, "now why'd I think a Maryland State Trooper could hit harder than that, huh?" Junebug's eyes lit up like road flares. He snorted and promptly unbuckled his watch band again. "Lezzz go another round, ya lil piss-ant, 'cause I'm gonna ssslap your sssorry ass into t'morrow!" he bellowed back. With a valiant last effort, Tony flung himself on the bar top and passed out. With a resounding belch, Junebug pushed away from the bar and aimed for the front door.

Several feet away, he abruptly stopped and looked back. Weaving back and forth, Junebug blinked and tried to focus his bloodshot eyes. An animal grunt escaped from his open mouth when he finally spotted it. Lurching over to the wall, Junebug positioned himself in front of the stuffed Canadian goose. He smiled and cooed lovingly, all the while gently patting the bird's head with his hand. After a fleeting moment of grace, Junebug suddenly jerked his arm back and smashed a fist into the desiccated bird. *Whack!* The hapless creature exploded, its feathered remnants fluttering down to the floor and over several tables. Junebug looked back at Dalton and broke into a drunken grin.

"Hey, ole buddy, juss wanted to put that poor ddduck outta its mizzwee OK?" Dalton grinned at him. "No problem, you big lummox, but your simple ass just showed me what fowl play really is," he shouted back. "Can't take you anywhere Junebug." They howled with laughter and wrapped arms around each other's shoulders as they meandered toward the front door.

Maybe tonight Junebug would force himself to behave more, Dalton hoped. Everybody in the county knew the popular homespun trooper, and they knew just about everything he did, too. Via the well-fed grapevine, they also knew much about what his virile buddy didn't do, but should have.

Even when he gauged the nature of the rural locale and the hordes of locals who attended the event, Dalton thought the Frog Pond Beach

Party in Greater Saint Leonard was nothing but surreal. The Frog Pond proprietors had several truckloads of filtered white sand brought in to fill a large area along the sidewalk in front of the bar. The perimeter adjacent to Route 2 was duly fenced off, and admission was charged.

Just outside the fence, cloistered in a tight group, Dalton saw several locals—wide-eyed, good-ole-boy farmer types in dirty bib-overalls and sweat-stained baseball caps. They were jabbing each other in the ribs and hooting up a storm as they gawked at the eye-candy and the enticing wonder in front of them. The place was jam-packed, with a long line of party people waiting to get in, and Dalton had already recognized a few rotten apples already. Maybe they'd stay to themselves and not get too asinine tonight. Being a cop, there was always that high-visibility problem when you lived and socialized in the same area you worked.

He noticed several multi-colored beach umbrellas near crowded plastic patio tables and strings of bright, multicolored party lights hanging from the Frog Pond's roof. A DJ was blaring out songs ranging from the Beach Boys and Jan & Dean to Caribbean steel drums. Ignoring the sticky humidity, and captured by the lively rhythm, the crowd was swaying and dancing in the sand.

Adding to the ambience, an inflatable wading pool had been set up near the fence. As Dalton made his way to the entrance, he noticed there were already three hairy-chested burley guys and two bikini-clad, tattooed biker-chicks frolicking in it, each of them gripping either a beer bottle or a plastic cup with a tiny umbrella sticking out of the mixed drink. They were loud and happy, shit-faced drunks who seemed content to splash water on each other, or on others who ventured too close. Perfect, he thought, maybe they also bought soap.

The Frog Pond had extra waitresses, and they all were barefoot and wore abbreviated cut-off jeans and tight white T-shirts with deliciously nothing underneath. In large, blazing pink and yellow letters, the slogan *Frog Ponder* was stenciled on both sides of the T-shirts. Each comely waitress also had a plastic-flowered leis draped around her neck for added effect, and all had smiles on their faces as they gamely worked the spirited crowd.

Dalton jostled his way into the packed bar and was surprised to find several inches of sand covering the entire floor. He had to watch where he stepped to avoid plastic iguanas and inflated crabs underfoot. The place was a loud carnival with wall-to-wall, scantily clad girls and guys singing and dancing up a storm. He'd recognized several people, the LE user-friendly types, and he heartily exchanged high-fives with them. With the smothering cloud of tobacco smoke tainted with a whiff or two of grass, electricity was in the air. It resonated, and soon enough, Dalton was caught up in it. And tonight, he couldn't help but notice an abundance of single, tantalizing babes for sure. Their sensuality oozed its way into his subconscious and his loins.

Someone shouted his name, and when he turned, a cold bottle of Bud was thrust into his hand. Junebug gave him a shit-eating grin, while he casually snaked his arm over the bare shoulder of the svelte, pony-tailed waitress who'd almost worked her way back to the bar before she was corralled. She forced a wane smile, after Junebug squeezed her tight enough to make her gasp. When he pulled her closer in a clumsy effort to kiss her on the neck, she yelped and wrestled free, stomping off annoyed. Junebug blew kisses at her rapidly departing, heart-shaped derriere. "She wants me, Dalton, I know she does. Just a lil busy, that's all. She'll be back later, she knows she will," Junebug shouted lustfully. "Damn, if she didn't give me a chubby though."

Placating his friend's despoiled barnyard pride, Dalton guided him toward an opening at the bar. After downing a few brews, Dalton loosened up, and he and Junebug started sizing up the flood of nubile babes parading in front of them. They loudly chided each other, comparing pluses and minuses, cleavages, contoured legs, tight buns, pretty faces and the overall sex appeal, before awarding each unknowing contestant a fitting numerical rating.

Their other trooper buddies who'd shown up earlier, the happily married, boringly-sane ones, had already left, Junebug told him, gauging their absence to mean that the pickings would be even better for just the two of them.

Dalton was amused by his friend's beer-infused bravado, but he was getting itchy about leaving before trouble found them. He also was planning to take his bombed, testosterone-packed cohort home again, too, but when he came back from the funky rest room, Junebug was gone.

Dalton was sipping the last of his beer, when the bouncy waitress with the ponytail threaded through the crowd. Standing on tippy-toes, she winked and whispered in Dalton's ear, telling him that Junebug had left the party, and she didn't think he'd be coming back. Damn, if that boy Junebug ain't a shark on a blood trail when it comes to women, Dalton mused, wondering if Junebug was homeward bound to duly service his insatiable, foxy-looking wife. He shrugged and smiled, trying hard to ignore the rising goose bumps on his forearm where one of the waitress's breasts had lightly brushed against him. She smiled and patted Dalton on the arm, before she was quickly swallowed in the crowd. She was indeed a cutie, and he'd been close enough to bask in her body heat. Too close!

With Junebug gone, Dalton thought it was wise to split—ala post-haste. The longer he stayed, the better the chances for getting into a mindless fracas with some drunk who'd put his ass on his shoulders. The need for a backup didn't concern him as much as the need for a witness in the form of a fellow trooper

Dalton was slapping tip money on the bar, when the pony tailed waitress returned and tapped him on the back. "This one's for you, trooper man, courtesy of your nurse pal from CMH. She thought you could use another one," the delectable trollop shouted, handing him the cold bottle of Coors. She turned to leave, but Dalton tugged on the sleeve of her T-shirt, his perplexed look begging for an answer. "Ok, she told me not to tell you, but I bet if you went outside, you'd probably find her and her nurse friend standing right next to the DJ's booth, OK? She'll be the, umm...tanned, frizzy-haired brunette wearing the aqua blue lei, and you didn't hear that from me, got it?" Dalton smiled at her and started for the door.

Dodging through the dancing, thrashing bodies, Dalton was soon standing next to the longhaired, grass-skirted DJ. A gay blade, but a hibernating one, he guessed—like it really mattered. Several nubile babes were mingling around the cluttered table, going through tapes, and he swiftly spotted the one the waitress had described. No way! She looked absolutely ravishing, and she was built like a bombshell to boot, but he didn't have the faintest rat's-ass clue as to who she was. Nope, he didn't recognize her, but the tall girl standing next to her *did* look vaguely familiar.

Dalton drifted closer, doing his best to feign indifference. Still, he couldn't place her, and besides, her attention seemed to be focused totally on the DJ's tapes.

He heard a shriek, followed immediately by catcalls and riotous laughter, and his attention turned to the dirt-balls cavorting nearby in the inflatable pool. To the amusement of several drunken onlookers, one of the biker-chicks had proudly taken off her bikini top, putting her prized high-beamers on display. Nice puppies that they were, Dalton was struck by two other things at the moment. First was the thought that maybe it was time to haul his lame trooper butt outta there. Second thing was an ice cube, which hit him soundly on the back of his head.

Momentarily startled, he looked around to see the frizzy-haired brunette with the aqua-blue lei pointing at him, keeled over in laughter. Collecting himself, he inched over to her. She was still giggling and teary-eyed, and as he closed the distance, she eased her head up and looked him in the eyes. Puzzled, Dalton studied her until it finally clicked. "You've gotta be kiddin' me," he blurted out to her. "Jamie...Jamie Cox, my favorite CMH nurse-buddy, is that really *you?*" She caught her breath long enough to nod yes. "Hey there, big guy," she said with an upraised eyebrow, "Now who the hell ya think it was, huh? Took ya long enough, didn't it? But than, I guess you've never seen me like this before, have ya, hon?"

Hell no! The voice in his other head, the one below his belt, silently teased back. She was wearing a pair of killer white shorts, very short and tight, and a red halter-top that strained hard to keep her firm cleavage in check. Visually stunned, Dalton was surprised at what great shape his petite twenty-eight year-old nurse-buddy was in. Beautifully tanned, tight, trim and firm, a solid nine-plus! And with her soft brown eyes, perky nose, full pouty lips and wild, frizzy hair, she was nothing but drop-dead gorgeous! In addition to the gold hoop earrings and gold chain anklet, what ratcheted up her allure were the cherry-red toenails peeking out from her straw sandals.

Dalton's beaming face obviously pleased her. Jamie smiled coyly at him, took the plastic lei from her neck and draped it over his head. Her face was a sun-kissed glowing beacon when she leaned over and kissed him lightly on the cheek. "Aloha, my blond feathered friend! Surf's up. Wanna hang ten with me, surfer boy?" she asked with a roll of an eye. "And *hey*, did you bring your handcuffs with you officer? I feel like I'm getting in the mood to be arrested by you, Sir...that is, if ya think you can come up with something kinky to charge me with!" With an impish smile, she playfully bumped him with her hip. Dalton shook his head and grinned. "Mon Cherie, you'd look utterly fantastic in *my* bracelets," he managed to squeak back at her, as both of his heads swirled with the scenario.

Tonight, she was out and about, and friskier then he'd ever imagined. The contrast was amazing! Back in the bland emergency room at CMH, with her hair in a bun and hidden under a nurse hat, minimal make-up, a stodgy nurse uniform and a prim demeanor, Dalton would have never guessed her to be the goddess he was devouring with his eyes right now.

Engulfed in the carnival atmosphere, they traded animated shits-and-giggles. Boosted by the brewskis, Dalton found himself becoming puppy-dog enamored with Jamie's arsenal of charms. In turn, she seemed to be thoroughly enjoying his undivided attention, even to the point of laughing at the lame old jokes he was having a hard time remembering. Her nurse pal had already perceived that she was on her own again, so she'd drifted away.

When Dalton finally dared to slip his arm around her waist, Jamie pulled herself closer and rested her head against his pounding chest. In turn, he lightly nuzzled her hair, and immediately felt relieved when she sighed and pressed herself tight against him. He savored her warmth, felt himself becoming intoxicated with the scent of her hair, which blended perfectly with the faint aroma of the Ambush perfume on her smooth, tawny neck. "Jamie," Dalton whispered in her ear, "you smell delicious, girl." She batted an eye and grinned. "And I'm *totally* delicious...you can take my word on that," she purred back, gripping his forearm tightly.

Although they did stay to watch the impromptu limbo contest, they traded hints about leaving to go—wherever. When the inevitable fight broke out between a shit-faced biker chick and a drunken local she-cat, Dalton knew it was time to split. The Frog Pond bouncers quelled the catfight quickly, but with the crowd getting rowdier, it'd be only a matter of minutes before Dalton's fellow troopers on night shift popped up. Expediency meant not being around when the cavalry arrived.

Yes, and begrudgingly so, it was time to put a pin to Dalton's over-inflated libido. He gave Jamie a hug, told her he was leaving, ("If I don't see ya in the spring, I'll see ya on the mattress!") then planted a soft goodbye kiss on her raised forehead. Good boy, you're doing great, he thought, as he reluctantly let go of her hand.

The key was barely in the ignition, when he heard the tap on the window. One look at her face, and a barely-audible sigh, before he leaned over and rolled it down. "Hey there, lover-boy, my ride left me high and dry some time ago. Guess she got lucky, maybe. Ummm, any chance of getting a ride home with ya?" Jamie pleaded innocently enough. She set her elbows on the window edge and winked at him. The palm of one hand propped up the chin of her pretty, pouty face, while the other gripped a full bottle of Boone's Farm Apple Valley wine. "I'll even show ya my new tattoo, if you'd like." The pout turned into a luring smile that melted away any restraint Dalton hoped to muster. At least, they hadn't been seen leaving together.

He quickly unlocked the passenger door. Jamie grinned, plopped herself down on the seat, and playfully gave him a peck on the cheek. She winked at him, then pulled her halter-top down a few sparing inches. Even in the dim light, he could still make out the faint outline of the miniature butterfly tattoo over her right breast. *Whew!*

"You can touch it if you want to, babe," she whispered, "it won't bite. I promise." Dalton leaned over and gave the butterfly a soft kiss, hoping it wouldn't get jumpy and fly away too soon. It didn't. He delicately flicked the tip of his tongue over it as a reward. Jamie's hand drifted around to the back of his head and she pressed him to her, encouraging his mouth to stay a while longer. It did. Aroused by her warmth, her sweet, delectable bouquet, and the pleasing taste of her smooth skin, his tongue rebelled and playfully forged its way further beneath her top. She caught her breath and brought his chin up for a fiery kiss. "Ummm, now *that* was *really* nice," she whispered as she rolled back and slumped down on the seat. Trying hard to ignore the growing sensation in his groin, Dalton focused and maneuvered the car onto the main road. With a nervous, unintentional grinding of gears, they were on their way.

In the middle of her aimless chit-chatting, Jamie pushed herself against the seat, arched her back, and stretched her arms over her head, allowing Dalton a quick side-glance of her firm breasts struggling against a skimpy halter-top. With a sigh, she lifted her legs and crossed them, then rested her bare feet on the dashboard. *Damn!* As they chatted, she casually kneaded her calves and plucked absentmindedly at her toenails. She lived in Scientists Cliffs, Gate A for starters, she confided. Dalton felt light-headed, and his face was warm and flushed, his heart pounding harder each minute.

Continuing down the winding road after passing through Gate A, he asked her how long she'd been living in the quaint, bay-side community. She snickered and turned to face him.

"Guess I told you a little white lie about that, hon," she chortled, resting a hand on a knee jutting from his blue-jean cut-offs. "Sorry about that one, but, hey, I *did* live here several years ago, if that counts. Truth is, I'm staying at my parents' place at Flag Harbor," she added with a shake of her head. Her fingers lightly traced ever-enlarging circles just above his knee. "Umm...I just thought it'd be, well, a nice night to go for a walk on a *real* beach, ya know?" she said nonchalantly. "Can't think of anyone else I'd rather kick sand with tonight, ya know?" Jamie bounced in the seat and waved a finger in front of his face. "Hey! Take the next left and go down the hill some and we'll have it all to ourselves. Wanna bet?" She was right.

The secluded beach below the cliffs was delightfully empty in the midnight hour. For several minutes, they sat and talked in his car, passing the bottle of Boone's Farm back and forth until it was empty. Dalton found himself getting more aroused by her, as his self-control continued to erode toward the point of no return. He felt the tension blowing away when they shared laughs over the inane thoughts that continuously popped into their heads. "Come, on lover boy! Let's go see if the surf's up!" Jamie suddenly shouted. Slapping his thigh for emphasis, she scampered from the car and walked toward the beach.

The bay was calm and quiet, and the clear night was speckled with bright stars. There was only a faint hint of a moon overhead, just enough light for them to pick their way along the murky shoreline. Far out on the bay, Dalton saw the red and green lights of some boats, and several miles to the south, along the cliffs of the western shore, the familiar floodlights of the nuclear power plant. He took a deep breath in a vain attempt to clear his racing heads, the primal one exhorting him on recklessly, the other urging him to dive back in his car and leave. He didn't bother pinching himself, knowing he'd probably never feel it. Instead, he forced himself out of the car.

For a long moment, he leaned back against the car door with his arms crossed, silently staring across the bay. When he sensed her mute siren beckoning to him, Dalton pushed himself off and ran to catch up with her. Sandals in hand, she was walking on the wet sand near the water's edge. He grabbed her hand and pulled it in tight, and she acknowledged by weaving her fingers between his. Hand in hand, they walked along the shore, passing rows of tended flowers, bushes and several Hobie Cat catamarans that had been pulled far off the beach.

Eventually, they came to a small grassy clearing bordered by a stand of tall bamboo trees. Jamie sat down on the cool, dewy grass and pulled her knees up to her chin. Dalton sat down next to her, making sure their shoulders touched. A cool, light breeze enveloped them with its ambrosia of late-evening scents—the tangy bay water, the wet sand and the rose mallows, beach plums and the swamp milkweeds that abounded under the majestic cliffs behind them. For a while, they chatted about those superfluous little nothings spawned from their lightheadedness.

Dalton soon found himself talking about his marital problems. Jamie listened patiently before she brought a finger to her mouth and kissed it. Smiling, she leaned over and placed it on his lips. "Shhhh," she mouthed in his ear. "We've already talked about all this during those idle times at CMH, haven't we, babe? You're a good guy, my own personal trooper-pal, and, hey...I believe you, so you don't have to rationalize things with me anymore, OK?" She smiled and pressed herself against him. He savored her warmth, her sensual abundance and pure womanly essence, before he spoke again.

"Jamie, I'm just trying to level with you so there's no misunderstanding here. I really, I mean, I *really* want you, it's just that I'm, I'm...!" She cut him off quickly. 'Hey, big guy, it's simple. We both like each other a lot, we're both obviously attracted to each other, and guess what? Yup, you got it, we're both here, all by our lonesome selves tonight, so it simply is what it is, no more, no less, and no strings attached."

Dalton turned and stared deep into her sparkling eyes. Even in the dim light, they burned, into his lusty heart. He felt a sudden stir, a flash of heat deep in his loins, and he shuddered. He took her hand from his chin and softly planted a kiss on her open palm. Jamie lay back on the grass, propped herself up on her elbows and shook her head, causing her hair to fluff up wildly. In aching silence, she stared back at him. His heart was pounding, and from deep within, his thin wall of resistance instantly collapsed. He rolled over on his side, took her in his arms and kissed her.

Wild-eyed, Jamie broke away for a moment and pulled on his T-shirt. "I need you to take this damn thing off for me," she rasped in his ear, as she helped him peel the shirt over his head. "Ummm, nice, real nice," she sighed, as her fingers danced teasingly across his muscular chest. After enduring her teasing long enough, Dalton pulled her to him and wrapped his arms around her. His lips eventually found the sweet softness of her neck, and after several light flicks of his tongue, she shuddered—so he stayed there and teased her until she gasped. Only then did he bring his lips up to kiss her lightly behind an ear. Slowly, he worked his way down her bare shoulders, planting warm, gentle kisses, which brought out goose bumps on her arms. He lingered for a while, and then returned to her open mouth to taste her deeply as he gingerly placed the palm of a hand flat against the hot, bare skin of her taut stomach. He felt her tremble, paused briefly, before using the tips of his fingers to slowly caress back and forth, from the top of her shorts to just below her halter top.

Dalton caught his breath when she trembled again. Another moan, a muffled one, escaped her lips when he lightly grazed the back of his fingers across her top where the two hardening buds were hidden. He let his fingers stray downwards until he reached the top of her shorts. His hand paused briefly before continuing on down to gently stroke the clothed V area between her parted legs. In response, she wrapped her arms tightly around him and opened her legs even further to encourage his roaming fingers to remain there. There were no doubts about his hunger for her now. His primal head ruled. To make sure she was fully aware of his need for her, he rolled over, arched against her, and shifted his hips. They kissed passionately, the heat building up with an urgency Dalton hadn't felt in too long a time.

Breathing heavily, almost out of breath, Jamie finally pulled away. She stood up abruptly, and brushed sand from her shorts, before positioning herself in front of him with her hands on her hips and her legs spread apart. His desire for her was unbearable, yet he was starting to think that perhaps she'd suddenly changed her mind now. For a brief second, he wished that someone, a misguided gargoyle of the night maybe, one with a charitable soul perhaps, would emerge from the darkness and shoot him in the head to end his misery.

"Jamie, you OK, girl?" he whispered softly between breaths. "No, damn you, I'm not OK," she answered in a thick voice. With a roguish smile, she nodded at him and lazily ran her fingers through her hair. She cocked her head and deftly removed both of her hoop earrings, then snugged them into a side pocket of her shorts. "Hope you don't mind if I change into something more comfortable," she whispered back. Dalton watched, in opened-mouth awe, as Jamie effortlessly slipped out of her shorts and halter-top, laying bare the indisputable proof that she did indeed have a splendid full-body tan.

Several blissful hours later, Dalton was in his driveway, slumped behind a steering wheel. In the stillness of the night, he reflected on the rapturous hours of before, thought about how alive and rejuvenated he felt. There was no guilt, only immediate gratification, a sense of redemption that allowed him to soar away from his quagmire of intimacy-starvation to a loftiness he never wanted to plummet from—

ever again. He stared in the rearview mirror and was instantly struck with an epiphany that finally acknowledged his overwhelming hunger for uninhibited sex, his absolute form of intimate communication, to make him feel so damned whole.

Dalton could still smell Jamie's womanly fragrance mixed with a trace of her perfume. Her alluring essence wafted from his skin and clothes, as his eyes drifted back to the looming shadow of his gloomy house. For several more precious minutes, he basked in the taunting elixir before he plucked a stale cigar from the glove box. He lit it and puffed several times, savoring the sweetness, before a cloud of smoke was exhaled beneath his still-damp T-shirt. He stayed in the car, blowing pungent tobacco smoke in an effort to mask his infidelity. Satisfied, and with a plausible cover story in his head, he entered the house and plopped down on the living-room couch.

While the strong cigar smoke had superbly masked any dead-giveaway fragrances, it couldn't conceal the mosquito-bite welts dotting his back and rear end. Nor could any smoke hide the thin, red fingernail-scratch lines on his back. Cindy, of course, would sense it all, but as usual, she'd ignore it rather than expose her anguish. When daybreak hailed, Dalton finally drifted off for an hour of sleep before his wristwatch alarm coaxed him awake. Minutes later, he was in the shower, reluctantly washing Jamie away as he prepped for another MSP early shift.

Dalton's dive into lust lasted only two months, but meanwhile he knew he was in Utopia City, simply heaven on earth! Once again, he was a whole, fully satiated renaissance man, a vindicated soul able to leap tall garbage dumpsters in a single bound, one who could scramble even faster than Hop-Along, the three-legged mutt who scampered after tossed fries at Hardee's. And *yes*, a man who couldn't put the brakes on a runaway heart, no matter how hard he didn't try—so blissfully alive again, for the first time in memory, maybe his entire life.

When they could, he and Jamie performed their covert trysts at one of the secluded beaches in the county's more-familiar south end. From a fellow trooper's desk drawer, Dalton also "liberated" keys to a BGE power line gate near Long Beach. Two miles from any road, and other than for a grazing deer or a high-flying red-tail hawk, very much undisturbed, they made their own sparks, had their own meltdowns, under the electrifying ambiance of the crackling, high-voltage nuclear plant power lines.

Unlike several of his gallivanting, lovelorn trooper-pals, Dalton's covert assignations weren't conducted on state time. In fact, the only infraction the MSP could ever jack him up on, was a one-count no-no involving the misuse of state property, his department-issued handcuffs. After Jamie curiously hinted to him several times about her fantasy of being helplessly restrained by the sterling steel bracelets, he finally convinced himself that she meant it. After her first and only such mind blowing experience, however, Dalton's love bunny discovered that she'd savored the erotic intensity entirely too much to chance a repeat performance.

Jamie blew softly on the tip of the jasmine incense stick. It glowed briefly and a thin tendril of the fragrant smoke spiraled upwards. Satisfied it would smolder on, she took Dalton's hand and led him towards the bed, only to stop before she clambered onto it. He watched in awe as her arms quickly flew behind her back to unfasten the slinky, black, sliding triangle bikini top she was wearing. It was tossed on the floor, but only after she'd taken her "oh-so-sweet" time removing it. Jamie gave him a sexpot smile and tucked her thumbs under the matching V-string bikini bottom. Ever so slowly she guided it down her svelte legs. With a deft kick, the tiny piece of fabric sailed across the floor. Knowing it'd be a perfect fit, Dalton had purchased the provocative bikini combo and a tube of flavored lip-gloss for her at a Victoria Secrets store as special gifts. Minutes before, he was ecstatic when she tore the box open and let out a delightfully rambunctious squeal to signal her appreciation. When she stripped off her shorts and top and hastily slipped the bikini on in front of him, he thought his heart would misfire.

With nimble fingers snapping over her head, she closed her eyes, bit her lower lip, and started gyrating her lissome body in a manner far more erotic and breathtaking than any striptease performance Dalton had ever feasted his eyes on. For a few fleeting moments, he basked in nirvana.

"You're next," she cheerfully chirped. Already shirtless, Dalton's hands darted to the waistband of his 'fruit-of-the-looms." "Hey...let me do that for you, Ok big guy?" she asked with innocent eyes. Jamie put her hands on her hips, and with the sensuality of an insatiable tigress on the prowl, she padded over to him. He held his breath as she nimbly tugged down his underwear, her body crouching below him as she did. For a sweet second or two, he felt her hot breath on him down there. And Oh My God, if the combination of her musk perfume mingled with the scent of her smooth, tawny skin wasn't driving him bonkers. With a gleeful shout, she tossed his fruity looms across the floor and triumphantly pointed at the bed.

Dalton sat facing her in breathless anticipation, his arms propped up in back, and his legs spread apart like she'd instructed. Jamie gave him a slinky look and shook her head, fluffing up her hair before easing forward. Effortlessly, she placed her legs over his and pushed herself closer to complete the teasing Kama Sutra foreplay position she'd been anxious to share with him. Dalton broke into a prurient grin, an apt response to the pair of fiery eyes searing into his, as she lazily applied the flavored "Hot Chocolate" lip gloss to her puckered lips. When she was done, Jamie lifted her chin and seductively licked her lips. "Mmm-uhh," she murmured in delight. "I've heard that chocolate's supposed to be good for ya....wanna taste, baby?" she whispered to him.

Wondrously au naturel in the waning evening hours, and shimmering with an eagerness fueled by two bottles of Cabernet Sauvignon—her preferred liquid panty remover elixir—they embraced in a passionate kiss. Led Zeppelin's flaming dirigible tape echoed in the background, as parted lips allowed frenzied tongues to wander while searching hands feverishly explored hot, flushed skin. With a devilish smile, Jamie untangled herself. Kneeling lightly on her knees with her heels tucked under the tight twin globes of her tantalizing bottom, she leaned over and teasingly kissed her way down his chest until her half-open mouth was just inches above the crux of his soaring manhood.

"My, oh my...now what do we have here, officer?" she murmured softly. She ran her tongue across her bottom lip, and paused to lock her glazed, kittenish eyes on his anxious face, all the while lightly raking her fingernails over his taunt stomach. He flinched when she worked her busy fingers on him, mere assurance to keep him suitably aroused in the requisite rigidity. Obviously pleased with the results, Jamie cradled him below with a cupped hand and slowly lowered her head. (Houston, we have a *perfect* landing!")

Dalton gasped and ran his fingers through her hair as she performed the light fandango on him. It was pure, unadulterated bliss until she felt his thigh tense up, a familiar signal that usually led to his irrevocable, fiery finale. With a lingering kiss, she abruptly scooted away.

Dalton was breathless, his heart beating wildly to match the throbbing ache in his groin. On her hands and knees at the end of the bed, Jamie smiled and bobbed her shoulders before wriggling her perfectly round, delectable rear end at him. "Ummm, hope I didn't do anything wrong here, officer," she innocently chided, with another tantalizing wriggle. "My nursing instincts just overwhelmed me and I just couldn't help myself, OK?" It took him a moment to collect his withering senses for any coherent words. "Well Miss Cox," he said shakily, giving her the sternest look he could muster, "as a matter of fact you most assuredly did violate the law...in spirit at least. They're arrest-able offenses too, come to think of it   Looks like I have no choice but to haul ya in for reckless teasing and failure to grant me right of way, violations of supreme expectations, they're called in the laws of this here Mason-Dixon state."

Dalton paused to snatch up the two sets of handcuffs from the nightstand. "Gonna come with me peaceful like, Miss Cox?" he asked with gleaming eyes. "Why of course, Trooper Bragg, sir, I fully expect to...mmmm, come with you, but I'm not too sure it'll be so peaceful when I do," she answered cheerfully, bouncing her way back across the bed. Jamie took a deep breath as Dalton snapped handcuffs on her offered wrists. She dreamily closed her eyes and surrendered another smile when he ratcheted them snugly; each loud click adding another beat to her racing pulse.

"But before I haul you in Miss Cox," Dalton said with a leery grin," there's this irksome matter of payback I need to settle with you, so I hope you don't mind the delay, OK?" "No problem sir," she eagerly replied, "I always make an extra effort to stay on the good side of those who enforce the law, especially when I'm dealing with those hunky, blonde hair, blue-eyed, trooper types."

With quick, forceful movements, Dalton spread her arms apart and clipped the other end of the cuffs to the two brass posts of the guestroom bed at her parent's summer bay-front cottage in Western Shores. She sighed as he quickly spread her legs apart with the back of his hands and tethered the straps tightly to the brass corner posts at the foot of the bed. She caught her breath, the ecstatic, wide-eyed look she gave him signaling her surprise. He propped her head up with two pillows so she'd see what he was going to do to her, then kissed her lightly on the forehead. "You're all mine now, beautiful," he whispered to her. Open-mouthed, Jamie shuddered and moaned softly, and her eyes glazed over.

Dalton took advantage of his love-bunny's vulnerability. Ignoring her breathless pleas for immediate gratification, he took his slow, sweet time toying with her in his diligent efforts to drive her wild, making sure his magic fingers pushed her to the brink of true bliss several times—slow then faster, before stopping for teasing interludes.

Jamie was shaking and covered with a light sheen of sweat when he finally removed his probing fingers from the wetness between her legs. Reluctantly, Dalton's mouth left the turgid, rosebud nipple of a perfectly sculpted breast. Showering her butterfly tattoo with kisses, he kissed his way down to her firm midriff again before returning to plant gentle kisses on the tip of her upturned nose, her closed eyes, and her gleaming forehead. A husky, animal-like moan escaped from her lips and she raised her hips when he took a pillow from under her head, folded it, and then snugged it under her. *Focus!*

Dalton knelt between her legs and traced the fingertips of one hand down the hot, flushed valley between her pert breasts while his other hand grazed lazily from the silkiness of an inner thigh. Like wayward moths drawn to the brightest light, his hands came together for another round of wild fingers. Totally captivated by her subtle, earthy ambrosia, Dalton slipped his hands under her firm derriere and lifted her closer to his yearning lips. He paused for a moment, then pressed the tip of his tongue against his upper lip and lowered his head. He felt her supple body jerk once, then again—a sweet reward for his efforts, and his hungry mouth performed more magic until she cried out and shook with unbridled pleasure.

Satiated, Dalton brought his head up and straddled her again. Jamie groaned and shivered when his rigid manhood brushed against her female essence. He paused for a few more delectably teasing moments before he flexed his hips and thrust himself into her. Instantly he was enveloped in the incredible heat of her flooding passion! Jamie cried out and arched her back, her head whipping wildly, side to side. Straining hard against the unyielding manacles, she balled her hands into fists, and with a few shared undulations, they brought each other to searing climaxes.

Even after he was spent and drained, Dalton forced himself to continue on, almost piston-like—teasingly slow, steady and deep, unmercifully coaxing more rippling cascades of sweet release from her writhing body. As the final euphoric waves faded away, Jamie moaned softly and her head floated back to the pillow. He felt her body flex and stiffen under him before she went limp and passed out.

In the sweet aftermath of their perfect storms, Jamie breathed lightly, her angel eyes still closed. Lying on his side with his head propped up on an elbow, Dalton softly caressed her shoulder and ran his fingers through the damp hair bordering her sweat-beaded forehead. He kissed her lightly on the cheek and mouthed an ear lob, allowing his tongue to have its gentle way with her there. Ummm.

After running the back of a finger lightly down the side of her face several times, her eyes flickered and she pursed her lips, signaling her return to consciousness, and her lover's attention. The startled look on her flushed face ripened into a warm, dreamy smile. She shook her head in silent disbelief before lazily draping a leg over his. "You went crazy on me baby...and I loved every damn second of it too," she said in a thick voice.

Dalton smiled knowingly and skimmed a finger back and forth over the inside of her thigh. The smile burst into a grin when he saw goose bumps emerging from his efforts. "Hey, hot stuff," he whispered to her with a wink, "ya ready for round two?" He kissed her shoulder and gently cupped a supple breast with a free hand. "Uhhhh," she groaned, her hand slipping between his legs to find out if he was serious. To her relief, he wasn't, at least not yet, and she merely smiled and nuzzled against his chest.

#

The inevitable guilt eventually swamped Dalton's conscience, and he found it hard to look Cindy in the eyes when he told her of yet another bogus stakeout or "special assignment" he'd have to take part in. During those moments, her discerning eyes told him that she knew all too well what was going on. Women always seem to have radar that tells them all they really don't want to know. She still had her pride, and Cindy never questioned him, though if she had, he knew he'd tell her. Dalton resented himself for the lies, the scheming and for the fidelity lapse that scarred his personal morality code. His once virtuous world was coming apart at the seams.

Of course, if he'd been aware of the rumors of an affair that his darling wife was supposedly having with an acquaintance of his, a fellow trooper, of all the gall, he might have felt a trifle less guilty. But no such rumors wafted his way until years later, unfortunately.

Dalton knew that things between him and Jamie would eventually have to end, as such liaisons usually did. Most ended ugly—at least that's what the other gallivanting, heart-struck troopers said, time after time. As unfulfilled as a husband could perchance feel, he still had strong feelings for his wife, and didn't want to hurt her any more than she was already hurting in her own turmoil. To add to his heart's dilemma, Dalton was genuinely becoming infatuated with his nurse friend too, and the feeling was undeniably mutual. He appreciated Jamie's joie-de-vivre simplicity, her openness and unpretentiousness almost as much as her raw sensuality. With his heart (and tenuous soul) feeling like a pinball in a runaway game from hell, it was Jamie who reluctantly ended it.

One early evening after she'd insisted on Dalton coming to her house to meet her parents—and after he'd adamantly refused—it all came tumbling down. Regrettably, inevitably, it was decision time.

Later, while holding hands and walking barefoot along the deserted Western Shores beach, they called it off. Before parting ways, Dalton gave her the shark tooth necklace he'd bought just hours before from "Tsunami" Parran, the jovial, beer-bellied shark-tooth vender on Route 4 near Lusby. He paused for a moment, then nimbly draped the necklace around Jamie's neck and kissed her lightly on the forehead. Jamie broke into a heart-stopping smile, wrapped her arms around his neck, and kissed him warmly before pulling away. A somber look suddenly crossed her face when she fixed him with imploring eyes.

"I've got something for you too, Dalton," she said in a silky, soft voice. She grabbed one of his hands and put it against her warm cheek. "It's the three words that I've been holding back from you, the three words you may not want to hear from me, but they're from the heart and I have to let you know." His mind racing in overdrive, Dalton knew what she was going to tell him, only wished she wouldn't. Hell, it was hard to deny it to himself any longer that he'd probably fallen in love with her too, but he couldn't bring himself to tell her those three pivotal words she was ready to say to him now.

Jamie sighed and relaxed her shoulders. "Dalton, I've been keeping this to myself far too long, and I don't know what to do about it, either." She bit her lower lip and pressed his hand tighter against her face. Waiting in mute resignation, Dalton shuffled his feet and lowered his head.

"I am *pregnant!*" she blurted out.

Dalton's knees gave out and his mouth dropped as the "deer in the headlights" look came over his stricken face. Instantly, the impact of her words hit him like a sledgehammer, causing his mind to run amok with heinous thoughts! Uhhh...*Houston, we have a real problem*! Now, just because of Captain Happy's runaway exploits, he'd have to drag himself home and tell his wife, his kids, his brothers and sisters, his parents, his close friends, and even his worthy dog Prince, how unworthy he was of their love and companionship. And, oh yeah, and by the way, his mind silently told him, my babe-a-luscious girlfriend's gonna drop our kid soon too, so it looks like we'll be getting' hitched up just as soon as you see a lawyer and ditch my sorry ass, OK, Cindy?

Oh, sweet Jesus, I'm gonna be just another one of those waylaid troopers doin' the ole child-support two-step boogie!

Jamie dropped her head. When Dalton heard her sobbing, he shook himself out of his daze. With an unsteady hand, he took her by the chin and slowly brought her head up until he saw her face. For several tense moments, she managed to look sorrowful, but when she saw the consternation scrawled over his tortured face, she couldn't hold it back any longer and she burst into hysterical laughter.

Dalton backed away when he saw the tears of laughter streak down her face. "Hey, big guy, I was only messin' with ya some, OK? Naw, nothing in the oven here, cause I've been poppin' those bad lil bye-bye-baby pills like candy," Jamie spouted to him between rogue laughs. "Heh, heh, heh! Sorry, babe, just couldn't help myself," she giggled. "If you could a only seen your face! (More laughter) Oh my God, I can't breathe! I can't breathe," she shouted as another wave of giggles hit. With the eight hundred pound gorilla suddenly jumping off his shoulders, Dalton felt lighter than air, more free than a 7-11 coffee to boot.

"Why, you crazy little bitch...!" With a loud whoop, he took off after Jamie who was giggling her lovely ass off as she sprinted down the shoreline. He tackled her on a sand bank, and they wrestled until they were out of breath. For a few minutes, they lay on their backs, listening to each other's heavy breathing. Jamie pushed her hair back, brushed a few grains of sand from her face and rolled over on her side to face him. 'OK, lover-boy blue, I think I know a better way for us to say the big Aloha to each other, but...ummm...I'm gonna need some help from ya if you don't mind," she whispered seductively.

Dalton broke into a smile when her teasing fingers danced beneath his polo shirt and flittered across his flushed, pounding chest. Nothing like going out with a big bang, Dalton decided not to say to her. With hungry eyes, he reached behind her, grabbed her firmly by the hair and guided her soft, warm lips to his for a long, tongue-tastic, toe curling kiss.

An hour later, feeling every bit the cad he never wanted to be, Dalton sat in his Pinto at the bottom of the hill below his house. He brooded in silence, a smoldering cigar stuck between the index and ring finger of his left hand. After he'd blown enough smoke down his polo shirt to gag a horse, he turned on the ignition and drove up the hill. Never again would he ever allow himself to stray into the enticing realm of perfidy, no matter how loud the siren beckoned.

#

Over the next several years, Dalton refocused, centering his priorities on the job, and on his deteriorating marriage. At home, he thought things would stay status quo for the most part, something he could live with—for the immediate future, perhaps.

With MSP, everything was finer than frog's hair. He thoroughly enjoyed being a corporal/road supervisor, and he devoted himself to his work group. The backbone of the MSP was the road patrol, and first-line road supervisor was a coveted position. Despite the exhausting shift work, and the ever-challenging job circumstances that contributed to the turmoil in his personal life, he strived in his revered MSP world. Rated high in his performance evaluation, Dalton concentrated on the upcoming sergeant's test.

For three tedious months, he pored over the patrol and administrative manuals, the criminal and motor vehicle law digests, special and general orders, the near-farcical "Keys to Knowledge" printouts, and the mind-dulling COMAR regs. Night shift, especially during the slow early-morning hours, turned into coffee-laced study sprees. After reams of crammed motor vehicle and criminal law data started seeping from his head like pus from a boil, Dalton blew out the flame of his apocryphal midnight study lamp.

Several weeks later, after getting his test results, the excited corporal startled Pearl, the barrack's secretary, with a loud whoop and a breathtaking bear hug before dashing madly out the back door. He was ranked number five on the Sergeant's list. On a dreary Friday late afternoon, four months after receiving his ranking, the promotion list was finally spat out by teletype. Three weeks later, with new sergeant stripes on his patrol jacket, Dalton reported to his new assignment, the newly designated College Park Barrack "Q." A desk sergeant who'd be supervising largely from the seat of his pants, Dalton was now a notch higher on the MSP totem pole, a position affording some extra padding for the inevitable ass reamings from those above.

###
(Purgatory Ridge)

The retiring sergeant opened his eyes and grunted loudly when he jacked himself up to his feet without spilling what was left of his beer. He worked his jaw back and forth, tasting the remnants of the stale beer and the blood in his mouth, blood seeping from the lip he'd been unconsciously biting. The sergeant swirled his tongue over the cut and cleared his throat, then quickly drained the can, involuntarily making a screwed-up face after swallowing the last flat dregs. With a loud belch, he crumpled the can and trudged over to the edge of the steep cliff. The wind was whipping up now, and there were agitated whitecaps on the tips of roiled waves. He could see dark, puffy clouds meandering in from the east. They signaled a gathering storm, maybe, but he wasn't sure, nor did he particularly care. Under blistering sun or pouring rain, his retirement party would go on regardless. Yes, they could piss on his parade all they wanted, but *today* his parade would go on until only *he* dropped the baton. That's the least he could do for himself, he reckoned.

They were great, though sometimes bittersweet, those corporal years were. He'd really enjoyed the first-line supervisory position, the "mother hen" buffer slot between his work group and the barrack's admin ranks. And, when the shit hit the fan, signaling show time, he prided himself by being with his troopers wherever the action was. The incident with Morgan, the crazy with the gun at Kenwood Beach, was a reminder of that. Mental cases (10-96 fruitcake calls), always got the adrenaline soaring instantly. Each such case offered up its own special potpourri of lunacy. For such a small county like Calvert, Dalton was continually amazed by the seemingly endless number of loonies who popped out of the woodwork whenever their wires short-circuited. And, as most cops eventually realize, a full moon does seem to bring them out in droves.

#
That following June, at a recruit class graduation ceremony held in the stuffy Pikesville gym, Dalton was awarded the Governor's Citation for his life-threatening performance under fire during that indelible

evening on the Calvert County pier. From then on, he'd wear the yellow and black striped ribbon on his uniform with unabashed pride. What meant so much more to him, however, was that he'd been there with his people when they needed him. Pomp and ceremonies were duly tolerated, but in actuality, he was never one to revel in the glory of the MSP limelight.

Reflecting on the incident, Dalton knew that if he'd been in similar circumstances in his recent years as a seasoned sergeant, he probably would have busted a cap on Morgan's ass when he first dared to wave the gun at them. Done deal—end of scene—Kaput-City! OJT experience and seasoning normally equated to tempered prudence when it came to the survival of his fellow officers. One for all, and all for one, *that* was the only way to go!

Respect and trust were earned begrudgingly from veteran road troopers, and Dalton was gratified when he knew he'd reached that status within his group. He was still dedicated to the department overall, but those particular years hadn't come without a cost, the effects of which he was reluctantly acknowledging. Sure, they all went through the convoluted menagerie of job experiences, tough transitions and the gut-churning tribulations, as most expected they would. Nobody ever promised anybody they'd be tiptoeing through a rose garden out there, that was certain. Depending on where they were assigned, most troopers probably had similar experiences; some, even worse. Many emerged completely unscathed from them, while others weren't so fortunate.

The reverberations of Donny Robert's slide into hell, the horrific ending of his girlfriend's life and his own, and the discovery of his friend and former shift mate's body, had shaken Dalton badly. Immediately afterward, the tremors and the macabre nightmares increased two-fold, and, for the first time, Dalton felt the "tiger" in his head blink its eyes and suddenly wake up. He thought he could wait it out, hoping it'd eventually tire of its restlessness, but it was never to be, so he did his best to quarantine the beast's petulance. Most of the time, he lost. He made sure that others, especially Cindy, never found that out. Troopers don't borrow each other's handkerchiefs, and a wife shouldn't see her trooper husband cry.

While the Donny Roberts ordeal was bad enough, the sudden, unexpected death of Colby Merson, his steadfast friend, had utterly stunned him. *God*—how he sorely missed him, his essence and dauntless spirit. The loss of Colby left him with a painful void that he could never fill, no matter how much he drank. And Dalton made sure he hid that well, too. And while the dents in his psychic armor accumulated, he found himself drifting even further away, as his wife sought shelter within herself, and his marriage experienced the early throes of its downward spiral. So, to compensate, he'd managed to let himself slip into an extramarital affair to let the sun shine in for those fleeting moments of life's invigorating bliss. But of course, it only made matters worse, because he could never come to terms about how he was able to self-inflict yet another unaffordable dent of tainted integrity in his armor.

The Sergeant stood there for several long minutes, arms hanging loosely at his side, and the wind blowing thorough his tousled hair, as he sucked in several deep breaths of cool air. His head started to throb, and he wished it were just another headache—but he knew better. He brought his hands to his face, palms up, and watched as his fingers started trembling in front of his bleary eyes. The tiger, his old antagonist, was stirring once again! Years ago, he'd learned not to panic from its restless padding. Damn! The last thing he wanted on the day of his retirement party was another episode of his rampaging nemesis to screw it all up!

Dropping to his knees, he crawled back to the oak tree. Gasping in relief, Dalton propped himself up against the rough trunk again. "Son of a bitch!" he yelled in the direction of the Eastern Shore.

He popped open another beer, took several gulps, and then picked up the Beretta again. This time he used a steady, two-fisted grip. *Blam!* The first round missed and eventually splashed harmlessly into the bay, well out of sight and mind. Instantly he felt a sharp pain shoot through his head, as the tiger snarled. *Blam!* The second shot did the trick, obliterating the top hoop of the "dream catcher," sending its remnants fluttering through the air and down the cliff. Ignoring the tiger's torment, Dalton blew away the residual smoke wafting from the gun barrel.

"Sorry about that one, Tonto, but the damn thing never worked for me anyhow," he quipped in resignation.

Chapter 10

DAYS IN THE LIFE OF A DUTY OFFICER
(Tribulations of a Certified Desk Jockey)

After the state opened a new 'Q" Barrack in College Park, the dingy Greenbelt Barrack facility was finally put to rest. The College Park Barrack was next to the beltway before Route 1. From the "merry-go-round," the MSP complex, with its concrete and stone amalgam exterior and low pitched, dark brown metal roof, looked foreboding—like a detention center or a truncated Bastille. Included was a detached three-bay garage, a carwash bay and a radio shop.

When *Sergeant* Dalton Bragg reported to the Beltway Bastille, he found that the "Q" zoo had a new keeper. Lt. Harrell and Dalton's archenemy, 2nd Lt Kurtz, were long gone. The barrack ringmaster was Lt. Dick Larsen, a balding, portly, old school type from Western Maryland. Dalton appreciated Larsen's easygoing manner and open candor, along with his penchant for spinning cheeky yarns about MSP and the country folk of Boonesboro, his hometown. Larsen could have hung up his Stetson years ago, a nagging aspect that gnawed on him now, and he longed to return to the Western Troop. Dalton half suspected that the department, in its nefarious "Send Em To Siberia" mode, had punted the free speaking, maverick commander from his snug home base for extra incentive in that regard.

Captain Jackson MacIntire, the new Metro troop commander, was an imposing man. Broad-shouldered, long-armed and ramrod trim, he towered over most troopers. The Captain had a distinct angular jaw and a cleft chin that complimented his long bony nose and steely blue eyes. His thinning sandy hair was slicked back, greatly accentuating his shiny forehead, a prominent forehead that earned the nickname Pontiac, the fabled Indian chief. He was born and raised on the Eastern Shore, the son of a waterman who didn't fancy pampering his offspring.

Jackson MacIntire's tough upbringing was apparent by his no-nonsense, rugged manner. Adding to his virile image, the Captain relished his Cuban cigars. To his secretary's disdain, there was always a stinky, smoldering cigar clenched in his teeth when he tromped into the barrack, and another one clamped between two stubby fingers when he left.

At times, the Captain turned arrogant, even pompous, when dealing with subordinates and weak-willed superiors. Dalton heard much MSP scuttlebutt about hardcore Captain MacIntire and his daunting persona. He was known as a strict, by-the-book stickler and one to be feared. Stetsons had to be worn by troopers, *anywhere*, even when they checked under the hoods of their cruisers on the barrack parking lot. A simple failure to sign in on the barrack log was considered heresy. The road troopers grumbled as they awkwardly danced to the Captain's strict music, and predictably, his imposing authority and starchy stodginess chafed away at the rambunctious members of the drug unit in a barrack basement. Tired of having their incorrigible, beer-bellied supervisor henpecked incessantly by Pontiac, they stewed amongst themselves and planned retribution.

Dalton was glad that the hard driving Bill Bowman, was now the barrack "first shirt," a good deal for the road pounders. Several of the senior troopers he knew from his Greenbelt days were now corporals serving as patrol supervisors. Dalton's only misgiving was that his new corporal had been involuntarily transferred in from a cream-puff special-services unit. Clueless to road patrol, he was back in uniform after a ten-year hiatus. Nevertheless, Terry Grasso, a lanky, deep-voiced, clean-cut sort from Harford County, was unabashed about being punted back to the road, and before long, Dalton was appreciating his sharp wit and take-charge style.

#

The MSP duty officer's slot was a hodgepodge of responsibilities, an unheralded position which Dalton years before had filled during his sergeant's absence. He'd never liked the catchall, in-house position, early on recognizing it only as a loathsome rung on his career ladder. Dalton's new work zone was the drab, always-cluttered DO's (duty officer's) pit. Upon entering the barrack, the first thing a Johnny Q

Citizen saw was a somber-faced uniform sergeant at a desk behind a slab of bullet-deflecting Plexiglas. The "pit" bristled with numerous shelves, trays, key boards, lock boxes and cabinets overloaded with reference books, logs and forms—most of which were daily ignored. The DO's desk was typically blanketed with paper, a half-filled coffee cup and the infernal, ever-ringing phone.

Having a knowledgeable, experienced PCO with a good attitude, one who diligently manned the radio and phones, was a godsend. A mentally-challenged PCO, the rare, dumbstruck dud who paid more attention to buffing her nails or jawboning on the phone, made for a daylong headache. When a star PCO was working, the DO was on auto-pilot, and if the star PCO happened to be an amiable, alluring *she,* clearing the radio room of salivating troopers was a never-ending task for the sergeant.

Dalton was blessed with a star PCO. Ginny Mae, a twice-divorced, winsome PCO stalwart, was known for her silky-sultry radio voice. Ginny Mae performed her job admirably enough, although she and Dalton had a few weeks of iciness between them when Ginny and Corporal Grasso had become infatuated with each other. The liaison soon blossomed into a falling-in-lust fiasco, which inevitably forced Dalton to upbraid his heart-struck corporal for spending too much time the radio room. But despite wanderings hearts, Dalton's shift was lucky to have Ginny Mae as their mother hen PCO.

Most weekday late and night shifts, when the brass was absent, passed smoothly. All too frequently, however, the duty officer was tagged with a hellish day that made him want to eat his gun. Phones rang off the hook, hordes of dour citizens paced the lobby, radio traffic was heavy and imploring, and the unchecked reports were endless, while the troopers ran from call to call. Meanwhile, the F/Sgt was locked in his office, pulling out what was left of his hair over the beastly master schedule, while the retirement-minded Lt. Larsen tried to entice the badgered sergeant into his office to reminisce on his glory days of yesteryears.

"Well, my young sergeant, I remember the days when you could tell who the hard-riding troopers were by the number of bugs they'd pull from their teeth after un-assing themselves from their motorcycles!

Damn straight! Took an hour just to blow all that gritty road dust outta your nose. Why, there was that time when I was alone and surrounded by a hopped-up gang of those city colored folks who..."

After those frequently frenetic days, Dalton left the barrack in a jaw-tight, volatile mood, usually with a pounding headache. He could almost hear his sphincter snap back and relax as soon as his cruiser raced across the Calvert County line.

#

Dalton's one-year sentence to the embattled Bastille passed quickly. Surprisingly, his transfer request back to Barrack "U" hadn't been "lost" in the void, as occasionally happened when the MSP Wizard of Oz was in one of his cantankerous moods. After a year at the "Q" Barrack, Dalton, Cap. MacIntire, Lt Larsen and a few others were ecstatically transferred back to their familiar turfs. None of them was more elated about returning than Captain MacIntire.

Providing an early impetus for the Captain's departure, the narcs finally came up with a suitable plan. Swearing to OMERTA-like secrecy in true narc fashion, and possibly influenced by some leftover coke dregs they'd sampled during an earlier buy, they activated their payback plan. It was a sophomoric prank, one destined for the books, Dalton learned. A week before the Captain's transfer, while he was savoring another closed-door, ass-chew session with Lt Larsen, the narcs "'liberated" the spare key to the Captain's unmarked car. Operating in stealth mode and wearing latex gloves, they filled the ashtray with gunpowder that had been removed from a dozen twelve-gauge shotgun shells. After topping the gunpowder with a thin layer of cigar ashes, they returned the key, undetected.

It was the barrack consensus that the Captain probably made it as far as the beltway and Route 50 before he set his smoldering cigar in the ashtray. Muttering obscenities, with his hands, face, and uniform covered in soot, Captain MacIntire rocketed back to the barrack in a full-blown tizzy. An internal investigation ensued, of course, and the irate Pontiac was on the warpath for scalps as the investigation plodded on. Due to the lack of credible evidence, and much to Pontiac's vexation, the investigation petered out. Mercifully, Captain Pontiac was transferred back to his Eastern Shore enclave.

#

Dalton was elated to be back with his old cohorts at the PF barrack, far removed from the beltway chaos. Lieutenant Rob Mister, the new commander, was a good ole boy—one of Calvert's favorite sons, an "aw-shucks," no-frills type who was greatly respected. Dalton had worked under the personable lieutenant years before, and while Lt Mister was a staunch supporter of MSP doctrine, he wasn't the type to step on anybody's back to get promoted.

Dalton especially enjoyed the company of stalwarts like Sgt. Elzy Shifflett, the gruff-talking Cpl Dan Collision, Sgt Ben Wiley, the unflappable Tfc. Harmes, Marty the Rat Rouser and good ole "Junebug" Buckler. It was harmony to his ears when he heard the familiar, shrill voice of Wanda Gatton, the Calvert Control chief, berating yet another trooper for rifling through her files without her queen-bee permission.

During the early 1980s, the barrack didn't have the usual MSP allotment of supervisors. Accordingly, the sergeants often alternated between the positions of shift supervisor and road supervisor. Dalton learned that with time and experience, a good sergeant, if sufficiently challenged, could bastardize just about anything to maintain status quo. Much to his liking, he found that the PF desk-bound duty officers slot was still in the future.

#

During the mid-eighties, the department, thanks to a new Superintendent, made a few long overdue changes. Colonel R.T. Muth, a heavy-set, bulldog-face veteran of thirty years, took the bull by the horns and made several notable decisions that directly affected the field troops. The troopers were truly heartened to get the boost in firepower from their new Smith & Wesson .357 magnum revolvers. The new four-inch barrel hand-cannons replaced the underpowered Colt .38s that had been issued for decades. However, the department, due to extraneous politics ("Holy shit, the troopers really have .357 magnums now?"), didn't issue the expected magnum rounds. While the majority of the disgruntled troops duly used the issued rounds, there were scores of others like Dalton, who bent the rules by loading up with magnums. They weren't about to let the department gamble with their lives when they were out there alone, answering to no one but themselves on the frequently unforgiving turf.

The second change under the new Colonel was the color of the State Police cruisers, from Chiquita-banana yellow (baby puke) to the more traditional light tan with the black and brown stripes. No longer would the troopers hear the mocking twang of truckers calling them "Tijuana taxis."

However, Colonel Muth earned Dalton's own Rotten-Egg Award for the *teddy bears.*

Somewhere along the periodically warped lines of communication, the MSP had inherited several hundred runt-size, russet-colored, furry teddy bears. After consulting with a harebrained guru in the Pikesville Crime Prevention Unit, Colonel Muth decided that *all* road troopers would have the fluffy little bastards in their cruisers. The idea fueling this crucial decision was that the teddies could be used to comfort any apprehensive toddler-tykes who had to be transported in a cruiser. Siding with the vast majority of the patrol force, Dalton thought the planners at Pikesville had gone bonkers again. When their shaky, yes-man southern troop commander later *ordered* his troopers to carry the teddy bears in their vehicles as assigned equipment, many were rankled. Junebug Buckler was the first in Dalton's group to sound off.

"So let me get this straight, Sarge. A kid's just seen his mashed-up momma hauled away in a meat wagon after her car kissed a tree, and on the way to CMH, I'm supposed to give him a frickin' teddy bear with a shit-eating grin to make him feel better?" Dalton rolled his eyes and shirked his shoulders. "Junebug, look at it this way," he said with a stone face, "Just be grateful that the Pikesville exalted ones inherited the teddies instead of Bo-Bo-the-Clown masks, OK?"

Most appropriately, it took less than a month for the fury little brown stuffed ones to migrate into the welcome arms of needy kids, trooper's girlfriends and several of the local drunks.

Just before dropping him off on an old logging road in deep woods near Adelina, Dalton bequeathed *his* teddy bear to the continually tipsy Cephas "Danny Boy" Height.

Danny Boy, a native Calvert son from Adelina, was a stocky black laborer of sorts who grudgingly worked for wine when he needed it. Otherwise, he was an obnoxiously brash, well-known beggar who was perpetually fantasizing his way back "home" to Louisiana Cajun country.

Danny Boy was the unofficial king of the band of haranguers on the Prince Frederick Shopping Center sidewalks. They loved to annoy the women-folk with never-ending mooching for spare change, which ultimately resulted in a bottle of Thunderbird or Ripple wine. Most troopers and deputies merely swept them off the streets and deposited them somewhere—*anywhere*—miles away from the shopping center. When no one of any discernable repute was near, troopers would occasionally hustle Danny Boy, or whomever, down the side alley. Away from curious eyes, the vagrants were unceremoniously stuffed into a cruiser trunk for a speedy trip to the woods. No way were they going to have Danny Boy or any of his foul ilk stink up their cruisers if they could help it. Avoiding the trunk routine, Dalton always kept a spray can of Lysol handy to disinfect the cruiser, and sometimes the passenger, after such odoriferous missions.

"Yo, Danny-Boy," Dalton shouted. Danny Boy woke up with a start and a bullfrog belch. Dalton deftly yanked the rousted drunk from his cruiser before he puked. "'Cause I'm in a good mood today, this time you get my teddy bear! Next time I have to cart your sorry ass away, you get dropped off in the quicksand at the end of Cypress swamp, got it?" Dalton shouted at deaf ears. "And, Danny Boy, no matter how much everybody says there ain't, there *are* some big-ass crocodiles back in that swamp, and most of em' are meaner then ole Judge Mackall when he finds out someone's been stealin' his bakker plants, hear me ?"

Dalton watched Danny Boy lean forward on wobbly feet and crane his head, trying to focus bloodshot eyes. He pulled away quickly when the stench of Danny Boy's wine breath assaulted his nostrils. The lush broke into a leer and let a loud fart. "Got ya, dogface," he spouted. Dalton smiled as he watched Danny Boy plant a sloppy kiss on the bear's black plastic nose. With his teddy gripped tight to his chest, Danny Boy did a quick two-step, tangled his legs and tumbled facedown in the dirt. Jamming drive, Dalton glanced in his rearview mirror to see Danny Boy for the last time. And if he'd known it was the last time he'd ever be able to lay eyes on the wino, Dalton would never have endowed him with his esteemed teddy bear.

Three weeks later, Danny Boy's eternally pending sojourn back to his beloved Louisiana bayou cabin was abruptly cut short. He was found in the outhouse of a shabby club near Dog Patch in neighboring Charles County. The single .32 round from the cheap revolver had plowed into Danny Boy's scarred forehead and through his brain, leaving him lifeless on the urine-soaked dirt floor. Danny Boy's checkout ticket had been overpayment for his drunken audacity to piss on the blue suede shoes of the incendiary Lemon Daniels, a fellow lush who was several shades of hell drunker than Danny Boy that night.

#

Considering the odds, it was bound to happen sooner or later, especially if a trooper's performance was aggressive. With over ten years of exemplary service, Dalton's tinseled image of his esteemed department suddenly jaded. Duty called, and he answered louder than most. Accordingly, Dalton was confident the department would unfailingly back him in return, trusting his actions and decisions. Color it naive or label it blind faith, that was not exactly how the game played out. His first seeds of trepidation within the MSP puzzle palace were planted by the manner in which a brutality complaint against him had been conducted. As his career unfolded, those seeds germinated into well-rooted qualms.

It was another sweltering early August eve, an overall quiet night for the troops, and the air was soupy, with most sane people hunkering down close to air conditioners or straining fans. Dalton, the late shift sergeant, was at the gas pump, when he heard the animated call from the Calvert Control center. *Great!* Just minutes left in the late shift, and yet another domestic call with no corporal and only two troopers working. Damn! He could almost taste his first welcome-home beer already.

Minutes later, the sergeant arrived at the Sunderland residence in the all-black community and was instantly immersed in a sea of chaos. In the dark shadows of the front lawn, he saw the frenzied crowd. Most were cussing and shouting, while others darted wildly back and forth, throwing punches and playing grab-ass with each other. *Not Good*! Dalton called for backup, grabbed his Kel-light, and sprang from the car.

Loud cries of "He's got a knife! Watch out for the mutha fucker!" sent shivers down his spine while the flashlight beam leaped back and forth, cutting through the dark. Adrenaline-pumped, Dalton spotted a lean, bare-chested black guy screaming in the face of the girl he clenched tightly by the throat. *Super!* Dalton effortlessly jerked the man away from the petrified girl. That Herculean one-handed action, of course, only inflamed the obviously hopped-up agitator, who brushed him back with his shoulder, and started after the girl again. Dalton whipped his left arm out, snared him around the neck, and jerked him off his feet.

For several pregnant moments, things looked encouraging, but when a lurker dashed from the shadows and grabbed Dalton's arm, the man he held in a headlock shrieked and turned bad-ass again. When Dalton turned his attention to the new threat, his hothead broke lose and punched him soundly in the chest. *"Oh, no you didn't!"* the sergeant's inner voice screamed. Dalton stumbled backward but was still able to yank the man back against his chest. When he flailed his arms in an attempt to break free, Dalton swung his flashlight at the closest arm. He missed. With a muffled thump, the flashlight ricocheted off the man's head.

In sickening silence, Dalton watched as the man slumped to the ground. Immediately, he was surrounded by an angry swarm of hotheads and a rising chorus of taunts. Dalton thought he heard a siren in the distance, but maybe not. Several times he shouted to those closing in, ordering them to stay back. From experience, he knew it was only a matter of time before one of the drunkest, the lone wolf skulking in the shadows, got bold enough to try to jump him. As if on cue, the man sprawled out on the ground screamed and lashed out wildly with his legs. No way in hell Dalton was going to do the solo dirt-dance with him amongst all those crazies.

To his instant relief, several people were flung aside like rag-dolls, when beefy Tfc. Harless Panos burst through the crowd like a fullback crossing a goal line. Another trooper, a new boot looking bewildered, joined them. When the moaning man on the ground leaped up, Dalton and Panos quickly pitched him face-first to the dirt, forced his arms behind him and slapped on the cuffs. Spitting and cursing, he was lugged over to Dalton's cruiser. After he kneed another trooper in the chest and tried to kick out the windshield, they lashed his legs together with a rope. The unruly arrestee refused medical treatment, and the sergeant was soon en route to the barrack with the cursing prisoner seated next to him.

Halfway there, the seething simpleton started spitting at Dalton again. With a life of its own, Dalton's right arm whipped out and backhanded him in the mouth. The prisoner's head flew back and bounced off the headrest, and snot blew out of an inflamed nostril. For a few gracious moments, there was silence. When the hothead hocked up another mucous glob and spit it on the side of his face, however, Dalton abruptly stopped the cruiser and slapped a big strip of duct tape over his mouth, causing his irate prisoner to up the ante by pissing himself. *Nice!* Thank *God,* he was able to rip most of the jerk's mustache off when he later yanked the duct tape off.

After processing, the prisoner was taken to CMH, complaining of a headache, but negative x-rays and no visible signs of injury dictated his release. Dalton subsequently charged him with assault on a police officer, disorderly conduct and resisting arrest, before taking him to jail for a county-paid overnighter. Hours later, the exhausted sergeant was homeward bound, convinced that he'd handled himself well under the circumstances.

Released from jail the next morning, Tyrone Mason rubbed the top of his head and smiled when he sniffed the sweet scent of easy money. Post-haste he contacted Odenton lawyer Nelson Friedman, and after a brief tête-à-tête, Tyrone promptly checked himself back in at CMH for his phantom headache. Friedman, a consummate ambulance chaser, promptly made a demanding inquiry to MSP headquarters about his client's wholly unwarranted injuries. Accordingly, the twittered MSP head honchos knee-jerked, as they always did whenever accosted by menacing attorneys and their nebulous complaints. The bold writing was splattered on the wall.

An Injury-to-Prisoner-investigation was conducted by First Sergeant Hutchinstuff, and with Lieutenant Mister's favorable endorsement, the reports were punted to the troop commander to begin a run up the MSP chain of command. Months dragged by with nary a peep from the palace, and since Tyrone Mason hadn't filed a brutality complaint, the incident gradually receded from Dalton's mind. In the interim, Mason had also been tried and convicted in district court on the assault charge and was now cooling his heels in the local pokey. The easy bus to Sue City had lickety split, leaving him choking in the dust.

After four months of lethargy, however, the puzzle palace wheels amazingly cranked a turn, and sullen phone calls heated up the hotlines. From the majestic third floor, the palace princes decreed that a full-blown, formal investigation would be conducted to determine if the sergeant from Prince Frederick had violated department policy pertaining to the misuse of force, a decision that put Dalton on the hot seat indefinitely.

Stung by the news, Dalton was dismayed, grasping that all Pikesville sniffed of the matter was that a white trooper, a *sergeant* at that, had slam-dunked a black man on the head with a metal flashlight. Done deal. Monday-morning quarter backing extraordinaire, and many months overdue at that.

Dalton only wished he could drag a few puzzle palace princes back to that ugly cluster-fuck call to test their own mettles on that August night. Yes, they'd experience the exploding pandemonium firsthand: hear it, smell it, have their mouths go dry and their stomachs cramp tight when the chills washed down their fickle spines. No doubt that certain princes, those pretentious, infinitely smarter, effete types— definitely not those like rugged Colonel Edwards who rose from the field ranks—*yes*, they'd be cringing in their own funk. He could see their anxious, ashen faces, their sweaty palms clenching steering wheels, as the craziness unraveled through their windshields. Paralyzed with fear and totally clueless, they'd await the arrival of real troopers.

As the inquest dragged on, Dalton shielded his pensive feelings around his fellow troopers. He could lose his job. Most had few clues as to how much it affected him, and he barely mentioned it to Cindy, since, not surprisingly, they were having communication problems again. As expected in the macho MSP realm, some troopers chided Dalton about it. Elzy even put D-cell batteries in his mailbox to razz him when he thought he needed a laugh. Hell, if he showed a thin skin, they'd only use it as an excuse to ramp up the frolics. For the first time in his career, Dalton felt doubted by his venerable department, which had shoved him under a scouring magnifying glass.

Of course he'd seen other troopers cope with such ordeals. It was never pretty, even when most were eventually exonerated, because the effect usually lingered to tarnish a trooper's reputation. For Dalton, a principled sergeant and supervisor, it weighed heavily. He started losing weight during those sleepless. Only Cindy could see how bad it was, evidenced by the slew of empty beer cans she found in the kitchen sink most mornings. Once again, the horrific nightmares kicked in, this time with a vengeance.

After several grinding weeks, the investigation ended, and the findings were sent to Pikesville. For several more months, Dalton felt like a scorched chicken on an eternal rotisserie. No matter how hard he tried to shrug it off, it wracked him, making it tough to focus on anything. *Hell*, if he knew it'd be such an ordeal, he sure as hell would've taken a Mickey Mantle home-run swing of his trusty Kel-light to make it worthwhile.

Ten months and five days after the Sunderland fiasco, Dalton was apprized that the MSP had closed the books on the matter. With the sage Pikesville palace princes nodding in accordance, it was decreed that his actions that summer night had been warranted after all. Much relieved, Dalton celebrated the event by going out and getting thoroughly trashed with Junebug, Elzy and Gary Rephan. Unsavory experiences regrettably came with the territory, but there would always be that residual, psychic scar, that nagging misgiving, which always reminded Dalton to never again hold blind allegiance to the department.

#

In 1988, the Calvert troopers moved into a new Barrack "U" complex on Main Street. When the MSP moved, the burgeoning Calvert County Sheriff's Office acquired their former abode, and the

Calvert Control Center moved to a new courthouse extension, separating it from both law enforcement departments.

The county was sprawling way too fast, according to many local hayseeds. From a population of 20,000 in 1970, it'd swelled to over 35,000 by the end of 1988. By the end of the next decade, the population would balloon to almost 51,000. Accordingly, emergency calls for police, fire and rescue services steadily mounted.

There was ample work for both LE departments. According to Pikesville's stats, the Prince Frederick barrack was the busiest full-service barrack in the state in 1987, a status that was no surprise to the troops on the front lines. Inevitably, when the Sheriff's Office emerged from under the wings of their "big brother" troopers, close rapport between the two departments faded, and the competition for service calls began in earnest.

The new barrack was a two-story brick structure topped by a flat, gravel covered, leak-prone roof. For the first time—praise the Lord—the PF troops had their very own garage and fuel pump. In the cluttered DO's pit, there was a small, split-screen TV monitor on the front desk, linked with cameras that monitored the main parking lot and garage complex, and the basement holding cells. The radio room, the barrack information hub behind the DO's pit, accommodated the radio console, large tape recorders, rows of file cabinets, charts and maps, and the coffee brewer. Shiny linoleum upper-level hallways led to offices that were all marked, military style, with lettered titles secured over doorframes. The gray carpeted secretaries' room was centered in the upper level, its walls flanked by long rows of file cabinets. The secretary's duties were efficiently managed by the chain-smoking, habitually outspoken Pearl, and her new co-worker, Cheryl Powers, the barrack's unflappable secretary.

Cheryl was a tall, good-looking woman who kind of grew on you. She had the auburn frosted, "big hair" thing going on, wore wire rimmed glasses propped low on her nose and chewed gum incessantly. Her husky, almost sultry voice added to her subtle sensuality, but what really stood out was her tight, beautifully sculpted body, a heavenly chassis that surpassed any brick shit house most troopers could envision—meaning that some of the horny, more impetuous troopers promptly put her on their "to-do lists. She was, however, very married, a vexing flaw they eventually learned when each perspective suitor's amorous overtures were tamped back down to wish-list status.

And it didn't take long for Pearl to seek an armistice with Cheryl, immediately following their first and last feud. Inevitably, Pearl had tried her hand at dominance, wholly ignoring the fact that Cheryl came from a hardworking tobacco-farming family in rural Huntingtown. Cheryl's outward composure and good looks masked an aggressiveness that could have easily landed her a job as a roller derby queen. Surprisingly, and to her credit, Pearl fully realized that if she'd pushed things any further that day, Cheryl would have dragged her outside to stomp her ass with minimal effort. Downright disappointing to those waiting to see a proper catfight, both secretaries kept a suitable equilibrium thereafter.

Adjacent to the secretaries' realm was the compact troopers' room where the road pounders waded through accursed paperwork. It was also where they held their scuttlebutt sessions, sessions which usually featured richly embellished road war stories, spectacular prowess on the softball fields and outlandish sexual exploits with the bodacious babes they encountered daily. Barrack "U," like most barracks, had its share of trooper groupies waiting to pounce on the hapless young men in Stetsons. While most troopers did their paperwork at the barrack, some preferred using the three satellite offices in the county. Better to be in Solomons, Huntingtown, or Chesapeake Beach, far away from the brass

The barrack lower level housed the prisoner processing room, an interrogation room (a special place where clandestine phone calls were made to girlfriends, or someone's straying wife), the holding cells, furnace room (Ernie the Caretaker's Cavern) and the conference room. Decorating the conference room walls were numerous engraved plaques and awards. Names were engraved under titles like: Barrack Trooper of The Year, Barrack Trooper of The Month, Highest Monthly DWI Producer and Barrack Top Shooter. The most cherished awards were the trophies won in the annual MSP softball tournament.

The spirited, two-day party-time softball tournaments, held at a tucked-away park near Frederick, were no trivial matters to the barracks hard-hitting, softball aficionados. Ultimately, the powerhouse teams like Northeast, Frederick or PF prevailed. It was also no small wonder that many troopers held well-founded hunches that certain-higher ups at Pikesville, those who lived in around Northeast in particular, would, year after year, go to the extent of actually recruiting, and then transferring, able-bodied ball players to barrack "F."

It was serious business for the majority of the MSP teams, excepting of course the incorrigible rogues from the Leonardtown Barrack. It was always enlightening to watch the drunken ball players of Barrack "T" tumble out of vans and cars at the tournaments early morning starting hour—always fun to watch them struggle to form a huddle just to hear and ignore the "go get-'em" pep talk presented by their soused coach through bloodshot eyes. .

Dalton was flabbergasted by the near-paralyzing effect that slow-pitch softball held over the barrack ball players. When the softball season arrived, and when the ball-player troopers were preening themselves, no one could have a decent conversation about anything else.

"Junebug, ya hear what Silver Tongue Wilkerson did yesterday while he was working the carnival assignment? Damn if the boy didn't mess himself up real good. There he was in uniform...the prima donna was profiling, ya know, trying to show how fast he could chuck a radar-clocked softball. And sure enough, Silver Tongue dislocated his shoulder when he hauled back and fired off a scorcher...damn if he didn't! Gonna be suckin' sick leave and light duty for two months or more at least. Who the hell we gonna get to play shortstop for us now, huh?" "Man-oh-man! Y'all shoulda seen ole Bull Brady kick his leg up and whack that ball into orbit for a bases-loaded homer! Sucker played his heart out in all three games today...and in all that scorchin' heat, too. Wanna bet he calls in sick for night shift again?"

Like bitch dogs in heat, the barrack soft ballers went bonkers discussing the trials and tribulations of their blessed sport. Dalton was certain that a few of them, like his bud Junebug, or the awesomely muscled, tobacco spitting slugger "Mad Dog" ('come on Mike, you know I don't do any steroids, don't ya?") Swisher, in all likelihood, probably even slept with their aluminum home run sticks.

On one side of the conference room was a small kitchenette, complete with double sinks, a microwave and a fridge. With the usual mountain of dirty dishes piled up in the clogged sinks, coagulated food splatters fermenting in the micro, and the various moldy, rotting foodstuffs long abandoned in the fridge—like the half eaten, partially putrefied, Leto's everything-on-it pizza, a musty container of leftover Egg Foo Yuck, half empty packets of greasy, marbleized Micky D funky fries, and lord knows what else, the trooper-ized kitchenette was nothing short of an e-coli incubation station.

At the far end of the room was the barrack TV and VHS recorder. The troops could watch training films when required, and, if lucky during the dull night shifts, they could ogle vid tapes like, "Debbie Does Dallas and Everybody Else, Too," until the sourpuss duty officer screwed things up by assigning them another piddly-ass to clear them out of the barrack.

Where Lt. Mister ever scrounged up Ernie Dorsey, the barrack's new caretaker would forever be a mystery. In the long run, however, the barrack greatly benefited from his unique mechanical savvy, or, perhaps more so, his supreme scavenging talents.

Ernie was born and raised in Wallville, a backwoods hole near St. Leonard. Being a homeboy gave him an advantage of knowing *whom,* to contact for *what,* for close to *nothing,* when he could wrangle it. When Dalton first saw him, he could easily picture "Ernie the pack rat" with glazed eyes and yawing mouth, rocking slowly on an old tobacco stained, wooden rocking chair on the garbage-strewn front porch of an Appalachian shack. Or perhaps more fitting, Ernie would have made an ideal scimitar-toting buccaneer, if, of course, he didn't have such a strong aversion to water.

He was a tall and lanky stick of a man in his late thirties, most people guessed, but his pock-mocked face, stubby scarred nose, deep-set vacant eyes, and heavy wrinkle lines on his forehead ending with crow's-feet at his eyes, branded him with the hardened look of someone much older. Ernie was distinctly bow-legged too, a condition which, along with other native characteristics, made him a candidate for being a true-blue SMIB (Southern Maryland Inbreed). His teeth, those few he still had, were crooked and yellow, his breath smelled like an over-populated chicken coop, and his thick, curly black hair was always dirty and unkempt. Strange looking flakes of dried food and tiny bits of weird looking insects fell from his head whenever Ernie ran his greasy fingers through his hair.

To be fair, Ernie would give you the shirt off his back, if you asked for it. And no one ever dared ask, because Ernie liked the fit of his blue chemise shirt so much that he'd wear it day after day without feeling the need to wash it. Ernie's command of the English language was scant, and he talked in a broken speech manner, but what offset his unflattering characteristics, was his positive spirit and down-home humor. At his command was an endless selection of barely tolerable two or three-liner dirty jokes.

"Hey, Sergeant Bragg, you know what the difference between sin and shame is? Huh, huh, do ya, Sarge?" Ernie muttered excitedly. "Heh, heh, I knew'd ya didn't. Well, it's a sin to put it in, but it's a shame to pull it out! Funny, huh, Sarge? Did ya get it? Huh, huh?" Ugh.

Contributing to the caretaker's warped sense of pride, the lieutenant eventually saw fit to anoint Ernie as the King of The Barrack Car Washers. That title of daunting authority meant that he oversaw the prisoner trustees and court-assigned community service car-washers when they washed police cruisers. What a treat it was to see Ernie with his puffed chest, strutting around like a peacock amongst the unfortunates serving under his broken-winged guidance. Overall, most at the barrack thought Ernie to be a likeable sort. Dalton thought if he ever dared to write a book some day, Ernie the Rogue would come alive again somewhere within its pages.

#

In the new Barrack "U," the TO (table of organization) was increased to the normal barrack allotment of five working groups, each group now having a sergeant and a road corporal. No longer were the sergeants free to roam the byways. Now they'd be spending most of their time as fixed targets in the duty officer's pit as glorified house boys. The starting lineup of duty sergeants—Elzy, Dalton, Dan Collison, Ben Wiley and Tom Long—was diverse and dependable.

Unknown to them of course, four of the five would remain at the barrack as sergeants for the rest of their careers, while the lieutenants and first sergeants above them, and a slew of corporals and troopers below, would come and go like the wind. In allotted manpower, the barrack had reached its high-water mark, with just under forty sworn MSP personnel. With the county resident trooper program on the chopping block, the number of troopers assigned to Barrack "U" would slowly decrease during the next decade.

Lieutenant Mister was able to lure two seasoned PCOs away from other barracks, and with the eventual hiring of three more PCOs, the barrack was up to par. Because they were scheduled on a limited rotating basis, each sergeant would eventually experience all of the PCOs—the good, the bad, the ugly, and the not-so-ugly-at all!

To Dalton and the other troopers in perpetual wanderlust, it was close to heaven when the cute and vivacious, super efficient, twenty-five year-old Barbi was the shift PCO. Working with the hard bodied little vamp during those long hours of night shift, watching her lean back smiling with her eyes closed, sighing wistfully as she lazily stretched her arms high over her long auburn tresses—the outline of a healthy pair of 34-Cs painfully coming into clear focus through a tight cardigan sweater—*yes*, it was pure torture.

Dalton would never admit it, and Lord knows he'd never allow her a hint, but if Barbi ever knew how often he'd come so close to shedding his sergeant persona to throw her over his shoulder and carry her to the spare bedroom for a quick bout of frothy, unbridled jungle sex, the lil heartthrob probably wouldn't have flirted with him like she did. Maybe not.

Alas, he was a slightly tarnished married man, and besides, it was common knowledge that Sergeant Don Collision had been knocking the bottom out of the sugar babe for the last several months.

Thanks to Barbi in all her lascivious splendor, that damned testosterone problem child always ran wild during those long night-shift hours. It was hell to traipse home with raging hormones, ready for a wild ride in the saddle, when your other half was still innocently dreaming of crossword puzzles in La-La land.

Dalton, of course, never had that rampaging problem when he worked with Herb, the surly old PCO veteran of maybe a few too many years behind the radio console. Beneath the scowls, the usual feigned grumpiness and the ever-present cloud of cigarette smoke, the mutton-chopped Herb unfailingly knew his stuff. If the DO working with this gentleman from Mississippi ever found the right keys to press, the perfect country music station to tune to, the hours drifted by easy-like.

Francis, forty-two years old, much older than most PCOs, was a different enigma. Married way too young and weighted down with twin baby girls, Francis hadn't seen much in the way of life experiences beyond the door of her shabby trailer set back on a dirt lot in the Hallowing Point trailer park. Taunted by an early mid-life crisis, Francis ventured out into the job world, surprising herself and her country-boy hubby by snagging a PCO job at the PF barrack. Endowed with a willowy figure and a narrow face which she excessively painted up with Dollar Store makeup, Francis was an innocent enough looking woman. Although her frizzy 'big hair" style and selected clothing gave her the outdated look of a sixties homecoming queen—the look of an extra in John Waters *Hairspray* movie—she was a disarmingly pleasant person to be around.

Unfortunately, it soon became apparent that the good-hearted Francis was just a few brain cells up from a garden rake, and the PCO job was an ever-evolving bewilderment to her. Although Dalton grew to like Franny Big Hair, he and the other sergeants didn't relish working an entire shift with her, simply because she amounted to something else to chafe about, a liability in the making and a source of smoothness, n*ot!* There were many Francis stories, and unfortunately, Dalton endured most of them.

During one draggy late shift, Dalton watched in amazement as Francis nervously stuttered into the radio mic a few times without bothering to use the transmit button. Her face turned beet-red when he patiently reminded her about the need to press the large, bright red button—the one looming in her face—to send a message.

"Sarge, you know I can't do two things at once," she answered feebly. He stifled a laugh when he noticed she was chewing gum. And the time she pressed the wrong button to answer an incoming phone call, via the internal page system, was a classic. Her voice echoed loudly over the entire PA: "This is the Maryland State Police, Prince Frederick barrack...Can I...ummm...help you? (Pause) Ohhh Damn! I pushed the wrong button again...I'm so sorry! (Click)!" Dalton lost it, keeling over in hysterical laughter. When he finally sat up, he rubbed his eyes and stared at her with a resigned look. Francis sheepishly gazed back. "Guess I did another blonde thing, didn't I, Sarge, huh?'

In the quiet early morning hours, when he worked night shift with Franny Big Hair, Dalton usually let her go home a few hours early. Francis was always grateful for that, and he was too, knowing that he'd be blissfully alone again, no longer suffering anymore from watching her stare vacantly at her blank computer screen, hoping vainly that it'd suddenly come alive and tell her what to do. And as soon as she left, Dalton sighed with relief and dashed lickety-split down to the radio room to switch the intercom radio frequency from the dull elevator music to a hard-rock station.

#

Since being a sergeant, Dalton had supervised four corporals, and he'd been satisfied with them all. Working a shift with a hard charging, dependable road corporal, and a star PCO, could tempt a giddy three-striper into doing a double back flip off the radio tower, maybe. While his current corporal didn't exactly set the world on fire, Dalton had to admit that Seth "Foozy" Taylor was one of the most personable, down-home guys he'd ever worked with. You just couldn't stay piqued with a corporal who always had a shit-faced grin on his mug.

Foozy took life at a much slower pace than most. Where many sweated the piddling stuff, Foozy didn't rattle, choosing to ramble on in his normal plodding manner. People like Foozy who were raised in St. Ingoes, a sleepy rural hamlet in St. Mary's county, tended to be that way. He was rather short and squat for a trooper, and he had those lazy-brown hound dog eyes and slightly drooping ears that would put one to ease the moment they met him. Foozy kept his sandy hair, what was left of it, cut short, but his wide, gray tinged sideburns were pushing the maximum length allowed by the MSP. With always-red cheeks on his round face, the corporal looked cherubic, most thought. Foozy also had a distinctly nasal, rasping voice that sounded whiny at times. It was pure southern Maryland dialect, and for most, it was entertaining to hear. With Foozy, oysters were "*arsters*," terrible came out "*turrble*," Washington DC was "*Worshintin*,"and Maryland was always "*Murlin*."

Dalton's thick bellied, beefy armed corporal with the habitual smile, was a short timer. He and the Foozy man had cleared the air on that aspect months ago, and Dalton decided to cut him some slack. When prodded from the barrack, Foozy did a decent enough job of tending herd on his group. When the fecal matter inevitably hit the fan, the troopers were always reassured when the cool-headed Foozy arrived on the scene. And when Foozy's eyes shrank down to dark angry slits and his ears turned red, nobody dared to mess with him, either.

At this epoch in his life, Foozy's waning MSP career was nearly a hobby to him. His heart was embroiled in his love for the water, beer guzzling and whacking softballs in the county league team he still played on. In his other off-duty hours, Foozy often helped on 'Lucy," his father's work boat, pulling crab pots and "arsters" culling from their beloved St. Mary's River. His leathery tough, calloused hands gave mute testimony to the hard days spent in pursuit of the delectable blue claws. In the fall, when the waters turned chilly and the brown autumn leaves started dropping, Foozy's stout form could be spotted easily from shore. There he'd be, standing shoulder to shoulder with his pipe-smoking dad, tonging for "arsters' at their favorite oyster bar. Ever so reluctantly, Foozy had given up chasing skirts years ago after his second divorce. To the benefit of the barrack vaunted MSP softball team, the forty-seven year-old corporal was still a viable softball player on the team roster.

Of all the corporals he'd ever work with, Dalton would remember Foozy as being the most "user-friendly," bar none.

Months after Dalton and his corporal had arrived at their mutual understanding, Kelly McKeon, the prudish female trooper in Foozy's work group, sidestepped her corporal's fatherly guidance to address an impending problem directly to Dalton, her sergeant. From his early corporal days, Dalton prided himself on his communication skills and his ability to interact effectively with countless number of troopers he'd rubbed elbows with. When he shut the door to the sergeant's room and invited the pensive female trooper to have a seat, he was confident he'd be able to resolve or clarify any problem she'd see fit to toss his way. On that belief, however, he was dreadfully mistaken.

Twenty-three years-old and on the job for less then two years, the medium built, brown-haired woman with the chatty personality was naive in many ways. Undoubtedly, Dalton knew that Trooper McKeon's job would be the most powerful one she'd ever have in a vertical position. As a road-pounding trooper, her performance was sadly lacking, and although she'd tried hard to adjust, done her best to be one of the guys, it was apparent to many that the comely woman wasn't cut out for the job. To further complicate matters, while many fellow troopers took her under their wings to guide her along, it'd been rumored that a few of the barrack's seasoned cock-hounds had taken her under the covers, too.

"Kelly, I'm all ears to you, OK?" Dalton told her after plunking himself down on top of his cluttered desk. Dalton locked eyes with her and immediately noticed she was fidgeting with one of her collar ornaments, and her lips were starting to quiver. She slumped in her chair, buried a fist in her cheek, and tapped her foot for an awkward moment—before exploding into tears. "Sarge, I've got a real, *real* bad problem," she blurted out with a sob, her head hanging low. Dalton pushed himself off the desk and put a hand on her shoulder. She looked up at him with teary eyes, her black mascara streaming down. "I'm pregnant, Sarge, and I'm not sure what I'm gonna do about it, so I think I need some advice."

Dalton remained somber-faced, but silently cussed himself out for not taking that personal leave day today, as he'd planned. "And I know my boyfriend isn't involved, because he *always* uses condoms when we screw...I make sure of that!" (La-la-la-la...too much information...I can't hear you, Dalton's inner voice called out.) His mind drifted beyond her echoing words to ponder about all the keeper bass he could have hooked by now at Judge Mackall's pond.

"OK, OK, and there's something else," Kelly rasped before she loudly blew her nose in the State of Maryland-issued napkin he'd handed her. "I guess you might know this...The father is one of the two married troopers I've been seeing, and both of them are friends of yours, too!" *Whoops*! Dalton just visualized himself trying to set the hook to Bubba, who'd just zoomed off with his new Power Bait eight-inch plastic worm dangling from his yawing mouth. The image blurred, and he coughed and gazed out the window for a moment before turning his divided attention back to her.

"Kelly, I've got lots of friends on the job," he said, faintly, wishing she'd suddenly vanish. "And you know what's the worst thing about it?" she asked with a childish look on her tear-streaked face. Dalton crossed his arms and fought to keep a deadpan face. "I know I love one of them, and I know he loves the hell outta me, too. Guess I was in the right place at the right time for that to happen, when I think about it, and, and, he says he's even gonna leave his fat-slug wife soon, too, so I may just keep his baby! Guess you know who I'm talkin' about, don't you, Sarge?"

Having guzzled way too many beers by now, Dalton saw himself flipping the boat over when he lost the struggle to stand up straight and piss his brains out. Forcing himself back to the moment, he stared forlornly at the trooper sitting in front of him, put a finger to his lips and let out a long, *Shhhh!* "Trooper McKeon, er, Kelly," he addressed her, trying hard to sound serious. "I think it's best that you keep that lil secret to yourself and just take the rest of the day off, so you can have a long, long weekend. Umm, you've got some rather...uhhh...challenging decisions to make, and some time off to think about them might do you good, right?" She nodded silently and got up to leave. "Oh, and Kelly, before you go," he added, watching her turn around with eager eyes, "be sure to turn in your performance report for me, OK?"

Several weeks later, the five-months pregnant trooper left the ranks of "Maryland's Finest," migrating to the sunny outskirts of Santa Fe, New Mexico, with her browbeaten boyfriend. Months later, the barrack received a postcard from her that was promptly tacked on the troopers' room bulletin board. Among the drivel in her familiar scrawled handwriting, she'd included the first name of her child, who, to no one's surprise, was named after the probable papa. But by then, however, most troopers already knew who that snake was, making it stale news in the scuttlebutt mill.

Due to political correctness being in its ambiguous infancy, those in the MSP puzzle palace never dared to acknowledge it, but to Dalton and many field troops it was readily apparent that when compared to their male counterparts, most of the female troopers, like Kelly McKeon, were having hard times hacking the strenuous demands of road patrol and shift work. Most female troopers who stayed on the job usually migrated to other non-uniform positions in the MSP enclaves where their attributes and job skills were better recognized and held in higher esteem.

#

Like most duty sergeants, Dalton was a certified Breathalyzer operator. Working night shifts on the busy weekends usually meant that the DOs would be steadily administering breath tests during the first few hours. Usually, the male DWIs were a decent sort to deal with. Sure, some of the macho, testy types put their asses on their shoulders every so often, but once they were taught the strict "house rules," they usually self-deflated and played nice. Of course it never helped when a rogue trooper, the bullying oaf type, needlessly teased and incited a fellow trooper's prisoner for shits and giggles.

The female DWIs were different. Many took the sympathy route, with flooding tears washing away dark eye makeup in nasty-looking rivulets, as the soused damsels tried to figure out where they were and what the hell was going on. Other starry-eyed femme fatales were brought in screaming and hissing like pissed-off alley cats. If that diplomacy failed, some of the wily cougars tried to alter the course of events by using time-honored powers of feminine persuasion.

"Hey there, trooper honey, bet ya didn't know that Trooper "Boogie" Perkins and I are real close friends, did ya, huh, trooper Boy? Ummm, if you're anything like him, you'd be an all-nighter for me, for sure! Bet ya never made it with a hot, married babe who can suck the chrome off a bumper hitch, huh baby? Tell ya what, good-looking...if I can't light your fire, your wood's all wet!"

Dalton *always* felt awkward giving breath tests to female DWIs. Often, when the woman wasn't giving an adequate breath sample, he had to advise her to, "Blow harder, More, More, *More!* Keep blowing, keep blowing...*harder!*"

On the night he gave those directions to Lisa, the tipsy barmaid from North Beach, her face turned ruby-red, and she suddenly stopped and burst out in hysterics. Regaining some control, she sloppily wiped away a few loose tears, smiled, and gave him a wink. "Sssugar babe... if I blowed any harder on that lil thang-a-ma-jig, that machine a yours ittth gonna have an, or...an org...aw hell, I got it...an *organism*, sure as shit! Sure like to see how the hell ya gonna write that report up, baby," she blurted out, slapping a hand on his leg. After several attempts, Dalton finally coerced a decent breath sample from her, but true to her nature, she turned into a total she-bitch afterward, granting her the privilege of being hauled down to the basement holding cell.

Dalton returned to the radio room to check in with good ole country gentleman Herb, the shift PCO. He was puzzled when he saw Herb's shit-faced grin. Herb coughed, snubbed his cigarette out and gestured at the TV monitor. The overhead holding cell camera was capturing it all.

"Got yourself a real whacko broad down there tonight, Sarge," Herb chuckled. Dalton peered at the monitor and turned up the volume. The starry-eyed North Beach babe was swaying side-to-side, leering up at the camera. She sputtered and cursed before breaking into an ear-to-ear grin. "OK, OK, I know y'all bees lookin' at me, damn sure if ya ain't," she yelled at the camera. "Well bbboys, if that's the way izz gonna be, might's well make it worthwhile for ya!"

Dalton shot a quick glance at Herb, who was gaping over his shoulder. Dumbstruck, they watched as the girl crossed her arms and nimbly pulled off her T-shirt! Into view popped a healthy set of firm boobies! She smiled coyly, blew a kiss, then cupped both breasts in her hands and offered them to the camera. "Say hello to my sssssweet lil darlins' why don't ya?" she shouted. Transfixed, they gawked openmouthed as she seductively wriggled her shoulders and hips for a few moments. Ever so slowly, she turned her back to the camera and bent over at the waist, placing her fingertips on the concrete floor.

"Holly Shit," Herb shouted, as Dalton gulped loudly in his ear. *"You go girlfriend!"* She had a fair, but rather hard-looking face, but the beach babe had nothing short of a killer bod. Spellbound, they watched as she stood up and lazily stretched her arms over her head. She gave an animated sigh then brought her hands down to the top of her khaki shorts. "Still with me, boys?" Without turning around, she effortlessly tugged the shorts down from a trim waist, revealing a magnificent set of tight, well-rounded buns. Dalton rubbed his eyes. "You gotta be shitting me," Herb gleefully exclaimed. Dalton elbowed him in the side and whispered hoarsely for him to shut up. 'This one's between me and you, right, Herb?" Herb smirked and nodded his head.

With a jubilant laugh, the babe brought her long, toned legs up and slipped them from her shorts. With her back still turned from the camera, she tossed the shorts over her shoulder and kicked off her lace-less sneakers. They watched tongue-tied as she slowly sauntered over to the back of the cell and sat down on the concrete ledge. With an inviting smile, she slumped back against the wall and spread her legs wide apart. Herb gasped.

"Sarge, don't know if the ole ticker can take much more, right now." The last image the gape-mouthed Herb saw, before Dalton turned the camera off, was her right hand inching down toward her shaved, totally bared, V junction. Reluctantly, Dalton ended the show to keep his PCO from going cardiac on him.

With help from the amused arresting trooper, Dalton finally managed to convince the North Beach queen that she'd passed her audition with flying colors. Satisfied, she pursed her lips and proudly stuck her nose in the air. Smiling triumphantly, she put her clothes back on just minutes before her weary-eyed, lawyer/ boyfriend, the forgetfully married Barry Branson, arrived at the barrack to take custody of her. After she hugged and sloppily kissed her frumpy-haired savior in the lobby, she turned and blew a kiss at Dalton, shook her boobs at him with a wink, then breezed out the door.

Lisa returned months later for community service ordered by visiting judge Stephen Lawrence Schultz, who was rumored to harbor a wandering libido. Washing police cars one Sunday and sweating bullets with several other petty malefactors, she complained to Sgt. Ben Wiley about working under the grueling sun. When she asked if he had any problem with her changing into something more accommodating, Ben offhandedly advised her to go for it.

It was a challenge, but when Franny Big-Hair, the shift PCO, wasn't looking, Ben zoomed in on the car washers with the outside camera. More precisely, Ben zeroed in on the sweaty, string-bikini-clad, heavenly-built Lisa, who, in her signature erotic style, was doing her best to show off her car-washing talents to her bedazzled fellow car washers and the handful of lusting troopers who'd drifted back to the barrack under the lame premise of finishing up paperwork.

The following Monday, Pearl, the honcho secretary, overheard the barrack scuttlebutt. Working herself into a full tizzy, she marched indignantly into Lt Mister's office for a major pow-wow. Riding a feigned wave of righteousness, Pearl complained vehemently to the weary lieutenant about the stripper from North Beach being allowed to wash cars in the nude over the weekend. Sadly, her animated tirades had the effect she'd wanted. Henceforth, the use of female court workers as barrack car washers came to a screeching, heartbreaking halt, Lisa's fame and glory never to be forgotten.

Yes indeed, there were endless stories surrounding the drunks, particularly their antics in the downstairs holding cells. From the strippers and masturbators, and the legions of screamers and head-bangers, to the imbeciles who crapped on the floors or clogged the stainless steel johns with toilet paper to flood the cells, the duty officers saw it all. Accordingly, there would be a bounty of bizarre tales for the troopers to share over beers.

Chapter 11

SPECIAL ASSIGNMENTS

Keeping the habitually chastised duty officer from chasing people around the barrack with a gun, the department early on conceived a two letter designation, "S/A," for Special Assignment, which was easily penned in on the master leave schedule to break up a crazed sergeant's monotony. There was always sick leave, court, training, and the occasional, badly needed, long lunch breaks to alter the routine, and to a trooper or corporal, "Special Assignment" could foster a major shit-fit. But for a harried sergeant, it usually meant a welcome un-assing from a well-worn chair in the DO's pit. Regardless of rank, during their MSP careers, troopers were assigned to countless "Special Assignments."

The all encompassing "S/A" could mean a tough day spent aboard a fellow trooper's boat, keeping well-oiled with Buds while partaking in a "Fishing for the Poor" program, or it meant being an LE torch-bearer in the annual Special Olympics run from Solomons to the Charles County line, or, maybe it was a chief's role barbequing a road-kill deer that was "appropriated" for the barrack stag party. Perhaps S/A could be disguised as a payback day for not claiming gads of overtime from the last pay period, or, maybe something actually job-related, like standing in the cold, pouring rain at an Annapolis street corner in class A uniform for the governor's inauguration—or a few days patrolling Baltimore City when the city's finest did their "blue flu" routine. Might even get to babysit prisoners at the PG County detention center when the guards walked off again, too.

Under the "Special Assignment" umbrella, you could join a phalanx of helmeted, raincoat and rubber glove-clad troopers and other allied LE brothers standing tall in thin ranks in front of the National Institute of Health compound in DC, patiently waiting for two thousand gay protestors to storm through the police lines during a nationally televised protest of cutbacks in AIDS research funds. (No...Lieutenant,

I swear, I have *no* idea which trooper was caught on camera dragging that spitting gay blade up the stairs by his hair, but I'm almost 99% certain it wasn't me, sir!")

Perhaps, if charmed, you'd find yourself suited up in bulky riot gear, sweating your butt off and bored senseless in a stuffed, dingy office under the Maryland State House. *Yes*, waiting endlessly for the *"Go"* signal, so you and the rest of the tact team herd could don helmets and make a mad dash outside, ready to flail away with your "defensive" PR-24 for some decent stick time on the unruly abortion protesters playing bad-ass whenever the TV cameras lit up. ("Ya want something to protest about, lil lady, huh? How's bout some mace in your pimply face to start things off right?" Elzy'd shouted at the dizzy college chick who shook the fake-blood smeared baby doll in his face.)

And there was always the yearly, inescapable CALVEX exercise, when the entire friggin barrack would be put on Special Assignment to coordinate the simulated evacuation of the county—a reality *if* one of the Calvert Cliffs nuclear reactors finally had an atomic orgasm oozing halfway to China. As dedicated as most troopers were, and most were innately impaired with that handicap, some wouldn't stick around to play the "blue canary" role. No, if Calvert's radioactive behemoths crashed, Dalton suspected those few would be northbound at a high rate, radio antennas bent back low from the g-forces, as they made their silent escape from the county.

But, "Special Assignment" could also mean that rare, vastly rewarding extradition, too! Nothing like a three-day, all expenses paid extradition, the more south and sunnier, the better, to recharge the spirits and calm the blood pressures. Years before, Dalton nabbed a decent sojourn to New Orleans, and with an ebulliently horny buddy trooper in tow, they got delightfully "lost" in the French Quarter for two days.

The extradition, which was Dalton's ultimate salvation from the DO's pit, was to retrieve Calvert fugitive Hezekiah Fowler from sunny Phoenix, Arizona. Totally baffling to both of them, Lt Mister paired Dalton and his buddy Junebug Buckler for the three-day mission to the

Tequila Sunrise state. Loaded with State's Attorney's expense money, they dutifully arrived at BWI airport. Boredom was never Junebug's forte, and with time to spare before the flight, he dragged Dalton to the closest lounge. After several drafts or more, both troopers were comfortably numb and gleefully carefree—until Dalton gaped at his watch and suddenly realized that the Southwest jet he saw taxiing away was their Phoenix flight.

"Damn, Junebug! "We're screwed big-time, now," he muttered, as they scurried over to the Southwest counter. "Naw, Sarge, just let the ole Bug handle this one, and you won't be frettin' none about losing a stripe...Got this shit down good, trust me." It wasn't *that* easy, but Junebug finally sweet-talked the comely female ticket agent into issuing them tickets for first-class red-eye flights later on. So it was back to the bar to toast their good luck.

After checking in with the Maricopa Sheriff's Office the next morning, they dove into a rental car and headed for the Phoenix outskirts. The unforgettable, stunning desert scenery— that majestic natural treasure—nearly proved to be the trip's highlight, Dalton thought. Before prowling out to the open desert, Dalton convinced Junebug to suck in some of the ambience by climbing a high mountain ridge overlooking Phoenix. When both winded troopers reached the top, Dalton knew he could stay there for hours, breathing in the sweet, clear air and taking in the splendid scenery spread out below: cobalt-blue sky, pastel painted mountains, prickly cactus decorating the slopes, the lush green valley and so much more.

Predictably within minutes, however, Junebug was bored. Shrugging his beefy shoulders, he signaled his growing restlessness by tossing a few large boulders down the mountainside. "Sarge, bowling for cactus," he hooted, after a big rock flattened a pronged cactus down below.

After the boulder barrage, Junebug eased himself up and brushed off his jeans. Dalton waved at him. "Come on, big boy, ya got your rocks off. Time to vamoose, before you get us busted for obliterating the Arizona state plant." Junebug howled like a happy coyote. "Ready to take that lil desert drive to that frontier town them Maricopa deputies told us about, hey, Sarge? Man works up a sweat chucking them big pebbles. Gotta feeling those cold Pearls we got stashed in the cooler might slake us cowpokes' thirst right about now," he added with a silly smirk. Dalton nodded and gave his buddy a thumbs-up.

"Sarge, but first, ya wanna challenge me to King of the Mountain before we head down? Huh, huh?" Dalton turned and stared at him. He winced when he saw the big lummox standing with his legs apart and his beefy arms crossed over a puffed-out chest. The veins on Junebug's thick neck were bulging cords, his nostrils flared, and his eyes beamed with anticipation. Dalton sighed and shook his head. "Naw, you win, hoss," he said mockingly before starting down the trail. Junebug snorted in victory. Moments later, Dalton dove off the trail, narrowly avoiding being flattened by another Junebug-propelled boulder. *Damn*! Just wish he'd quit playing that dumb-ass Rambo shit.

Silverwood, the makeshift frontier town near Scottsdale, was perfect. The tipsy duo eventually stumbled into a genuine imitation of an old-time western cantina and feasted heartily on mesquite-grilled buffalo steaks and side orders of almost anything else cowboy-like they could stuff down. Hell, why not, since the extradition cost would be tacked onto Hezekiah Fowler's court sentence later? In the spirit of justice, they happily toasted the dirt-ball they'd soon be rescuing from a dank Arizona prison cell.

The overhead sign read "Lazy-J's." From the outside, at least, it seemed to be just the rowdy looking saloon they remembered from the cowboy flicks of their Red Ryder days. Dalton half suspected that ole squinty-eyed Clint Eastwood might be in there, sipping a whiskey and calmly puffing away on a stogie. To his dismay, the smoky bar section was filled with cowboy-costumed dandies and a handful of gawking tourists—no hardcore Clints.

Sauntering into the back gambling room, Junebug's attention was instantly riveted on the winsome waitresses and nubile dancing girls. Dalton nudged him after he spotted drool forming at the corner of his mouth. "Hey Sarge...don't have any choice over what I see, OK? Gotta move like a cheetah to get where I have to go, know what I'm sayin'?" Junebug shouted over the hard-rock music blasting from the not-so-wild-west jukebox. Dalton eyed Junebug with mixed curiosity when he puffed out his chest and flexed his meaty biceps.

All the young babes wore different, scanty costumes: Indian squaws, dance hall girls, to Annie Oakley garb. Several wore NFL cheerleader outfits. Both troopers drifted over to the glitzy bar and grabbed two vacant stools to scope out the enticing scenery. Dalton was nursing his Coors draft and behaving himself—until he did a double take at the approaching waitress.

She was a tall, tanned, outrageously gorgeous blonde, packed tight in a body-hugging pair of blue star-studded, white mini shorts! She was also wearing a star-studded, blue and white matching halter-top that exposed much of her bountiful cleavage. He didn't need to see her white cowboy boots to confirm that she was dressed as one of his most treasured symbols of pure femininity—a *Dallas Cowgirl Cheerleader!* Swooning badly, Dalton peered at her nametag. The name Cheyenne was centered over one of the most perfect boobs he'd ever seen. For a fleeting moment, he was googly-eyed and mushy. Feeling close to heaven, he stuttered out an order for two more beers.

Dalton was so wildly enamored with his bubbly Cowgirl angel that he hadn't seen Junebug stalk over to the cluster of NFL cheerleaders at the end of the bar. Dalton wasn't sure if it'd been when Junebug's amorous advances were rebuffed by the Forty-Niner's cheerleader, or the voluptuous Washington Redskinette, but regardless, Junebug traipsed back with his head hung low like a whipped puppy. Dalton almost panicked when his antsy cohort announced he was splitting, but he calmed Junebug down with a quick time-out.

Yup, it was time for Dalton to make a last second, fourth-and-long, field goal attempt at his captivating Dallas Cowgirl. When Cheyenne asked him if they needed anything else, Dalton blinked stars from his eyes and broke from his one-man huddle. Reaching out, he took her hand and kissed it, then wrapped an arm around her waist and gently sat her down on his lap. Oh, God help me, he thought, when her Obsession perfume engulfed him like a cloud from heaven. He felt his face flush, as that tingly, debilitating feeling rushed over him again. Above the driving sound of ZZ Top's, *She's Got Legs*, reverberating from the juke, Dalton found his nerve and blurted out a request for

Cheyenne to perform a private lap cheer for him, or something close to it; he'd probably remember later. She broke into a heart stopping smile, wriggled her shoulders, then leaned over and whispered into his ear. After she deftly blocked his last-second field goal attempt ("Thanks for the invite Buckaroo, but I don't hike the football with anyone but my fiancé), both deflated troopers scooted from the saloon to find their four-banger Toyota steed.

As they drove down the lonely desert road back toward Phoenix, the crimson sun was slipping behind the majestic mountains on the faraway horizon. In the early evening, Dalton was mesmerized by the desert's subtle beauty. For miles, he saw nothing but scrub brush, prickly cactus of all sizes and shapes, rock-strewn arroyos and the magnificent, earthy pastels of the west he thought he'd never see. He fiddled with the radio knob until a station came in clear. He found *Vayas con Dios* in Spanish, the singers caressing the ballad with soft, flowing words. Seizing the moment, Junebug flexed his biceps and belched loudly, as he handed Dalton another chilled Pearl. Dalton grinned at his sunburned partner, and they tapped beer cans in a sloppy salute. "Don't get no better than this, right, Junebug?" he shouted. Hey, a toast to Hezekiah, the dude who made this all happen, OK?"

Junebug fetched another beer and settled back in the seat. "Yeah, Sarge, things are A-OK round these parts...Feel close to being in desert paradise, matter of fact," he said facetiously. "But ya know, if you'd turn this lil pissant car around and take our asses back to Lazy J's...that saloon with the Redskin's cheerleader...I know I'd be back in true paradise for damn sure! Yup, I *know* that girl wanted me, bet my ass on it, too...But, but, she just didn't know how to show it, know what I mean?"

Dalton laughed at his buddy trooper. "Ain't turning around for no floozy Washington Redskin cheerleader, but I gotta admit to ya, Junebug, I *am* thinking awfully hard about that pretty lil Dallas Cowgirl again," he countered. Junebug made a squeamish face. "Your Cow-babies suck this year, and the Skins are kicking ass big time, Sarge, even *if* the Cow-pukes did beat em' twice, OK?" Shaking his head, Dalton decided against rehashing their football feud and jacked up the radio instead.

For several miles they traveled on—before Dalton suddenly brought the Toyota to a tire screeching halt. Junebug looked quizzical as he studied his pal, who was deep in thought. He pulled a few times on the bill of the ten-gallon cowboy he'd bought earlier and drummed his fingers on a hand-rest. Using his best pseudo-cowboy voice, Dalton shouted a loud, high-pitched "Yee-haw!

"We're goin' back to Lazy-J's for some sudden-death overtime, Junebug," he yelled. "But how's bout doin' me a favor and taking off that stupid-ass cowpoke hat, OK? Ain't no self-respecting Redskin cheerleader gonna make time with you lookin' like ole Gabby fuckin' Hayes, trust me on that one, partner!" Dalton glanced over at his buddy's cowboy hat and laughed. The emblem on front read, "Liquor Up Front, Poker In The Rear." Junebug let out a loud war whoop and passed his cohort another Pearl, after Dalton floored the gas pedal and spun tires in a piss-poor imitation of a power turn. Jerking hard on the steering wheel, he forced the car back on the happy trail leading to Lazy J's.

Eighteen hours later, after dumping off fugitive Hezekiah at the Calvert County "Ritz," both extraditionalists were home again, trying to convince their wives how exhausted they were from the jet lag and the demanding rigors of the remarkably dull trip.

#

There was, however, one type of Special Assignment that troopers utterly dreaded, and if a trooper attended one of them, it was one too many—the funerals of fellow troopers, his brothers or sisters who'd died in the line of duty. Dalton had attended five MSP funerals in his career so far, and each one had taken another modest piece of his soul away, but the experiences had also strongly emphasized the sacrifice and reinforced the roles that "Maryland's Finest" played in protecting the citizens of the Old Line State.

Months after his Phoenix extradition, Dalton attended yet another funeral for a fellow trooper. This funeral, the funeral of another classmate, would affect him more than any other. For the prestigious MSP, it was a very sad, tragic event.

Corporal Mike Fox didn't have to work the graveyard shift that night, but the Glen Burnie barrack would have bare minimum manpower if he didn't, so he duly reported in. The highly decorated, forty-two year-old veteran of seventeen years would have it no other way. Mike Fox had to be out there with his fellow troopers where the action was. Any thoughts of being promoted to sergeant, to languish behind a desk, were dismissed by the energetic road corporal.

He was feeling great about life that night, still basking from the limelight of the night before, when he'd been honored at a local awards banquet. Tonight, all Mike wanted most was for the eight hour shift to zip by so he could slip home to his wife Doreen and his two sons. Maybe, if his timing was right, he could chat and share his usual breakfast of bacon, easy-over eggs and whole-wheat toast with Doreen before he hit the sack. It was always fun, a bonding factor too, when he was able to shoot the hoops or play pickup basketball with his boys after he normally woke up, just about the time they got home from school.

Mike stifled a yawn when the barrack PCO radioed the station ID and 0330 time check. Lowering the volume of the AM/FM radio, which was tuned to a Baltimore moldy-oldies station, he tried to finish off the last few dregs of coffee. Fitting to his nature, the corporal liked his coffee black and strong, but now it was bitter and galling, so he dumped the rest out the window. He stretched his back against the front seat and rubbed his aching eyes with stiff fingers.

Twenty minutes later, on that disarmingly quiet March morning, Corporal Fox set up his marked cruiser in the median strip of northbound MD Route 3 just north of Crofton, just six miles south of the Baltimore beltway. He'd already run the cruiser through his pre-marked VASCAR course for calibration, and now, comfortably alone, he waited for wayward speeders.

A half hour dragged by, and so far no speeders worth stopping. He didn't expect much at this hour, since traffic was so light, but as his father said, "You don't catch any fish unless you fish, son," so he patiently waited. When the corporal saw the speeding car's headlights pass the first small traffic cone he'd placed on the shoulder, he flicked the timer knob on the VASCAR unit. Seconds later, he flipped it down when the vehicle passed the second cone. Instantly the digital speed display flashed eighty-three miles an hour. *Ahh, finally, a decent arrest*! He hit the emergency lights, floored the gas pedal, and swung the cruiser around in pursuit of the streaking red Mustang.

To the corporal's satisfaction, the driver immediately pulled onto the fast shoulder of the divided highway and glided the Mustang to a quick stop. An experienced road corporal, Mike's gut told him that nothing seemed out of place about the car, so he didn't bother to call out the traffic stop. He was close to the barrack anyhow, and, like most nightshift troopers, he was getting tired of hearing the weary PCOs gripe about having to write down every traffic stop in the radio log. Besides, he was a supervisor, a corporal-at-large and in charge, and he felt confident on his own—just the way he liked it. After switching on the high beams and centering the spotlight on the car in front, Corporal Fox put on his Stetson, grabbed his Kel-light, and jumped from the cruiser. Approaching the Mustang, he cautiously shined the flashlight throughout the interior, and the beam picked up nothing even remotely suspicious.

Two people were in the car; the young driver and a medium-built, bearded man with a baseball cap tucked down close to his ears. His eyes were closed, and his breathing was deep, apparently sound asleep. The corporal immediately sensed that the slightly built Hispanic-looking driver with the wavy black hair seemed like an OK sort of guy. He had a warm, easy smile, and was close to falling over himself, sputtering apologies for having a lead foot. When he displayed his New Jersey driver's license, and what appeared to be a state-issued security guard photo ID, the relaxed corporal jokingly razzed him about the security job routine. He was also impressed when the driver told him that he'd recently applied to the Newark City PD.

When the driver demurely asked permission to take a peek at the VASCAR unit, a speed-enforcement tool he'd never seen before, Corporal Fox smiled and gestured for the "wannabe" cop to follow him back to P-32, his cruiser. The man sitting next to the corporal peppered him with VASCAR questions as the traffic citation was filled out. .

Everything was going smoothly, the citation almost complete, when, on afterthought, Corporal Fox decided to radio the barrack for a registration check on the Virginia tag. Initially he wasn't going to—was just going to rely on what the apologetic driver had told him, but force-of-habit kicked in. Earlier, the driver had laughed and innocently shrugged his shoulders after declaring that the car registration card had gone AWOL on him. Corporal Fox gazed through the windshield and fixed his eyes on the Mustang's tag as he grabbed the radio mic. The mic was inches from his mouth, a finger resting on the transmit button, when he froze in place!

An icy chill ran down his back, and his eyes shot wide open while internal sirens shrieked in his head, piercing his senses and screaming at him that something was horribly, horribly wrong! He jerked his head to the right, when he heard the ugly metallic click of the hammer being cocked back on the steel revolver. There was a blinding, ear-shattering blast! Instantly, he felt a searing pain in his right side that stole his breath away. The second shot came immediately, the hollow point .38-caliber round slamming hard, tearing through his neck. The corporal gasped. On reflex, his legs shot out and his back slammed against the front seat. With an animal cry, he slumped over the steering wheel.

Satisfied, the shooter reached over and grabbed his license and the bloody citation book from the corporal's lap. "Ahora tu suenas con los muertos!" (Now you dream with the dead) he muttered with a sneer. As if he didn't have a care in the world, the killer calmly exited the cruiser, tucked the snob-nose pistol under his belt, and then sauntered back to the stolen Mustang and his sleeping crony. Seconds later, the Mustang was barreling north toward the Baltimore beltway.

Corporal Fox coughed and fought hard to clear his head. The searing pain was overpowering, and he felt weighted down and drained. His head swirled in a howling storm that got darker and louder with each moment. Slumped over the steering wheel and unable to move his legs or raise his head, he felt the radio mic in his hand. With all his waning fortitude, the MSP corporal edged it close to his mouth and pressed the transmit button with a trembling finger. "Sss...ssig...signal tthirteen Glen Burnie!" he rasped out. He coughed and spat out a bright red stream of blood. Fighting to stay conscious, his breath came in gasps. "Signal Thirteen! I...I've been shot! Rrroute three...Glen

Burnie...*SIGNAL THIRTEEN!* " The radio mic dropped from bloody fingers, and with a final groan, his body tensed and went limp.

Satan performed his gruesome work with ruthless efficiency in the fading hours of the graveyard shift that cold morning in 1989. Moments after making the Signal 13 call, Corporal Mike Fox was dead.

Thanks to the dogged efforts of tenacious Captain Terry Shelton and his seasoned, hardcore team of MSP detectives, the cold-blooded killer and his witless colleague were eventually tracked down and arrested in New Jersey. Both were soon extradited to Maryland to stand trial for the murder of the trooper.

The funeral of Corporal Michael Fox was held four days after his shocking death. Like his fellow troopers, Dalton was stunned when he heard the news of his classmate's death. The MSP family closed ranks and mourned their fallen comrade, but it would be a long time before it recovered from the dreadful experience. Dalton Bragg, and scores of other troopers, never did.

From allied police departments as far away as Kansas and Maine, a sea of several thousand grimfaced fellow law officers, all attired in immaculate dress uniforms of gray, brown, green and blue, joined the ranks of the troopers attending the funeral service of the fallen comrade. Due to the immense turnout, several hundred troopers and allied officers stood outside in formed ranks during the hour-long service. It was a cool, misty day, overcast with occasional glimpses of sunshine, but few felt the chill. Amongst his brother troopers, Dalton stood outside in the ranks at parade rest.

Dalton felt detached, like being in a bizarre movie. Maybe the whole eerie scene would suddenly come to a grinding halt in the form of an obscene April Fool's joke? The stark reality, however, dictated otherwise, vividly evidenced by the coal-black shroud on his badge. His eyes drifted up from the badge and shifted side to side, focusing on the ranks of police officers in front of him. They remained rigid with their backs straight, hands clasped behind them and their heads riveted forward. Several troopers twiddled their fingers, a few idly shifted their weight from leg to leg, and, like Dalton, some were eyeballing others, trying to gauge their reactions to the sorrowful ordeal

The sermon was piped out through loudspeakers, but Dalton's attention was elsewhere, his mind flashing with memories of his friend Mike Fox. How motivated and determined Mike was in the academy! Such athleticism! There were few who could match him, especially in the boxing ring. Mike was tough in competition, a straightforward type who dauntlessly performed at his best. *Always!*

Although they'd been assigned to different troop areas since the academy, Dalton had heard much about Mike's stellar career. It intrigued him back in many years past when they both were selected as the "Trooper of the Year" for their respective barracks. To those who knew him, Mike was *the* perfect road trooper, a cop's cop kind of guy. He'd achieved an excellent reputation in the agency, and when he shed his uniform, he was a loving husband and father, and a caring community member, too. Undoubtedly, Dalton thought as he flexed cold fingers, of all his academy classmates, he'd respected Mike Fox the most. So how did his death, and the dark repudiation of mortality which most of them were so self-assured of, make any damned sense at all?

The plaintive wailing of the bagpipe playing *Ireland I'll Not Tell Her Name* brought Dalton back to the moment. At the front of the formation, an MSP captain called the troopers to attention. Dalton watched in silence as the six-man MSP honor guard, bearing rifles and unfurled flags, came to attention. One of the somber-faced troopers cradled a Stetson adorned with a gold cord that signified a missing comrade. As the eight MSP pallbearers carried the corporal's flag-draped casket from the church, Dalton felt a chill run down his spine. "Present arms!" the Captain's voice rang out. Instantly, several hundred white gloves shot up in unison, touching the tips of Stetsons, as the casket was carried to the hearse. After Corporal Fox's family and the various dignitaries were guided to the idling cars, the law officers returned to their vehicles to form the funeral procession.

And what a glorious procession it was—the largest ever in the history of the Maryland State Police! Local and national newspaper accounts reported that the procession was longer than eighteen miles, as it wound its way to his final resting place near Towson. There were more than 850 gleaming police cruisers in the queue. Dalton was buried in deep thought when he joined up with several of his BK "U" buddies to take a back seat in a cruiser. Uncharacteristically quiet and numb, he was having a hard time dealing with his old friend's death. Many images of better days raced in his head, and the imagery of the funeral pageantry was starting to fade. Red and blues flashing, the MSP motorcycles were first, followed by the black hearse, a few dignitary limos, then the long caravan of police cars.

It was unexpected by almost all who took part in the funeral procession that day, when the meaning of it all suddenly became crystal-clear. It also jerked Dalton out of his near-stupor when he saw it. As they traveled north on the beltway, the surprised troopers saw cars and trucks parked along the shoulders of the inner loop. People were standing beside them, typical citizens mixed with scores of upper-class well-wishers, all somber-faced and sullen. Some waved while others cried.

The outer loop traffic on the beltway had come to a complete standstill, as motorists stopped to gawk at the long line of police cars. Dalton heard the honking car horns mixed in with the loud salutary blasts of eighteen-wheeler air horns. Up ahead, on a beltway overpass, he saw dozens of people waving. A lump formed in his throat when he saw the cardboard sign an old man was proudly holding. It read, "God Bless Corporal Mike Fox." On the next overpass, two fire trucks were parked facing each other with their black-shrouded extended ladders crisscrossed to form the platform for a large Maryland flag. Passing underneath, Dalton saw crowds of people lining the railing, waving to them as they passed. Some held their hands over their faces as they wept.

Mile after mile, the beltway scene was repeated. Most troopers would later recall how overwhelmed they were by the outpouring of public support for their fellow trooper, one of "Maryland's Finest." And in the moment's reality, as most troopers felt that day, Dalton was never more proud of being a Maryland State Trooper.

Amidst much fanfare, the procession slowly snaked its way to Dulaney Valley Memorial Gardens, the fallen trooper's final resting place. The contingent of officers quickly assembled in ranks and surrounded the tent at the gravesite. In stone silence they watched as the ruddy-faced Maryland governor and other dignitaries filed in to take their seats in rows of folding chairs. When the MSP color guard slowly advanced to the gravesite, the ranks were called to attention for another salute. Behind the color guard came the flag draped casket carried by the grim-faced pallbearers, eight troopers and close, personal friends of their fallen comrade. Following the casket was Mike's wife, Doreen, her sons and family members. Dalton took a deep breath when he caught a glimpse of Doreen's blank face as she gripped the hands of her sons. Obviously overwrought with heartbreak, she steeled herself to persevere.

The law enforcement brothers and sisters stood stiffly at parade rest throughout the half-hour service. Although his eyes were fixed mostly on the blouse of the trooper standing in front of him, Dalton occasionally eyeballed the scene around him. As one, the ranks were stoic, but the all-pervasive feelings of loss and sorrow covered them like a thick blanket. When the service ended, the rank and file silently watched as two MSP pallbearers diligently folded the Maryland flag and presented it to the new widow. Dalton averted his eyes and clamped his jaw tight when the emotional waves hit.

From a distance, they heard the mournful bugle playing *Taps*, and as the bugle faded out, Dalton heard faint sobs coming from the ranks. His misty eyes spotted several troopers openly weeping, an understandable contrast to the others who did their best not to. Soon, they heard the familiar, high-pitched whine of a Dauphin medevac helicopter. As it flew closer, Dalton heard the loud droning sound of the chopper blades cutting thin air. In a final tribute to their fallen comrade, the MSP helicopter drifted low overhead. When it flew from sight, the air suddenly crackled with the echoing of a radio broadcast coming from the outside speaker of an MSP cruiser parked close by. The querying female voice of a Glen Burnie barrack PCO rang out crisp and clear.

"Glen Burnie, P-32! (long pause) Glen Burnie, P-32! " Another long pause before the call was answered. "Pikesville to Glen Burnie!" the gravelly voice of the headquarters' duty officer boomed out. "P-32 is 10-42 (end tour of duty)...Forever!"

Many of the more stoic officers who'd been able to hold their emotions in check before, had tears streaming down their faces after they heard the riveting farewell message. As hot tears welled up in his eyes, Dalton heard coughs mingled in with sobs. After what felt like an eternity, the formation of officers was dismissed, signaling an end to the gravesite service. For Dalton, it was a long ride back to Calvert County that dreary afternoon, the day his classmate Corporal Mike Fox was buried. Alone and in grateful silence, he headed south to the much needed sanctuary of his home.

Later that evening, after both daughters were asleep, Dalton related the day's somber ordeal to his wife. Cindy was moved, as evidenced by tears in her eyes. Gradually, Dalton sensed her drifting away from him, escaping into her comfort zone, wherever that was. With a hollow expression, she hugged him and quietly retired to their bedroom. After she left, Dalton was instantly reinforced with the understanding of what all troopers eventually realized; only a brother or sister officer could truly relate to what they encountered, absorbed, sacrificed and lost during their careers. Losing one of their own was sacred.

In the reassuring glow of the living room fireplace, Dalton broke out several beers and drained them, one right after the other. He closed his eyes, but the day's stark images reappeared, yanking him right back to the reality he'd been trying so hard to suppress. It was all such a waste, such a horrendous loss for all of his fellow cops who strived so hard to protect and hold the line against *them*—the evil ones—the predators of society's good and decent. And all for what? He pondered in silence.

From deep within, he suddenly felt the ominous stirring of rage. He balled his hands into hard fists and gritted his teeth to confront the swelling anger. For the first time in his life, he wanted to kill in cold blood, felt beyond doubt that he could and would. It'd be pure Nirvana in his life right now to grab Mike's cold-blooded killer by the neck with his bare hands. He'd smile in his face, his eyes searing into the killer's bulging eyes, as he slowly took his miserable, meaningless life from him. Yes, he'd squeeze and squeeze until he saw the swelling veins in the scumbag's temples close to bursting, until he felt the windpipe collapse, until his death rattle was music to his ears. Then, he'd squeeze even harder. He'd finish up by pounding that shocked, ugly, lifeless face into pulp! No need for some pontificating, emotionally detached, black-robed judge to pass a politically correct sentence on such earthly scum. Yes, that's what he'd like to do to make the pain go away!

Instead, Dalton pushed himself from the easy chair, and quietly ambled down the wood steps to the basement. He paused, listening for any telltale sounds in the kitchen above, before opening the fishing tackle box that harbored his weekly, half-empty pint-bottle of tequila. He pulled the stashed bottle out and groped through the darkness until he bumped against the weight bench. Relieved, Dalton gingerly sat down on the padding, unscrewed the cap, and took a long swig.

After the bottle had been inverted a few times, he screwed the cap on and slid it back in the tackle box beneath a pouch of plastic worms. Satisfied that the coast was still clear, he emerged from the basement. With a sigh of relief, he slumped back into the easy chair and closed his eyes. Yes indeed, he'd just let the buzz and the welcome warmth of the fire do its best to coax him down from his phantom executioner's role. Since his friend's callous death, he hadn't slept well, nor could he even make a feeble attempt to put much food into his tightly balled stomach. Maybe things would be better tomorrow. Dalton felt the moist, warm muzzle of Prince, the family's faithful golden lab, brush against his right hand. His perceptive canine pal whined softly, then plopped himself down at the feet of his master, who was already nodding off.

Shattering through his fleeting tranquility, the "tiger" in the sergeant's head suddenly leaped to its feet, signaling the start of the first nightmare he'd had in months. With a thunderous roar, the angry beast attacked. From somewhere deep within his reeling mind, the unearthly screams echoed from the fog, reaching a horrific peak. He felt the hideous presence of death once again, as the torturous horror unfolded all around him. The dank, musty odor of human fear and the acrid copper stench of fresh blood attacked his sense of smell, and he gagged to shut it out. The unspeakable terror was all-pervasive, lying just beyond the bloody hands grotesquely sticking out from the wall of swirling fog—waving at him, urging him on, ever so close and closer.

His body jerked violently enough to roust him from the horror. Sweat oozed off his forehead, and his breath came in harsh gasps. Dalton felt the tendons in his wrists aching from his white-knuckle grip on the easy chair. When he heard whimpering sounds, he jerked his head around. The fire had died, leaving glowing embers, but in the dim light he spotted Prince cowering near the sliding glass door. The poor dog's paws were wet from standing in a pool of urine. Dalton called out to him in a soothing voice, but his perceptive canine buddy shook even more and refused to approach him.

"So, the tiger upset you too, did he?" he whispered to Prince, hoping for a tail wag or any other sign of acknowledgment. Nothing. "Let's keep this one to ourselves, my friend, just between you and me," Dalton added as he rose from the easy chair. Yes, the nightmares had returned with a vengeance all right, only this time they'd never leave.

#

At the end of 1990, the MSP heralded a new leader, the second one in two years, after Colonel Muth abruptly decided to retire and whack golf balls forever. Accordingly, the new MSP chief hastily buffered himself with yes-men while making the usual changes in leadership style that normally caused ripples amongst those alienated from the know-and-flow. The Prince Frederick barrack also endured another lamentable changing of the guard, and several of the old salts had either retired or been promoted and transferred elsewhere. Lt Rob Mister, the revered Andy Griffith-like barrack commander, was on the retirement springboard, and F/Sgt Hutchinstuff somehow got himself promoted and was suitably punted to another troop area.

In addition, Dalton's incorrigible cohort, Sgt Lester Elzy Shifflett, had also begrudgingly retired, joining recent retirees Sgt Tom Long and Dalton's corporal, "Foozy" Taylor. Undeniably in his blood, Elzy would eventually drift into private detective, super-snoop work, but for now, he was on a badly needed sabbatical, throwing down easy money at racetracks. Sgt Long's exodus proved the demise of the barrack's renowned fall and spring stag parties he magnificently coordinated over so many years. In all likelihood, his departure probably resuscitated a few troopers' waning marriages, too.

All that "Foozy" Taylor wanted to do with his life beyond the MSP (and surprisingly, there was such an existence), was to crab and "arster" with his dad. To Dalton's surprise, even Marty Metzger, his old sidekick, decided to cash in his chips and exit the ranks. True to his nature, Marty winnowed a special disability retirement (66 and 2/3 final tax-free salary, don't ya know) due to an old "warrior wound' he'd suffered in his early sprite years.

According to filed medical reports, Marty had supposedly wrenched his back while wrestling with a feisty, fat hog which had escaped from a meat locker plant in old Prince Frederick. Naturally, the traffic-snarling swine had only gone bonkers after Marty whacked it on its voluminous butt with a shovel—but only after he'd emptied a canister of tear gas on the bewildered beast. Unknown by his fellow troopers, the phantom back injury had ostensibly haunted the wily trooper ever since. Dalton's best guess had Marty selling used cars just days after his retirement, but with Marty, one never knew.

With the departure of those "old gang" troopers, the barrack received another crop of new blood. Pearl, the honcho secretary, reluctantly resigned herself to the role of breaking in yet another new barrack commander and first sergeant. Dalton inherited a brandnew, starry-eyed corporal, and the barrack received four more baby faced recruits. Dalton, along with fellow sergeants Dan Collison and Ben Wiley, couldn't help noticing how the new boots looked younger than ever—like eager-eyed, peach-fuzz kids just out of high school. Shrugging their shoulders, the stalwart NCO trio tried hard to ignore the creeping times that had inevitably overtaken them, as they'd evolved into the old salts.

A sergeant for more than seven years, Dalton was getting antsy about the looming promotion list. Several months before, he'd disciplined himself, wracking his brains out prepping for the next First Shirt's test. Both daughters were blossoming in their early teens, and, with their emerging hormones bouncing off the walls, concentration wasn't easy when phones rang off the hooks with girlfriends, boyfriends and wannabes calling round the clock. Nonetheless, Dalton hunkered down in his usual relentless manner. Sure, attaining the next rank would be another status step and another badly needed salary boost, but that wasn't the driving force behind his promo quest. It was shift work, more than twelve years of unstable hours and missed weekends, which had caused family havoc, an irksome aspect he longed to change. To that effect, he continually assured Cindy that better times were just ahead, kept urging her to hang on while he surrendered his off-duty hours to flip through the mountains of study material and associated pablum—the beef of the upcoming written test. Dalton's last evaluation had far exceeded his expectations, and he had a half-suspicion it was a farewell gesture from retiring Lt. Mister, but regardless, he couldn't look a gift horse in the mouth at this career junction.

Weeks after taking the F/Sgt's test, Dalton learned that his score was the fourth highest, statewide. Several weeks later, the evaluation scores were combined for a final ranked list. Dalton was giddy after Lt Mister gleefully dragged him into his office to tell him he was number twelve on the First Sergeants list. Both realized that Dalton would be wearing another stripe soon, and with the changing barrack dynamics, and his rocky marriage, it couldn't happen soon enough.

(Purgatory Ridge)

And now, the tiger, his old nemesis, was trying to put a damper on his retirement hoopla, the bastard! The veteran sergeant rubbed his temples in an effort to ease the emerging pain of another headache. With a groan, he slumped back against the oak. It was harder to focus his thoughts when his roaring marauder restlessly padded about, looking for another spat, but true to his nature, he had to confront it. Dalton slapped another mag into the Beretta and jacked in a hollow-point JP round to spite his feline antagonist. God, how he liked the reassuring feel of that Berretta baby when his hand wrapped around her beckoning butt. For a fleeting moment, he almost wished his true-life girlfriend was with him now to share in the festivities, but the wistful thought evaporated as soon as it flashed. He knew she'd understand—some day.

He shook his head and he reached into the knapsack for another rum river crook. After licking the end, he stuck the twisted little cigar in his mouth and surprised himself by lighting it on the first try. Lifting his head, he sucked in a mouthful of the sweet smoke, then slowly exhaled. The wind from the east was blowing hard now, making a mess out of his thinning blond hair. Dalton closed his eyes and took a deep breath, savoring the bay's tangy, salty essence.

There were more and more dark clouds swirling in to blot out the late-afternoon sun sinking behind him. Fleeting shadows danced behind trees, as the tiger in his head twitched its tail and growled, waiting impatiently for the cage door to open. He spited the beast again by taking another long drag from the cigar, then teased it even more by trying to blow a few smoke rings into the wind.

"Ahhh, those early sergeant years," he murmured in the direction of the Eastern Shore. They were trying times, but he thought the transition had worked out suitably well. Sure, the brutality complaint had ruffled his feathers some—*No*—a lot, but despite the tormenting interval between that chaotic night and the ultimate MSP "exoneration," things had eventually turned out OK. Still, as many seasoned troopers knew, the department traditionally went overblown ape-shit with internal investigations. It took a while to become clear, but Dalton eventually concluded that if the MSP performed as diligently in its criminal investigations as in investigations of its own troopers, the department's criminal-case closure rate would be almost one hundred percent.

The horrible, unexpected death of his academy classmate, Mike Fox, was a painful loss, an abhorrence that continuously plagued him. He tried hard to shrug it all off, but he finally realized that with more than eighteen years on the job, he'd radically changed from the experience.

And, there was the specter of those irretrievable "glory days" that had haunted him unmercifully. It was dismally accepted overall, but still nettling, when he finally had to acknowledge it. Those "glory days," as one of the young-buck troopers out there running with the herd, exalting in the camaraderie of it all, *yes*, inevitably, they'd all come down to an end. The once eternal "one for all and all for one" MSP spirit of yesteryears were his best years on the job. In the final picture, he really missed them—far more than he'd ever admit.

True, in addition to stalwart friends like Junebug Buckler and one or two others, he still had his fellow supervisors to bounce off of, to commiserate with. Aside from his best friend Gary, however, he realized that as far as the MSP brotherhood was concerned, he was drifting off on his own, like many did when they started the downhill side of their careers.

The new recruits seemed a different breed, with less affinity for the revered old-school ways. It was more like, "Ask not what you can do for the Maryland State Police, but what the Maryland State Police can do for you." But he also fathomed that the new boots were merely representing a rapidly changing society that was riding the crest of the high-tech boom, and for the most part, he begrudgingly accepted such differences. Hell, that's what the old-timers probably thought about his breed of upstarts, the kids of the sixties, when they became the "New Centurions."

In his treasured hours of solitude, during those special moments when he reflected on better times, Dalton especially missed those on the job he'd allowed himself to get close to, those who'd been ripped away from their lives and his friendship forever. He'd shared priceless experiences with them, and now they were gone, kaput, end of story. From his academy roommate Mel Purvey and fellow classmate Mike Fox, to his sidekick and confidant Colby Merson, and Nate Odom, his trooper first class mentor during those tumultuous early corporal days at College Park. And *yes*, even Donny Roberts, before his spiraling descent into his own world of hell—he missed them all, missed their spirit and companionship more than he'd ever admit to any living soul. And there were those other now deceased, less familiar colleagues who'd earlier passed through his life, and he missed their essence too. If only he could shrug it off and just chalk it up to his mother's Black Irish roots, the deeply complex, emotional side of the genetics mix that never fully healed from such grievous wounds. An easy rationalization, albeit an impossible fix.

But the growing onslaught of nightmares—*No*—they came from the ugly job experiences, and he'd be hard-pressed to blame them on anyone but himself for his decision to become a trooper. When the last eighteen years were all wrapped up, and despite the toll—the losses, ordeals, and shaken beliefs—Dalton was still damned proud of being one of Maryland's Finest. But, of course, it'd cost him dearly, the extent of which he couldn't fathom yet. And the MSP never issued the troops crystal balls either, so he dutifully marched on as the ominous downward spiral of his destiny picked up speed.

"Yeah, you marched on, all right...right into a minefield of shit, ya dumb ass," the old-salt sergeant growled. He coughed to clear his throat, before taking another sip of warm beer, then another. Closing his eyes again, he pondered on. "Yeah, you kept most of it inside, didn't you, Sarge? Ya didn't want 'em to know how bad things were getting, and now look where you are...all by your lonesome self, just the way ya never thought it'd go," he grumbled to the Beretta. He knew he'd been playing with fire for too many years, knew full well that he'd let his marriage and family life go down the tubes, while he was metaphorically trying to keep his head above water, standing on his tip-toes, as the relentless high tide kept surging in. Hell, he didn't have to tally every day's empty beer cans and pint bottles to figure that one out any more.

Still, he'd been confident about toughing it out long enough to cross the finish line standing, and by golly, damn if he hadn't done it, too! No, just too much pride to admit to others he was having a hard time handling it all. Suck it in, troop, *suck it in!* No, *that* stigma, that weakness, was for wimps and wussies. And he was goddamned sure he'd never go out like some did—those who sucked up the sixty-six and two-thirds disability retirement after months of feigning phantom injuries or highly-ambiguous, stress-related afflictions.

He felt ashamed of the bare audacity of those he knew who went out on *that* gravy train, smiling ear to ear, joyfully milking the system on their quest for cushy, tax-free pensions. No, he'd hold his head higher than any of those cheating malingerers, simply because he owed it to his himself not to do otherwise. "What the hell did y'all think you'd be getting into when you joined the force anyhow, you bunch of wimps...a friggin rose garden or something?" Dalton chortled to his cigar butt. No, he'd decided long ago that he was going out on hard time, even if it killed him.

The sergeant shook his head and stared blankly at the wind-whipped bay. He blinked reflexively when he saw the first flash of lightning strike the water near the tip of Walnut Point, the south end of Tilghman Island on the Eastern Shore. He strained to focus his unsteady eyes on the angry gray and black-smeared bank of ragged clouds massing several miles across the bay at the mouth of the Choptank River. Towering high above them, a colossal thunderhead formation, a puffy white, flat-topped cumulonimbus—a name he could spell, but never pronounce correctly—was slowly spreading and spiraling upward. From that distance, Dalton thought it looked like an albino version of a nuclear mushroom cloud.

"It's about damned time they got around to nukin' the frickin' Eastern Shore, land of the web-footed ones," he chuckled in jest, knowing the Delmarva Peninsula and its bounty of nature would always be dear to him. He took another gulp of tepid beer and gazed listlessly at the mushroom cloud. The wind from the east was picking up noticeably, and he realized the ominous storm was definitely coming his way now. Still, Dalton thought there was ample time to finish his retirement party before he was thoroughly drenched. Several more jagged bolts shot down from the roiling clouds, but since he hadn't heard any rumblings of thunder yet, he eased back to kill off the rest of the beer.

Maybe it *was* a good idea he hadn't opted for the two-hour paddle across the bay to hold his retirement party on what was left of the steadily eroding James Island. Twice before, his stable, hybrid Cayuga kayak had made the blissful trip to that uninhabited, wind-swept pair of islands he'd shared with no one else. Nobody, except those resting eternally in the ancient remains of a family cemetery on a ridge farther inland. Other than a rogue band of skittish sika deer, a few protesting seagulls and pesky black flies, the magnificent little island kissing the mouth of the Little Choptank River was all his. Those were better days then, calm and forgiving, quite the contrary to what it was like now on the bay and in his life.

He feverishly rubbed his temples when the sharp pain hit again, and growled a loud curse at the tiger before aiming the Beretta at the empty can in front of him. Beautiful sight alignment, squarely in the middle of the shiny aluminum target. OK, let the breath out real slow, then a smooth squeeze of the trigger, and—No—*wait!* Dalton jerked his head up. Of course! How could he forget? The sergeant set the handgun on the ground, patted it, then pulled out his wallet from his worn jeans. Smirking, he hastily snatched his good luck silver dollar and held it out in front of him at arm's length. He studied his bequeathed charm for a few minutes, turning it end-over-end in solemn reflection.

With a loud, protesting grunt, Dalton forced himself to his feet and trudged over to a sapling close to the cliff edge. After wedging the coin between the V of two small branches, he picked up the Beretta again and marched back to within a few feet of the sapling. This one had to be just right—for his father's sake. This time, he used a steady two-fisted grip. The sight alignment weaved back and forth, finally coming together for that brief moment of sweet, elusive perfection. *Blam!* The silver dollar zinged from the notch, instantly airborne! His face beamed with satisfaction, as the perforated coin sailed beyond the edge of the cliff and dropped from sight.

The tiger trapped in his head roared louder then ever before, as it lunged forcefully against the gates of its taunting keeper. Again and again it smashed its powerful body against the weakening portal in an attempt to get out, but its efforts were fruitless, and the snarling beast soon tired.

Dalton cleared his throat and spat on the ground. "That the best you can do, ya big pussy?" he cried out with contempt. Suddenly, he was laughing so hard that he was close to pissing himself, as he envisioned a wayward shell-collector stumbling upon his once-cherished memento some day. Maybe the damned thing won't be cursed anymore. His beer supply exhausted, he rummaged through the knapsack and brought out the half-pint of tequila. Nasty stuff, but he'd finally acquired a taste for the volatile cactus juice after all those gut-wrenching years of half-ass effort. He took a healthy sip and squeezed his eyes shut, as the liquor went down hard. After a few more sips, he'd probably feel inclined to present himself with a retirement award or two perhaps, but for now, he'd stick with the routine and go on with the show. Grinning broadly, Dalton screwed the cap back on and tossed the bottle to the ground.

\

Chapter 12

OUTSIDE THE GRID

The long-awaited "Christmas List" was a bloated whale, and while Sergeant Dalton Bragg wasn't on it, he'd scooted up to the number four slot on the F/Sgt's list, a virtual shoe-in within the year.

At the barrack, things were status quo. Pearl, the fussy queen bee secretary, was having major conniptions schooling the new independent- minded barrack commander to the realities of how things worked at *her* barrack. Lt Don McCauley, a tall, lumbering, Dudley Do-Right sort, was a barrack road trooper years before, and he was quite familiar with Pearl's overbearing tendencies and petty nuances. Being the new commander, he vowed never to allow Pearl to yank *his* chain again. As predicted, their fiery exchanges nicely spiced up monotonous days.

Overall, Dalton's MSP world's status was copasetic, as many of the troops jested when conditions were barely tolerable. On the home front, however, behind a facade of complacency, strained sentiments, nil communiqué and passable civility, conditions steadily eroded. When the life-renewing days of spring finally arrived, it happened. Cindy decided it was time to catch up with herself—Sooo—acting on her long-sought secret agenda, she flew the coup with both daughters. Dalton wasn't at all shocked by her forthright departure.

Deep in his heart, he knew that his troubled wife wasn't content with her life, knew full-well Cindy was struggling with an inner battle she wasn't ready to fight, let alone win. Perhaps surprising to her, if she'd ever allowed herself to dwell on it, Dalton was quite aware of his own contributions to the decline of their tenuous relationship.

It should have been apparent by the painfully obvious signs of stress he'd been dragging home. The effect was accentuated by the rotating shifts, his drastically increased drinking and dour mood swings, and the demons that emerged from his ghastly nightmares. It was undeniable, even to himself, that he'd drastically changed during the last few years. No, he certainly couldn't point a finger at her, without jabbing one hard into his own chest first. Maybe it *was* time for that time-out in their marriage after all, to let things settle and maybe heal.

Still, when his family left, it shook him more than he'd anticipated. Their absence left him in a bleak funk, a gut-wrenching void that quickly ate at his core. Within days, he felt wired, found it hard to concentrate on anything, especially his job. Although he could readily bounce his innermost feelings off his younger brother Jon and good friends like Gary Rephan and "Junebug," Dalton's pride forced him to keep the core of his personal vexations to himself.

Six interminable months later, after weeks of sweet overtures and cajoling, he persuaded his indisposed wife to return home and try again. For several months thereafter, the sun shone brightly on their newly thawed relationship, the daughters perked up, and once again there was a trace of bliss. But deep inside, Dalton fostered a premonition that the renewal of marital nirvana would inevitably fade again. And Cindy remained resolute, believing it was only a matter of time before they'd once again crash and burn as a family. For now, however, she'd resume playing the dogged wife and doting mother role until she simply couldn't stand it any more

#

While his personal life returned to a tolerable, but fragile equilibrium, the Maryland State Police world took a major hit when the dedicated men and women of "Maryland's Finest" were abruptly confronted with a sudden turn that shook them to the core.

During the late summer months, a chorus of rumors surrounding the state's looming budget crisis circulated in the legislative chambers, and soon enough, the rumors were rampant throughout the entire state government. Widespread warnings of massive cuts in state departments and agencies reverberated from the Annapolis statehouse, and MSP scuttlebutt ran wild with threats of possible trooper layoffs and barrack closures. The troopers were already used to constraints, having endured the last several years without salary increases or even cost-of-living parity pay. Many old-salt troopers merely shirked off the nagging rumors as hearsay. Few, however, were prepared for the wrath of

Maryland's volatile governor, a consummate politician who never shied from playing hardball.

In October, to conceivably offset the fiscal fiasco, Governor Daniel J. Shipley directed hefty cuts across the board. This time, in an effort to jolt the legislature and citizens, he whacked a line drive into the slackened solar plexus of the high profile State Police. For the first time in its history, the Maryland State Police was ordered to terminate the employment of troopers. More than one hundred sworn personnel were destined for the axe, and the MSP was directed to promptly shut down two barracks, along with several aviation sections, whose helicopters flew the medevac missions.

As expected, morale in the department sank like a rock. Consequently, the predicted outcry from concerned citizens and vocal members of the General Assembly mounted, just as the bombastic governor had expected.

Historically, the troopers had accepted those years without pay hikes and better equipment. It wasn't so long ago when most lower-rank troopers actually qualified for food stamps. No, the majority of them certainly hadn't signed up for the modest salary, that was certain. As banal as it may have sounded to any outside critics, the members of the Maryland State Police sacrificed much while going that extra mile to serve and protect. In the extreme, some sacrificed their lives, too, but they all knew the inherent dangers, and they persevered. It was the MSP heritage and loyalty that mattered to those who wore the Stetsons of "Maryland's Finest."

From their inception, they were a sitting governor's ever-ready whipping boys, the dauntless force he'd send to the cities and counties whenever they were needed—when the prison riots got out of hand or when the local police walked off their jobs in "blue flu" mode during salary disputes. They were the loyal ones who stood tall on the front-line crises and catastrophes anywhere in the state. And now, for the first time in their history, "Maryland's Finest" found themselves being used as pawns in a political chess game stunt masterminded by a cantankerous, thin-skinned, goateed governor who was willing to let his ill-disguised disdain for them jeopardize public safety.

Like his fellow troopers, Dalton was stunned when the department's cutbacks were announced. Ironically, Dalton was beginning to admire the "tell it like it is" street-brawler style of the former Prince George's County politician, aptly nicknamed "Cue Ball" for his shiny baldpate and nutty, off-the-wall antics. This time, however, Cue Ball's mulish game of power politics was overplayed. For the first time ever, the rank and file of the MSP galvanized to protest a Maryland Governor's cuts that adversely affected their mission to serve and protect fellow Marylanders. Coordinated by the Maryland Troopers Association, plans were drawn up to protest in the sympathetic court of public opinion. Letter-writing campaigns were fostered to flood the offices of state lawmakers, and troopers visited local legislators face-to-face, while TV, radio and newspapers were warned of threats to public safety from the cutbacks.

Along with his Prince Frederick cohorts and many other troopers, Dalton participated in several high visibility "public-awareness" activities. The milestone event which eventually stuck in the governor's craw was the MSP show of force at the colonial State Capitol in Annapolis. As many anxiously predicted, the affair was misconstrued by the state's head honcho as intimidation fostered by an armed, unruly, renegade tribe of wayward state employees who wore those silly cowboy hats.

More than four hundred off-duty uniformed and plainclothes troopers swelled the ranks that crisp, fall evening. The phalanx conducted a somber candlelight march from the Naval Academy stadium to the capitol, where special budget meetings were in session. After the press and TV filmed the group in front of the capitol with their white, dripping candles, the troopers filed into the gallery of the in-session senate chamber as a silent protest.

To the governor, the demonstration was a personal affront, *no*, a direct assault on his colossal ego, and a challenge to his authority. His trooper bodyguards privately affirmed that the event left "Cue Ball" stroking his stringy goatee, seething at the lack of control the sympathetic MSP superintendent had over his "misled" troopers. Despite all efforts to rescind the cuts, the hellbent governor still muscled most of them through, although public outcry and pressure persuaded him to limit the loss of troopers to the current academy class. While much of the MSP budget cuts, including the two barrack closures, were eventually restored, the troopers' trust in the security of their careers remained shaken for many years to come.

Alas, governor Shipley's mercurial wrath hadn't waned, as most thought it would, and the ex-marine drill sergeant still seethed with a "fire in the hole" mentality. Within the MSP ranks, a bothersome scent of change hung in the air. It took months of unrelenting pressure, combined with several "on the carpet" heated clashes, before the efforts of the governor and his relentless staff finally prevailed. After serving admirably for over four years, Colonel Tom Carpenter, under fire and wholly undermined, resigned as superintendent.

And so, after a month-long nationwide search, which presumably combed through dozens of superbly qualified candidates, the governor made his pliant choice. Actually, staffers in the governor's close fold already knew who the next MSP goaltender was going to be, despite the ballyhooed nationwide search. Nonetheless, the usual dog-and-pony-show of Maryland politics was appropriately played out to sidetrack needless controversy. The governor's influential UYMR (Ultimate Yes-Man Requirement) loyalty factor made it a done deal, but the choice still flabbergasted many troopers. And miraculously, the governor's selection was plucked from within the recalcitrant ranks of MSP itself!

Captain Harry T. Lyons was known as an amiable guy, who, years before, had escaped road patrol to land a cushy slot in the department's specialized Truck Enforcement Division. Through rumored family ties and influences, the squat, barrel-chested trooper sporting the spiffy flattop and signature choirboy smile, eventually skated into the MSP's elite Executive Protection Unit (EPU) which guarded the governor and a few other prominent politicos.

Providing security in EPU was ambiguously defined. The road-pounding troops mostly referred to the handpicked EPU troops as go-fers, door openers and chauffeurs, definitely *not* bona-fide Maryland State Troopers. Rubbing elbows, endlessly fetching newspapers and coffees and running other such "vital" errands for the upper politicians did wonders for careers. Over the years, Governor Shipley grew to appreciate the simple, loyal character of one particular trooper from the once-quaint village of Severna Park. Harry T. Lyons had pervasive qualities that caught his eye. "I know the boy's just an average Joe," the governor admitted to a close aide, "but when I say *jump*, he only asks how high, and that's good enough for me!

Fast-forwarding to the current, "Buffalo," as Captain Lyons was aptly nicknamed for his beefy, humped-over posture and dogmatic traits, hit the jackpot and was crowned the new MSP Superintendent! Like many prior head honchos, Colonel Lyons promptly shielded himself with a close core of MSP disciples who were promptly bequeathed with promotions. Armed with the governor's mandate, and much to the chagrin of one miffed, high-ranking palace prince who thought that the only way "Buffalo" Lyons could ever be a leader would be to find a parade and get in front of it, the new MSP leader set out on his mission to reign in his impetuous troops.

Initially, Dalton was laissez-faire about any politics. But over time, he, like most troopers, grew disillusioned with the internal partisan politics running amok in the department. MSP was becoming rife with self-serving troopers bent on schmoozing their way up the promo ladder.

Ignoring the disparities, and with his looming promotion a virtual done deal, Dalton remained optimistic. While some idealistic troops hung on to the whimsical belief that the MSP promotional system was based solely on ability and merit, it was widely acknowledged, and begrudgingly accepted, that many promotions were inevitably made from certain political considerations; a "nature of the beast," as the old salts put it. The Maryland constitution actually granted the Superintendent the unique power to make any and all promotions as he saw fit. Past MSP leaders cloaked themselves behind it when they made dubious promotions, and "Buffalo" Lyons was certainly no exception.

Months later, after "Buffalo" and his trusty princes stampeded from the Pikesville Palace on a sullen Friday afternoon, Dalton's naive trust in the MSP leadership was betrayed, evidenced by the new promotion list. Dalton got the somber phone call at home from fellow sergeant Ben Wiley.

Immediately afterward, he dashed from the house and took a long, brooding, hike in the woods. Incensed, he fought off the anger clouding his thoughts. Although he'd been number four on the F/Sgt promo list, Dalton was stunned when Ben told him his name wasn't among the sixteen promotions to that rank. Wiley read the entire list to him, adding expletives when he came across another flunky who'd been oddly promoted. Dalton didn't feel so aggrieved when he learned that several minority candidates had been promoted over his head, despite two of them being ranked below 150 others on the list.

He accepted minority promotions as plausible payback that would continue until the racial disparities afflicting MSP were resolved— maybe on some brilliant, sunny day in the distant future. It'd taken a while, but Dalton eventually recognized that, subtle or not, the agency had more racial discrimination problems than he'd realized. No, he could live with that call. But to get jumped by yes-men, the favorite sons and the politically embroiled boy scouts, was an affront. Hell, rumor had it that several who'd been promoted weren't even *on* the eligible list. *Bah!* After a bitter tromp through the woods, ripping off branches and karate-chopping trees, Dalton made his decision.

During "Buffalo" Lyons several-year tenure under quirky "Cue Ball" Shipley, promotional aspirations, fostered under the ghostly MSP merit charade, were dicey ones at best. No, unlike many disgruntled troopers who pissed and moaned and swore they'd never take another promotional test again—*but did*—Dalton wasn't playing the "Alice in Wonderland" promo game anymore. In doing so, he sentenced himself to the sergeant rank forever, but to do otherwise was unpalatable. Relegated to the sidelines, Dalton's once-proud days of being an MSP shooting star were over.

#

Just two months after Sergeant Dalton Bragg pushed the self-destruct button at MSP, his personal life exploded—again. After silently mulling over the one-year anniversary of her dubious return, Cindy, in deja-vu style, evacuated herself and both daughters from the home front again. This time, it was a done deal, signaling the end of their bumpy family life. Dalton knew it was going to happen again, knew their relationship had disintegrated, day by day, and month by torturous month. The walls separating them had again grown higher, and, except for a short-lived, random flare-up over some minuscule annoyance, they'd become incommunicado. Dalton felt a chill whenever they were alone together.

Unlike the last separation, however, Dalton couldn't find it within himself to urge her to stay this time, especially after she'd dismissed his repeated requests to seek marriage counseling. Although he held strong feelings for her, knew he was in love with her still, he realized it'd be like pumping air into a flat tire.

The final separation brought that dismally familiar, ugly void that quickly wreaked havoc with his shaken mind. Coming home to an uninhabited, cold and empty tomb of a house, ravaged his spirit, especially during those dreaded late evening hours when the insufferable silence taunted him with unfailing vengeance. His daughter's radios weren't blaring as usual, no phones ringing with boyfriends, no TV screaming commercials at him, no nothing—save for the ungodly loud tick-tick-ticking of the damn kitchen clock. The constant ticking never failed to mock him, always reminded him that life was still passing by in spite. So, Dalton cracked open the beers. After a few quick gulps of the third or maybe the sixth one, he'd traipse over to the TV and turn it on to nullify the empty, bedeviling silence. He stuck to the sterile news channels, painstakingly avoiding any amorous soaps or lovey-dovey movies. All radios and tape players in the house also remained silent.

No time for any of that woebegone, "My wife done left me, and it's cold outside, my dawg's gone too, and the whiskey bottle's empty," lamentable horse shit. Sometimes it worked.

When it didn't, he felt the warm, wet snout of his canine buddy Prince grazing along the back of a hand. Dogs always felt their master's pain, and Prince always did his simple-minded best to cheer him up. Dalton even gathered up all the family pictures, photo albums and other such memorabilia, and squirreled them in a closet, away from his dreary eyes.

Too late for the guitar, though. Recently, during an unchecked sentimental mood, he'd taken the battered six-string down with him when he sat in front of the wood stove again. He smiled, remembering how much pleasure it gave him when he played the three or four-chord songs to both smiling daughters who sat at his feet, happy-faced, listening in awe. After three beers and too much fiddling with stretched-out strings, Dalton finally had the mahogany wood beast tuned enough for a decent play. He tried to ramble through some oldies like *Proud Mary*, the Beatles' *Not a Second Time* and the Animals' *House of the Rising Sun*. They all came out tinny, flat, and clunky, his voice shaky and hesitant, forcing him to stop in mid-verse.

He heard a clap from the hands of a child, followed by another, and soon there was clapping in unison, deafening to his ears. "Encore! Encore!" the phantom audience screamed. "More! More!" Dalton felt the blood pulsing in his temples, his head close to bursting, as the cacophony of cheers and clapping built up to a smothering roar. *"More Daddy—More!"*

With both hands he suddenly grabbed the guitar neck in a strangle hold and shot from the chair! In a move that would have turned Pete Townsend, The Who's lead guitarist, green with envy, Dalton wind-milled the guitar against the concrete wall. *Crack!* Instantly the stage lights flickered out, and the raucous cheering stopped, leaving him in stillness amid the litter of splintered wood, metal frets and unfettered wire strings.

As anticipated, within weeks after the final separation, the adverse effects blanketed Dalton with waves of anxieties. Insomnia set in like a disease. His knotted stomach zilched his appetite and he began losing weight. If he was able to force down a half can of tuna, a power bar or a handful of stale crackers and a cup of fruit juice without retching, he was grateful. Combined with his dark, sunken eyes and distant personality, it was apparent to those at the barrack that another trooper was going through another marital ordeal. Dalton had already seen how agonizing that had been for several already, and he strived to keep it all together, vainly hoping that the others weren't perceiving how bad it was for him. He was a *trooper,* and troopers were supposed to take the pain!

Hoping to offset his rankled mind, Dalton pushed himself hard with a daily physical regimen. Several times a week he pumped iron for hours, punishing himself with extra sets of heavy bench presses, grueling biceps curls and taxing upper-lat exercises. Other days he'd seek relief by running those long miles along the shoulders of Broomes Island Road near his house. Donning his sunglasses and slipping his preferred running tape, U2's *Zooropa*, into his Walkman, Dalton felt he could run in the sun forever on those special days. On the all-too-frequent dispirited days, he had to drag himself over to his jogging shoes, as random thoughts of throwing himself in the road to do a speed bump imitation danced wildly in his head.

Soon enough, Dalton found that the alternating shift-work hours had become his nemesis. Night shift, with its loooong hours of thought-provoking placidity, turned into a troglodyte zone, while late shift meant that he'd go home to that wretchedly cold, empty bed again, an ordeal he faced, but only after downing a few sleep tabs and too many beers.

At work, it was hard to focus on much of anything. Irritability traded places with anxiety pangs that would suddenly shoot up from nowhere, turning the simplest tasks into unmanageable burdens. He frequently misplaced his keys and notebooks, missed paperwork deadlines, and worse, he continuously found himself unable to give adequate attention to his shift's activities. During his last burst of night shift, he'd even been late for work several times, having slept through the blaring alarm clock. Fellow sergeant Don Collison had to send two wary troopers to wake him up with shrieking sirens, after several phone calls to the house went unanswered.

Troopers caught their prostrated sergeant with both hands in his pockets jiggling his keys, as he stared aimlessly at blank walls, or gazed in a daze through the DO's Plexiglas window in stone silence. At times, Dalton looked like a zombie, as he sleepwalked through the entire eight-hour shift. He felt a paralysis come over him whenever Lt McCauley queried him about work matters. The look on his face told the story, after he answered them with yet another burst of semi-coherent babble. As always, Dalton unfailingly assured him that things in his life were simply copasetic. ("Yeah, buddy! Welcome to the worst fuckin' month of my life, Lieutenant! But have no fear, Sir...Things are finer than frog's hair with me...And...umm...w*hen* were those asinine de-centralized inspection reports due again, ya say? You're kiddin' me, I didn't hand in my performance report a*gain*, Sir?'").

Dean Fulton, Dalton's new corporal, was an easygoing, upbeat guy who, quickly sensing his sergeant's predicament, assumed many of Dalton's supervisory duties. Amazingly, Dalton had even become emotionally immunized to Pearl's daily tantrums, too. For a while, he had a hint that Pearl, perhaps sensing his plight, was purposely playing the low-key act with him.

Weeks and months flew by, but time just wasn't living up to its healing aspects as Dalton had hoped. Very little in life seemed to have meaning anymore. Each day he found himself shutting down more, edging ever so closely toward convincing himself there was no way out. And on those stifling nights at home with the walls closing in, his faithful savior arrived in chilled cans. *No*, he wouldn't go to the Frog Pond or the Calverton Room to soak up suds, sympathy and unneeded attention. *Yes*, he'd do even worse—he'd drink alone!

First, he'd unplug that bastard, the tick-tock kitchen clock. Then, all by his lonesome self, he'd dilute his agony with copious cold brew. With a little help from his aluminum-clad buddies, Dalton's near-instant transformation blessed him with the feelings of serenity and peace on earth, while he stared passively at the smoldering fireplace embers. But soon enough, with a slew of empty beer-can buddies shining back at him, it'd happen again. Faithfully tenacious in its piteous quest, the 'tiger" in his head started twitching, signaling the onset of another long, fitful night, another bout with those wretched nightmares.

At least Dalton felt some comfort knowing that his friends and cohorts still weren't aware of his "tiger" or the god-forsaken nightmares that inevitably trailed in the beast's path. Only Prince, his trusty golden retriever, was so frightfully aware of those monstrosities. No, those hideous secrets he'd never divulge to anyone. *Never!* It was his fight, and his alone, win or lose.

Later than sooner, Dalton finally arrived at another conclusion; he didn't particularly relish bouncing off the walls or being alone anymore. It was a dire status he hoped to deal with ASAP, once he established a few elusive strands of understanding with his estranged wife Cindy. With Calvert being the close-knit county it was, it wasn't long until Dalton learned through the grapevine that his estranged beauty had already jumped into the dating arena, the impetus needed to signal his overdue liberation to do likewise. Wishful thinking at best, he was hoping that another "special other" in his life might serve as a tonic to his doldrums. Initially, his optimism would be duly rewarded. Although he dreaded the daunting rebound-dating game, he dreaded his self-imposed desolation more so.

So, after lunging from the starting blocks before the gun went off, Dalton promptly dived in headfirst to fall in lust with the first enticing woman he met who didn't wear a wedding ring. He knew it'd be a tiresome task to mold any normal dating around his shift work, and he was also well aware that many datable women had an aversion to lawman-types, although others, for whatever bizarre reasons, readily succumbed to the superman-in-uniform syndrome.

Regardless of the hurdles, Dalton felt up for the challenge—Yes, indeedy! The dire need for a libidinous re-energizing, an ultra-intimate connection, or even just a thorough cleaning of his pipes to assure they still worked, suddenly turned paramount. With his good buddies combing the area for prospects and with his babe radar finely tuned to the max, the hunt began in earnest.

Rhapsody of the Rebounds

Angie, the cutesy-friendly, long-legged, forty year-old, blue-eyed, blonde he met a few days later while searching for sharks' teeth along the Flag Ponds beach, was on the rebound too. Unfortunately, the swanky, gold-hearted woman from Port Republic was in his carnal knowledge picture for only three months—just long enough for her cocky ex-boyfriend, the ragamuffin snot, to sniff out the fact that she'd finally found the audacity to see someone else. That stupefying discovery had energized him enough to streak back into her life and propose marriage, something the clod had been loathe to do ever since they'd first goggle-eyed each other over a pitcher of beer a few years before. Dalton was unfazed, however, owing to the discovery of his new flame, the charming Joanie.

Joanie, his next ricochet infatuation, was a familiar figure in the PF courthouse, the Peyton Place of Calvert County which barely edged out the nuclear plant in Lusby as the county's reigning realm of salacious hanky-panky. Joanie's familiar figure was indisputably one of the best-maintained ones in the county, too. The petite woman with the cinnamon-brown hair, pert nose and easy smile was also the most genuine and good-natured of all the clerks in the thin-walled courthouse. As luck would have it, she'd been separated from her lawyer-hubby for close to a year, after the egotistical charlatan had strayed off the path to shack up with his twenty-one year-old sexpot secretary.

Dalton knew Joanie of course, and ever since he'd first laid eyes on her, he'd had a magnetic attraction to the effervescent strumpet from Dare's Beach. Sweet prudence prevailed, however, to hamstring his lechery, and he'd never gone beyond musing about the possibilities. Now that they both led estranged lives, Joanie glowed like a sunburst, and Dalton soon succumbed. His resourceful buddy Junebug had worked his unfailing magic, and within days of Dalton's inquiry about her, Junebug proudly presented him a card with her phone number.

("Hey, Sarge, the county's got plenty of hot babes out here for the taking, if you just do some trolling, don't ya know! Lordy, when my old lady found this three-by-five card on me, she blew a major shit-fit, too...but when I told her I was tryin' to fix Joanie up with *you*, she lightened up on my ass, some. You owe me big time, buddy!")

For two sinfully delightful months, Dalton and his new flame couldn't get enough of each other. It was nonstop bliss, fireworks galore, heaven on earth, and "I'll be yours till the end of time," until the fairy dust of lust settled enough for them to catch their breaths. When they did, it was Joanie who realized their delectable tryst was destined to be "two ships passing in the night."

One lazy afternoon, just after they'd worn each other out in another amorous marathon, she tearfully told him. The type of woman who took extravagant pains to guard her personal life, Joanie knew it was time for them to part before they became fodder for the county's rumor mill. Besides, her lovelorn lawyer-hubby had suddenly seen the light and was making strong overtures about returning faithfully to her side for the last time—again.

Donna was an accident that didn't wait to happen. Dalton met her at an accident scene a few weeks after Joanie's disheartening exit. Donna's rusty 1988 Mustang had been rear-ended hard enough to need a tow to Rayford Fowler's Prince Frederick garage. Dalton, her savior in the form of an empathetic paladin, had gallantly offered her a ride back to her rented bungalow in Huntingtown. The ride evolved into coffees and a chummy chat over her kitchen table that led to a dinner-date the next evening.

Donna was a pleasant looking, warmhearted single mom in her late thirties, a blue jeans and loose T-shirt type who was trying to make ends meet as a bartender and waitress at the Gold Dust Inn just south of Prince Frederick. With her delicate, lithe frame complimenting her near-perfect alabaster skin, sparkling green eyes, flowing red hair and a laid-back style, Dalton was drawn to her. She also had the best-looking pair of pencil erasers he'd ever laid his eyes on.

After their first dinner date, an Italian extravaganza served under dripping candlelight at cozy Mama Francesca's in North Beach, they cheerfully returned to her place to polish off a magnum of red claret. Donna loosened up and playfully suggested that the appropriate dessert could be had on the heated waterbed in her bedroom. Accompanied by the slushy sounds of the heaving, unbaffled aqua berth, Donna's shy persona quickly faded, replaced by a fiery, pent-up passion. Although Dalton felt seasick after each frothy session, he enjoyed his bosom-mate immensely.

Five weeks after they met, Donna finally worked up the nerve to ask him the thorny question of where their relationship was going. It was a question he hadn't really thought about, one he certainly wasn't prepared to answer while the foundation of his own life was Jell-O. It was timing, always the dreaded timing—people needing to go somewhere with their infernal time-clock agendas, which proved to be so damned detrimental to such promising relationships, Dalton concluded after they reluctantly split up that night.

But it was Angelica Ames, the thirty-six year-old part-time healer and full-time sorceress, who finally put the brakes on Dalton's rebound roller-coaster ride. In the beginning, of course, he hadn't the faintest clue she was an authentic, one hundred-percent, dyed-in-the-wool witch, nor was he aware of her being in the recovery throes of a second nervous breakdown! No, Angelica shrewdly took things slow, but once she thought she had him ala hook, line and sinker, her humanistic charade drifted away.

With her long blonde tresses whipping in the brisk wind, the statuesque Angelica looked every bit the true Nordic goddess, when he first saw her that sunny day sauntering barefoot along the North Beach boardwalk. She wore a multi-colored Caribbean serape over her skin-tight, one piece turquoise bathing suit. Dalton felt the herds of butterflies go berserk in his stomach when the tall, buoyant beauty stopped to engage him in a whimsically cheeky, icebreaker chat. She was new in the county and was renting a cottage in Chesapeake Beach while she took a sabbatical from her busy fashion designer career in the DC area. Most important, Dalton learned that she was unattached at the moment, having just ended a stormy relationship with an insanely jealous boyfriend. The more their animated chats continued, the more Dalton found himself becoming enchanted. She was humorous, intelligent and more perceptive than any other femme-fatale re-bounder he'd met thus far in his quest to fill the void in his heart and bed. Consequently, it didn't take long before the emerging chemistry worked its magic.

For several months, Dalton knew he'd discovered paradise. Angelica was educated, well read, worldly and chic in so many ways, almost as passionate about her culinary talents as she was with her tireless dexterity between the sheets. In bed, and during the slack times out of it, she seemed to be the most talented woman Dalton had ever been entangled with. But ready or not, and as providence decreed, her angelic veneer melted away in front of his eyes as the months eked by.

OK, truth be told, he could live with her insistence that she had more guardian angels hovering over her than he did. Granted, she *had* softened the declaration, had even thrown Dalton a bone, in fact, by assuring him that "Dirk," his strongest guardian angel, was one of the most bad-ass guardian angels she'd ever encountered. And no, he wasn't going to allow any of her trivial thoughts about her true professed savior, "Cyber-Goth," the esteemed veteran of the angel wars, intervene with their budding relationship. In all likelihood, Dalton thought he could do the angel thing indefinitely with her, just as long as she continued to amaze him with her innovative libidinous endeavors.

Her need for *The Exorcism* to be performed in his basement, however, finally sent Dalton reeling back into conventional reality.

Angelica's emerging ethereal manner and unpredictable behavior had already gained his incredulously undivided attention on several occasions. Sometimes, when he spent the night at her cottage, he'd inexplicably jolted himself awake to find her standing in the dark at the edge of the bed, dressed in nothing but her bedazzling birthday suit. It was an unnerving sight that assaulted his sleepy eyes when he focused them better. As if spellbound, both of her arms were crossed over her supple breasts, and her wide-open eyes beamed wildly at him, as she mouthed unspoken words in the silence of the bedroom. For several really creepy moments, Dalton suspected that she was trying to turn him into her personal gargoyle, or maybe she was just trying to test her powers of levitation on him—scary thoughts that made him grip the sheet with nervous fingers in hopes of thwarting a possible ascension. When she sensed he was awake and felt his eyes dissecting her transcendental adjurations, she merely shook her blonde tresses and, with no explanation, gingerly crawled back into bed to cuddle next to him.

On those bizarre nights when she whispered softly to her angels about him, it would take a while before the staccato beating of her heart and the heaving of her chest calmed down enough to allow sleep to overtake her. Angelica had also freaked out in public a few times during their outings.

Dalton was flabbergasted when, on that till-then uneventful day, she suddenly gasped and slammed herself hard against the wood plank wall of the Drum Point lighthouse at the Calvert Marine Museum in Solomons. He watched her face turn stark white, and he gaped in open-mouth amazement when her body started shaking and trembling, and the pupils of her eyes slid up until only the whites were showing.

"I can feel their lost souls...the ones who lived here before! Oh my God! *No! Nooo!* I can feel their pain...They're being slaughtered by the boat people!" she cried out, before collapsing on the floor with a loud groan. It took him a twelve-pack and a weary two-day respite, before he entertained the thought of calling her again.

Later one night, after they'd made amends and performed a few minutes of frenzied aerobics on her kitchen floor, she eased up and told him how she'd become an authentic, ordained faith healer. Yes, she was one who could take away the everyday pain and stress most mortals suffered, but only *if* they'd at least *try* to tune in to *her* lofty frequency, of course. Dalton's mind raced with amusement as she matter-of-factly described her widespread assortment of healer-talents to him. Later, very much agitated, perhaps from his resounding silence, Angelica indignantly shoved a manila envelope into his hands and scooted him from her cottage. The crinkled envelope contained a packet of fresh sage, a small vial of rosewood and a card with her hand-scrawled instructions.

Angelica Ames was finally gonna have him exorcize his demon-invested basement! Sure, he'd steeled himself and reacted nonchalantly, after she'd gone spastic with fright in his basement a week before, but she'd truly rattled him when she started screeching about the basement being possessed by the unearthly evils of the living dead. His basement would be doomed for all eternity, she told him—unless he performed the needed cleansing, the *Exorcism.* Dalton dismissed her bizarre outburst, blaming it on the two bottles of cheap Shiraz wine they'd shared earlier. But now, in an alcohol-fogged consternation, he was speeding home to expel the nasty demons from his boogieman basement.

After stumbling down the basement stairs with a lit candle, Dalton arranged the sprigs of sage in a loose circle on the cold cement floor. He then sloppily dumped the vial of rosewood oil over the sage and took out the card bearing the exorcism guidelines. Prince, his trusty canine pal, cocked his head with curiosity. Delirium suddenly hit, and

Dalton broke into bellyaching laughter. Yes indeed, Angelica Ames was a certified loony, all right, and he was teetering close to being certified too, if he dwelled under her freak-ass spells any more. Wracked with hysterics, Dalton was still able to scoop up most of the sage. Together with the empty vial and the instruction card, he jammed the eerie mess back into the envelope and blew out the candle before tromping upstairs to plunk himself down on his bed.

The next night after late shift, Dalton brought the unused exorcism items back to Angelica and off-handedly told her that he'd failed miserably in his aborted attempt to cleanse his basement of the boogie men. He watched in stupefied awe, as her face turned into a crinkled red ball of fiery rage.

"Oh-my-God! You simple, simple man! You have no idea what you've done!" she shrieked in his startled face. "You've broken the spell! You've broken the spell! *Get out! You must leave at once!"* He saw her body start to convulse, and he gaped with disbelief when she tore wildly at her hair while ungodly moans escaped from her trembling mouth. When Dalton reached out to calm her, she hissed at him like an angry snake and ran screaming to her bedroom, where she slammed the door and bolted it. And with that parting display of lunacy, Dalton thought it best to levitate himself from the clutches of his comely sorceress, once and for all.

On his way home, Dalton stopped at Stinchcomb's in Chesapeake Beach for some badly needed brewskis. The landmark bar and restaurant, which catered mostly to the blue-collar types with the calloused hands, was one of his favorite twin beach watering holes. Just to lay an elbow on the varnished bar top, and eavesdrop on the leather-faced watermen jostling each other about the day's misfortunes, was ample amusement in itself. Much to his liking, Stinchcomb's also had the coldest draft beers in the county, too. As Dalton ruminated over a drained beer mug, Marie Odella, the gray-haired, golden-hearted barmaid sage who'd worked at Stinchcomb's since at least the Civil War, waltzed over and fixed him with her all-knowing eyes. "Don't look like yourself tonight there, hon," she cackled. Marie paused for a second, squinty-eyed, and patted down her hair with one hand while plucking the half-smoked cigarette from her lips with the other.

"Lordy, hon, almost looks like you've seen a ghost or something, to me at least!"

The ancient barmaid shrugged her shoulders and blew a cloud of smoke from the side of her mouth. Dalton stared idly into his beer mug for a moment before lifting his weary head. "Naw, just a witch, that's all, Marie," he muttered with a faint smile. "Momma told me there'd be days like this, Marie, but she didn't tell me jack shit about any damned witches!" Marie bit her lower lip in deep thought and wiped the bar top with an old rag. "Yeah, the beaches have more than a few of those ugly-ass witchy-women around, you can believe that one," she said, "but it's them weird, pardon my French, fuckin' warlocks hanging out at the Stonehenge that you better keep an eye out for, and that's the truth of it, don't ya know!" she added with a straitlaced smile.

Dalton smirked and pointed at his empty beer mug. "Marie," he sighed, "some days in my life, I'm beginning to think it's not even worth chewing through the restraints, ya know what I mean?" he asked, knowing she probably didn't have the faintest clue. Marie gave him a wrinkly grin and took another long drag on her cigarette. "Yeah, you got that one right, babe," she replied, patting him lightly on the hand. "Next one's on me, Ok? Ummm, ever chugged down a boiler maker, hon?"

Although his rebound-dating escapades were winding down after a three-year run, Dalton still ventured an occasional date, albeit on a more user-friendly level. The "once bitten, twice shy" syndrome had blanketed him with caution. It took much longer than expected, but he was finally able to rein in his raging hormones enough to allow most of his cognizant thinking to be derived mainly from the head on his shoulders, rather than from the one below his belt. He'd survived The Battle of The Little Big Head intact—but just barely.

#

And just when that irksome hindrance seemed under control, Diane Coulson re-entered his radarscope. At first he didn't recognize her at all in the "hatch-momma" flashy garb she wore for the covert assignment she was working in St. Mary's county. He only knew that the cute trooper with the sparkling white teeth and strawberry-blonde, Rita Hayworth hair—the babe wearing the gaudy "hooker" boots, and the skimpy, come-hither skirt displaying a pair of finely toned legs, was a member of the MSP's vaunted Intelligence Unit. When he first saw her skittering around the radio room, milking the computers for data, Dalton did his best not to stare and drool on his tie.

Several days later, he decided to break the ice and approach her in the parking lot. She was gassing up her covert "hooptie" car, a ragged-out, early-eighties Opel enhanced with a chain-bordered license plate, three shiny plastic hubcaps, countless window decals, cheap add-on window tinting and an exhaust pipe secured by a coat hanger.

Diane tossed back her curly locks with a laugh, her baby-blues suddenly sparkling with recognition. The zany-acting sergeant chatting with her, maybe even drifting close to hitting on her, was the same nice-looking corporal with the broad shoulders she'd remembered from the College Park barrack many years before. Dalton thought that Diane had gotten better looking since then. It was tantalizingly, no, *sinfully* obvious she worked hard to stay in great shape, too.

In their ensuing chats over the next few days, he realized that the once-quiet and shy military brat had a good head on her shoulders and had become a competent, seasoned investigator. Beneath the buffered LE veneer, she still fostered a cheerful personality and a daring sense of adventure. After he garnered the inside scoop that Diane was currently unattached, Dalton stealthily made a game plan to snare her attention.

One small fruitful step led to another, and within a few weeks they were seeing each other exclusively. Dalton had never considered dating anyone on the force, especially after hearing some of the rumors swirling through the grapevine surrounding such a dicey matter. "Ya better damn well expect that almost any female comin' on this job is a full-blown, carpet munchin' dyke!" Elzy spouted out to him one day, in the midst of another one of his politically incorrect tirades. The idea of his becoming involved with a "sister" trooper seemed almost unorthodox at first.

As their relationship blossomed, however, such incestuous musings were happily proven baseless. And, they could bond and bounce off each other when it came to sharing war stories. Despite their fifteen-year age disparity, they had other commonalities. When it came to partying and clinking beer mugs or chugging down shots of who-knows-what, Dalton discovered that Diane harbored a hollow leg, an asset making her wholly capable of holding her own with him. And Diane had a zany sense of humor, too, a tonic for his recent lagging spirits. When the timing was right, and the stars were in correct alignment, they eagerly took advantage of the sparks that flared up between them. Eventually, they became more like comfortable buddies who relished their own independent traits and personal needs.

They were especially synchronized when they were immersed in the natural world. Over the ensuing years, there were many unforgettable trips they shared with Diane's family at their rustic log cabin on a mountain slope overlooking Virginia's Shenandoah Valley. For hours on end, they enjoyed watching the whitetail deer graze in the meadows below, while the hawks above soared lazily on the warm air currents. They also shared the thrill of white-water rafting on the scenic "Yough" river in Pennsylvania, hiking the beaches of Chincoteague Island in Virginia, skiing Canaan Valley in West Virginia and lazing on beaches of the outer banks in North Carolina. But of all their favorite "nature fix" niches, the shell-covered beach beneath Calvert Cliffs just north of Long Beach, was their favorite.

Unfettered, they perched on the sandbanks, rubbing shoulders in front of a driftwood fire, savoring the peace of mind. Between sips of Pinot Grigio and morsels of nuts, dried fruit and smoked cheese, they marveled at the ospreys hurtling down with sweptback wings to the shallow waters, hoping to snag an alewife. They also watched the gawky blue herons as they keenly stalked along the water's edge. And, every so often, the silence was shattered by the percussive rattle of a kingfisher. The bluish-gray bird with the compact body and crested head hovered briefly before plunging into the water to spear its prey. Schools of snapper blues or young rockfish, the sun flashing off their silver sides, whipped the glassy surface of the bay into a frenzy in their pursuit of bait fish, and the air was filled with the squeals of seagulls as they spastically dipped and soared, diving down every so often to snatch leftovers.

But what really captivated their attention, what took their breaths away every time, was the occasional bald eagle drifting low overhead on broad wings. The moments would be short-lived, as the wise birds never seemed to loiter in one place, but the humbling effect of the eagle's "salutes" to them remained for hours.

On those crystal days when they could see for miles—those days when the rare phenomenon of atmospheric refraction made the boats appear to hover above the water, and the Eastern Shore features seemed so much closer—they'd stay on the beach and wait for the setting sun to be blocked out by the majestic cliffs behind them. In awe, they gazed across the bay and watched the ebbing sunrays turn the illusory outline of the Eastern Shore into a panoramic brilliance. And if the wine held out, and driftwood was found for the waning fire, they'd stay hours longer.

With Dalton and his spirited girlfriend, there was no rush, pressure or pesky requirement to find out where they were going, nor was there an implicit need to shack up with each other. As a detached twosome, they were content to share their shits and giggles to the extent they felt they could, wherever and whenever.

#

A year after their final separation, long after any possible reconciliation thoughts had vanished, Dalton reluctantly filed for a divorce. Up until then, he and Cindy had remained cordial to each other, mainly for their daughters. When the lawyers came into play, however, the game changed, and they became icy adversaries. Both teenage daughters had problems coping with the life changes, the adverse affects translating into pain, alternating bursts of anger, and almost daily incidents of rebellion. Schoolwork suffered drastically, as stability and discipline in their lives deteriorated. Since the last separation, and for the next few years, Charlene and Anne Marie would alternately live with one or the other parent, ping-ponging between them, as the stress grew and disagreements flared.

When one or both daughters lived with him, Dalton did his best to maintain a semblance of domestic life, but with the continuous shift work, it proved to be daunting and nearly impossible. If possible, between MSP calamities during the late shifts, he'd come home to fix them a quick dinner, inquire about homework, then dash back to the barrack. Other times, he'd have to settle for phone call checkups, or if *really* suspicious, especially during the vulnerable night shifts, he'd make unannounced visits to the house to assure no wayward boyfriends lurked in the house. Dalton found it extremely difficult to juggle his obligations and a growing desire to spend more time with Diane, but eventually, things settled down.

Shouldering their deep-rooted emotional wounds, both daughters inevitably flapped from the coop on crippled wings to get on with their lives however they could. Under the trying circumstances, Dalton almost felt satisfied knowing he'd done what he could. Deep inside, however, he knew it hadn't been enough, and he'd always regret how much the family instability and collapse affected them. Still, he couldn't hold his estranged wife wholly responsible for the breakup. No, they both had to share high-fives for screwing that up.

Dalton loathed leaving the two-level saltbox house on the five wooded acres adjoining St Leonard Creek. He would sorely miss watching the foraging deer, the random wild turkeys, the clownish raccoons and squirrels, the varieties of birds and the other creatures that made the place so special to him. But there were too many wretched memories, and he knew he couldn't stay there.

Scouting around St Leonard for rentals, Dalton found a modest, quaint, two-bedroom cottage in a secluded area of Calvert Beach. His newfound abode was on a small lot close to the community beach, and for the time being he labeled it home. Diane, ever the supreme organizer, helped him set up house on moving day. Afterward, they had two bottles of her favorite Chardonnay and polished off a hastily made salmon dinner before testing the sturdiness of the teak platform bed in the cramped knotty-pine bedroom.

Later in the evening, hours after Diane had left in her backfiring "hooptie" car, it wasn't long before the shrinking cottage walls left him in total solitude. Dalton took two beers from the fridge, snapped the pop tabs and set them on the pine coffee table he'd handcrafted years before. He lit the three-wick vanilla candle, turned off the floor lamp, then wearily flopped down on the couch. When the "tiger" visited again, when the God-forsaken nightmares emerged as they always did, he'd be more susceptible now. No longer would he feel that warm, comforting snout muzzling his hand. Several weeks before, when he realized that his fourteen year-old, ever-faithful companion Prince was suffering, Dalton reluctantly had the ole dog put down. Now, in a late-night moment, he really missed his furry, tick-ridden stalwart.

After too many beers, two Unisom sleep tabs and way too much pondering, Dalton blew out the candle and called it a night. Maybe someday he'd be lucky enough to find another pal like Prince, he thought wistfully. But that thought was readily dismissed. No, it just wasn't in the cards, since he'd already made up his mind not to get attached to anything, or maybe even anyone—ever again.

#

It was an ominous fog, a thick, hanging mist reeking of an unknown peril the likes of which he'd never felt before. Any horror-movie set with its billowing dry ice fog, howling sound machines and light effects, couldn't match this scary soup, Dalton thought, as he steadily tromped along the edge of the mucky cornfield. In the eerie murk, he could only see a few feet ahead.

Calvert Control Center received the call from the tenant farmer's frantic sister during the waning hours of a boring night shift, a grave-yard shift so monotonous that even the voluptuous *Penthouse* Pets in the sizzling new issue failed to keep Dalton and Elzy from nodding off. Both troopers were nudged awake by the zombie-like Ozzie Albright, Wanda "Battle Axe" Gatton's zaniest PCO. No one had seen or heard from her elderly brother for three days. The venerable two-trooper night shift dutifully shook the zzzs from their heads and were soon en route to the dilapidated tenant house on Skinners Turn Road in Owings.

The hovel lacked electricity and running water, and, unsurprisingly enough, it was unlocked. After a quick search by flashlight, they also found it empty, except for a few humongous rats that shrieked and scurried into shadows. Elzy's instincts kicked in big time. It was all wrong—he could smell it, could feel it. They decided to split up and search the cornfield perimeter, planning to meet back at the house. Dalton held the mag-light at chest level, swinging it back and forth through the white soup as he forged on. He felt it now, too. Something was wrong.

Suddenly, he heard a mournful cry from some close-by, ungodly night creature. The hair on his neck tingled, and he froze in his tracks.

Dalton watched in awe as a scraggly red fox emerged ghostlike from the fog ahead. Its mouth hung open, and a limp tongue dangled from one side as it passed. The fox was panting, eyes fixed and blazing red in a trance, ignoring him. He shuddered when the animal shattered the stillness with another long, eerie wail before vanishing back into the haze. Dalton stood straight up, took a deep breath and nervously whacked his leg with the flashlight before moving on. (You *really* didn't see that, did you, Trooper Bragg? Fuck it, right?) After several minutes of sluggish progress, he was at the corner of the field. Great! Just a short pause and he'd be turning back. Still, he was too edgy, his senses still ramped up on high alert.

The flashlight cut through the fog just in time to keep him from stumbling over it. Dalton gasped when the beam danced across the body lying at his feet! He'd found the old black farmer all right, but he was stone dead and board-stiff. Dressed in dirty, worn coveralls and a torn checkered wool shirt, the body lay face-up, spindly arms and legs grotesquely curled up, like a dead insect. The old man's toothless mouth was wide open, locked in a horrific grimace, and full of white, slimy maggots, and more of them squirming in the putrefied eye sockets.

Dalton spotted several small, vaguely discernible, bite marks on the bloated face and hands. Chest wildly pounding, he gagged when the stench reached his nostrils. "OK, bring it down, my man," he muttered. "You've seen worse than this before, you bet ya!" But what were those small, dark holes in his coveralls? He wanted to call out for Elzy, but quickly dismissed the thought. No, not yet. Dalton took a deep breath and squatted down beside the body, training his flashlight on the man's coveralls near his chest. .

Shotgun blast, sure enough! "Jesus H Christ!" he heard himself shout, "Prince Frederick's got itself another damned homicide!"

As if on cue, the mass of maggots in the dead man's mouth was suddenly coughed into the trooper's face, followed by a loud, piercing shriek! When Dalton sputtered and tried to wipe his eyes, two icy-cold claws grabbed him violently by the throat and locked him in a vise grip. He tore desperately at the slimy hands, but it was no use. He was powerless, couldn't even get to his gun. When he tried to scream, nothing came out but a low, muffled gurgle. *No! Nooo*! Despite desperate attempts to fight it, his head was being forced closer and closer to the rancid corpse's shrieking mouth. He felt a paralyzing dizziness when his windpipe collapsed, felt his bladder release and his body shake uncontrollably as his neck bones cracked and caved in. He knew his life was oozing away when fleeting images of his mother flashed across his fading thoughts. *Oh My God—Nooo...!*

Dalton woke up with a start, his body drenched in a cold, damp sweat. His panicked mind raced uncontrollably, and his heart pummeled his chest in a frenzied reaction to yet another cursed nightmare. He groped blindly in the dark for the lamp switch and wiped the sweat from his forehead with the back of a trembling hand. While he forced himself to take deep breaths, his flaring eyes focused on the lazily twirling ceiling fan.

Yes, if there was anything he could always count on in his convoluted life right now, it was those infernal nightmares. Dalton could easily recall every gruesome, haunting job experience they were twisted from. All of them—every damned one—was seared in his mind forever.

He'd chalk up tonight's grotesque entertainment, a rare combo event, to the "suicide" corpse in the ravine near Lower Marlboro, while the search-in-the-fog episode came from the murdered old tenant farmer in the Owings cornfield. The decomposed corpse in the ravine had rotted for several days by the time Dalton and another trooper contacted the farmer who led them to it. The good-ole-boy hayseed had seen the turkey vultures circling high overhead. Suspecting that one of his missing Herefords may have perished in the heat, he trudged across the rye grass to find out otherwise. Clusters of maggots squirmed in the suicide victim's frozen-in-death, wide-open mouth, and others slithered across the bloated purplish-black face. And the rotten stench was overpowering. It hadn't helped matters much when Dalton slipped and rolled down the ravine to land against the emulsified thing.

When the corpse's pureed arm sloughed off the jelly-like torso and landed in the dirt with a sickening splat—when what was left of the head threatened to do the same as the remains were bagged—Dalton gagged and fought the urge to puke. The rancid, soggy mess they'd hauled up in the black body bag was a sixty-two year-old NSA employee who, for whatever reasons, had "apparently" blown his brains out with a double-barrel shotgun years before his time.

The search for the missing old tenant farmer had been a chilly, near-ethereal experience that macabre night. Both he and Elzy intuitively sensed the essence of death lingering somewhere nearby, just waiting to be coaxed into its horrid discovery. While searching the crude cabin, Elzy had fallen partially through the rotten floor in the old man's makeshift bedroom, after jumping over the half-filled bucket of rank fecal matter next to the filthy mattress on the floor. Nervous laughs and a few choice "mutha fucks!" lessened the tension.

In fog thick as soup, the two troopers searched along most of the cornfield perimeter that night before turning back. The next day, an investigator determined that if Dalton had ventured just a few more steps that ghoulish night, he would have stumbled over the grotesquely sprawled out murder victim. Instead, he'd turned back after the wild-eyed, deranged fox from hell (rabid?) had eerily passed him in the dismal fog.

Yes, all his incessant nightmares had his morbid job experiences scorched in them, one after the other. No matter who or what entered his life, Dalton knew they'd never stop plaguing him now. He also knew he couldn't dare share his demons with Diane for fear she'd think he was losing his mind. Undoubtedly, she'd leave him like a bad dream itself, if she found out how bad it was. He only hoped that when they spent those infrequent nights with each other, she wouldn't be too spooked if the "tiger" emerged and snared him again. She was smart, too savvy for her own good, and he knew he'd be hard-pressed to rationalize his wild, nocturnal outbursts if they happened more than once.

He'd been lucky so far in that regard. Diane had brought a lot of sunshine into his life since they'd met. Despite her warmth, however, he felt the clouds of despair drifting back in to reclaim dominion over his disquieted soul. Dalton resigned himself to fight the onslaught for as long as he could, but the downward slide into the vortex of his personal Hades was unstoppable, this he already sensed. If nothing else, he'd do his best to camouflage it from the others any way he could. From now on, he'd insulate himself deeper within his crumbling, self-protective walls, hoping to hold out long enough to devise a suitable game plan for what lay ahead.

#

Sergeant Dalton Bragg's last few Maryland State Police "sunset" years were grinding down—considerably slower, however, than most retirees had predicted. On the MSP center stage, Colonel "Buffalo" Lyons had been jettisoned by a new governor. His successor was Colonel Donald C. Mooney, the former Anne Arundel County Police Chief who'd worked under his current boss when the future governor was the lauded A.A. County Executive.

While county police chief, Mooney had earned a stellar reputation for leadership. Following the dubious tenure of Colonel "Buffalo," the new, highly resourceful MSP leader was considered a saint. Consequently, Colonel Mooney made great progress in revamping the department during his first two years. After enduring too many years of substandard salaries and pinched budgets, the troopers were *finally* being compensated with overdue pay increases and better equipment.

To his everlasting credit, Colonel Mooney also restored integrity to the formerly abused promotional system. Although promotional selections customarily fluctuated through the years to counter supposed inequities, under the new Colonel it was firmly established that once the promotion list was final, certified and cast in stone, there would be strict adherence. Well, maybe ninety-six percent of the time. Along with enhanced salaries, the restoration of a credible promotional system was a major plus for the MSP, and the troopers' morale soared.

#

With his retirement fast approaching, and his mindset in a quagmire, Dalton knew it was too late for another decent stab at promotion. Nonetheless, the new promo system was a godsend to his fellow troopers who now held redeeming faith in their careers. Any ambivalence he held in that regard was cast aside when his good friend Gary Rephan was promoted to the rank of major on Colonel Mooney's second official promotion list. All hoped the inglorious days of the Wizard of Oz Promotional Follies were finally over.

Inevitably, no earthly being walks on water too long. Predictably, Colonel Mooney amassed detractors, several of them from within the higher echelons; the more conniving Pikesville Palace Princes. Alas, the self-respecting MSP boss had a penchant for iron-fisted rule, and while most lower ranks were insulated from it, MSP scuttlebutt revealed that the testy Colonel was arrogant and overbearing with his truculent subordinate commanders. Those who dared to voice contradictory opinions, or attempted to stand their ground against the chubby-cheeked taskmaster, were duly slighted and openly ridiculed. Amongst the troops, it was rumored that their stoop-shouldered "Soup" who kept his dyed blond hair combed over bald spots, had a fragile but immense ego that required constant soothing from his specially chosen aide-de-camps (gofers). It was commonly known that Colonel Mooney thrived on publicity and was, unquestionably, the most politically oriented leader the MSP ever had.

Troopers serving in the field, however, felt that he genuinely cared about them. Almost to the man, those who wore the Stetsons thought that Colonel Mooney had arrived at the right time and right place.

Despite his self-indulging quirks, Colonel Mooney's tenure would have been an exemplary one—had it not been for that not-so-anonymous Pikesville Prince from the Eastern Shore who gleefully spoon-fed a *Baltimore Sun* newspaper columnist the juicy details about a few adulterous shenanigans and off-track betting improprieties the Colonel was embroiled in. The published stories culminated with Colonel Mooney being investigated by a special state prosecutor. After beating his chest raw and roaring loudly in expressed indignation—which bounced off deaf ears—the crestfallen State Police head abruptly resigned. Those in the know grasped that Colonel Mooney's incentive for his jackrabbit departure was to deflect any further publicity about the affair he was having with his hot stuff, feline Pikesville Palace secretary. His loyal wife had been tormented enough already.

#

At this point in the twilight of his career, Dalton had served under four governors and seven superintendents. Colonel Mooney was his last superintendent, though if he'd stuck around longer, as his buddy

Gary Rephan had urged, he'd have been pleasantly surprised by number eight. The governor, piqued and deeply embarrassed, took pains to make sure he played it safe on his next choice. After scrutinizing the credentials of countless candidates, a new leader was plucked from the MSP ranks—again. This time, they got it right.

If Dalton had stumbled across a spare crystal ball, he might have shelved his retirement plans long enough to see his old sidekick Gary Rephan raise his right hand and take the oath to become the next Maryland State Police Superintendent. It would have been more entertaining than a barrel of rabid chimpanzees, just to see how Gary, in his characteristic buzz-saw manner, cleaned house on the Puzzle Palace third floor. It'd be a declared open season on malingerers, brown-nosers, self-servers and goldbricks, big-time.

More than likely, Gary would have also followed through with his veiled threat to have Dalton join him as a trusted ally at Pikesville, too. That dreadful aspect was jokingly brought up during a beer-infused, left-field discussion many months before, when Gary was mellow enough to talk trash about his MSP aspirations. Dalton's confidant had dropped by his cottage that afternoon for an impromptu visit after he hadn't heard from Dalton for a few days. Sensing that a few cold brews were the ticket, the old sidekicks were soon perched atop familiar bar stools in the Calverton Room.

"Yeah, Dalton, my good man, if I ever got plucked out of a hat to be the "Soup," I'd make ya my loyal butler, just like that squirrelly, bald-headed lieutenant who's Colonel Mooney's lapdog up there now. You know, that baby-face lieutenant what's-his-name who fetches Mooney's bottle of Avian water, the one who daintily opens his pack of banana-nut granola bars before those stupid-ass commanders' T-MAS meetings we're forced to endure. Yeah, the frenzy-eyed dude who bolts ahead to open doors and fetch Mooney's lil can of hair spray before any pictures are allowed to be taken...Come on, you know 'im," Gary chided.

Dalton howled and draped an arm over his pal's shoulder. "Got a strong aversion to Pikesville, my friend. You, of all people know *that* for shhhsure," Dalton slurred back. "Besides, this ole trooper's definitely splittin' this candy-ass outfit when he's done his twenty-six year burst...give or take a minute or two. Got me a few good job offers to follow-up on, too, as a matter of fact," Dalton said wistfully, with a false hint of pride. Gary set his beer mug down, wiped his mouth, then shot him an inquiring look. "OK, my friend, enlighten me. I'm all beers!" Dalton took another gulp and put on the best serious face he could muster.

"Yup, it's a toss-up between the two, but I'm gonna try to snag me a cushy job down on that warm, bohemian-infested island of Key West...I think. Yeah, buddy, for one rare and righteous moment, I'm gonna put down that Hurricane drink with that cute lil umbrella doo-hicky thing sticking out of it, and raise a free hand to swear allegiance to the Conch Republic. Me's gonna be the head-honcho driver of that pink and yellow Conch Train that hauls all those touristy-types around, damn straight!" Gary tapped a finger on the bar top and stared at him in wordless wonder. "Umm, and if that falls through, I may just try a shot at that "in-flight missile repairman" gig the US of A's Army is advertising at the Aberdeen Proving grounds, maybe. Either way's my ticket to paradise, the way I figure it," Dalton said, breaking into an ear-to-ear grin. Gary shook his head and jabbed him in the side with an elbow. "Think you'll be needing a conductor for your lil conch choo-choo train, maybe?" he asked sheepishly. Amidst lingering laughter, both troopers clinked mugs and toasted each other's dubious futures before skedaddling home.

No, sir, Dalton didn't need any old, friggin' crystal ball to tell him what his game plan was. That plan had already been set in stone, and come hell or high water, it sure as didn't include being sentenced to any hard time at Pikesville, *that* was certain.

#

The burn-out years of playing the duty officer/ barrack houseboy role had predictably settled in, adding to Sergeant Dalton Bragg's growing inner turmoil. While his personal friends and most others thought his turbulent days had passed, Dalton knew otherwise. He steeled himself, taking great pains masking his deepening funk from those closest to him, the influential ones who could help him—if he'd let them. But pride denied that distasteful option. With protective walls locked in place, they'd never discern the extent of his personal hell, which steadily intensified with each abhorrent nightmare, each tiresome bout of inexplicable gloom that added to his detachment.

The drinking sprees alone, in the false sanctuary of the cottage, had increased drastically, in his attempt to stave off the torment long enough to allow a few elusive hours of rest. Only his brother Jon, maybe his best friend Gary and perhaps Diane had the faintest suspicions that all wasn't quite "Ocean King" with him. So far, he was winning—but for how much longer?

At the barrack level, the lifeblood and tempo had changed significantly during Dalton's last few years. Morale at the PF barrack was, well, OK, but with the absence of the, once frequent barrack parties, Dalton had seen much better spirits in days long gone. Only the barrack ballplayers during softball season displayed the zest of PF's infamous yesteryears. And with another MSP musical chairs game, the barrack was endowed with a new F/Sgt and D/Sgt, some new NCOs and a handful of baby-face troopers. This time, Pearl and Cheryl, the ever-faithful secretaries, *both* tore out their hair trying to accommodate the newest arrivals.

Dalton's personal pride mandated a conscientious job performance. Yup, he was going out the right way with his head held high! No way would he let himself turn into a two hundred and forty-pound paperweight, as others had done when they'd gotten so tantalizingly close to retirement. He'd juggle the plethora of duty officer responsibilities all right, but he sure as hell wouldn't be stressing out anymore about those piddling annoyances that always found a way to fall through the cracks and bite him on the ass. Those anxious days of scurrying around like Chicken Little to get things done earlier then *yesterday,* just so some Pikesville Prince numb-nuts could have the report languish on his desk gathering dust, were all over. No more playing the caged lion role, with the taunts and jabbing sticks. Dalton's overwhelming concern now was the welfare of his "brothers in arms," those troopers in the trenches who gave their all. Yes, they were the ones he still held allegiance to.

Long ago, he'd reluctantly crossed the supervisory line to side with the hard-pressed lower ranks, hoping to insulate them as much as possible from the department's growing dirge of follies. He'd even managed to mentally immunize himself from the endless frivolities of daffy Francis, his nice, but still quite inept PCO, too. For whatever reasons, however, the most irritating peeve that still wrangled its way through his duty officer's veneer was the increase in the barrack's walk-in traffic. Inherently, the barrack was open for business on a 24/7 basis, making it a target for the loonies when they came out of the woodwork during the normal troglodyte hours. And when the loonies in the lobby became overly belligerent and put their asses on their shoulders, Dalton's temper shot up to the chokehold level.

He only wished that the barrack commanders had taken him seriously when he implored them to install an electric shock mat in the lobby and a gong bell in the duty officer's pit to rectify such nuisances. One gong, a fifteen-second delay to allow a retreat, then a resounding bug zapper-like *"Zzzit!"* for those crazies who dawdled.

With the transfers and retirements of trusty stalwarts during the preceding years, Dalton and fellow Sergeant Ben Wiley were the barrack's only silverback troopers left from the early seventies. As Ben succinctly put it one day when they were commiserating about old times, "Yup, it's you and me now, ole buddy! We're the last of the fuckin' Mohicans now, that's us!" Both silverback Mohicans bounced off each other constantly, comparing notes about the new troopers looking younger every year. They agreed that most of the recruits were smart and had more computer savvy, but they also thought they were maybe a little *too* straight-laced and lacking in certain areas such as grammar in report-writing, and in God-given, simple common sense.

"Dalton, ole buddy, when these sad-sack kids go home after putting in their exact eight hours or less, most of 'em' drink soda or fruit juice...Can you believe that shit?" Ben grumped to him. "Yeah, pretty messed-up bunch a pansies, huh, Ben?" Dalton replied, rolling his eyes and shaking his head. "Well, I got so tired of using my red magic marker on Trooper Lowery's reports, that I went out and bought the moron a pocket dictionary," Dalton told him. "Ya know what he asked me, partner?" Ben looked out the window with vacant eyes and shrugged his shoulders. "Stupid son a bitch asked me how he was supposed to look up a word if he didn't know how to spell it in the first place!" Ben keeled over, howling with laughter. His face was beet-red when he finally came up for air.

"Lowery? Is that the goofball who had his dog's name tattooed on his right shoulder? The guy who came in one day with the bleached-blonde Mohawk?" Ben asked. "Yup, sure is, and here's another one of his brain farts: You know how a lot of the troops end their CIRs with the standard, 'the area was canvassed for clues, spiel?" Dalton queried. Wiley nodded. "Well, Lowery indicated on his last destruction-of-property report that 'the area was canvassed but all my hard exertions in the matter had to cease and desist because I ran out of canvas and clues.' Not kiddin' ya, Ben, so help me God!"

As time slipped by, Dalton and his silverback cohort vented more about the new breed of troopers being catapulted into the field. To the seasoned three-stripers, the new boots didn't have much of the old team spirit at all. To them, it seemed that most young troopers wanted to chart their own agendas, with too many questionable voids and variables between. But if the two silverbacks had been honest about it, they'd probably be forced to admit that the old-timers who paved the way before *they* got on the force probably grumped about their new generation too. Every jawbone session strongly reinforced the belief that every day they were getting ever so closer to the day they'd be hanging up their Stetsons for good.

One barrack stalwart who beat both of them was Tfc. Craig Harmel. No one else Dalton had ever worked with, with the exception of his friend Gary perhaps, had commanded his respect more than the practical-minded, soft-spoken black trooper. Time after calamitous time, Harmel had proven himself as the barrack's most reliable, cool-headed trooper whenever the bad stuff hit the fan. His modest self-assurance set the bar high for others who tried to follow him. When Harmel told his PF buddies he was retiring to run for the recently vacated Calvert County Sheriff's position, few took him seriously. However, when the tightly-contested election was held a year after Sheriff Almos Jett left to go fishing forever, it was former trooper Craig Harmel who raised his right hand to be sworn in as the new sheriff.

#

The loss of Junebug Buckler, Dalton's intrepid compatriot and a barrack top dog, was a tough one. Dalton was glad he wasn't working the night his hard-charging pal had that ghastly departmental accident.

The highspeed chase started on northbound Route 4, just north of Prince Frederick. Junebug was cruising down Dalrymple Road in Sunderland, when he heard the broadcast. It was 1:05 AM, and he'd just cleared a domestic complaint, which ended with him rapturously consoling the big-breasted, distraught young woman who'd just dumped her boyfriend after discovering he'd been doing the nasty with her younger sister. The night shift corporal working radar at Hunting Creek Hill was in hot pursuit of an early-model Plymouth Fury at speeds above one hundred miles an hour.

Junebug kicked into it, hoping to get to the Route 2 and 4 intersection in time to set up a roadblock. When the corporal radioed he was northbound at Sunderland Hills, Junebug excitedly blathered out an imperceptible microburst message in an effort to apprize the corporal of his roadblock intentions. Unsure of Junebug's verbal diarrhea, the corporal barreled on. Approaching the junction at warp-speed, Junebug made a crucial split-second decision. With his hair on fire, he jerked the steering wheel sharply to the left and zipped the wrong way down the one-way exit ramp from Rt. 4. When the corporal suddenly spotted Junebug's cruiser hurtling down the ramp, he yelled in the mic—but it was too late. At eighty-some miles an hour, the Plymouth Fury slammed head-on into the speeding MSP cruiser.

The accident scene was an ugly, tangled mess of torn metal, mangled flesh, shattered glass, steamy leaking fluids, shrieking sirens and wildly flashing emergency lights. The ghastly spectacle was chaotic, as rescue squad members and police officers feverishly worked against time. The teen-age driver of the Fury was stone drunk, yet limber enough to escape with a few broken bones. Junebug, however, was trapped in the steaming wreckage of his cruiser for an hour before he was cut free with the "Jaws of Life" rescue tool. Covered in blood, but alive and mumbling incoherently, Junebug was flown out by MSP helicopter to the Baltimore shock trauma unit, where he remained in stable, but critical condition for several long days.

In addition to severe internal bleeding, both of Junebug's legs and his right arm were fractured, several ribs were broken, and he had several head lacerations. Tfc. Jim Buckler was as tough as they come, however, and he stayed at the trauma center for only a few days before being shipped to CMH, the county hospital. While he was at the trauma center, Dalton visited him and was encouraged by his good friend's spirit. "Yeah, Sarge, I guess I shoulda zigged when I zagged, huh, ole buddy," Junebug said in a choked voice hampered by the thick plastic tube stuck down his throat. "Well, at least I kept my perfect record and never lost a 10-80, didn't I?" he joked. Sheila, his exhausted wife, smiled gamely and squeezed his hand. "Weird thing though, Sarge," Junebug muttered after she walked beyond earshot, "That son a bitch was the first one I ever played chicken with who didn't back off from me, the crazy muthafucker!"

Despite months of agonizing physical therapy and several surgeries, Junebug was eventually determined to be permanently disabled, and, with no hope of staying on the job, the disheartened trooper was medically retired from MSP. For the rest of his life, Junebug Buckler would receive sixty-six and two thirds of his final trooper's salary; tax free—small comfort to the highly decorated trooper with the can-do spirit. Dalton would forever recognize his friend as one of the rare few on the job who not only talked the talk, but also walked the walk.

Police work ran thick in Jim Buckler's blood. "Gonna get my PI license soon, Sarge, and who the hell knows, I just might even try a run for sheriff some day, too, if I get too bored, maybe," the starry-eyed Junebug excitedly told Dalton one night over too many beers. "Yeah, buddy, and I'll probably see pigs sprout wings and fly before that ever happens," Dalton chided him before breaking out in a shit-faced grin. To Dalton, Junebug's shattered invincibility would forever serve as yet another stark reminder of the steep price many of his fellow troopers paid for being one of "Maryland's Finest."

\#

While the departure of Dalton's friend Junebug Buckler was tough, the sudden, shocking death of Tfc. Toby K. Hunter, just a year later, stunned the entire Prince Frederick barrack As Hunter's shift sergeant, Dalton took his loss hard. "TK," as he was called, had been a road-patrol trooper for more than fifteen years, and Dalton had been his group supervisor for five of them.

Raised in an impoverished Baltimore slum, the easy-going teenager had found a home in the US Navy as a corpsman before joining the MSP. Over the years, TK, despite his idiosyncrasies, had bloomed into a credible road trooper. True, he was plagued by a case of the slows, and he continually fell behind in the essential road-patrol stats, but what made the good-natured trooper shine brighter than most was his quirky personality. It wasn't just the way the slightly built soul brother cheerfully greeted everyone with that smile and that lazy, comical hand salute. The troopers all smiled and shook their heads in disbelief when TK, his Stetson cocked back on his head, diddy-bopped into the room in his usual happy-go-lucky manner while crooning a few off-key lines from a gospel hymn he favored at the moment. And like flies on shit, the sergeants jumped on TK constantly about why his brass looked like it'd been polished with a Hershey bar, or why his olive-drab MSP trousers looked like he'd slept in them. But nobody fostered ill feelings toward him for very long. It was the bizarre myriad of consternations trailing behind him that turned TK into a barrack legend.

As his sergeant, who was having a hellacious bad-hair day, Dalton had begrudgingly assigned TK to a theft complaint in Neeld's Estates near Huntingtown. Not hearing from him for some time, Dalton called the residence for a status check. The owner of the house, a woman who sounded ditzy and way too happy, spouted out that "Trooper TK" had been teaching her mesmerized daughter how to play the piano during the last two hours. With her falsetto voice echoing in the phone, she pleaded with Dalton to allow her to keep TK for a while longer, if possible, to further his "investigation" of her missing mailbox—and perhaps her ditzy dizziness.

Tfc. Toby Hunter was also blessed with unusually bad luck with animals. He held a place in his heart for all critters, but the feelings of God's creatures weren't reciprocal. The reminder was the permanent horseshoe welt, which, in the right light, could be seen on the top of TK's shiny bald head. "Yeah, uh-huh...Years ago, my auntie down at

Wallville done nicknamed me 'Lucky" after an ugly-ass mule done kicked me in the head when I was cleaning out a stall. Yup, bent down to pick up the harmonica that fell outta my pocket, and *wham...*The damn mule done went and kicked me side the head somethin' God-awful fierce. Onlyest thing lucky that day, Sarge, was the mule, uh-huh, 'cause I was gonna put the pitchfork to the ornery bitch, but my aunt snatched it outta my hands fo' I could stick it! Lucky, my ass!"

Dalton almost peed himself from laughing the day he overheard TK's encounter with the deer playing out over the MSP radio. The free-spirited trooper was driving slowly down Chaneyville road that crisp, late fall afternoon, when he spotted a four-point whitetail buck trotting along the edge of a cornfield next to the road. The deer was just yards away, loping aimlessly ahead while matching the cruiser's speed. The rutting season was in, and as rural-country troopers knew from experience, it was kamikaze time for the lusty bucks. TK sped the cruiser up and watched with amusement as the buck broke into a full run, straining to keep up. Poor dumb critter can't hold on too much longer, TK thought, as stomped on the gas pedal.

Seconds later, the buck jerked sharply and bounded into the air to explode through the passenger window of TK's cruiser! In an instant, the kicking, convulsing deer was wedged tight between the windshield and the front seat! Moments later, the hapless trooper was howling on the radio. With one hand juggling the steering wheel and the radio mic, TK started whacking the agitated buck on the head with the first thing he got his free hand on—a citation book, as he braked the patrol car to an abrupt halt.

"U-41 Prince Frederick! *U-41...Prince Frederick!"* he screeched over the radio. "I'm being assaulted by a crazy god-damn deer on Chaneyville Road! Holy Jesus! Need me some back-up...and...er, make it 10-18 (quickly)!" TK shouted, as he continued slamming the citation book on the head of the agitated buck. In a frenzy to free itself, the deer was steadily demolishing the cruiser's vinyl dashboard and radio console with its pointy antlers and flaying, knife-sharp hooves. Dalton and Francis, his dumbstruck PCO, listened gleefully, as TK radioed a running account of his battle with the buck.

"I've got it by the horns, Prince Frederick...but, but I can't hold out too much longer! *Aggghhh!* OK, Prince Frederick, I'm outside my unit and I'm pullin' on it's back legs now, so's I can get the crazy thing to stop kicking so much!" Finally: "U-41 Prince Frederick! *U dash forty-one Prince Frederick!* Request permission to shoot this damn thing!" TK railed.

Dalton kept himself in check just enough to signal Francis to give him the A-OK. Before she could hit the transmit button, however, TK came back on the air. Breathlessly, he advised the barrack that the berserk buck had untangled itself from the MSP unit and was thrashing its way back through the cornfield.

When he wrote up the endorsement to TK's departmental, Dalton had to restrain himself from indicating on the report that the accident could have been avoided if TK had simply "passed the buck" when he first saw it. Indeed, with TK around, there was never a dull moment. But now he was gone.

From all indications, nothing seemed to be plaguing TK during that humdrum late shift on the last day of his life. As most agreed, Tfc. Toby Hunter was the epitome of a laissez-faire guy who didn't fret the small or big stuff. Problems just seemed to roll off him—or so it appeared. Even his stunned, distraught wife swore she never saw it coming.

After securing from late shift that August night, TK went home to his wife and her pre-teen daughter at the tranquil Bay Side Trailer Park in Huntingtown. They were fast asleep, and he thoughtfully closed their bedroom doors so they wouldn't be disturbed when he turned on the TV in the cramped living room. After taking off his gun belt and clip-on tie, he unbuttoned his uniform shirt and lazily kicked off his shoes. Picking up the remote, he switched on the late news before meandering over to the kitchen to microwave a bag of popcorn. While the popcorn was being nuked, TK drifted back into the living room and picked up the Bible from the coffee table. He stared at the dog-eared, black leather-bound tome for several long moments, smiled to himself, then gently set it back down. With glazed eyes, he listened dispassionately to the Washington DC Channel Four news.

His mind made up, TK gingerly eased the .40-caliber Beretta from its holster, checking to see if the tiny red indicator on the side plate still showed. Red was the color that confirmed the chambered round. Satisfied, he opened the side door of the mobile home and stepped outside under a lustrous, star-filled sky. He eased the door shut behind him, shuffled down the steps to the gravel sidewalk and filled his lungs with the clean night air. He smiled when Otis Redding suddenly materialized to serenade him with his all-time favorite, *Sittin' On The Dock of the Bay*. As he slowly exhaled, the cold barrel of the weapon settled against the side of his head. High tide, low tide, don't matter to me anymore... With the simple flexing of his right index finger, Tfc. Toby K. Hunt blew his life away.

The investigation of TK's suicide never developed any explicit reason why the tormented Maryland State Trooper took his life. What investigators discovered later was that TK's personal computer tower was never brought to the Annapolis PC repair outlet, as he'd told his wife earlier the day he killed himself. Any possible answers to the endless questions surrounding his self-extermination were hidden within the mangled pieces of his Gateway Intel PC lying on the bottom of thirty-seven feet of murky Patuxent River water next to the Route 231 Benedict Bridge.

Trooper First Class Toby Hunter's funeral was heartrending. Dalton felt drained, devoid of emotions, as he joined the scores of brother troopers, family members and friends attending the ceremony. While the reverend performed the eulogy, Dalton zoned out and recalled the preserved memories he embraced of his unique former shift member. A chill came over him as the image of TK looking down the shiny barrel of his Beretta suddenly sprang into his mind. In his painful recollection, Dalton was conducting the monthly inspection, checking out TK's service weapon only three days before the happy-go-lucky trooper used it for the last time. Dalton shook the ugly memory from his head, and instead of joining the others at the Barstow cemetery, he made a spur-of-the moment decision and returned home.

Shortly after arriving there, Dalton Bragg hastily shed the MSP costume, donned a pair of faded blue jean cutoffs and a mesh tank top, slipped into a grungy old pair of sneakers. Snugging the flask in his back pocket, he rushed back out into the welcome fresh air. Soon, he was picking his way through the shell and rock-strewn beach, aiming for the looming cliffs up ahead. Except for a lone shark tooth collector searching the shoreline far to the south, the beach was empty.

He'd been running and hiking along the beachfront for some time now, and he'd found it to be a haven, one he could readily turn to when things had to be sorted out in his jumbled life. Today was one of those days when he needed the answers to more questions he knew he'd never understand.

The brooding, ash-gray sky easily matched his dour mood. He stopped for a moment and turned to face the bay. In the far distance, out in the shipping channel, he saw a tugboat pulling a loaded barge through the indigo water, traveling north to Baltimore, he suspected. White specks in the far distance, several power boats with outriggers stretched high above flying bridges, carved through the water, bound for fishing spots or still undecided destinations. Overall, the bay was calm, with hints of light breezes from the southwest brushing the surface, sending ripples skittering aimlessly. It was low tide, the water was fairly clear, and only gentle swells licked at the shoreline. An odor of stale must, earthy smells from the cliff sediment mixed with decaying beached seaweed clumps, hung in the air.

Dalton kicked off his sneakers, tied them together, and slung them over his shoulder. He waded shin-deep into the water and started sloshing north again. The tepid water felt good on his legs, and the smooth, sandy bottom made the going easy enough. Several times, alarmed by his sudden intrusion into their realm, small crabs—"blue claws"—darted away to deeper water, fleeing sideways with one claw dragging straight behind. And once, he almost waded into the pulsating, bell-shaped gelatinous head of a translucent sea nettle with long threads of stinging tentacles trailing behind it. He waded for a long time, slowly becoming uncharacteristically oblivious to most of his surroundings, as wistful thoughts of the amiable enigma he knew as TK flooded his mind with memories—and one giant, sorrowful question mark.

"Damn You! God Damn you, TK!" He shouted at the silent cliffs he suddenly faced. He thought briefly about climbing up to his Purgatory Ridge refuge, high above, but instead, he picked up a handful of smooth stones and craggy oyster shells. One by one, he angrily hurled them out into the bay. He set his jaw and fought hard to keep his eyes from misting up, as he turned around again. "Why, TK? You of all people! Why? Why end your life?" Dalton cried out to the chalky fossil shells in the thick blue clay of the cliff base. "Ain't none of us getting out of this gig alive, my friend, but why the hell ya have to rush it? Why didn't you let us know…*Why?*" he rasped through gritted teeth.

When he finally tired himself from bombarding the Chesapeake with stones and shells, Dalton somberly trudged over toward a downed tree hugging the shoreline. The tree was one of several that had recently tumbled from the cliff, after its roots finally lost their tenuous grip in the rain-soaked soil. The sergeant vaulted over the tree trunk and walked the shore for a few more minutes, until he spotted a sun-bleached log on the beach, several feet back from the waters edge.

Perfect place for a respite. He slumped down on it, then crossed his legs and stretched them out in front, allowing a bare heel to dig into soft, warm sand. The flask top was unscrewed, and Dalton tilted his head back to take a long swig of the tequila. In no time, he managed to guzzle down close to half of the burning liquor. Satisfied for the time being, he set the flask between his legs. Dalton gazed mindlessly at the lone blue heron silently stalking through the shallows nearby. Moments later he shifted his unfocused eyes toward the raucous fish crows. The scavengers were picking through the silver carcass of a keeper rockfish, likely gut-hooked, that had washed ashore further down the beach. With his head in his hands, alone and far removed from the presence of others, the sergeant allowed himself to quietly mourn the loss of another good friend and fellow trooper—and another piece of his soul.

Chapter 13

SIGNAL 13

Dalton eased his cruiser into a slot near the MSP gym, and then checked himself to make sure his stuff was suitably spiffy. Satisfied, he centered his Stetson, exited the cruiser, and walked briskly toward building "C," the familiar three-story brick headquarters housing the academy and personnel division. It was an early Monday morning; his last week on the force, and Dalton planned to review his retirement papers to avoid any last-minute glitches. Despite a strong aversion to being anywhere near the Pikesville complex, today seemed gloriously different, since it'd be his last visit.

Approaching the gym, Dalton abruptly stopped and focused on the redbrick four-story executive building looming on his right. Ahhhh, the MSP Puzzle Palace, the all-knowing, wisdom-spewing antithesis of the once-revered KISS acronym (Keep It Simple, Stupid). And in the overall scheme, all he'd amounted to them was a twenty-six year, four-number PIN (Personal Identification Number) for them to screw with. Dalton scowled at the palace for a few moments before breaking away.

Spotting the open side door of the gym, he backtracked down the walkway and curiously poked his head in. Good, no one there. Shoulders back and head held high, Dalton sauntered in. Awash in memories, he stood motionless, studying the familiar interior. A hint of a smile creased his face when he realized the place hadn't changed all that much in the twenty-six years since he'd toiled there with his fledgling academy classmates. The wretched chin-up bars were still there, bolted to the side walls, the loathsome, sweat-maker circuit training devices were stowed near the front entrance, and the thick, worn-out navy-blue judo mats were all neatly folded over. The wood gym floor was immaculate as always, and the torturous climbing ropes still dangled from high overhead. Dalton closed his eyes and took a deep breath. Christ, it even had the same funky smell, too—floor polish, vinyl and rubber scents, tinged with the unmistakable eau-desweat of the hundreds who'd trained so hard to become Maryland State Troopers. For a fleeting moment, he thought he heard the sadistic instructors barking out orders and taunts at the woeful recruits who could never do anything right or fast enough. Dalton grinned. With a dismissive headshake, he left the gym and strode over to building "C."

Climbing the steps to the main lobby, Dalton decided to make a quick impromptu visit to the academy second floor, the infamous dormitory. Again, he was lucky. The trooper candidate class was somewhere else. Dalton quietly meandered down the hallway until he came to room 204, paused, then looked in. Damn if they still weren't using those surplus metal dressers and chairs, and the lamentable metal beds with the thin mattresses and the ash-gray, heavy wool blankets! And as expected, everything was shipshape. Stuck in a moment, Dalton drifted back to distant memories. Mel Purvey, his long-deceased roommate, soon floated into view. Sprawled on his bunk, Mel was joking with him as usual in that low, staccato voice, while a twenty-six years younger Dalton hunkered down to review the day's motor vehicle law lesson with him. Once again they were bantering like young roosters, all the while having no idea, no queasy trepidations at all, about what lay ahead.

Catching himself quickly, Dalton reeled away and darted down the stairwell. He stopped to gaze at the glass-enclosed law-enforcement patch collection, the enormous MSP shield over the front door and the slew of MSP class plaques lining the walls, before continuing to the personnel section. After saluting and exchanging muted greetings with a haughty, preppie-face captain he'd neither seen or heard of before—the type who performed a mirror check every few minutes to make sure his precious hundred-dollar toupee was still in place—a gum-smacking secretary extracted his retirement papers from a cabinet and reviewed them with him. Everything seemed in order, and when Dalton asked to review his personnel file, the bubbly secretary retrieved the voluminous folder from a creaky revolving file rack, then ushered him to a vacant room.

Dalton took his time gleaning the thirty-plus letters he'd received over his career from the people who counted most, the grateful citizens of Maryland. Although Dalton greatly appreciated the multitude of

MSP awards he'd received, what made him glow even more was that batch of appreciative letters from the people whom he, and his fellow troopers before and after him, had sworn to serve. *That* was the whole ballgame, all it was really about, bottom line.

Leaving the room, Dalton was heartened to know that despite the setbacks on the job and in his personal life, he just might have made a small difference, after all. He gave the file back to the obliging secretary and thought about having one last, dank coffee in the MSP cafeteria for old times' sake. Coming to his senses, he dismissed the thought outright, realizing he'd probably run into some brass there—an unneeded thrill he felt obliged to avoid. Instead, he walked back into the lobby and left the academy from the front entrance.

Stepping outside, he blinked and squinted when the brilliant, late-morning sun hit him. Slowly, the images in front evolved into a familiar panorama that had changed little over the years. The tranquil, grassy courtyard with the nosy squirrels cavorting under the oaks, the red-brick headquarters buildings bordering the courtyard, the flagpoles with waving flags, everything was the same—until the surprising spectacle of something he'd heard about, but had never seen, slowly materialized. He walked down the steps, his eyes glued on the shiny, walnut-brown, pyramid shaped Maryland State Police "Fallen Heroes" memorial in front of the academy building. The memorial was the product of efforts by several MSP alumni who'd toiled for years to make their dreams come true. Immersed in thought, Dalton drifted down the white brick walkway. Suddenly, his mouth went dry, and his fingers twitched, as his eyes settled on the gold-tinged words under the outline of the Maryland State Trooper's badge:

They gave so such ...For their sacrifice the People of Maryland will always be grateful. Their dedication, contribution and memory will always be part of the Maryland State Police.

Like a magnet, Dalton drew closer to the white granite memorial base to read the sculpted brass names of the thirty-seven fellow troopers who'd sacrificed their lives in the line of duty. Of the more recent fallen heroes, there were several he'd known but had never directly worked with. When he came to Sgt Randall Branham's name, Dalton knelt down on one knee and lightly traced a finger over the nameplate of the renowned Eastern Shore trooper he'd known too briefly. Still kneeling, he scanned the names for the two fallen-hero troopers who were his academy classmates. His fingertips first rested on the nameplate of his roommate Mel Purvey. He paused, let out a sigh, then stretched his arm out and settled his shaking fingers on Mike Fox's cold nameplate. Instantly, his jaw quivered, and a hard lump formed in his throat. Dalton swallowed and took a deep breath, then unpinned the Governor's Citation ribbon from his uniform shirt. "This is yours now, brother," he whispered as he set the ribbon over Mike's nameplate.

Dalton blinked his glistening eyes and struggled back to his feet. Backing up several paces from the memorial, he snapped his heels and stood at ramrod attention. For the last hand salute he would ever render in his MSP career, Dalton Bragg crisply saluted his fallen comrades, then turned and briskly walked away. Under the hastily donned sunglasses, he felt confident that no one had seen the pained, glazed-over eyes of a veteran MSP sergeant.

On his way back to Calvert County, Dalton decided against returning to the barrack, knowing full well that the "first shirt" never expected to see him the rest of the day, anyhow. Tired of listening to FM rock, he turned off the radio and broke out a small cigar. Time to ruminate a bit about his MSP past and his fate beyond the department. "Bittersweet" was the kindest word he could think of to describe his distorted sentiments at the moment. He took a shortcut at Wayson's Corner, then Rt 4 south to Calvert County. Two miles into the county, he smiled when he spotted several Canadian geese grazing in a cornfield beside Yellow Bank Road. On his left, directly across the lanes of the busy dual highway, a new, bustling McDonald's stood in sharp contrast to the opposite side's rustic scene.

Yup, with all the new developments sprouting up like crabgrass, this county's going to hell in a hand basket for sure, Dalton mused. He took a last drag on the cigar butt, killed it in the ashtray, and then flipped it out the window. Just before Dunkirk Plaza, he made a right turn on Ferry Landing road and continued until he came to the gravel driveway of the peaceful Presbyterian Church. Dalton parked the cruiser in back, unsnapped his seatbelt, but left the engine running. For a few reflective moments he stared blankly through the windshield, until his fingers came alive to drum on the steering wheel, synchronizing with the staccato clicks of the turn signal he'd left on. With a weary sigh, he turned the ignition off, exited the cruiser and strode through the grove of tall oaks in front of the sunlit Asbury cemetery. On the way to his friends' resting place, his eyes took in the name on each headstone he passed.

Surprisingly, a familiar name jumped out, and he paused to fixate on the headstone at his feet that bore the engraved name of Mike Garber. "Sooo, this is where you finally wound up, you ole warhorse," Dalton murmured at the marker. He knew that Garber had died a few years ago, but he never knew where they'd taken him for his eternal dirt nap. Some of his reminiscing friends felt that "Iron" Mike died of a broken heart, while most others insisted that the bottle had done him in for sure. Whichever, Dalton felt remorse, knowing that the gregarious former North Beach Police officer had departed in his mid fifties—way before his time. He tipped his Stetson and smiled, remembering when "Iron" Mike once joked to him about how he wanted nothing but a parking meter showing an *expired* sign over his grave when he finally kicked the hell out of the bucket. Instead, only a cold granite slab stood vigil over him now.

Dalton trudged on until he'd almost reached the wood-line. A few steps further and he was staring at Colby Merson's headstone. Someone had draped a white plastic-bead necklace over the granite marker, and there was a bouquet of multi-colored, sun-faded plastic flowers propped against the base. Dalton fumbled in his shirt pocket and brought out one of the MSP collar ornaments he'd saved for the occasion. Being the thankless barrack supply officer gave him certain pilfering advantages. He removed the clasps from the ornament posts then knelt down and gently pressed the MSP shield into the grass, just inches from his friend's headstone.

Dalton patted the side of the headstone and stood up, but before leaving, he leaned over and plucked the bead necklace from Colby's marker. With a muttered curse, he tossed it deep into the woods. Next, he yanked the bouquet of plastic flowers out of the ground and lobbed it into the woods also. 'No, my friend, with your outrageous zest for life, you were far, far away from being a plastic persona, at least in my eyes," he whispered.

Dalton roamed aimlessly until he finally found Donny Roberts' grave. The flat granite plaque in the ground was weed-choked and half hidden. He pulled the weeds back to see the name Roberts, and then pressed another MSP collar ornament into the grass in front of the plain marker. Too many unanswered questions, so many stale postulations about what so dreadfully happened in his short life. To Dalton, however, Donny had been a fellow trooper, an obliging older brother who'd bonded with him when he was just a boot trooper many years ago, at a time when Donny needed them all more than they ever knew.

Lost in thoughts, Dalton trudged back to the cruiser and left the churchyard to head south. When he arrived at Hallowing Point Road in Prince Frederick, he turned right and continued for several miles until he came to the small, fenced-in cemetery bordering the quaint Barstow Methodist Church. Several large cedar trees were scattered throughout the graveyard, making it difficult to spot the burial site he was looking for, but minutes later he was standing in mute silence next to Toby Hunter's grave.

For a fleeting moment, Dalton listened to the mesmerizing wind whisking through the cedar boughs overhead. The lolling serenity was punctuated by the snapping of the fluttering American flag planted next to Toby K. Hunter's headstone. Dalton's gaze slipped from TK's engraved name to the inscription beneath, "Ours for the brief moment, now with Jesus and the angels forever."

Maybe someday, somehow, he'd be able to visualize the full light of the Lord, but for now, Dalton only saw the loss of a good friend and fellow trooper, nothing more, nothing less.

As if on cue, he suddenly felt a strange chill in the air, a hint of a hazy premonition that made him uneasy. He jerked his head around and gazed back at the church, his skittish eyes immediately darting up to the burnished metal cross atop the steeple. Staring at the holy symbol, his mind raced back to those unfathomable, certain-death times he'd experienced over his long career. Including the Kenwood Beach incident, there were more than a handful. Somehow, against the odds, he'd survived them all, when he knew, deep down, that he shouldn't have. Probably happened to most troopers and LE types during their careers, but some of his fellow officers, of course, hadn't been so fortunate, and they'd paid the ultimate price.

Dalton nodded at the cross in a vain effort to acknowledge his lukewarm belief in what it exemplified to him. "Whatever you are, God, Mohammed, and Buddha or maybe even the Great Spirit in the Sky...and for whatever you stand for in this world and in my life," he murmured, "I owe you for the divine intervention, OK?" Dalton casually saluted the cross with a two-fingered peace sign and turned his attention back to TK's grave. The last collar ornament was gently pressed into the ground between TK's headstone and the wind-blown American Flag. His mission done, Dalton left the desolate graveyard and set out for his Calvert Beach cottage.

There were several phone messages—one from Diane, good buddy Gary, and a funny blurb from his brother Jon. He picked up the phone and started mashing buttons to call Diane first. Catching himself, he eased the phone back down. Maybe later. As an afterthought, he sifted through the day's mail. When he found the current issue of the quarterly *Trooper* magazine, he almost opened it, but tossed it on the coffee table instead. For now, he just wasn't in the mood for the glossy, vanilla essence the Maryland Trooper's Association magazine imparted to its MSP family. Hats off to them for trying, though. Shedding his gun belt and uniform, Dalton slipped into jogging shorts and a ragged "Sloppy Joe's" T-shirt.

Minutes later, he was ambling barefoot along the warm, sandy beach, hoping that another vitalizing walk in the sun might diffuse pressing issues. For a few unfettered moments, Dalton felt at peace with himself, although at best, he knew he was just one railcar short of being a psychological train wreck waiting to happen. The early June sky was clear, and the offshore breeze shimmering across the water brought him the sweet, piquant smell of the Chesapeake. There was freedom, temporary at best but freedom nonetheless, out here in the splendid openness, almost enough to make him feel very much alive again—for a while. Yes, he could flop down on a sand bank, throw his endless dreams and dashed aspirations at the Eastern Shore, and just watch the boats, birds and the rest of the world slip by forever, if he dared.

Hours later and somewhat re-energized, Dalton dragged himself from the beach and back to the cottage. Tomorrow was his last late shift on the job. Tonight, up to and well past the midnight hour, he'd be afforded with another blessed evening of imbibing. Damn the nightmares and full speed ahead, he reckoned, as the first of too many beers was liberated from the fridge.

#

On that Friday late shift, Dalton's last day to wear an MSP costume and hand-cannon, things evolved smoothly for the silverback sergeant. En route to the barrack, Dalton stopped at the Prince Frederick Post Office and slipped the passel of letters into the drive-through slot. Days before, he'd finally finished them all, despite the building angst surrounding his fast-approaching last day. Crossing the street, he guided the cruiser to the rear of the dimly lit Prince Frederick library, where he removed half a dozen bulky cardboard boxes from the trunk. One by one, the unwieldy boxes were lugged to the back door.

Moments later, Dalton was at the barrack. He punched the combination buttons on the back door lock and entered the lower foyer, dutifully signing in on the log as Jimi Hendrix, making sure to add the exact time Jimi Hendrix arrived. Never did fathom why the troopers had to sign in on the barrack log, when the PCO recorded them in the radio log after they radioed they were at the barrack. Another MSP quirk. Dalton stared up at the long flight of steps leading to the first floor. With a weary look, he clambered up the stairs and ambled down the hallway to the duty officer's pit.

It had been a quiet day, with neither the first sergeant nor the lieutenant working, and, accordingly, both secretaries were long gone. Other than to let Dalton know that his group had miraculously reported in (It *was* a Friday afternoon), Ben Wiley, the early shift DO, had little to brief him on. Before leaving, Ben reminded Dalton that he was picking him up the following Friday to take him to the supply division for his uniform and equipment turn-in. Dalton was momentarily surprised, but he caught himself quickly. "Yeah, buddy, I'll be a-waitin' for ya with bells on my fingers and rings on my toes...maybe one in my nose, or some shit like that," Dalton quipped to his erstwhile cohort. Idle chatter tapered off, and Ben left after playfully slapping his short-timer pal on the back.

Dalton sorted through his mailbox and played catch-up with paperwork before calling in Barney Stuart, his last-ever road corporal, to fill in as the DO. His easygoing corporal had few qualms about sitting behind the desk, especially since it gave him a chance to hobnob more with wacky Francis, the late-shift PCO. After sharing a few lame jokes with Stuart, Dalton retreated to the sergeant's room. While he cleaned out his desk and file cabinet, the sergeant reminisced about the past few years. But when he felt a tinge of sappiness seeping through, he jerked himself out of the mushy mind-set. No room for any whoosie time today, big guy, he told himself. Dalton boxed up everything that wasn't trashed, and then stashed the boxes in U-17, his 1998 Ford Crown "Vic" cruiser.

Back inside the barrack, Dalton wandered through the lower level for a last, obligatory look-see. He lingered in the conference room for a while, marveling at the numerous plaques and trophies lining the walls. Good ole Barrack "U" Prince Frederick! Of all the other full-service barracks throughout the state, Dalton couldn't imagine any of them coming even close in comparison to his legendary Prince Frederick barrack. Returning to the upper level, Dalton meandered through the troopers' room, pausing to chuckle at the cross-eyed "Jack-a-lope" head mounted on the wall, before continuing on his barrack tour.

As a final salute to the new barrack commander, Dalton taped a glossy *Playboy* playmate of the month foldout to the back of the lieutenant's open door. Perhaps when the next rogue Pikesville Palace Prince came down for another closed-door bitch-session, his lieutenant's attention would be gratefully diverted for a few precious moments. Before he made it back to the DO's pit, Dalton stuffed his coveted Dallas Cowboys Cheerleader Calendar and a recent *Power Realm* weight-lifting magazine into an envelope and shoved it in Ben Wiley's file cabinet. He stealthily made his way out to the secretaries' office and slipped two cards halfway under Pearl and Cheryl's desk blotters before meandering into the first sergeant's office. With mischief lighting up his face, he unscrewed the desk phone's bottom section and taped over the small microphone holes with heavy-duty Scotch tape. Laughing out loud, Dalton screwed the section back on and artfully dusted black fingerprint powder over the top end of the receiver. He waited in the dark office for several minutes while his laughter died down, before he traipsed over to the detective sergeant's office.

As always, Detective Sergeant DeLauder, sage sleuth that he was, kept his office door locked to evade the barrack jesters. Unable to mess with the D/Sgt's beloved computer, Dalton thought about squirting crazy glue into the keyhole. He decided against it, then turned around and did it anyway, making sure to drain the tube's entire contents.

He'd already taken care of Ernie the caretaker days before, when he presented him a 60's era National Beer lighted clock he'd recently found at a yard sale. Ernie always thought that the National Beer logo on the clock, "From the Land of Pleasant Living," was the Maryland State motto. He watched in amusement as Ernie's face exploded into a wide, semi-toothless grin.

"Sarge...Sergeant Bragg...Ya done got me good with this here Natty Bo clock," Ernie spouted, as Dalton tried to sidestep him. "Aw, Sarge, for that, er...I gotta tell ya my newest joke yet, OK?" Dalton paused to placate him. "Ok, looky here, ummm...Let's see how that one went." Ernie pulled on his stubbled chin, deep in thought. "Yeah, I got it now, Sarge! OK. How's can ya tell if a lawyer's well-hung, huh, Sarge, huh?" Dalton shirked his shoulders and raised his eyebrows. "Got ya on this one, I knows I do, Sarge, heh, heh. Ok, the onlyest way you can tell if a lawyer's well-hung, is when you can't fit your finger between the rope and his dick!"

Ernie guffawed loudly and stomped his feet. Dalton merely stared at him with a blank expression until the caretaker finally blew his nose, signaling the end of his hysterics. "Ernie, you mean his *neck* , not his dick, right?" Ernie looked at him sheepishly for a moment, his face turning red. With a nervous cough and a few lame "Heh-heh-hehs," he fingered the bill of his greasy ball cap. "Yeah, I guess that was it, come to think of it. Anyways, thanks for the clock, Sarge. Ya know, I'm gonna go right home and hang this here sucker over my bed," he sputtered back. He probably will, Dalton thought as he smiled and walked away, wondering how on earth he'd ever be able to endure the rest of his life without Ernie being in it.

Finally, everything was in order, and after squaring things away with Corporal Stuart, Dalton blew a grossly exaggerated kiss to Francis who sat stoop-shouldered at the radio console, primed to resume her one-sided conversation with the numb-looking corporal. She waved back as Dalton strode from the lobby to patrol away the last few hours of the shift. Later, when Francis checked her file drawer again, he hoped she'd be pleased with *The Road Less Traveled* self-help book he left for her. Maybe she'd have better luck with it than he had.

His farewell present for his corporal, a set of sergeant's stripes, had been stuffed into an envelope and left in his mailbox. Dalton hoped that Stuart, the dexterous supervisor that he'd become, would be wearing them soon enough. And for each road trooper in his motley shift, Dalton shoved black-ink ballpoint pens in their mailboxes to assist them in their ever-demanding MSP writing endeavors.

For his farewell parade, the retiring sergeant aimed U-17 north on Route 4 and zipped away from Prince Frederick. He took a hard, tire-squealing turn onto Plum Point Road and followed it down to the Route 261 split. At the split, Dalton veered left and continued down the winding, single-lane country road at a high rate until he came to the hilly straightaway leading to the twin beaches. Slowing down, he drove through quiet Chesapeake Beach.

He'd almost reached the town limit of North Beach, when he got caught up in a moment and pulled the cruiser off the road. In a flash, the driver's window zipped down. Yeah, buddy! Despite the ongoing renovations and the surge of new condos and office buildings built in the twin beaches over the last twenty years, he could always count on one feature to remain status quo—that funky, all-pervasive swamp-gas sulfur smell that perfumed the area whenever the bay tides ran low.

He slowly cruised along the North Beach main drag. Except for a scantily clad, heavily tattooed, drunken biker babe who licked her lips and shook her bloated butt at him when he passed, he found nothing exciting, so he swung his mechanical steed back down the main drag. At the Route 261 and Route 260 intersection, the sergeant left the twin beaches, following Route 260 to its end at Route 4 and the Calvert County line. Gunning the cruiser enough to squeal tires and lay down some decent rubber, he whipped left onto Route 4 to start his trek back south.

Dalton switched on the FM radio and fumbled with the knobs, searching for some suitable ambience. After passing over several droning country-music stations—and barely missing a terrified possum that was crazily jerking back and forth in the fast lane—Dalton found a decent-enough station. Thank his lucky stars! It was a hard-rock station playing moldy oldies, a station from Easton across the bay, and he locked it in. Other than for routine calls and the half-hour time checks, the MSP radio was dead quiet. Mountain's *Mississippi Queen*, one of his all-time favorites, started blaring, and Dalton cranked up the volume to savor the hard-driving ditty. *"Mississippi Queen!* You *go,* girlfriend!"* he shouted, as he drummed a loose hand on the steering wheel to match the thundering tempo accented by that funky cowbell. In no time, he zipped through Dunkirk flats. By the time he was streaking down Hall's Creek Hill, the *Queen* had fled the airwaves, replaced by a wretched old bubble-gummish Barry Manilow tune—so the volume was instantly jacked down.

Rolling through Huntingtown, Dalton pondered on the profuse changes that had overtaken the quiet, rustic "Charm of the Chesapeake" since his boot trooper arrival at the PF post that summer of 1974. For starters, the population had quadrupled, as the suburbanites, hoping to flee from the hustle and chaos of PG County and beyond, continued their southern migration in droves. With the skyrocketing influx, demand for services mounted drastically, and the county government was going bonkers to keep up. From two traffic lights in 1974, now there were two dozen, with many more on the state's drawing boards. More schools were built, with several others in planning. Morning and evening rush hours on the Route 4 main corridor had turned it into a high-speed raceway for the local natives who dared to venture out during those precarious hours.

From the birth of Hardees's, once the county's only fast-food outlet, to the current plethora of McDammit's, Wendy's, Arby's and a dozen other major franchises, most of the Honey Suckle Café home-style cooking eateries were gone, except for the delectable Frying Pan in Lusby and maybe one or two others. The waning days of warm and friendly personal service had been eclipsed by speedy indifference.

"Hey, hon," the chummy waitress at the Honey Suckle Café would whisper, catty-like, to those she knew well as she poured coffee, "Have you heard that Trudi's aunt Jenny done went and dyed her hair platinum-blonde last week? I coulda slapped her upside the head myself, and Lordy be if that po' woman ain't catchin' holy hell from her snippity-minded bowling team members now! And geez oh mighty, hold on ta yourself now! Ya heard the newest about that lil tramp Anna Belle Turner gettin' it on with that weasel-eyed lawyer, Barry-what's-his name? Them two wuz in bed doin' the nasty the minute his wife took off for that weeklong Florida family vacation. Somethin' goin' on there, you bet ya!"

No More.

Home-cooked, mouth-watering meals and sumptuous homemade deserts, all filling victuals made with care by native hearts, had been superseded by boorishly automated fast-food quarter-pounders, buckets of greasy fried chicken, limp French fries, soggy Mex-Tex burritos and assembly-line milkshakes. Whatever fast food conveniences the fleeing suburbanite refugees were accustomed to, were expected to follow them down. Those homey, wood-floored mom & pop country stores that once provided most of the staples for the locals, those unique stores that displayed counter top glass jars of reddish-pink pickled pig's feet soaked in brine, whole cucumbers in tangy vinegar mix and those soft boiled eggs cured in who knows what, felt the pressure, as the Wal-Mart and K-Mart super twins arrived to signal their inevitable death knells.

With the exploding invasion of the "bedroom community" masses, land development had mushroomed. Farmers working and living on ancestors' estates felt the rising pressure to sell, as land values and property taxes soared, and many of the hard-pressed natives eventually succumbed to the tempting overtures of the ravenous developers. Since the early seventies, it was apparent to most that the rush for land had kicked into high gear. Few, however, could imagine that by the end of the nineties, there would be fewer tobacco fields remaining in the county than there were county commissioners.

There were other subtle signs, of course: No more of the once-prolific "Keep Calvert Country" bumper stickers, either.   Sadly, "Culvert" County, the once alluring "Charm of the Chesapeake," was being eroded by the inevitable onslaught of "progress."

And when hard-core farmer Judge Mordeci G. Mackall, one of the most rooted of all "Culvert" countians, finally pulled the plug and sold his farm to escape the madness and alight on thirty acres of peace in the Blue Ridge mountains, the not-so-subtle message resonated loud and clear. Ole Issac Silverman, the county's once premier statesman, just had to be sputtering in his grave.

On the public-safety side, the calls for service skyrocketed, taxing the limited resources of all emergency services. As the increasingly proficient Sheriff's Department swelled in numbers to answer the demand, Dalton, and most of the barrack's old salts, realized the MSP presence in the county would, at best, remain stagnant, as it had during the previous fifteen years.   By the mid nineties, the Sheriff's Department had overtaken MSP in manpower and service calls.

After passing through Prince Frederick, Dalton pulled over and lit up a stogie. He puffed until it glowed bright red, and then zipped down the driver's window so he could spit out a few sprigs of loose tobacco. It was a super-clear night with a starry sky, and traffic was almost zilch. Dalton coughed and blew out a mouthful of smoke, when he heard the beginning stanza of *Born to be Wild* burst from the radio. For a fleeting moment he thought he'd pass it up, but for old time's sake, he knew he couldn't.   Before turning the FM up full-blast, he called to the MSP south patrol unit. "U-17, U-31...10-20?"   Brief pause.   "U-31, U-17, I'm at the Solomons office with Deputy Evans...You have a message, sir?" the lethargic voice answered. "Negative, U-31, I'll contact you later, 10-4?" *Super!* Both south patrol units were out of the picture. Dalton jacked up the radio and revved the engine.   "Got my mojo running...!" He took a long drag on the stogie, tossed the soggy butt out the window, and checked the rearview. One car swooshed by, and when he saw the taillights fading away, the coast was clearer than the sky overhead.

"Lookin' for direction...and whatever gets in my way!" A grin captured his face, and his pulse shot up like a spastic rocket. *"Aw screw it!"* he shouted. Dalton switched the high beams on and mashed down on the gas pedal, aiming the barreling cruiser into the southbound fast lane. Damned Crown "Vic" was way overdue for a "carbon check," anyhow. When the speedometer read eighty, he gripped the steering wheel with both hands and straddled the broken middle-lane markings. His pulse rocketed, as the roaring air assaulted the windshield again. "Kickin' ass, my man...*You're kickin' ass!"* Dalton yelled with unfettered glee. *Born to be wild!*

Warping to triple-digit speed, he spotted the glowing pair of eyes owned by the bedazzled, elephant-size, twelve-point buck standing in the middle of the southbound lanes. The electrified sergeant hit the siren switch and sighed with instant relief as the frantic whitetail bounded back into the woods. "Jesus H Christ!" he thundered at the windshield. "That's all I needed...a frickin' departmental with the Arnold Schwartzeneger of all deer...And on my last day, too!" During his career, Dalton had managed to splatter three of the white-tailed kamikaze car-demolishers; all three splattered in good ole Calvert County.

Faster and faster, the cruiser careened down the highway, the sergeant all the while maintaining his white-knuckle grip on the steering wheel, trying hard to rivet his shaky attention on the rushing road ahead. "Just a born wild child, baby!" When the cruiser finally hit the bottom grade at Parker's Creek, the speedometer was pushing one hundred and twenty-five, and Steppenwolf's legendary song of the sixties was fading out. Nice fare-thee-well rush, Dalton thought, as he shot past German Chapel road.

Still, it hadn't quite compared to the adrenaline rush he'd treated himself to after one late shift in '76 on that special moonlit night when he'd performed a spur-of-the moment, lights-out "carbon check" on the Bay Bridge on his way home. That night, the speedometer on the specially souped-up 1973 Dodge Polara read one hundred and thirty-six, and the sleek, unmarked cruiser was steadily accelerating toward mach one when Dalton backed it off before hitting the Eastern Shore terra firma. Ahh, those times ya never forget, he mused.

Dalton was zooming down St Leonard Hill, still on route 4, when Free's *All Right Now* hit the airwaves. For a split-second he thought about doing another "carbon check." Instead, he reluctantly reached over and turned off the radio. Two "carbon checks" in one night was supposed to be beaucoup bad luck, according to Marty Metzger, his incorrigible shift-mate from the early days.

For several more miles, Dalton rode in pensive silence. When he crested the rise at Dowell road, he saw the blinking red lights of the prominent Thomas Johnson Bridge linking Calvert to St. Mary's, her sister county. Dalton's mind drifted back to the Spring of 1977 when he watched the heavy-lift helicopters fluttering back and forth, low over the river, hauling huge buckets of concrete for the bridge pilings. The bridge, a southern county evacuation route in the event of a nuclear plant fiasco (major cluster-fuck ala MSP jargon), assured that the county's south end would build up and sprawl.

Dalton gunned the cruiser when he passed the new Patuxent Shopping center and its fast- food outlets, then tooled down the main drag leading to Solomons Island. For a moment, he thought about scooting down to the tip of the island to the Chesapeake Biological Lab, thought about parking the cruiser along the bulwark to watch the late-night touch-and-go antics of the test aircraft across the river at the bustling Patuxent Naval Air Station. Instead, he pulled off just before the bantam causeway bridge, which qualified Solomons Island as a true island. Nope, not tonight.

He kicked U-17 into a gravel-churning U-turn and headed north again. Of course, he'd always appreciate the Calvert Marine Museum exhibits, along with the Light Tower Inn, Jesse's Fisherman's Wharf and Yvette's superb China Coast restaurant—and he'd always have a forever place in his heart for the Kon Tiki bar and Bowen's Café, too— but tonight, he just didn't feel like driving down the flashy, bar-strewn gauntlet again. Maybe in another life.

Minutes later, the sergeant maneuvered the cruiser up a dark, off-road ramp several hundred yards north of the nuclear power plant entrance. He backed up to the wood line, zipped the driver window down, and turned the ignition off. Nice, obscure niche, out of view from any traffic. Dalton jacked up the police radio until it squelched, turned it down a hair, then snatched another cigar from under the visor. After a crucial "station identification" nature call in the wood shadows, he lit up and sauntered back to the cruiser.

Propped against the driver's door, he took a few short drags and lazily gazed up at the stars. Several commercial jets passed high above, and the Little Dipper was clear, but for the moment, he zoned them out. The music had been a diversion, but it hadn't masked the remembrances of his twenty-six years in MSP. Maybe it was the handful of scattered homemade crosses, some arrayed with garlands of flowers, balloons and pictures, others landscaped with stone—the decorated shrines alongside the highway that were left as memorials to the road crusaders who'd perished before their times. *Yes,* maybe they'd foisted the melancholy mood on him.

During his final tour as a sworn trooper, Dalton passed many scenes along the way, each bringing back deep memories. There was that grisly double fatal at the county line many years ago. It was so bitterly cold that night that the pooled blood, yellowish brain matter, and fragments of stark-white, blood-speckled skull, had frozen solid before the two mangled bodies were cut out from what was left of the Toyota Corolla. So cold, that both his and Trooper Newman's pens froze up right after they pulled them from their pockets. And *there,* in that yellow split-level house perched high on the bank overlooking Route 4 in Dunkirk, was the house where he'd investigated his fifth suicide, a very untidy, twelve-gauge, rifled slug-to-the-stomach deal back in '77. The acrid smell of cordite and the blanketing cloud of chalky gun smoke still hung in the air, while the dead teen's lifeless eyes were fixed on the blaring TV.

And there were all those other maelstroms—the domestics and fight calls, knifings and shootings at the Collard Club in Huntingtown and the Twin Cedar Bar in Lusby, the rowdy fiascos in the twin beaches and various other raucous spots in the county. How about those drag racing, testosterone-charged teens who kissed their lives away that early spring evening when both of their cars went airborne into the woods just before Hunting Creek Bridge? Talkin' about some serious Hamburger-Helper on that bloody scene, folks. Hard to forget the countless horrors of LE experiences that he and his fellow troopers and deputies had seen over the years.

And how could he easily shrug off the reality that the Cypress Creek Bridge, marking Colby Merson's fatal accident, was only a few hundred yards from where he stood alone in the dark right now? *God*, how he'd sorely missed Colby and his all-pervasive exuberance over all those slow passing years. What haunted him relentlessly was that he'd missed them *all* so much. Too much! From Mel Purvey, his academy roommate, and TK, a shift favorite, to Mike Fox, another academy mate, Sergeant Branham, Donny Roberts, Nate Odom and all his other long-gone MSP brothers and sisters. Over the years, they'd *all* become irreplaceable. If only he could turn back time, if only he could re-visit those earlier days of naiveté and die-hard camaraderie. If only—!

Dalton took a last drag from the cigar stub and cleared his throat. He ground the glowing cigar tip into the macadam, then craned his head up for a look at the Little Dipper hanging high overhead. "Enough of this dumb ass horseshit, Sergeant," he muttered to Ursa Minor glittering back at him, as he fumbled in his pocket for the keys.

Dalton was soon back at the cottage in his sweat pants and T-shirt, his crossed legs resting on the coffee table in front of a blank TV screen, and an eighteen-pack of Busch nestled beside him on the ragged-out leather couch. What wasn't guzzled tonight, was extra hooch for tomorrow's retirement party. The blinking red light on the phone pod signaled messages. With an annoyed grunt, Dalton rose from the couch and yanked the phone jack from the outlet. No more diversions needed.

God, if only he'd met Diane earlier, long before the wretched desolation and despair had so totally paralyzed him. In the sunny days of those better years, she would have fit into his life like a warm glove. Before he snapped the first beer tab, Dalton turned off the floor light, leaving the cottage in comforting darkness. Satisfied, he popped the tab and gazed idly through the living room plate-glass window. Other than the lone streetlight partly veiled by a lofty pine tree, there was nothing to see. Thankfully, it was all Dalton wanted to see on the night before the big shindig marking his departure from the MSP world. Soon enough, the demons would surface to attack him with another hellacious nightmare, and the "tiger" would angrily twitch itself awake again, just like every dreadful night he'd endured the past few years. For the fleeting moment, he basked in the soothing tranquility while he could.

(Purgatory Ridge)

The silverback Barrack "U" sergeant squinted his bloodshot eyes and raised the pint bottle of tequila up high against the background of ugly, black storm clouds gathering across the bay. *Damn!* Empty bottle. He cursed and drained the last drop of cactus nectar into his gaping mouth. Tossing the bottle aside, Dalton frowned and ransacked the knapsack again, hoping to find more reinforcements. Arrgghhh! SOL there, he mouthed a silent curse and picked up his trusty Beretta again.

Fighting fuzzy vision and the emerging throes of a searing, kick-ass headache, the sergeant surprisingly maneuvered the gun into reasonable sight alignment—he hoped. *Blam!* The first shot zinged wide to the right. With a loud roar, eyes blazing with cold fury, the "tiger" in his head leaped to its feet! Dalton closed his left eye and focused hard with his right, as the empty tequila bottle wavered in the sights. "Hold still, lil baby," he muttered softly, "One more time for Pappa, OK?" *Blam!* Another miss, and worse yet, the frickin' gun jammed! Instantly, jagged pain shot through his temples, signaling the "tiger's" rage. OK, OK, he remembered it now. "Gotta do that "rrrrap, sssslap and tttap" crap, to clear the damn bbbbitch," he slurred aloud. Dalton fumbled through the routine once, then again, finally slapping his hand against the back of the slide in a frenzied effort to make things right. Glancing down, he realized that the gun hadn't jammed at all. The Beretta was empty, emptier than the Tequila pint bottle, as evidenced by the locked back slide and a barren chamber. Dalton ejected the magazine, then thumbed the release and slammed the slide forward before tossing his trusty metallic friend on the knapsack. With a weary sigh, he shut his woody eyes and rubbed his aching forehead with shaking hands.

Yeah, no doubt about it, those last few dragged-out MSP years were tough bitches. When added to the crumbling family life, those years became a recipe for disaster. But nonetheless, he doggedly persevered and stayed in the game. All told, those naive, indelible first few years on the job—the potpourri of better times in his life—were the ones he'd cherish forever. Too bad the ugly reality of it all translated into the stark awareness that there never was that "somewhere over the rainbow," right Mom?

In the distance, Dalton heard the approaching thunder, felt the goose bumps rising on his taunt forearms, as the howling winds announced the oncoming storm. The rumbling monster was less than halfway across the bay, and moving fast. Dark, ugly masses of angry clouds were swirling together, forming a solid line of attack. " *Turn out the lights, the party's over, 'cause Elvis is leavin' the building, folks!"* The sergeant grunted and launched himself from the base of the tree. Struggling to stay upright on shaky feet, he shook his head and fell back against the tree trunk, but steadied himself enough to stand up tall.

Dalton flinched and nearly dropped the Beretta, when the twin-pronged, white lightning bolt streaked from the sky to strike the bay surface several hundred yards off. The deafening thunderclap followed immediately, and he recoiled from the close shock. Still, he was on his feet. *Crack!* Another jagged spear of unharnessed electricity, followed a split-second later by its horrendous peal, jolted him violently. The sergeant smirked and shook his head when he spotted the approaching sheets of rain pelting the whitecaps of the troubled bay. "Ya know," he muttered in resignation, "it really, *really* sucks to be me, sometimes!" He never did feel comfortable about toasting himself anyhow, he mused, stooping over to pick up the knapsack.

He hadn't reckoned with the ire of his enraged "tiger," however, and his adversary from hell hated being spurned. A wave of pain, a red-hot, jarring pain worse than he'd ever felt in his head before, drove him instantly to his knees. Dalton closed his aching eyes, and with a loud animal cry, clasped both hands tightly over his ears. Slack-jawed and gasping for air, he rocked back and forth in a crazy, possessed manner. He heard piercing screams, tortured lost souls wailing in agony. He wasn't sure if the screams were his, or if they were the eternal screams of the old couple helplessly trapped in the wreckage of their fully engulfed car in Sunderland on that warm spring afternoon in 1980. Dalton and the other trooper arrived too late to save them, but they'd arrived just in time to hear the last of their blood curdling shrieks in the ravaging flames.

Seconds were hours, as the excruciating pain in his head lingered. Trying to tough it out, he found himself tumbling into a black void. As suddenly as it came, the pain lifted, allowing him time to funnel his splintered thoughts. "Get up, Troop! Get your lame ass *up!*" ordered the stern voice in his head. Dalton struggled to focus his eyes on the knapsack lying next to him. When the blur cleared, he picked up the Beretta and wedged it firmly under his belt. The howling wind battered the saplings and branches unmercifully, but the sergeant forced himself to his feet again and faced the oncoming storm. Even in all its formidable fury, the sight of it was frightfully exhilarating, magnificently awesome! Dalton stumbled and bent over low, trying to shield his squinted eyes from the whipping wind. Cautiously, he shuffled closer to the edge of the cliff.

Crack! Another lightning flash, this one on his immediate right, followed by an ear-shattering thunderclap! The ground shook like jelly, and his body trembled from the concussion. A spear of white-hot pain shot through his head, announcing the "tiger's" outrage. "Come on, you furry striped bastard...That the best you can do?" he yelled into the wind. Dalton shook his head and crouched, spreading his unsteady legs farther apart. Fighting for balance, he fumbled around in a pocket of his jeans until his fingers closed on what they sought. With vacant eyes, he stared down at the gold MSP badge clenched in his hand. On a sudden, angry impulse, he curled his index finger around the top of the badge and whipped his arm back, ready to hurl the cursed medallion into the wind.

Helplessly frozen in place and gasping wildly, Dalton battled the bedeviling sentiments whirling in his head. After several anxious moments, the veteran sergeant breathed a sigh of relief and slowly swung his arm back around. For a long moment he stared wide-eyed at the badge in disbelief. He rubbed his thumb lightly over the embossed outline of the ever-vigilant, spread-winged eagle perched over the *Trooper* inscription. His eyes shifted to the motto, *Fatti Maschi Parole Femine* (Strong deeds, gentle words), engraved below the Maryland emblem, just above the *State Police* inscription. Finally, with the hint of a smile, the sergeant brought the badge up to his face and pressed it tightly against his lips.

The familiar odor of fresh summer rain mixed with ozone was all-pervasive now. When he heard the first raindrops spattering on the ground, Dalton craned his head up, letting a few of them splash on his face. Satisfied, he solemnly pinned the badge on his T-Shirt, just above his heart. Dueling with the gusting wind, Dalton freed the Beretta from his belt and swung it around in a smooth, robotic motion. He ejected the empty magazine clip into his free hand, then wedged the handgun between his left arm and side while he searched the small coin pocket of his jeans with his index finger.

He gazed listlessly at the shiny JP round for a pensive moment before pressing it into the magazine. The clip was slapped back into the butt of the weapon. Using a well-practiced motion, the sergeant yanked the slide back and released it with a metallic clang to chamber the round. With the tip of the cold, black muzzle, he lightly traced an elongated circle around the breast badge before centering the front sight an inch below it. He dropped the butt to angle the barrel up, and his right index finger automatically settled on the grooved trigger.

Once again, he felt a knife-like pain shoot down both sides of his temples, and his head throbbed unmercifully as the "tiger," muscles coiled and tense with anticipation, crouched to spring. "No, you bastard, this is my call," he rasped at his antagonist as his index finger tightened. The sergeant paused and took a deep breath. He closed his eyes and slumped his head down on his chest as the first torrent of chilly rain washed over him.

#

Diane unlocked the front door to her boyfriend's cottage with the key he kept over the door, and, like a typical girlfriend, she started checking things out. Oddly, they hadn't connected with each other during the last two days for their normal catch-up talk, so on a whim, she dropped by right after her covert assignment in Charles County. Other than the normal disarray—empty beer cans cluttering the sink, bed a disaster, clothes strewn about, etc—nothing seemed out of the ordinary at first glance. When she read the funny message he'd scrawled on the chalkboard for her, her eyes brightened a bit.

As usual, he'd ended the note with a "happy face" and his customary two-finger peace-sign salute. She could always count on his zaniness to lift her doldrums on those two or three days a month when she knew she should have stayed in bed, preferably snuggled up in his strong, reassuring arms.

Even though the MSP cruiser and his Honda Accord in the driveway told her he was probably close-by, and while she knew he usually hiked along the beaches or adjoining woods almost daily, his absence still gnawed at her. As intuitive as she was, she couldn't quite put her finger on it yet. And there was the matter of that storm brewing across the bay, something that resonated loudly, after she heard the rumbling of distant thunder. Maybe he was already hotfooting his way back. Retirement from a job— *any* job—let alone the MSP after twenty-six years of blood, sweat, tears, cheers and too many beers, had to be daunting, she imagined. Perhaps her unsettled feelings could be chalked up to the nonchalance he seemingly displayed toward his impending life changes, maybe. No doubt, *that* was why he'd become so quiet and pensive around her during the last few months. Still, her detective's instincts nagged her enough to tell her things just weren't right.

In his bedroom she noticed several open cardboard boxes on the floor, all packed with MSP uniforms, manuals and other issued gear. OK, nothing fishy there. When she wandered into his spare bedroom, however, she froze in shocked disbelief. Where was the collection of books, his cherished books that were normally stacked in the bookcases and piled high up on the closet shelves? *All his books were gone!* From his treasured collection of Hemingway, Joseph Conrad, Stephen Ambrose and James Michener novels, the vast assortments of wildlife and nature books, to his military history books, the collection of *National Geographics*, even to the Bible his mother gave him when he was a total hellion in elementary school, the one book he didn't have time to read any more—*they were all gone*! *No!* There was *No* way he'd part with them, unless, unless—!

Her mind racing, Diane bit her lip and dashed from the room to snatch the spare keys off the hallway credenza and rush outside to search Dalton's cruiser and Honda. She found nothing to lift her spirits. In the cruiser ashtray, however, she did find a tornup three-by-five card. When she pieced it together, she could clearly make out more than a dozen written names, including hers, which had been neatly crossed out. The list of names started with his two daughters, then hers, his parents, brothers and sisters, Gary Rephan, Jim Buckler, her own parents and a few other friends, most of whom she knew.

Seconds later, Diane was back in his bedroom rummaging through dresser drawers, file cabinets and boxes in a frenzied search for the one item she so desperately had to find. Nothing there. She shoved the closet doors apart and fixed her eyes on the folded Sam Browne belt on the closet top shelf. In a heartbeat, she yanked it down—only to find an empty holster. *Not Good!* She dropped the belt and raced back to the living room for the phone. For a frenetic moment, the blinking red message light diverted her attention from the yellow lined notebook next to the phone receiver. When she grabbed the phone to call either Gary or Dalton's brother Jon, she wasn't sure which one yet, her eyes took in the red-inked words and numbers scribbled on the pad. There were at least half a dozen of them scrawled out, each line the same, and they'd been traced over several times:

SIGNAL 13! SIGNAL 13! SIGNAL 13!

Diane gasped and slapped her hand to her chest, as it all came together in one terrifying picture.

"Oh my god! *No!* Please, please dear God...*Noooo!*"

She slumped against the wall, dizzy and suddenly short of breath. *OK, hold it!* Now's *not* the time to go the panic route, she quickly told herself, forcing her mind back into the leather-tough LE mode. No time to mess with any damned phone calls, either. Grim-faced and determined, Diane burst from the cottage and dashed down the road leading to the beach.

By the time she reached the wind-swept beach, her lungs were on fire. Diane slumped over, her face flushed and chest heaving hard as she tried to catch her breath. The shrill wind whipped her hair across her face when she turned to study the south shoreline. She held her hair back and squinted her eyes, shielding them from the blowing sand, while she scanned the beachfront all the way down to where it ended at the rock jetty next to the Flag Harbor inlet, a half-mile away. Other than a few skittish seagulls hunkered down behind a wall, and a young couple perched on a nearby sand dune, she saw no other living entities.

Startled by another thunderous boom, Diane quickly shifted her attention to the mass of dark, roiling clouds swirling over the choppy whitecaps to the east. It was an ugly, powerful-looking storm, growing uglier in front of her dazed eyes, and it was moving fast and furious. From all indications, it also looked like the brunt of the storm was going to pass to the north of where she stood now. She brought a hand up to shield her eyes, and searched the long expanse of broken shoreline under the cliffs in the vain hope of catching a glimpse of his familiar figure traipsing back. Nothing.

Ungodly frustrated as never before, Diane felt her eyes tear up, felt the tightness in her shoulders and a sudden, sharp ache in her stomach. She shook her head and gritted her teeth. "No time for that now!" the voice in her head screamed. On a hunch, she started walking along the shore to the north, crouched and bent over low to study the sandy beach closer to the water's edge. High tide was coming in. Combined with the crashing, storm-driven waves, much of the beach was washed over already.

Bingo! Despite the blowing wind and relentless, stinging sand, she finally spotted a partly obscured set of jogging-shoe prints along the beachfront. To be sure, she placed one of her sneakers over an imprint. She knew he was a size twelve at least, and this print was at least that big. Her face crinkled into a tight scowl when she saw that the set of footprints trailed north to the massive cliffs.

Just a week ago, Dalton had taken her there again to watch the eagles, his "baldies," as they cavorted on the warm air currents. Later, they searched for shark's teeth and other fossils amidst the bounty of shells, stones and driftwood. It was a beachcombing excursion on another picture-perfect day. But while she enjoyed his company as always, Diane was intimidated by the imposing cliffs that rose high above her head. It was hardly soothing when Dalton pointed out the masses of large clay boulders, mounds of dirt and fallen trees from recent cliff cave-ins. At Dalton's favorite spot, his Purgatory Ridge, he'd even goaded her about climbing the high cliffs with him so they could sit and bask in the awesome view on that gorgeous, sun-drenched day. To avoid the ordeal, she'd feigned she was tired, and he wisely let the matter go.

Diane stood up straight, put her hands on her hips and glared at the treacherous shoreline again. No doubt in her mind now. Yes, he'd be up ahead, high above at his special Calvert cliffs overlook! She flinched and jerked her head when a jagged lightning bolt suddenly arched from the storm clouds. Seconds later, the rolling thunderclap echoed loudly. The threat of the cliffs wasn't her only problem now. There was no other choice, and no time for any chicken-shit contemplations either. Diane filled her lungs with several deep breaths and started jogging along the beachfront.

Despite the buffeting wind and crashing waves that soaked her sneakers and ankles, she made decent progress for the first few hundred yards. When she came to the first eminent section of the cliffs, however, the going got rougher as the beach narrowed. Soon, she was sloshing shin-deep in the surging waves. She hadn't bothered to roll up her cargo pants, and now they were soaked, but she paid scant attention to the chilly wetness. Loud thunder exploded in her ears again, and she cringed instinctively, her shoulders hunching up close to her head. From the corner of an eye, she saw driblets of sand and clumps of clay cascading from the cliffs. Every second golden, she fought back her fears and forged ahead.

With a loud curse, Diane grabbed onto the upright branch of a large fallen poplar that blocked her way and effortlessly hoisted her wiry frame onto the trunk. When she edged closer to the edge to jump, her long-sleeve T-shirt snagged on a broken limb. *Damn!* She tore wildly at the snag with her fingers, and freed herself just as twin bolts of lightning shot down and struck the water close by. Startled by the brilliant blue flash and the ear-splitting thunderclap, she lost her balance and landed facedown and hard. Momentarily stunned, she lay sprawled in the shallow water, as the angry waves crashed over her. With a start, she coughed and sputtered, clearing the brackish water from her mouth before yanking herself back onto her feet again. On shaky legs, she paused to wipe the gritty, wet sand from her eyes and mouth before moving on.

Like a runaway freight train from hell, the roaring wind and thunder intensified as the dark, threatening storm clouds hurtled closer. Her heart raced, and her breath came in painful gasps, as she fought to control the paralyzing fear building up inside. "This can't be real. This just can't be real! Dear god, help me...*Please!*" In defiance of her silent plea came a blinding white flash and the sharp *Crack* of a close lightning strike! Diane slapped her hands over her ears and braced herself for the thunder. When it came, she stifled a cry, as a huge section of the cliffs—several tons of red dirt, clay boulders, trees and underbrush, and a bounty of ancient fossils—broke away and tumbled down to the bay just yards from where she crouched. Instantly she felt a rising surge of panic, and she trembled. *"Nooo!"*

With a willpower and perseverance honed from years of facing adversity, Diane steadied herself. She balled her hands into fists and started sloshing through the water toward the heap of debris blocking her way. Halfway there, she heard the loud, clapping sound of the approaching rain, the cloudburst pummeling the water on a race to land. There was no way she was going to make it past the mass of dirt and trees, she could see that clearly, but damn if she wasn't going to give it one hell of a try! If she remembered correctly, the path leading up to his favorite perch on the cliffs was probably just beyond the earthen barrier.

She flinched when another spiny lightning bolt struck a tall tree on the cliff top just up ahead. If it hadn't hit his location, it was too awfully damn close. She heard a loud, droning *Bzzzzt*—followed by a piercing *Crraak!* For one long, unbelievable moment, the gigantic, pulsating bolt of blinding white lightning seemed glued to the edge of the tree line. For a split-second she thought she spotted the outline of a human figure standing near the edge of the cliff, but maybe her strained eyes were playing tricks on her. She watched, dumbstruck, as a fork of the white lightning splintered off and streaked back up through the sky to vanish into the angry black clouds. And in that bizarre instant, from somewhere deep within her feminine psychic, it hit her like a bomb, bringing the ethereal encounter into crystal-clear clarity. Diane suddenly realized he was beyond her help now, knew full well that he'd torn himself away from their lives forever.

Stunned, and feeling disoriented and numb, she sunk to her knees, the cold, slashing rain showing her no mercy. She jerked her head up and searched frantically for some shelter from the chaos around her. Pushing herself to her feet, she lurched toward a large tree that had tumbled from the cliff. Exhausted and drained of strength, she dropped down against the side of the tree and rolled herself into the shallow gap beneath it. Her body shook violently, and her teeth chattered uncontrollably when she curled herself into a tight fetal position to ride out the storm. Only then did she allow herself to cry.

For what seemed a lifetime, the storm vented itself in relentless fury. Ever so slowly, the rolling thunder tapered off, and the pelting rain and wind diminished. Diane waited for the rain to stop, before she rolled out from her improvised shelter. In place of the howling winds, she felt only a light breeze on her face. To her relief, the bay was calming down, as the broken gray clouds deserted in the wake of the violent summer storm. Soaked to the bone and shaking, she stood up and forced herself to flex her stiff joints and knead her aching arms. Not bothering to look back, Diane started threading her way back to the community beach.

Half an hour later, hobbled with a limp and an aching dullness in her chest, Dalton's girlfriend emerged from the realm of the cliffs to stand beside the rock jetty marking the perimeter of the community beach. To the west, the late afternoon cobalt-blue sky was devoid of clouds, and the welcome, redeeming sun had already slipped below the stand of tall oaks, mute sentinels that rose beyond the beach. The wind had died down, allowing the bay to rid itself of the furious whitecaps, which had earlier contributed to its ageless cycle of havoc.